At only 26, Matthew Reilly is the No. 1 bestselling author of three novels, *Contest*, *Ice Station* and *Temple*. He wrote his first two books while studying Law at the University of New South Wales, and now spends his time writing novels, big-budget Hollywood screenplays, and creating television series.

Ice Station and *Temple* were both runaway No. 1 bestsellers in Australia. Publishing rights to the two novels have been sold to over ten countries. Film rights to Matthew's first book, *Contest*, were optioned early last year. He lives in Sydney.

TEMPLE

MATTHEW REILLY

PAN

Pan Macmillan Australia

This is a work of fiction. Characters, corporations, institutions and organisations mentioned in this novel are either the product of the author's imagination or, if real, used fictitiously without any intent to describe actual conduct.

First published 1999 in Macmillan by Pan Macmillan Australia Pty Limited
This Pan edition published 2000 by Pan Macmillan Australia Pty Limited
St Martins Tower, 31 Market Street, Sydney

Copyright © Matthew Reilly 1999

National Library of Australia
cataloguing-in-publication data:

Reilly, Matthew, 1974– .
Temple.

ISBN 0 330 36214 3 (pbk.).

I. Title.

A823.3

Typeset in 10/11.5 pt Palatino by Post Pre-press Group
Printed in Australia by McPherson's Printing Group

For my brother, Stephen

Acknowledgements

Special thanks are due to several people this time round.

To Natalie Freer—she is always the first person to read my pages and she reads them in 40-page chunks. Thanks again for your extraordinary patience, generosity and support. To my brother, Stephen Reilly—for his unsurpassed loyalty and his razor-sharp comments on the text. (Have I ever mentioned that he has written the best screenplay I have ever read?)

To my parents, as always, for their love, encouragement and support. To my good friend John Schrooten for being the guinea pig for the third time. (John is the first person to read my books *in toto*—I still remember him reading *Ice Station* while we were watching a cricket match at the Sydney Cricket Ground.) Also to Nik Kozlina for her early comments on the text and to Simon Kozlina for letting me give the hero of this book his face!

Lastly, mention must be made of the good folk at Pan Macmillan. To Cate Paterson, my publisher, for—well—making all of this possible really. Her endeavours to publish mass-market thriller fiction in this country are unmatched. To Anna McFarlane, my editor, for bringing out the best in me. To every single sales rep at Pan—they're out there, every day, working the front lines in bookstores around the country. And last of all, a very special thank you to Jane Novak, my publicist at Pan, for guarding me like a mother hen and for seeing the irony when Richard Stubbs and I talked about her—our mutual publicist—on national radio!

Well, that's it. Now, on with the show . . .

INTRODUCTION

From: Holsten, Mark J.
        Civilization Lost—The Conquest of the Incas
        (Advantage Press, New York, 1996)

'CHAPTER I: THE CONSEQUENCES OF CONQUEST

. . . What cannot be emphasised enough is that the conquest of the Incas by the Spanish conquistadors represents perhaps the single greatest collision of cultures in the history of human evolution.

Here was the most dominant seafaring nation on earth—bringing with it all the latest *steel* technology from Europe—clashing with the most powerful empire ever to have existed in the Americas.

Unfortunately for historians, and thanks largely to the insatiable gold lust of Francisco Pizarro and his bloodthirsty conquistadors, the greatest empire to have inhabited the Americas is also the one about which we know the least.

The plunder of the Incan empire by Pizarro and his army of henchmen in 1532 must rank as one of the most brutal in written history. Armed with that most overwhelming of colonial weapons—gunpowder—the Spaniards cut a swathe through Incan towns and cities with "a lack of principle that would have made Machiavelli shudder" to use the words of one twentieth-century commentator.

Incan women were raped in their homes or forced to work in filthy makeshift brothels. Men were routinely tortured—their eyes would be burned out with hot coals or their tendons cut. Children were shipped to the coast by the hundred, to be loaded onto the dreaded slave galleons and taken back to Europe.

In the cities, temple walls were stripped bare. Gold plates and holy idols were melted into bars before anyone even thought to inquire as to their cultural significance.

Perhaps the most famous of all the tales of quests for Incan treasure is that of Hernando Pizarro—Francisco's brother—and his Herculean journey to the coastal town of Pachacámac in search of a fabled Incan idol. As described by Francisco de Jérez in his famous work, the *Verdadera relación de la conquista de la Peru*, the riches that Hernando plundered on his march to the temple-shrine at Pachacámac (not far from Lima) are of almost mythic proportions.

From what little remains of the Incan empire—buildings that the Spaniards did not destroy, golden relics that the Incas spirited away in the dead of night—the modern historian can only garner the barest of glimpses of a once great civilisation.

What emerges is an empire of paradox.

The Incas did not have the wheel, and yet they built the most extensive road system ever seen in the Americas. They did not know how to smelt iron ore, yet their metalwork with other substances—in particular, gold and silver—was second to none. They had no form of writing, and yet their system of numerical record-keeping—multi-coloured string formations

4

known as a *quipus*—was incredibly accurate. It was said that the *quipucamayocs*, the empire's feared tax collectors, would know even when something so small as a sandal went missing.

Inevitably, however, the greatest record of everyday Incan life comes from the Spaniards. As Cortez had done in Mexico only twenty years previously, the conquistadors in Peru brought with them clergymen to spread the Gospel to the heathen natives. Many of these monks and priests would ultimately return to Spain and commit what they saw to writing, and indeed, these manuscripts can still be found in monasteries around Europe today, dated and intact . . .' [p. 12]

From: de Jérez, Francisco
      Verdadera relación de la conquista de la Peru
      (Seville, 1534)

'The Captain [Hernando Pizarro] went to lodge, with his followers, in some large chambers in one part of the town. He said that he had come by order of the Governor [Francisco Pizarro] for the gold of that mosque, and that they were to collect it and deliver it up.

All the principal men of the town and the attendants of the Idol assembled and replied that they would give it, but they continued to dissimulate and make excuses. At last they brought very little, and said they had no more.

The Captain said that he wished to go and see the Idol they kept, and he went. It was in a good house, well painted, decorated in the usual Indian style—stone statues of jaguars guarded the entrance, carvings of demonic cat-like creatures lined the walls. Inside, the Captain found a dark foul-smelling chamber, in the centre of which stood a bare stone altar. On our journey, we had been told of a fabled Idol that was housed inside the temple-shrine at Pachacámac. The Indians say that this is their God who created them and sustains them, and who is the source of all their power.

But we found no Idol at Pachacámac. Just a bare altar in a foul-smelling room.

The Captain then ordered the vault in which the pagan Idol had been housed be pulled down and the principal men of the town be executed at once for their dissembling. So, too, the attendants to the Idol. Once this was done, the Captain then taught the villagers many things touching our Holy Catholic Faith, and taught them the sign of the cross . . .'

From: The *New York Times*
        December 31 1998, p. 12

Scholars Go Ga-Ga Over Rare Manuscripts

TOULOUSE, FRANCE: Medieval scholars were presented with a rare treat today when monks from the San Sebastian Abbey, a secluded Jesuit monastery in the Pyrenees Mountains, opened up their magnificent medieval library to a select group of non-ecclesiastical experts for the first time in over three hundred years.

Of key interest to this exclusive gathering of academics was the chance to see first-hand the abbey's renowned collection of handwritten manuscripts, notably those of St Ignatius Loyola, the founder of the Society of Jesus.

It was, however, the discovery of certain *other* manuscripts—long since believed to have been lost—that sparked cries of delight from the select group of historians who were granted entry to the abbey's labyrinthine library.

The lost codex of St Aloysius Gonzaga, or a heretofore undiscovered manuscript believed to have been written by St Francis Xavier, or—most wonderfully of all—the discovery of an original draft copy of the fabled Santiago Manuscript.

Written in 1565 by a Spanish monk named Alberto Luis Santiago, this manuscript commands almost legendary status among medieval historians—principally because it was assumed to have been destroyed during the French Revolution.

The manuscript is believed to outline in the most stark, brutal detail the conquest of Peru by the Spanish conquistadors in the 1530s. Famously, however, it is also understood to contain the only written account (based on its author's first-hand observations) of a murderous Spanish captain's obsessive hunt for a precious Incan idol through the jungles and mountains of Peru.

Ultimately, however, this was to be a 'look-but-don't-touch' exhibition. After the last scholar was (reluctantly) escorted from the library, its massive oak doors were firmly sealed behind him.

One can only hope that it won't be another three hundred years before they are opened again.

TEMPLE

PROLOGUE

**San Sebastian Abbey
High in the French Pyrenees
Friday, January 1 1999, 3:23 am**

The young monk sobbed uncontrollably as the cold barrel of the gun was placed firmly against his temple.

His shoulders shook. Tears streamed down his cheeks.

'For God's sake, Philippe,' he said. 'If you know where it is, tell them!'

Brother Philippe de Villiers knelt on the floor of the abbey's dining area with his hands clenched behind his head. To his left knelt Brother Maurice Dupont, the young monk with the gun to his head, to his right, the other sixteen Jesuit monks who lived in the San Sebastian Abbey. All eighteen of them were on their knees, lined up in a row.

In front of de Villiers and a little to his left stood a man dressed in black combat fatigues and armed with a Glock-18 automatic pistol and a Heckler & Koch G-11 assault rifle, the most advanced assault rifle ever made. Right now the black-clad man's Glock was resting against Maurice Dupont's head.

A dozen other similarly garbed, similarly armed

men stood around the wide dining room. They all wore black ski masks and they were all waiting upon Philippe de Villiers' response to a very important question.

'I don't *know* where it is,' de Villiers said through clenched teeth.

'*Philippe* . . .' Maurice Dupont said.

Without warning, the gun at Dupont's temple went off, the shot ringing out in the silence of the near-deserted abbey. Dupont's head exploded like a watermelon and a wash of blood splattered all over de Villiers' face.

No-one outside the abbey would hear the gunshot.

The San Sebastian Abbey lay perched on a mountaintop nearly 6000 feet above sea level, hidden among the snow-capped peaks of the French Pyrenees. It was 'as close to God as you could get', as some of the older monks liked to say. San Sebastian's nearest neighbour, the famous telescope platform the Pic du Midi Observatory, was nearly twenty kilometres away.

The man with the Glock moved to the monk on de Villiers' right and placed the barrel of the gun against his head.

'Where is the manuscript?' the man with the gun asked de Villiers a second time. His Bavarian accent was strong.

'I don't know, I tell you,' de Villiers said.

Blam!

The second monk jolted backwards and smacked down against the floor, a puddle of red liquid fanning out from the jagged, fleshy hole in his head. For a few seconds, the body shuddered involuntarily—spasming violently—flopped against the floor like a fish that had fallen out of its bowl.

De Villiers shut his eyes, offered up a prayer.

'*Where is the manuscript?*' the German said.

'I don't—'

Blam!

Another monk fell.

'Where is it?'

'I don't know!'

Blam!

All of a sudden, the Glock came around so that it was now pointed directly at de Villiers' face.

'This will be the last time I ask you this question, Brother de Villiers. *Where is the Santiago Manuscript?*'

De Villiers kept his eyes closed. 'Our Father, who art in heaven, hallowed be thy—'

The German squeezed the trigger.

'Wait!' someone said from the other end of the line.

The German assassin turned and saw an older monk step up and out from the line of kneeling Jesuit monks.

'Please! *Please!* No more, no more. I will tell you where the manuscript is, if you promise you will kill no more.'

'Where is it?' the assassin said.

'It is this way,' the old monk said, heading off into the library. The assassin followed him into the adjoining room.

Moments later both men returned, the assassin carrying in his left hand a large leather-bound book.

Although de Villiers couldn't see his face, it was clear that the German assassin was smiling broadly behind his black ski mask.

'Now, go. Leave us in peace,' the old Jesuit said. 'Leave us to bury our dead.'

The assassin seemed to ponder that for a moment. Then he turned and nodded to his cohorts.

In response the squad of armed assassins raised their G-11s as one and opened fire on the line of kneeling Jesuit monks.

A devastating burst of supermachine-gun fire cut the remaining monks to ribbons. Heads exploded, jagged rags of flesh were ripped clear from the monks' bodies as they were assailed by a force of gunfire never before witnessed.

In seconds, all of the Jesuits were dead, save for one: the elderly monk who had brought the Germans the manuscript. He now stood alone in a pool of his comrades' blood, facing his tormentors.

The lead assassin stepped forward and levelled his Glock at the old man's head.

'Who *are* you?' the old monk said defiantly.

'We are the *Schutz Staffeln Totenkopfverbände*,' the assassin said.

The old monk's eyes went wide. 'Good God . . .' he breathed.

The assassin smiled. 'Not even He can save you now.'

Blam!

The Glock went off one last time and the assassins swept out of the abbey and into the night.

A whole minute passed, then another.

The abbey lay silent.

The bodies of the eighteen Jesuit brothers lay sprawled on the floor, bathed in blood.

The assassins never saw it.

It was high above them, hidden *within* the ceiling of the enormous dining room. It was a loft of some sort, an attic in the ceiling that was separated from the dining room by a thin, wood-panelled wall. The individual panels of the wall were so old and shrivelled that the cracks between them were wide.

If they had looked closely enough, the assassins would have seen it—peering out through one of those cracks, blinking with fear.

A wide-open human eye.

3701 North Fairfax Drive, Arlington, Virginia
Offices of the US Defense Advanced Research
Projects Agency
Monday, January 4 1999, 5:50 am

The thieves moved fast—they knew exactly where they were going.

They'd picked the perfect time for the raid. Ten minutes to six. Ten minutes before the night guards were due to clock off. Ten minutes before the day guards were due to clock on. The night guards would be tired and looking at their watches, looking forward to going home. They would be at their most vulnerable.

3701 North Fairfax Drive was an eight-storey red-brick building just across the street from the Virginia Square Metro station in Arlington, Virginia. It housed the offices of the Defense Advanced Research Projects Agency—DARPA—the cutting-edge research and development arm of the United States Department of Defense.

The thieves ran down the white-lit corridors with their silenced MP-5SD submachine guns held high, SEAL-style—their folding stocks pressed firmly against their shoulders, their eyes looking straight down their barrels, searching for targets.

Thwat-thwat-thwat-thwat!

A hailstorm of silent bullets ripped down yet another Navy guardsman, number seventeen. Without missing a beat, the thieves leapt over his body and headed for the vault room. One of them swiped the cardkey while another pushed open the huge hydraulic door.

They were on the third floor of the building, having already breached seven Grade-5 security check-points—checkpoints that had required four different cardkeys and six different alpha-numeric codes to open. They had entered the building via its under-ground loading dock, inside a van that had been expected. The underground gate guards had been the first to die. They had been followed soon after by the van's drivers.

Up on the third floor, the thieves hadn't stopped moving.

In quick succession they entered the vault room—an enormous lab chamber bounded on every side by six-inch-thick porcelain walls. Outside this porcelain cocoon was another, outer wall. It was lead-lined and at least twelve inches thick. DARPA employees called this lab 'the Vault' and for good reason. Radio waves couldn't breach it. Directional listening devices couldn't touch it. It was the most secure facility in the building.

Was the most secure facility in the building.

The thieves fanned out quickly as they came into the lab chamber.

Silence.

Like the womb.

And then, suddenly, they stopped dead in their tracks.

Their prize stood before them, occupying pride of place in the centre of the lab.

It wasn't very big, despite what it could do.

It was maybe six feet tall and it looked like a giant hourglass: two cones—the lower one pointing upwards, the upper one pointing downwards—separated by a small titanium chamber which held the core of the weapon.

A collection of coloured wires snaked out from the titanium chamber in the centre of the device, most of them disappearing into a laptop computer keyboard that was crudely attached to its front section.

For the moment, the small titanium chamber was empty.

For the moment.

The thieves didn't waste any time. They removed the entire device from its power generator and quickly placed it on a custom-made sling.

Then they were moving again. Out the door. Up the corridor. Left then right. Left then right. Through the brightly lit government maze, stepping over the bodies they had killed on their way in. In the space of ninety seconds, they arrived back at the underground garage, where they all piled back into the van, together with their prize. No sooner were the last man's feet inside than the van's wheels skidded against the concrete and the big vehicle peeled away from the loading dock and sped out into the early morning light.

The team's leader looked at his watch.

5:59 am.

The entire operation had taken nine minutes.

Nothing more. Nothing less.

FIRST MACHINATION

Monday, January 4, 0910 hours

William Race was late for work. Again.

He'd overslept and then the subway had been delayed and now it was ten after nine and he was late for his morning lecture. Race's office was on the third floor of the old Delaware Building at New York University. The building had an ancient wrought-iron elevator that travelled at a snail's pace. It was quicker to take the stairs.

At thirty-one, Race was one of the youngest members of staff in the Ancient Languages Department at NYU. He was of average height—about five-foot-nine—and handsome in a very unassuming kind of way. He had sandy-brown hair and a lean physique. A pair of wire-rimmed glasses framed his blue eyes and an unusual facial mark—a triangular brown birthmark situated directly below his left eye.

Race hurried up the stairs, a thousand thoughts running through his mind—his morning lecture on the works of the Roman historian Livy, the parking fine from last month that he still had to pay, and the article that he'd read in the *New York Times* that morning saying that because 85 per cent of people based their ATM numbers on important dates like birthdays and the like, thieves who stole their wallets—thus obtaining not only ATM cards, but also driver's licences containing the owners' dates of birth—were finding it easier to break into their bank accounts. Damn it, Race thought, he was going to have to change his PIN number.

He came to the top of the stairwell and hurried out into the corridor.

And then he stopped.

Two men stood in the hallway in front of him.

Soldiers.

They were decked out in full battle dress, too—helmets, body armour, M-16s, the lot. One stood halfway down the corridor, nearer to Race. The other was stationed further down the hall. He stood rigidly to attention outside the door to Race's office. They couldn't have looked more out of place—soldiers in a university.

Both men snapped around immediately when they saw him burst out from the stairwell. For some reason, in their presence, Race suddenly felt inferior—somehow unworthy, *undisciplined*. He felt stupid in his Macy's sports coat, jeans and tie, carrying his clothes for a lunchtime baseball game in a battered old Nike sports bag.

As he approached the first soldier, Race looked him up and down—saw the black assault rifle in his hands, saw the velveteen green beret slouched on his head, saw the crescent-shaped patch on his shoulder that read: SPECIAL FORCES.

'Uh, hi. I'm William Race. I—'

'It's okay, Professor Race. Please go in. They're expecting you.'

Race continued down the corridor, came to the second soldier. He was taller than the first one, bigger. In fact, he was huge, a mountain of a man—at least six-feet-four—with a soft handsome face, dark hair and

22

narrow brown eyes that didn't miss a trick. The name patch on his breast pocket read: VAN LEWEN. The three stripes on his shoulder indicated that he was a sergeant.

Race's eyes drifted to the man's M-16. It had a state-of-the-art PAC-4C laser sighting device mounted on its barrel and an M-203 grenade launcher attached to its underside. Serious stuff.

The soldier stepped aside promptly, allowed Race to enter his own office.

Dr John Bernstein was sitting in the high-backed leather chair behind Race's desk, looking very uncomfortable. Bernstein was a white-haired man of fifty-nine and the head of the Ancient Languages Department at NYU, Race's boss.

There were three other men in the room.

Two soldiers, one civilian.

The two soldiers were dressed and armed in much the same manner as the guards outside—fatigues, helmets, laser-sighted M-16s—and they both looked extremely fit. One appeared to be a little older than the other. He held his helmet formally, wedged firmly between his elbow and his ribs, and he had close-cropped black hair that barely reached his forehead. Race's sandy-brown hair fell constantly down into his eyes.

The third stranger in the room, the civilian, was seated in the guest's chair in front of Bernstein. He was a big man, barrel-chested, and dressed in shirtsleeves and trousers. He had a pug nose and dark heavy-set features that were weathered with age and responsibility. And he sat in his chair with the calm assurance of someone who was used to being obeyed.

Race got the distinct impression that everyone had been waiting in his office for some time.

Waiting for *him*.

'Will,' John Bernstein said, coming around the desk and shaking his hand. 'Good morning. Come on in. I'd like you to meet someone. Professor William Race, Colonel Frank Nash.'

The barrel-chested civilian extended his hand. Strong grip.

'Retired. Good to meet you,' he said, looking Race over. He then indicated the two soldiers. 'This is Captain Scott and Corporal Cochrane of the U.S. Army Special Forces Group.'

'Green Berets,' Bernstein whispered respectfully in Race's ear.

Then Bernstein cleared his throat. 'Colonel—er, I mean, *Doctor*—Nash is from the Tactical Technology Office at the Defense Advanced Research Projects Agency. He's come here seeking our help.'

Frank Nash handed Race his photo-ID card. Race saw a mug shot of Nash with the red DARPA logo on top of it and a whole lot of numbers and codes beneath it. A magnetic strip ran down one side of the card. Beneath the photo were the words: FRANCIS K. NASH, U.S. ARMY, COL. (RET.). It was a pretty impressive card. It screamed: *important person*.

Uh-huh, Race thought.

He had heard of DARPA before. It was the primary research and development arm of the Department of Defense, the agency that had invented the Arpanet, the military-only precursor to the Internet. DARPA was also famous for its participation in the *Have Blue* project in the 1970s, the top-secret Air Force project that had resulted in the construction of the F-117 stealth fighter.

In fact, truth be told, Race knew a little more about DARPA than most, for the simple reason that his brother, Martin, worked there as a design engineer.

Basically, DARPA worked in partnership with each of the three branches of the U.S. armed forces—the Army, the Navy and the Air Force—developing high-technology military applications appropriate to the needs of each force: stealth technology for the Air Force, ultra-high-tensile body armour for the Army. Such was DARPA's status, however, that its accomplishments often became the stuff of urban legend. It was said, for example, that DARPA had recently perfected the J-7—the mythical A-frame rocket pack that would ultimately replace the parachute—but this had never been proved.

The Tactical Technology Office, however, was the spearhead of DARPA's arsenal, the jewel in its crown. It was the division in charge of developing the *big* stuff—high-risk/high-return strategic weaponry.

Race wondered what DARPA's Tactical Technology Office could possibly want with the Ancient Languages Department at NYU.

'You want our help?' he asked, looking up from Nash's photo-ID card.

'Well, actually, we came here specifically seeking *your* help.'

My help, Race thought. He lectured in ancient languages—mainly classical and medieval Latin—with a little bit of French, Spanish and German on the side. He couldn't think of a single thing that he could help DARPA with.

'What sort of help?' he asked.

'Translating. Translating a manuscript. A four-hundred-year-old Latin manuscript.'

'A manuscript . . .' Race said. Such a request wasn't unusual. He was often asked to translate medieval manuscripts. It *was* unusual, however, when it was asked in the presence of armed commandos.

'Professor Race,' Nash said, 'the translation of the document in question is a matter of extreme urgency. In fact, the document itself is not even in the United States yet. It is en route as we speak. What we would require of you is to meet the document at Newark and translate it in transit to our destination.'

'In transit?' Race said. 'To where?'

'I'm afraid that is something I am unable to tell you at this stage.'

Race was about to argue when suddenly the door to the office opened and another Green Beret entered. He carried a radio pack on his back and he walked quickly over to Nash, whispered softly in his ear. Race caught the words: '—been ordered to mobilise.'

'When?' Nash said.

'Ten minutes ago, sir,' the soldier whispered back.

Nash looked down quickly at his watch. 'Damn it.'

He swung back to face Race.

'Professor Race, we don't have much time, so I'm going to give this to you straight. This is a very important mission, a mission that seriously affects the national security of the United States. But it is a mission that has a very short window of opportunity. We *must* act now. But in order to do that, I need a translator. A medieval Latin translator. You.'

'How soon?'

'I have a car waiting out front.'

Race swallowed. 'I don't know . . .'

He could feel everyone's eyes on him. He felt suddenly nervous at the prospect of travelling to destination unknown with Frank Nash and a team of fully armed Green Berets. He felt like he was being railroaded.

'What about Ed Devereux at Harvard?' he said. 'He's a lot better at med-Latin than I am. He'd be faster.'

Nash said, 'I don't need the best and I don't have the time to travel up to Boston. Your brother mentioned your name to us. He said you were good and that you were in New York and quite frankly, that's all I need. I need someone close who can do the job *now*.'

Race bit his lip.

Nash said, 'You'll have a bodyguard assigned to you for the entire mission. We'll pick up the manuscript at Newark in about thirty minutes and get on the plane a few minutes after that. If all goes well, you'll have the document translated by the time we land. You won't even have to get off the plane. And if you do, you'll have a team of Green Berets looking after you.'

Race frowned at that.

'Professor Race, you won't be the only academic on this mission. Walter Chambers from Stanford will be there; Gabriela Lopez from Princeton; and also Lauren O'Connor from—'

Lauren O'Connor, Race thought.

He hadn't heard that name in years.

Race had known Lauren back in his college days at USC. While he had studied languages, she had majored in science—theoretical physics. They'd dated, but it had ended badly. Last he heard, she'd been working at the Livermore Labs in their nuclear physics department.

Race looked at Nash. He wondered just how much Frank Nash knew about Lauren and himself—wondered if he had dropped her name deliberately.

The thing was, if he had, then it worked.

If Lauren was anything, she was street-smart. She wouldn't go on a mission like this without a good reason. The fact that she had agreed to be a part of Nash's adventure gave it instant credibility.

'Professor, you will be amply compensated for your time.'

'It's not that—'

'Your brother is also part of the mission team,' Nash said, taking Race by surprise. 'He won't be coming with us, but he'll be working with the technical team at our offices in Virginia.'

Marty, Race thought. He hadn't seen him in a long time—not since their parents had divorced nine years ago. But if Marty was also involved, then maybe . . .

'Professor Race, I'm sorry, but we *have* to go. We have to go now. I need an answer from you.'

'Will,' John Bernstein said, 'this could be a tremendous opportunity for the university—'

Race frowned at Bernstein, cutting him off. Then to Nash: 'You say it's a matter of national security?'

'That's right.'

'And you can't tell me where we'll be going.'

'Not until we get on the plane. Then I can tell you everything.'

And I'm going to have a bodyguard, Race thought. *You usually only need a bodyguard when somebody wants to kill you.*

The office was silent.

Race could feel everyone waiting for his response. Nash. Bernstein. The three Green Berets.

He sighed. He couldn't believe what he was about to say.

'All right,' he said. 'I'll do it.'

Race walked quickly down the corridor behind Nash, still dressed in his jacket and tie.

It was a cold and wet winter's day in New York and as they made their way through the maze of corridors toward the westernmost gate of the university, Race caught the occasional glimpse of the heavy rain falling outside.

The two Green Berets who had been in the office walked ahead of him and Nash; the other two—the two who had been out in the corridor—walked behind. Everyone was moving quickly. It felt to Race like he was being pulled along by a strong current.

'Will I get a chance to change into something a little less formal?' he asked Nash. He had brought his sports bag along with him. It had his change of clothes inside it.

'Maybe on the plane,' Nash said as they walked. 'All right, now listen carefully. See the young man behind you. That's Sergeant Leo Van Lewen. He'll be your bodyguard from here on in.'

Race looked behind himself as he walked, saw the mountain-sized Green Beret he had seen earlier. Van Lewen. The Green Beret just gave him a curt acknowledging nod as his eyes swept the corridor all around them.

Nash said, 'From now on, you're a real important person and that makes you a target. Wherever you go, he goes. Here. Take this.'

Nash handed Race an earpiece and a wraparound throat microphone. Race had only ever seen them on TV before, on footage of SWAT units. You strapped the throat mike around your neck and the microphone picked up the vibrations of your voice box.

'Put it on as soon as you get in the car,' Nash said. 'It's voice-activated, so all you have to do is talk and we'll hear you. If you get in any trouble, just say the word and Van Lewen here will be at your side in seconds. You got that?'

'Got it.'

They came to the western entrance of the university, where two more Green Berets stood guard at the door. Nash and Race stepped past them, out into the pouring rain.

It was then that Race saw 'the car' that Nash had said was waiting out front.

On the gravel turnaround in front of him stood a motorcade.

Four police motorcycle outriders—two at the head of the line of cars, two at the rear. Six plain-looking olive-coloured sedans. And wedged in the middle, cocooned by the outriders and the sedans, were two heavy-duty armoured vehicles—Humvees. Both were painted black and they each had deeply tinted windows.

At least fifteen heavily armed Green Berets stood with M-16s at the ready all around the motorcade. The pouring rain hammered down against their helmets. They didn't seem to notice.

Nash hurried over to the second Humvee and held the door open for Race. Then he handed Race a thick manila folder as he stepped inside the big vehicle.

'Take a look,' Nash said. 'I'll tell you more when we get on the plane.'

The motorcade sped through the streets of New York.

It was mid-morning, but the eight-car procession just raced through the soaking city streets, whipping through intersection after intersection, getting green lights all the way out of the city.

They must have set the traffic lights like they did for the President when he visited New York, Race thought.

But this was no presidential procession. The looks on the faces of the people on the sidewalk said it all.

This was a different kind of motorcade.

No limousines. No flapping flags. Just two black heavily-armoured Humvees hovering in the middle of a line of drab olive cars, slicing their way through the pouring rain.

With his bodyguard seated beside him and his earpiece and throat mike now in place, Race stared out the window of the speeding Humvee.

Not many people could claim to have experienced a clear passage out of New York City in the middle of the mid-morning rush, he thought. It was a strange experience; otherworldly. He began to wonder just how important this mission was.

He opened the folder that Nash had given him. The first thing he saw was a list of names.

CUZCO INVESTIGATION TEAM

CIVILIAN MEMBERS

1   NASH, Francis K—DARPA, project leader, nuclear physicist

2   COPELAND, Troy B—DARPA, nuclear physicist

3   O'CONNOR, Lauren M—DARPA, theoretical physicist

4   CHAMBERS, Walter J—Stanford, anthropologist

5   LOPEZ, Gabriela S—Princeton, archaeologist

6   RACE, William H—NYU, linguist

ARMED FORCES MEMBERS

1   SCOTT, Dwayne T—United States Army (GB), Captain

2   VAN LEWEN, Leonardo M—United States Army (GB), Sergeant

3   COCHRANE, Jacob R—United States Army (GB), Corporal

4   REICHART, George P—United States Army (GB), Corporal

5   WILSON, Charles T—United States Army (GB), Corporal

6   KENNEDY, Douglas K—United States Army (GB), Corporal

Race turned the page and saw a photocopy of a newspaper clipping. The headline was in French: MASSACRÉS DES MOINES AU MONASTÈRE DU HAUT DELA MONTAGNE.

Race translated. 'Monks massacred in mountaintop monastery.'

He read the article. It was dated 3 January 1999—yesterday—and it was about a group of Jesuit monks who had been slaughtered inside their monastery high up in the French Pyrenees.

French authorities believed it to be the work of Islamic fundamentalists protesting against French interference in Algeria. Eighteen monks in all had been killed, all of them shot at close quarters in the same manner as in previous fundamentalist slayings.

Race turned to the next item in the folder.

It was another newspaper clipping, this one from the *Los Angeles Times*. It was dated late last year and the headline screamed: FEDERAL OFFICIALS FOUND MURDERED IN ROCKIES.

It said that two members of the U.S. Fish and Wildlife Service had been found murdered in the mountains north of Helena, Montana. Both officials had been skinned. The FBI had been called in. They suspected that it was the work of one of the local militia groups who seemed to have a natural enmity toward any sort of Federal agency. It was thought that the two Wildlife officials had stumbled upon some militiamen hunting illegal game for their pelts. Instead of skinning the animals, the militiamen had skinned the rangers.

Race winced, turned the page.

The next sheet in the folder was a photocopy of an article from a university journal of some kind. The article was in German and it was written by a scientist named Albert L. Mueller. It was dated November 1998.

Race scanned the article, rapidly translating the German in his head. It was something about a meteor crater that had been found in the jungles of Peru.

Underneath the article on the meteor crater was a police pathologist's report, also written in German. In the box marked 'NAME OF DECEASED' were the words 'ALBERT LUDWIG MUELLER'.

Beneath the pathologist's report were some more sheets of paper, all covered with various red stamps— TOP SECRET; EYES ONLY; U.S. ARMY PERSONNEL EYES ONLY. Race flicked through them. Mostly, the sheets were filled with complex mathematical equations which meant nothing to him.

Next, he saw a handful of memos, nearly all of them addressed to people he'd never heard of. On one of the memos, however, he saw his own name. It read:

3 JAN 1999 22:01 US ARMY INTERNAL NET 617 5544 88211-05 NO.139

From:	Nash, Frank
To:	All Cuzco Team Members
Subject:	SUPERNOVA MISSION

Contact to be made with Race ASAP.

The motorcade arrived at Newark airport. The long line of cars raced through a gate in the cyclone fence and quickly made its way to a private airstrip.

An enormous camouflaged cargo plane stood on the tarmac waiting for them. At the rear of the plane, a cargo ramp was lowered so that it touched the ground. As the motorcade pulled to a stop alongside the massive aircraft, Race saw a large Army truck being driven up the ramp into the rear of the plane.

Led by Sergeant Van Lewen, he stepped out of the Humvee, into the rain. No sooner had he emerged from the big black vehicle, however, than he heard a monstrous roar from somewhere high above him.

An old F-15C Eagle—painted in green and brown camouflage colours and with the word 'ARMY' emblazoned on its tail—came roaring in overhead and screeched to a landing on the wet tarmac in front of them.

As Race watched the fighter plane wheel around on the runway and taxi back in his direction, he felt Frank Nash grab him gently by the arm.

'Come on,' Nash said, leading him toward the big cargo plane. 'Everyone else is already on board.'

As they approached the cargo plane, Race saw a woman appear in a doorway on its side. He recognised her instantly.

'Hey, Will,' Lauren O'Connor said.

'Hello, Lauren.'

Lauren O'Connor was in her early thirties, but she

didn't look a day older than twenty-five. She'd cut her hair, Race saw. Back at USC, it had been long, wavy and brown. Now it was short, straight and auburn. Very late nineties.

Her big brown eyes were still the same, though, as was her fresh clear skin. And standing there in the doorway to the big cargo plane—leaning casually against the frame with her arms folded and her hips cocked, dressed in heavy-duty khaki hiking gear—she looked the way she had always looked. Tall and sexy, lithe and athletic.

'It's been a long time,' she said, smiling.

'Yes, it has,' Race said.

'So. William Race. Expert linguist. Consultant to the Defense Advanced Research Projects Agency. You still play ball, Will?'

'Just socially,' Race said. Back in college, he'd lettered in football. He'd been the smallest guy on the team, but also the fastest. He'd lettered in track too.

'How about you?' he said, noticing for the first time the ring on her left hand. He wondered who she'd married.

'Well, for one thing,' she said, her eyes lighting up, 'I'm very excited about this mission. It's not every day you get to go on a treasure hunt.'

'Is that what this is?'

Before Lauren could answer, a loud whining sound made both of them turn.

The F-15 had pulled to a halt about fifty yards from the cargo plane and no sooner was its canopy open than the pilot was leaping down onto the wet tarmac beneath it and running toward them, hunched over in the drenching rain. He carried a briefcase in his hand.

The pilot came up to Nash, handed him the briefcase. 'Doctor Nash,' he said. 'The manuscript.'

Nash took the briefcase and strode over to where Lauren and Race were standing.

'All right,' he said, ushering them inside the cargo plane. 'Time to get this show on the road.'

The giant cargo plane thundered down the runway and lifted off into the rainsoaked sky.

It was a Lockheed C-130E Hercules and the interior was divided into two sections—the downstairs cargo hold and the upstairs passenger compartment. Race sat in the upstairs section with the five other scientists going along on the expedition. The six Green Berets accompanying them were down in the cargo hold, stowing and checking their weapons.

Of the five civilians, Race knew two: Frank Nash and Lauren O'Connor.

'We'll have time for introductions later,' Nash said, sitting down next to Race and hauling the briefcase onto his lap. 'What's important right now is that we set you to work.'

He began unclasping the buckles on the briefcase.

'Can you tell me where we're going now?' Race asked.

'Oh yes, of course,' Nash said. 'I'm sorry I couldn't tell you before, but your office just wasn't secure. The windows could have been lased.'

'Lased?'

'With a laser-guided listening device. When we speak inside an office like yours, our voices actually make the windows vibrate. Most modern office towers are equipped to deal with directional listening devices—they have electronic jamming signals running through the glass in their windows. Older buildings like yours don't. It would have been way too easy for someone to listen in.'

'So where are we going?'

'Cuzco, Peru—capital of the Incan empire before the Spanish conquistadors arrived in 1532,' Nash said. 'Now it's just a large country town, a few Incan ruins, big tourist attraction, so they tell me. We'll be travelling non-stop, with a couple of mid-air refuellings on the way.'

He opened the briefcase and extracted something from it.

It was a stack of paper—a loose pile of A3 sheets, maybe forty pages in total. Race saw the top sheet. It was a Xerox of an illustrated cover sheet.

It was the manuscript Nash had spoken about earlier, or at least a photocopy of it.

Nash handed the stack of paper over to Race and smiled. '*This* is why you are here.'

Race took the pile from him, flipped over the cover sheet.

Now, Race had seen medieval manuscripts before—manuscripts painstakingly reproduced *by hand* by devoted monks in the Middle Ages, back in the days before the printing press. Such manuscripts were characterised by an almost impossible intricacy of design and penmanship: perfect calligraphy—including wonderfully elaborate leading marks (the single letter that starts a new chapter)—and detailed pictographs in the margins that were designed to convey the mood of the work. Sunny and gay for pleasing books; dark and frightening for more sombre tales.

Such was the detail, it was said that a monk could spend his entire life reproducing a single manuscript.

But the manuscript that Race saw now—even in black-and-white photocopied form—was like nothing he had ever seen.

It was magnificent.

He flicked through the pages.

The handwriting was superb, precise, intricate, and the side margins were filled with drawings of gnarled snaking vines. Strange stone structures, covered in moss and shadow, occupied the bottom corners of each page. The overall effect was one of darkness and fore-boding, of brooding malevolence.

Race flicked back to the cover page. It read:

NARRATIO VERA MONACHI IN TERRIS INCARUM: OPUS ALBERTI LUIS SANTIAGO ANNO DOMINI MDLXV

Race translated. *The true relation of a monk in the land of the Incas: A manuscript by Alberto Luis Santiago.* It was dated 1565.

Race turned to face Nash. 'All right. I think it's about time you told me what this mission of yours is all about.'

Nash explained.

Brother Alberto Santiago had been a young Franciscan missionary sent to Peru in 1532 to work alongside the conquistadors. While the conquistadors raped and pillaged the countryside, monks like Santiago were expected to convert the Incan natives to the wisdom of the Holy Roman Catholic Church.

'Although it was written in 1565, well after

Santiago's eventual return to Europe,' Nash said, 'it is said that the Santiago Manuscript recounts an incident that occurred around 1535, during the conquest of Peru by Francisco Pizarro and his conquistadors. According to medieval monks who claimed to have read it, the manuscript recounts a rather amazing tale: that of *Hernando* Pizarro's dogged pursuit of an Incan prince who, during the height of the siege of Cuzco, spirited the Incas' most venerated idol out of the walled city and fled with it into the jungles of eastern Peru.'

Nash swivelled in his seat. 'Walter,' he said, nodding to the bespectacled, balding man sitting on the other side of the centre aisle, 'help me out here. I'm telling Professor Race about the idol.'

Walter Chambers got up from his seat and sat down opposite Race. Chambers was a mousy little man, three-quarters bald and bookish, the kind of guy who'd wear a bow tie to work.

'William Race. Walter Chambers,' Nash said. 'Walter's an anthropologist from Stanford. Expert on Central and South American cultures—Mayans, Aztecs, Olmecs and, especially, the Incas.'

Chambers smiled. 'So you want to know about the idol?'

'It would seem so,' Race said.

'The Incas called it "the Spirit of the People",' Chambers said. 'It was a stone idol, but one that was carved out of a strange kind of stone, a shiny black stone that had very fine veins of purple running through it.

'It was the Incan people's most prized possession. Indeed, they saw it as their very heart and soul. And when I say that, I mean it literally. They saw the Spirit of the People as more than a mere *symbol* of their power. They saw it as the actual, *literal*, source of that power. And indeed, there were stories about its magical powers—how it could calm the most vicious of animals, or how, when dipped in water, the idol would sing.'

'Sing?' Race said.

'That's right,' Chambers said, 'sing.'

'*O-kay.* So what does this idol look like?'

'The idol's actual appearance has been described in many places, including the two most comprehensive works on the conquest of Peru, Jérez's *Relación* and de la Vega's *Royal Commentaries.* But descriptions vary. Some say it was a foot high, others only six inches; some say it was beautifully carved and smooth to the touch, others say it had rough, sharp edges. One feature, however, is common to all descriptions of the idol—the Spirit of the People was carved in the shape of a snarling jaguar's head.'

Chambers leaned forward in his seat. 'From the moment he heard about that idol, Hernando Pizarro wanted it. And all the more so after the attendants at the idol's shrine at Pachacámac whisked it away from under his nose. See, Hernando Pizarro was probably the most ruthless of all the Pizarro brothers to come to Peru. I imagine today we would call him a psychopath. According to some reports, he would torture whole villages on a whim—just for the sport of it. And his hunt for the idol became an obsession. Village after village, town after town, wherever he went he demanded to know the location of the idol. But no matter how many natives he tortured, no matter how many villages he burned, the Incas wouldn't tell him where their precious idol was.

'But then—somehow—in 1535 Hernando discovered where the idol was being kept. It was being kept

41

inside a massive stone vault inside the Coricancha, the famous Temple of the Sun, situated in the centre of the besieged city of Cuzco.

'Unfortunately for Hernando, he got to Cuzco just in time to see a young Incan prince named Renco Capac make off with the idol in a daring ride through the Spanish and Incan lines. According to those medieval monks who read it, the Santiago Manuscript details Hernando's pursuit of Renco following the young prince's escape from Cuzco—a dazzling chase that wound its way through the Andes and out into the Amazon rainforest.'

'What the manuscript also allegedly does,' Nash said, 'is reveal the final resting place of the Spirit of the People.'

So they were after the idol, Race thought.

He didn't say anything, though. Mainly, because it just didn't make sense.

Why was the U.S. Army sending a team of *nuclear physicists* down to South America to find a lost Incan idol? And on the basis of a four-hundred-year-old Latin manuscript. They might as well have been following a pirate's treasure map.

'I know what you're thinking,' Nash said. 'If someone had told me this same story a week ago, I'd have thought about it the same way you do. But then, up until a couple of weeks ago, nobody even knew where the Santiago Manuscript was.'

'But now you have it,' Race said.

'*No*,' Nash said sharply. 'We have a *copy* of it. Somebody else has the original.'

'Who?'

Nash nodded at the folder in Race's lap. 'Did you see the newspaper article in the folder I gave you before? The one about the Jesuit monks who were killed in their monastery in the Pyrenees?'

'Yeah . . .'

'Eighteen monks killed. All of them shot at close range with high-powered weapons. At first glance, it looks like the work of your garden variety Algerian terrorists. They've been known to attack isolated monasteries and their favoured m.o. is to shoot their victims at very close range. Sure enough, the French press reported it that way.

'*But*'—Nash held up a finger—'what the press don't know is that during the carnage, one monk managed to escape. An American Jesuit on sabbatical in France. He managed to hide upstairs in an attic during the whole thing. After the French police debriefed him, he was passed on to our embassy in Paris. At the embassy, he was debriefed again, only this time by our CIA Chief of Station.'

'And?'

Nash looked Race squarely in the eye.

'The men who stormed that monastery weren't Algerian terrorists, Professor Race. They were commandos. Soldiers. *White* soldiers. They all wore black ski masks and they were all armed to the teeth with some pretty awesome weaponry. And they spoke to each other in German.

'What's more interesting,' Nash continued, 'is what they were after. Apparently, the commandos gathered all the monks together in the abbey's dining room and made them get down on their knees. Then they grabbed one of the monks and demanded to know the location of the Santiago Manuscript. When the monk said he didn't know where it was, they shot two monks—one on either side of him. Then they asked him again. When he again said he didn't know, they killed the next two monks. This would have gone on until they were all killed but then someone stepped forward and said he knew where the manuscript was.'

'Jesus . . .' Race said.

Nash pulled a photograph from his briefcase. 'We have reason to believe that the man responsible for this atrocity was this man, Heinrich Anistaze, formerly a major in the East German secret police, the Stasi.'

Race looked at the photo. It was an eight-by-ten glossy of a man getting out of a car. The man was tall and broad-shouldered, with short black hair that was brushed forward and two narrow slits for eyes. They were hard eyes, cold eyes, eyes that seemed to be set in a perpetual squint. He appeared to be in his mid-forties.

'Notice the left hand,' Nash said.

Race looked at the photograph more closely. The man's left hand rested atop the car door. Race saw it.

Heinrich Anistaze had no left ring finger.

'At one time during the Cold War, Anistaze was captured by members of an East German crime syndicate that the Stasi was trying to shut down. They made him cut off his own finger before they sent it off in the mail to his superiors. But then Anistaze escaped, and returned—with the full force of the Stasi behind him. Needless to say, organised crime was never a problem in communist East Germany after that.

'Of more importance to us, however, are his methods in other circumstances. You see, it seems Anistaze had a peculiar way of making people talk: he was known for executing the people on either side of the person who failed to give him the information he wanted.'

There was a short silence.

'According to our most recent intelligence,' Nash said, 'since the end of the Cold War, Anistaze has been working in a non-official capacity as an assassin for the unified German government.'

'So the Germans have the original manuscript,' Race said. 'How did you get your copy then?'

Nash nodded sagely.

'The monks gave the Germans the original manuscript. The actual, undecorated, *handwritten* manuscript written by Alberto Santiago himself.

'What the monks didn't tell the Germans, though, was that in 1599—thirty years after Santiago's death—*another* Franciscan monk began transcribing Santiago's handwritten manuscript into a more elaborate, decorated text that would be fit for the eyes of kings. Unfortunately, this second monk died before he could complete his transcription, but what remains is a second copy of the Santiago Manuscript, a *partially completed* copy that was also kept at the San Sebastian Abbey. It is this copy of the manuscript that we have a Xerox of.'

Race held up his hand.

'Okay, okay,' he said. 'Wait a minute. Why all this murder and intrigue for a lost Incan idol? What could the U.S. and German governments possibly want with a four-hundred-year-old piece of stone?'

Nash gave Race a grim smile.

'You see, Professor, it's not the idol that we're after,' he said. 'It's the substance that it's made of.'

'What do you mean?'

'Professor, what I mean is this: we believe that the Spirit of the People was carved out of a meteorite.'

'The journal article,' Race said.

'That's right,' Nash said. 'By Albert Mueller of Bonn University. Before his rather untimely death, Mueller was studying a one-mile-wide meteor crater in the jungles of south-eastern Peru, at a site about fifty miles south of Cuzco. By measuring the size of the crater and the speed of jungle growth over it, Mueller estimated that a high-density meteorite about two feet in diameter impacted with the earth at that site some time between the years 1460 and 1470.'

'Which,' Walter Chambers added, 'coincides perfectly with the rise of the Incas in South America.'

'What is more important for us,' Nash said, 'is what Mueller found in the *walls* of this crater. Deposited in the walls of the crater were trace samples of a substance known as thyrium-261.'

'Thyrium-261?' Race said.

'It's a rare isotope of the common element thyrium,' Nash said, 'and it is not found on Earth. In fact, thyrium has only been found here in petrified form, presumably as a result of previous asteroid impacts in the distant past. It is indigenous to the Pleiades system, a binary star system not far from our own. But since it comes from a *binary* star system, thyrium is of a far greater density than even the heaviest of terrestrial elements.'

Things were beginning to make a little more sense to Race now. Especially the part about the Army sending a team of physicists down to the jungle.

'And what exactly can you do with thyrium?' Race asked.

'*Colonel!*' a voice called suddenly.

Nash and Race turned in their seats to see Troy Copeland, one of the other scientists, come striding quickly down the centre aisle from the cockpit. Copeland was a tall man, lean, with a thin, hawk-like face and intense, narrow eyes. He was one of the DARPA people—a nuclear physicist, Race recalled— and he appeared to Race to be a completely humourless individual.

'Colonel, we have a problem,' he said.

'What is it?' Nash said.

'We just caught a priority alert from Fairfax Drive,' Copeland said.

Race had heard of 'Fairfax Drive' before. It was shorthand for 3701 North Fairfax Drive, Arlington, Virginia. DARPA headquarters.

'About?' Nash said.

Copeland took a deep breath. 'There was a break-in there early this morning. Seventeen security staff dead. The entire night crew killed.'

Nash's face went ashen white. 'They didn't—'

Copeland nodded seriously. 'They stole the Supernova.'

Nash stared off into space for a second.

'It was the only thing they took,' Copeland said. 'They knew exactly where it was. They knew the codes to the vault room and had cardkeys for the clampdown locks. We must assume that they also know the codes to the titanium airlock on the device itself, and maybe how to detonate it.'

'Any idea who it was?'

'NCIS are there now. Early indications are that it might be the work of a paramilitary group like the Freedom Fighters.'

'Shit,' Nash said. '*Shit!* They must know about the idol.'

'It's likely.'

'Then we have to get there first.'

'Agreed,' Copeland said.

Race was just watching this conversation like a spectator at a tennis match. So, there had been a break-in at DARPA headquarters, but what exactly had been stolen was a mystery to him. Something called a Supernova. And who were these Freedom Fighters?

Nash stood up. 'What's our lead?' he asked.

'Maybe three hours, if that,' Copeland said.

'Then we have to move fast.' Nash turned to Race. 'Professor Race, I'm sorry, but the stakes in this game have just been raised. We don't have any more time to waste. It is now imperative that we have that manuscript translated by the time we fly into Cuzco, because when we hit the ground, believe me, we are gonna hit it running.'

With that, Nash, Copeland and Chambers moved off to other areas of the plane, leaving Race alone with the manuscript.

Race looked at the cover page again, scanned the rough texture of the photocopier's ink. Then he took a deep breath and turned the page.

He saw the first line, written in fine medieval calligraphy:

NOMINUS MEUS ALBERTO LUIS SANTIAGO ET EL RELATIO
MEA . . .

He translated.
My name is Alberto Luis Santiago and this is my story . . .

FIRST READING

FIRST READING

On the first day of the ninth month in the year of Our Lord 1535, I became a traitor to my country.

The reason: I helped a man escape from a prison of my countrymen.

His name was Renco Capac and he claimed to be an Incan prince, the younger brother of their supreme ruler, Manco Capac, the man they called the Sapa Inca.

He was a handsome man, with smooth olive skin and long black hair. His most distinctive feature, however, was a prominent birthmark situated directly below his left eye. It looked like an inverted mountain peak, a ragged triangle of brown skin that sat atop his otherwise clear complexion.

I first met Renco on board the *San Vicente*, a prison hulk that lay out in the middle of the Urubamba River, ten miles north of the Incans' capital, Cuzco.

The *San Vicente* was the foulest of all the prison hulks that lay at anchor in the rivers of New Spain—an old wooden galleon no longer fit for ocean travel that had been dismasted and hauled overland for the sole purpose of housing hostile or dangerous Indians.

Armed as usual with my prized leather-bound Bible—a three-hundred-page handwritten version of the great book that had been a gift to me from my parents upon my entering the Holy Orders—I had come to the prison hulk to teach these heathens the Word of Our Lord.

It was in this capacity as a minister of our Faith that I met the young prince Renco. Unlike most of the others in that miserable hulk—foul, ugly wretches who, owing to the shameful conditions my countrymen imposed on them, looked more as dogs than men—he was well spoken and educated. He was also possessed of a most unique sensitivity the likes of which I have not seen in any man since. It was a gentleness, an understanding, a look in his eyes that penetrated my very soul.

He was also of considerable intelligence. My countrymen had been in New Spain for but three years and he could already speak our language. He was also eager to learn of my Faith and understand my people and our ways, and I was happy to teach him. In any case, we soon struck up a friendship and I visited him often.

And then one day he told me of his mission.

Before he had been captured, so he said, this prince had been charged with travelling to Cuzco and retrieving an idol of some sort. Not an ordinary idol, mind, but a most venerated idol, perhaps *the* most venerated idol of these Indians. An idol which they say embodies their spirit.

But Renco had been waylaid on his journey to Cuzco, captured in an ambush set up by the Governor with the aid of the Chancas, an extremely hostile tribe from the northern jungles that had been subjugated by the Incan people against their will.

Like many other tribes from this region, the Chancas saw the arrival of my countrymen as a means of breaking the yoke of Incan tyranny. They were quick to offer their services to the Governor as informers and as guides, in return for which they received muskets and metal swords, for the tribes of New Spain have no concept of bronze or iron.

As Renco informed me of his mission and his capture at the hands of the Governor, I saw over his shoulder a Chanca tribesman who was also being held captive inside the *San Vicente*.

His name was Castino and he was an ugly brute of a man. Tall and hairy, bearded and unwashed, he could not have been more dissimilar to the young articulate Renco. He was an utterly repulsive creature, the most frightening human form I have ever had the misfortune to lay my eyes upon. A sharpened piece of white bone pierced the skin of his left cheek, the characteristic mark of the Chancas. Castino always stared malevolently at Renco's back whenever I came to visit the young prince.

The day he told me of his mission to retrieve the idol, Renco was extremely distressed.

The object of his quest, he said, was locked inside a vault inside the Coricancha, or sun temple, at Cuzco. But Renco had that day learned—by eavesdropping on a conversation between two guards on board the hulk—that the city of Cuzco had recently fallen and that the Spaniards were inside its walls, sacking and looting it unopposed.

I, too, had heard of the taking of Cuzco. It was said that the looting taking place there was some of the most rapacious of the entire conquest. Rumours abounded of Spaniards killing their fellow soldiers in their lust for the mountains of gold that lay inside the city's walls.

Such tales filled me with dismay. I had arrived in New Spain but six months previously with all the foolish ideals of a novice—desires of converting all the pagan natives to our noble Catholic Faith, dreams of leading a column of soldiers while holding forth a crucifix, delusions of building high-spired churches that would be the envy of Europe. But these ideals were quickly dispelled by the wanton acts of cruelty and greed that I witnessed of my countrymen every day.

Murder, pillage, rape—these were not the acts of men fighting in the name of God. They were the acts of scoundrels, of villains. And indeed at the moments when my disillusionment was at its greatest—such as the time when I witnessed a Spanish soldier decapitate a woman in order to seize her gold necklace—I would wonder whether I was fighting for the right side. That Spanish soldiers had taken to killing each other during their plunder of Cuzco came as no surprise to me.

I should also add at this juncture, however, that I had heard rumours about Renco's sacred idol before.

It was widely known that Hernando Pizarro, the Governor's brother and chief lieutenant, had put up an incredible bounty for any information that led to the discovery of the idol's whereabouts. It was to my mind a tribute to the reverence and devotion that the Incans paid their idol that not one of them—not a single one of them—had betrayed its location in return for Hernando's fabulous reward. It shames me to say that I do not believe my countrymen, in similar circumstances, would have done the same.

But of all the tales I had heard of the looting of Cuzco, nowhere had I heard of the discovery of the treasured Incan idol.

Indeed, if it had been found, word would have spread faster than the wind. For the lucky foot soldier who discovered it would have been instantly knighted, would have been made a marquis by the

Governor on the spot and would have lived the rest of his life back in Spain in unreserved luxury.

And yet there had been no such tale.

Which led me to conclude that the Spaniards in Cuzco had not yet found the idol.

'Brother Alberto,' Renco said, his eyes pleading, 'help me. Help me escape this floating cage so that I can complete my mission. Only I can retrieve the idol of my people. And with the Spaniards holding Cuzco, it is only a matter of time before they find it.'

Well.

I did not know what to say. I could never do such a thing. I could never help him escape. I would be making myself a hunted man, a traitor to my country. If I were caught, I would be the one imprisoned inside this hellish floating dungeon. And so I left the hulk without another word.

But I would return. And I would talk with Renco again—and again he would ask me to help him, his voice impassioned, his eyes begging.

And whenever I contemplated the issue more closely, my mind would always return to two things: my total and utter disillusionment at the despicable acts of those men I called my countrymen, and—conversely—my admiration of the Incan people's stoic refusal to disclose the secret location of their idol in the face of such overwhelming adversity.

Indeed, never had I witnessed such unfailing devotion. I envied their faith. I had heard tell of Hernando torturing entire villages in his obsessive search for the idol, had heard of the atrocities he had committed. I wondered how I would act if I were to see my own kinfolk butchered, tortured, murdered. In those circumstances, would I disclose the location of Jerusalem?

In the end, I decided that I would and I was doubly ashamed.

And so despite myself, my Faith and my allegiance to my country, I decided to help Renco.

I left the hulk and returned later that night, bringing with me a young page—an Incan named Tupac—just as Renco had instructed me. We both wore hooded cloaks against the cold and kept our hands folded inside our sleeves.

We came to the guard station on the riverbank. As it happened, since most of my country's forces were at Cuzco partaking in the looting there, only a small group of soldiers were on hand in the tent village near the hulk. Indeed, only a lone night guard—a fat slovenly thug from Madrid with liquor on his breath and dirt under his fingernails—guarded the bridge that led to the hulk.

After taking a second glance at young Tupac—it was not uncommon at that time for young Indians to serve as pages for monks like myself—the night guard belched loudly and ordered us to inscribe our names on the register.

I scratched both of our names in the book. Then when I had finished, the two of us stepped onto the narrow wooden footbridge that stretched out from the riverbank over to a door set into the side of the prison hulk in the middle of the river.

No sooner had we stepped past the filthy night guard, however, than the young Tupac whirled around quickly and grabbed the man from behind and twisted his head, breaking his neck in an instant. The guard's body slumped in its chair. I winced at the sheer violence of the act, but strangely I found that I felt little sympathy for the guard. I had made my decision—had pledged my allegiance to the enemy—and there was no turning back now.

My young companion quickly took the guard's rifle and his *pistallo*—or 'pistol' as some of my countrymen were now calling them—and, last of all, his keys. Tupac then affixed a stone weight to the dead guard's foot and dropped the body into the river.

In the pale blue moonlight, we crossed the rickety wooden footbridge and entered the hulk.

The interior guard leapt to his feet as we entered the cage room but Tupac was far too quick for him. He fired his pistol at the guard without missing a step. The explosion of the gunshot in the enclosed space of the prison hulk was deafening. Prisoners all around us awoke with a start at the sudden terrifying sound.

Renco was already on his feet as we came to his cage.

The guard's key fitted perfectly in the lock of his cell and the door opened easily. The prisoners all around us were shouting and banging on the bars of their cages, pleading to be released. My eyes darted around in every direction and in the midst of all this uproar, I saw a sight that chilled me to my very core.

I saw the Chanca, Castino, standing in his cell—standing perfectly still—staring at me intently.

His cage now open, Renco ran over to the dead guard's corpse, grabbed his weapons and handed them to me.

'Come on,' he said, awakening me from Castino's hypnotic stare. Dressed only in the barest of prison rags, Renco quickly began to undress the dead guard's corpse. Then he hurriedly put on the guard's thick leather riding jacket, pantaloons and boots.

No sooner was he dressed than he was on his feet again, unlocking some of the other cages. I noticed that he only unlocked the cages of Incan warriors and not those of prisoners from subjugated tribes like the Chancas.

And then suddenly Renco was dashing out the door with a rifle in his hand, ignoring the shouts of the other prisoners, and calling for me to follow.

We dashed back across the rickety footbridge, amid a crowd of running prisoners. By this time, however, others had heard the commotion on board the hulk. Four Spaniards from the nearby tent village arrived at the riverbank on horseback just as we leapt off the bridge. They fired at us with their muskets, the reports of their weapons booming like thunderclaps in the night.

Renco fired back, handling his musket like the most seasoned Spanish infantryman, blasting one of the horsemen from his mount. The other Incan prisoners ran ahead of us and overpowered two of the other horsemen.

The last horseman brought his steed around so that it stood directly in front of me. In a flashing instant, I saw him register my appearance—a European helping these heathens. I saw the anger flare in his eyes and then I saw him raise his rifle in my direction.

With nothing else to call on, I hastily raised my own pistol and fired it. The pistol boomed loudly in my hand and I would swear on the Good Book itself that its recoil almost tore my arm from its socket. The horseman in front of me snapped backwards in his saddle and tumbled to the ground, dead.

I stood there, stunned, holding the pistol in my hand, staring fixedly at the dead body on the ground. I endeavoured to convince myself that I had done no wrong. He had been going to kill me—

'Brother!' Renco called suddenly.

I turned on the moment and saw him sitting astride one of the Spanish horses. 'Come!' he called. 'Take his horse! We have to get to Cuzco!'

The city of Cuzco lies at the head of a long mountain valley that runs in a north-south direction. It is a walled city that is situated between two parallel rivers, the Huatanay and the Tullumayo, which act rather like moats.

Situated on a hill to the north of the city, towering above it, is the most dominant feature of the Cuzco valley. There, looking down over the city like a god, is the stone fortress of Sacsayhuaman.

Sacsayhuaman is a structure like no other I have seen in all of the world. Nothing in Spain, or even in the whole of Europe, can compare with its size and sheer dominating presence.

Truly, it is a most fearsome citadel—roughly pyramidal in shape, it consists of three colossal tiers, each one easily a hundred hands high, with walls constructed of gigantic hundred-ton blocks.

These Incans do not have mortar, but they more than make up for that deficiency with their extraordinary abilities in the art of stonemasonry. Rather than bind stones together with pastes, they build all of their fortresses, temples and palaces by fashioning enormous boulders into regular shapes and placing them alongside each other so that each boulder fits perfectly with the next. So exact are the joins between these monumental stones, so perfectly are they cut, that one cannot slip a knife blade between them.

It was in this setting that the intriguing siege of Cuzco took place.

Now, it is at this point that it should be said that the siege of Cuzco must rank as one of the strangest in the history of modern warfare.

The strangeness of the siege stems from the following fact: during it the invaders—my countrymen, the Spaniards—were inside the city walls, while the owners of the city, the Incan people, were positioned outside the city walls.

In other words, the Incans were laying siege to their own city.

To be fair, this situation came about as the result of a long and complicated chain of events. In 1533, my Spanish countrymen rode into Cuzco unopposed and, at first, they were friendly to the Incans. It was only when they began to perceive the full extent of the riches within the city walls that any pretence of civility vanished.

My countrymen pillaged Cuzco with a frenzy never before witnessed. Native men were brutally enslaved. Native women were ravaged. Gold was melted down by the wagonload—after which time the Incans began calling my Spanish countrymen 'gold-eaters'. Apparently, they thought that my countrymen's insatiable lust for gold stemmed from our need to eat it.

By 1535, the Sapa Inca—Renco's brother, Manco Capac—who had until that time been conciliatory in nature toward my countrymen, fled the capital for the mountains and assembled an enormous army with which he planned to retake Cuzco.

The Incan army—100 000 strong, but armed only

with sticks and clubs and arrows—descended upon the city of Cuzco in a fury and they took Sacsayhuaman, the massive stone citadel overlooking the city, in a day. The Spaniards took refuge inside the city walls.

And so the siege began.

It would last for three months.

Nothing on this earth could have prepared me for the sight that I beheld when I rode through the enormous stone tollgates at the northern end of the Cuzco valley.

It was night, but it might as well have been day. Fires burned everywhere, both within the city walls and without. It looked like Hell itself.

The largest force of men I have ever seen filled the valley before me, an undulating mass of humanity pouring down from the citadel on the hill toward the city—100 000 Incans, all of them on foot, shouting and screaming and waving torches and weapons. They had the entire city surrounded. Inside the city walls, fires could be seen ravaging the stone buildings situated there.

Renco rode ahead of me, right into the seething mass of people, and like the Red Sea for Moses, the crowd parted for him.

And as it did so, an enormous roar went up from the Incans, a cheer of rejoice, a shout of such fervour and celebration that it made the hairs on my neck stand on end.

It was as if they had all recognised Renco instantly—despite the fact that he was dressed in Spanish clothing—and stood aside for him. It was as if every single one of them knew of his mission and would do their utmost to allow him every possible haste in effecting it.

Renco and I charged through the teeming mass of people, galloping at tremendous speed as the hordes of cheering Incans opened up before us and urged us on.

We dismounted near the base of the mighty fortress Sacsayhuaman and walked quickly through a crowd of Indian warriors.

As we walked through the Incan ranks, I saw that numerous stakes had been driven into the ground all around us. Mounted on top of the stakes were the bloodied heads of Spanish soldiers. On some stakes, the entire bodies of captured Spaniards had been impaled. Their heads and feet had been hacked off. I walked quickly, mindful to stay close behind my friend Renco.

Then all at once, the crowd in front of us parted and I saw, standing before me at one of the entrances to the giant stone fortress, an Indian dressed in a most glorious manner. He wore a dazzling red cape and a gold-plated necklace and on his head sat a magnificent jewel-encrusted crown. He was surrounded by an entourage of at least twenty warriors and attendants.

It was Manco. The Sapa Inca.

Manco embraced Renco and they exchanged words in Quechuan, the Incans' language. Renco later translated it for me thus:

'Brother,' said the Sapa Inca. 'We were anxious as to your whereabouts. We heard that you had been captured, or worse, killed. And you are the only one who is permitted to enter the vault and rescue the—'

'Yes, brother, I know,' said Renco. 'Listen, we have no time. I must enter the city now. Has the river entrance been used yet?'

'No,' said Manco, 'we have refrained from using it as you instructed, so as not to alert the gold-eaters of its existence.'

'Good,' said Renco. He hesitated before he spoke again. 'I have another question.'

'What is it?'

'Bassario,' said Renco. 'Is he inside the city walls?'

'Bassario?' Manco frowned. 'Well, I . . . I do not know . . .'

'Was he in the city when it fell?'

'Well, yes.'

'Where was he?'

'Why, he was in the peasant prison,' said Manco. 'Where he has been for the past year. Where he belongs. Why? What need have you of a fiend like Bassario?'

'Let it not concern you now, brother,' said Renco. 'For it will matter for nothing if I do not find the idol first.'

Just then there came an almighty commotion from somewhere behind us and both Renco and I turned.

What I saw filled my heart with unimaginable horror: a column of Spanish soldiers—no fewer than three hundred of them, resplendent in their forged silver armour and distinctive pointed helmets—came charging into the valley from the northern tollgates, their muskets firing. Their horses were covered in heavy silver plating and, thus protected, the mounted Spanish troops cut a swathe through the ranks of the Incan warriors in front of them.

As I watched the column of conquistadors hack their way through the Incan ranks, trampling the Indians before them, I beheld two of the riders near the head of the procession, both of whom I recognised. The first was the Captain, Hernando Pizarro, the Governor's brother and a most cruel man. His distinctive black moustache and unkempt woolly beard were visible even from where I stood, four hundred paces away.

The second horseman was a figure whom I recognised with some degree of dread. Indeed, so much so that I took a second glance at him. But my worst fears were confirmed.

It was Castino.

The brutish Chanca who had been in the *San Vicente* with Renco. Only now he rode with his hands unmanacled—free—alongside Hernando.

And then all at once I understood.

Castino must have overheard my conversations with Renco . . .

He was leading Hernando to the vault inside the Coricancha.

Renco knew this, too. 'By the gods,' said he. He turned with haste to his brother. 'I must go. I must go *now*.'

'Speed to you, brother,' said Manco.

Renco nodded curtly to the Sapa Inca and then turned to me and said in Spanish, 'Come. We must hurry.'

We left the Sapa Inca and hastened around to the south side of the city, the side furthest from Sacsayhuaman. As we did so, I saw Hernando and his horsemen charge in through the city's northern gate.

'Where are we going?' I inquired as we strode quickly through the angry crowd.

'To the lower river,' was all my companion said in reply.

At length, we came to the river which ran alongside the southern wall of the city. I looked up at the wall on the other side of the stream and saw Spanish soldiers armed with muskets and swords walking the ramparts, silhouetted by the orange light of the fires burning behind them.

Renco strode purposefully toward the river and, to

my great surprise, stepped boots-and-all straight into the water.

'Wait!' I cried. 'Where are you going?'

'Down there,' said he, indicating the body of water.

'But I . . . I can't. I can't go in there with you.'

Renco gripped my arm firmly. 'My friend Alberto, I thank you from the bottom of my heart for what you have done, what you have risked to allow me to complete my mission. But now I must hurry if I am to succeed in my quest. Join me, Alberto. Stay with me. Complete my mission with me. Look at these people. While you are with me, you are a hero to them. But while you are not, you are just another gold-eater who must be killed. And now I must go. I cannot stay behind with you. If you stay here, I will not be able to help you. Come with me, Alberto. Dare to live.'

I looked at the Incan warriors behind me. Even with their primitive sticks and clubs, they still looked fierce and dangerous. I saw a Spanish soldier's head on a stake nearby, its mouth open in a grotesque yawn.

'I think I will go with you,' said I, turning and stepping waist-deep into the water next to him.

'All right, then. Take a deep breath,' said he, 'and follow me.'

And with that Renco held his breath and disappeared under the water. I shook my head and, despite myself, took a deep breath and followed him under the surface.

Silence.

The chants and shouts of the Incan hordes were gone now.

In the darkness of the murky river I followed Renco's kicking feet into a circular stone pipe that was set into the underwater wall of the city.

It was difficult to pull myself through the submerged cylindrical tunnel, its confines were so narrow. And it seemed to go on for an eternity. But then, just when it seemed as if my lungs would burst, I saw the end of the pipe and the rippling waves of the surface beyond it and I pulled myself harder through the water toward them.

I arose inside an underground sewer of some kind, lit by flaming torches mounted on the walls. I was standing waist-deep in water. Damp stone walls surrounded me. Square-shaped stone tunnels stretched away into the darkness. The foul stench of human faeces filled the air.

Renco was already wading through the water away from me, toward a junction in the tunnel system. I hurried after him.

Through the tunnels we went. Left then right, left then right—thus we made our way hastily through the underground labyrinth. Never once did Renco seem lost or doubtful—he just turned into each tunnel with confidence and purpose.

And then all at once he stopped and stared up at the stone ceiling above us.

I just stood behind him, perplexed. I could see no difference between this tunnel and any of the other half-dozen that we had just come through.

And then for some reason unknown to myself, Renco ducked underneath the foul-smelling water. Moments later, he came up with a rock the size of a man's fist. Then he climbed up out of the water and stood astride the narrow ledge that lined the tunnel and with his newfound rock began to hit the underside of one of the stone slabs that formed the ceiling of the tunnel.

Bang-bang. Bang.

Renco waited for a moment. Then he repeated the same sequence.

Bang-bang. Bang.

It was a code of some sort. Renco stepped back down into the water and we both stared up at the wet stone ceiling in silence, waiting for something to happen.

Nothing happened.

We kept waiting. As we did so, I noticed a small symbol carved into the corner of the stone slab that Renco had been assailing. It was a carving of a circle, with a double 'V' inscribed within it.

And then all of a sudden—*boom-boom, boom*—a series of muffled whumps could be heard from the other side of the ceiling. Someone repeating Renco's code.

Renco sighed with relief. Then he stood up on the ledge again and pounded out a new sequence of thumps.

Moments later, the whole square-shaped section of the ceiling slid away, grinding loudly against its neighbours, revealing a dark, cavern-like space above us.

Renco immediately climbed up out of the water and disappeared into the hole in the ceiling. I followed.

I came up inside a most splendid room, an enormous vault-like chamber, lined on all four sides with magnificent golden images. All four walls of the chamber were made of solid stone blocks, each one ten feet wide and probably as thick. There was no obvious door, except for a smaller stone—this one only six feet in height—set within one of the sturdy walls.

I was in the vault of the Coricancha.

A single flaming torch illuminated the cavernous space. It was held by a burly Incan warrior. Three other equally large warriors stood behind the torchbearer, glaring at me.

There was another person in the vault, however. An elderly woman, and she had eyes only for Renco.

She was a handsome woman, with grey hair and wrinkled skin, and I imagined that in her prime she must have been a strikingly beautiful woman. She was dressed simply, in a white cotton robe and a gold-and-emerald headdress. And I must say that in her simple white attire, she looked angelic, almost heavenly, like a priestess of some—

Boom!

I spun at the sudden noise. Renco did, too.

Boom!

It seemed to come from the other side of the walls. Someone pounding on the outside of the stone door.

I froze in horror.

The Spaniards.

Hernando.

They were trying to get in.

The old priestess said something to Renco in Quechuan. Renco replied quickly and then he gestured toward me.

Boom! Boom!

The old priestess then turned hurriedly to a stone pedestal behind her. I saw on the pedestal an object covered with a purple silk-like cloth.

The priestess picked up the object—cloth and all—and despite the insistent pounding on the walls, handed it solemnly to Renco. I still could not see what lay beneath the cloth. Whatever it was, it was about the size and shape of a human head.

Renco took the object respectfully.

Boom! Boom!

Why was he moving so slowly, I wondered incredulously, as my eyes darted to the shuddering stone walls around us.

Once the object was safely in his hands, Renco slowly removed its cloth.

And I saw it.

And for a moment, I could do nothing but stare.

It was the most beautiful, and yet at the same time the most fearsome-looking idol I had ever seen.

It was completely black, carved out of a square block of a very unusual type of stone. It was rough and sharp at the edges, the workmanship crude, uneven. Out of the middle of the block had been carved the visage of a fierce mountain cat with its jaws bared wide. It looked as if the cat—deranged with rage and fury—had managed to *push* its head out of the very stone itself.

Imperfections within the rock—thin rivulets of the most lustrous shade of purple—ran vertically down the cat's face, making the image appear even more fearsome, if indeed such a thing were possible.

Renco covered the idol once again. As he did so, the old priestess stepped forward and placed something around his neck. It was a thin leather cord with a dazzling green gemstone attached to it—a magnificent shining emerald that was easily the size of a man's ear. Renco accepted the gift with a solemn bow and then turned quickly to face me.

'We must go now,' said he.

Then, with the idol under his arm, he made for the hole in the floor. I hurried after him. The four burly warriors all took hold of the great stone slab that would cover our exit. The old priestess did not move.

Renco climbed down into the sewer. I lowered myself after him. As I did so, however, I noticed something quite peculiar.

The vault was silent.

The pounding outside had stopped.

And as I pondered this curiosity some more, I realised with some dread that the pounding had in fact ceased some goodly time before.

It was then that the entrance to the vault exploded inwards.

A great flash of white flared out around the edges of the huge stone doorway, and an instant later, the whole six-foot doorstone just blasted out into a thousand fragments, showering the vault room with fist-sized rocks.

I couldn't explain it. A battering ram could not possibly have fragmented so large a stone so instantaneously . . .

And then the smoke and dust in the doorway cleared and I saw the great black barrel of a cannon in the space where the doorstone had been.

My mind reeled.

They had blown open the vault door with a cannon!

'Come on!' Renco called from the sewer beneath me.

I immediately started lowering myself into the hole, just as the first Spanish soldiers came charging in through the dustcloud, firing their muskets in every direction.

And as I disappeared through the hole in the floor, the last thing I saw was the Captain, Hernando Pizarro, striding into the vault room with a pistol in his hand. His eyes were wild, and his head turned this way and that as he searched the vault for the idol that he so longed for.

And then, in a single horrifying instant, I saw Hernando look down in my direction and stare directly into my eyes.

I sloshed madly through the dark sewer tunnels, trying with all my might to keep up with Renco. As I did so, I heard shouts in Spanish echoing off the hard stone walls of the tunnels, saw long ominous shadows stretching out around the corners behind us.

Ahead of me, Renco just plunged onward through the filthy water with the Incan idol under his arm.

We hastened through the tunnels, waist-deep in the water, ducking left, bending right, weaving our way through the dark stone labyrinth back toward the river entrance and freedom.

After a while, however, I began to notice that we were racing in the wrong direction.

Renco was not heading back toward the river entrance.

'Where are we going!' I called forward.

'Just move!' he called back.

I turned a corner just as a torch on the wall above my head was blasted from its mount by a musket shot. I turned and saw a team of six conquistadors wading through the tunnel behind me, the flaming torchlight of the passageway glinting off their helmets.

'They're right behind us!' I called.

'Then run faster!'

More musket shots rang out, loud as thunderclaps, deafening my ears. Their projectiles exploded against the damp stone walls around us.

Just then, ahead of me, I saw Renco leap up onto a ledge and push up with his shoulder against a stone slab in the ceiling—a slab which I saw bore in its corner the same mysterious symbol that I had seen before, the circle with the double 'V' inside it. I leapt up onto the ledge after him and helped him heave the stone upward, revealing the starry night sky.

Renco climbed out first and I followed immediately behind him. We were standing in a narrow cobblestoned street of some sort. Impenetrable grey walls lined both sides of the alleyway.

I hurriedly began to replace the stone slab when all of a sudden, a musket shot from within the tunnel pinged against the edge of the hole, narrowly missing my fingers.

'Never mind. Come on, this way,' said Renco, pulling me down the tiny street.

The walls on either side of me became indistinguishable blurs of grey as we all but flew through the crooked alleyways of Cuzco with Hernando's soldiers ever close behind us.

As we evaded our pursuers, every now and then we would see brigades of Spanish troops running through the streets, racing for the ramparts.

We also—I am ashamed to say—saw stakes not unlike those outside the city walls. They were set up in every one of the city's plazas, row after row of stakes, upon which were impaled the horribly mutilated bodies of captured Incan warriors. These warriors had had their hands, heads and genitals hacked off.

In one such plaza, Renco saw an Incan longbow hanging from one of the desecrated corpses. He seized it and the quiver full of arrows on the ground beside it and then ducked back into the maze of alleyways. I just followed close behind him, not daring to let him out of my sight.

At length, however, Renco turned abruptly and entered a building of some sort. It was a squat stone structure, remarkably solid. In fact, so solid it almost looked fortified.

We passed through several outer rooms before we descended a flight of stone steps and came to a very large subterranean hall.

The hall was divided into two levels—one wide lower level and an upper landing that was little more than a balcony that ran around the circumference of the hall.

But it was the lower storey that held my attention.

There were nearly one hundred holes in the dirt floor of this hall—pits over which a network of thin stone bridges passed. With a surge of dread, I realised where we were.

We were in an Incan dungeon.

I was reminded of the fact that these Incans had not yet discovered metallurgy, hence they had no bars to create cages. A pit, I saw, was their answer to this dilemma.

I looked up at the balcony that overlooked the lower floor. It was a guard-walk, for the prison guards to patrol while they looked down on the prisoners.

Renco didn't miss a step. He just marched out onto one of the narrow stone bridges and peered down into the holes beneath it. Wails and shouts erupted from below, from the wretched, starving prisoners who had been left in their pits when the siege had begun a week earlier.

Renco stopped above one of the pits. I followed him

out onto the stone bridge and looked down into the dirty hole and, truly, this is what I saw.

The pit itself must have been at least five paces deep, with sheer earthen walls. Escape was impossible. At the bottom of the dirty well sat a man of average size, but filthy and putrid. Although he was thin, this man did not seem distressed, nor was he shouting like the rest of the poor, forlorn creatures in the prison hall. He just sat with his back pressed up against the wall of his pit, looking, if anything, relaxed and at ease. His composure—that wanton coolness of criminals around the world—made my skin crawl. I wondered what Renco could want with such a character.

'Bassario,' said Renco.

The criminal smiled. 'Why if it isn't the good prince Renco . . .'

'I need your help,' said Renco directly.

The prisoner seemed to find this humorous. 'I cannot imagine what the good prince could possibly want with my skills,' the criminal laughed. 'What is it, Renco? Now that your kingdom is in ruins are you thinking of embarking upon a life of crime?'

Renco looked back toward the entrance to the underground chamber, watching for Spaniards. I shared his concern. We had been in this dungeon too long already.

'I will only ask you this once, Bassario,' said Renco firmly. 'If you choose to help me, I will take you out of here. If you do not so choose, then I will leave you to die in this pit.'

'An interesting choice,' remarked the criminal.

'Well?'

The criminal Bassario stood. 'Get me out of this hole.'

Renco immediately went to fetch a wooden ladder resting against the far wall.

For my part, I was worried about Hernando and his men. They could arrive at any moment and here Renco was bargaining with a convict! I hurried over to the door through which we had entered the prison hall. When I got there I peered around the stone door-frame—

—and saw the dark demon-like figure of Hernando Pizarro striding down the stairs toward me!

My blood curdled at the sight—the wild brown eyes, the hooked black moustache, the scraggly black beard that had not been shaved for weeks.

I whirled back inside the doorway and started running. 'Renco!'

Renco had only just lowered the ladder into Bassario's pit when he turned and saw the first Spanish soldier come charging into the prison hall behind me.

Renco's hands moved quickly and in an instant he had his longbow raised with an arrow drawn back to his ear. He let fly with the missile and it streaked across the room, careering right for my head. I ducked and the arrow smacked into the forehead of the soldier behind me. His feet flew out from under him and he was thrown to the floor in a heavy heap.

I rushed out onto the network of stone bridges, ran quickly over the foul dungeon pits.

More conquistadors entered the prison hall behind me, Hernando among them, firing their muskets wildly.

By this time Bassario had emerged from his pit and now he and Renco were running across the wide section of dirt floor at the far end of the prison hall.

'Alberto! This way!' Renco called, pointing at the wide stone doorway at that end of the dungeon.

I saw the opening at the other end of the hall, saw a

solid squared-off boulder suspended above it by a pulley-like mechanism. It wasn't a big boulder—it was roughly the size of a man—and it was exactly the same size and shape as the doorway beneath it. Two taut lengths of rope held it above the doorway, each rope weighed down by stone counterweights, making it easier for the prison guards standing on the elevated guard-walk to raise and lower the boulder into the opening.

I ran for the door.

Whence I felt a terrible weight slam against my back and I was thrown forward. I fell heavily onto one of the narrow stone bridges and saw to my surprise that I had been pummelled from behind by a Spanish soldier!

He knelt astride my body, drew his dagger and was about to run me through when abruptly an arrow struck him in the chest. In fact the arrow hit the soldier with such force that it knocked his peaked steel helmet clear off his head and threw him bodily off the bridge and into the pit beneath us!

I looked down into the pit after him, only to see four bedraggled prisoners converge on him as one. I lost sight of the hapless soldier, but an instant later I heard a scream of the most utter and absolute terror. The starving prisoners in the pit were eating him alive.

I looked up just in time to see Renco slide to the ground next to me.

'Come on!' said he, grabbing my arm, pulling me to my feet.

I got up and saw that Bassario had arrived at the far doorway.

Musket fire rang out all around us, the rounds kicking up bright orange sparks as they bounced off the stone bridge beneath us.

Just then, a stray round hit one of the ropes that held the squared-off boulder suspended above the stone doorway at the far end of the hall.

With a sharp *twang* the rope snapped . . .

. . . and the boulder began to lower itself into the doorway!

Beneath it, Bassario looked up in horror, then back at Renco.

'No,' Renco breathed as he saw the descending boulder.

The doorway—forty paces away from us, and the only way out of the dungeon—was being sealed up!

I evaluated the distance, took in the speed at which the boulder was grinding down into the square stone opening.

There was no way we could make it.

The doorway was too far away, the boulder descending too rapidly. In a few moments, we would be sealed inside the dungeon, trapped and at the mercy of my bloodthirsty countrymen who were at that very moment racing out onto the network of stone bridges behind us, firing their muskets.

Nothing could save us now.

Renco obviously did not see it that way.

Despite the roaring body of musketeers behind us, the young prince quickly looked about himself and spied the pointed steel helmet of the Spanish soldier who had fallen into the pit beneath me.

Renco dived for the helmet, grabbed it, and then turned and threw it side-handed, sliding it across the dusty floor of the dungeon *toward* the rapidly-closing doorway.

The helmet slid across the dirt floor, spinning laterally as it did so, its silver pointed peak glinting in the firelight.

The boulder in the doorway kept descending, grinding against the sides of the stone opening.

Three feet.

Two feet.

One foot.

At which moment the rapidly-spinning helmet slid into the threshold of the doorway and wedged itself perfectly in between the descending boulder and the dirt-covered floor, stopping the boulder's downward movement! Now the thin boulder stood poised a bare foot above the floor, balanced on top of the helmet's pointed steel peak!

I looked at Renco, astonished.

'How did you do that?' said I.

'Never mind,' said he. 'Go!'

We ran off the bridge together and dashed across the wide section of dirt floor that led to the partially-open doorway—where Bassario stood waiting for us. In a dark corner of my mind, I wondered why Bassario hadn't just run away while Renco was occupied saving me. Perhaps he thought he stood a better chance of survival staying with Renco. Or maybe there was some other reason . . .

Frighteningly loud musket fire rang out all around us as Renco dropped down onto his behind and slid feet-first through the narrow gap between the boulder and the floor. My slide was somewhat less graceful. I dived head-first onto the dust-covered floor and wriggled clumsily on my chest through the gap and out into a stone-walled tunnel on the other side.

I was getting to my feet just as Renco kicked the helmet out from under the boulder and the great square-shaped stone completed its sealing of the doorway with a loud *whump*.

I sighed, breathless.

We were safe. For the moment.

'Come, we must hurry,' said Renco. 'It is time we farewelled this wretched city.'

Back in the alleyways. Running posthaste.

Renco led the way, with Bassario behind him and me last of all. At one point in our runnings, we came across a stockpile of Spanish weapons. Bassario took a longbow and a quiver full of arrows; Renco, a quiver, a rough leather satchel—into which he placed the idol—and a sword. For my own part, I took a long glistening sabre. For indeed, although I may be a humble monk, I hail from a family that has bred some of the finest fencers in all of Europe.

'This way,' said Renco, charging up a flight of stone steps.

We hurried up the stairs and came to a series of uneven roofs. Renco hastened out across the rooftops, hurdling low dividing walls, leaping across the small gaps between the different buildings.

Bassario and I followed until at last Renco fell to the ground, behind a low wall. His chest heaved as he breathed, rising and falling quickly.

He looked out over the low wall above him. I did the same. What I saw was this:

I beheld a wide cobblestone plaza filled with perhaps two dozen Spanish troops and as many horses. Some of the horses were freestanding, while others stood harnessed to a variety of wagons and carts.

On the far side of the plaza, set into the outer wall of the city, stood a large wooden gate. This gate, however, was not indigenous to Cuzco, but was rather an ugly appendage affixed to the city's stone gateway by my countrymen after the city had been seized.

Positioned directly in front of the enormous wooden gate was a large flatbed wagon drawn by two horses who faced in toward the city, away from the gate itself. Mounted on the back of this wagon was a sizeable cannon pointed in the other direction.

Nearer to us, at the base of the building on which we now sat, stood about thirty miserable-looking Incan prisoners. A long length of black rope was threaded through the steel manacles that each prisoner wore around his wrists, binding all of them together in a long dejected row.

'What are we going to do now?' I inquired of Renco anxiously.

'We're leaving.'

'How?'

'Through there,' said he, indicating the gate on the far side of the plaza.

'What about the sewer entrance?' said I, thinking it to be the most obvious escape route.

'A thief never uses the same entrance twice,' said Bassario. 'At least, not once he has been detected. Isn't that right, prince?'

'Correct,' said Renco.

I turned to appraise the criminal Bassario. He was in fact a rather handsome man, despite his grimy appearance. And he smiled broadly, his eyes twinkling—the smile of a man happy to be part of an adventure. I could not say that I shared his joy.

Now Renco began to rummagé through his quiver. He pulled out some arrows whose points had been wrapped in cloth, creating round bulbous heads.

'Good,' said he, looking about himself and finding a lighted torch hanging on a nearby wall. 'Very good.'

'What are you planning to do?' I inquired.

Renco did not appear to hear me. He merely stared

out at three horses standing unattended on the far side of the plaza.

'Renco,' I pressed, 'what are you planning to do?'

At which point Renco turned to face me and a wry smile crossed his face.

I stepped out into the wide-open plaza with my hands folded inside my saturated monk's cloak, my sodden hood pulled low over my wet hair.

I kept my head bowed as I crossed the plaza—stepping deftly aside as clusters of soldiers ran past me, ducking quickly as horses wheeled about in my direction—desperate not to sport any attention.

Renco guessed that the soldiers in the plaza would not yet know that a renegade Spanish monk—me—was aiding the Incan raiding party. As such, so long as they did not notice my soggy clothing, I should be able to get near the three unattended horses and bring them over to a nearby alleyway where Renco and Bassario could mount them.

But first I had to clear a passage to the gate, which meant getting the flatbed wagon with the cannon on it out of our path. That task would be harder. It required that I 'accidentally' scare the two horses harnessed to the wagon. Thus I carried concealed within my sleeve one of Renco's sharply pointed arrows, ready to—God forgive me—surreptitiously jab one of the poor creatures as I walked past them.

I crossed the plaza slowly, careful to keep my eyes averted, not daring to lock eyes with anyone.

85

As in the other plazas around the city, this one had stakes driven into the ground all around it. Severed heads were impaled upon them. The blood on the heads was fresh and it trickled down the stakes to the ground. My fear was extreme as I passed them—such would be my fate if I didn't get out of Cuzco soon.

The gate came into my view and with it the flatbed wagon that stood in front of it. I saw the horses and tightened my grip on the arrow inside my sleeve. Two more steps and—

'Hey! You!' barked a coarse voice from somewhere behind me.

I froze. Did not look up.

A large soldier with a pot belly stepped in front of me, so that he stood in between myself and the two horses. He wore his pointed conquistador's helmet perfectly and his voice was laced with authority. A senior soldier.

'What are you doing here?' said he and curtly.

Said I, 'I am sorry, so sorry . . . I was trapped in the city and I . . .'

'Get back to your quarters. This isn't a safe area. There are Indians in the city. We think they're after the Captain's idol.'

I couldn't believe it. I was so close to my objective and now I was being turned away! I reluctantly made to leave when suddenly a strong hand landed on my shoulder.

'A moment, monk—' the soldier began. But he cut himself off abruptly as he felt the dampness of my cloak.

'What the—'

Just then, a sharp whistling sound filled the air around me and then—*thwack!*—an arrow smacked into the big soldier's face, shattering his nose, causing an explosion of blood that splattered all over my face.

The soldier dropped like a stone. The other soldiers in the plaza saw him fall and whirled about, searching for the source of the danger.

Suddenly a second whistling sound filled the air, and this time a *flaming* arrow flew down from one of the darkened rooftops surrounding the plaza and shot low over the flatbed wagon in front of me and slammed hard into the big wooden gate behind it.

Shouts filled the air as the conquistadors opened fire on the shadowed source of the arrows.

I, however, was looking at something else entirely.

I was looking at the cannon on top of the flatbed wagon, or more particularly, at the fuse protruding from the breech of the cannon on top of the flatbed wagon.

The fuse was alight.

The flaming arrow—I did not know at the time, but I understand now that it was Bassario who fired it—had been so well aimed that it had *lit the fuse* on the cannon!

I did not wait for what would happen next. I just ran for the three unattended horses as quickly as I could, for no sooner did I reach them than the cannon on the flatbed wagon went off.

It was the loudest noise I had ever heard in my life. A monstrous blast of such intensity and power that it shook the world under me.

A billowing cloud of smoke shot out from the cannon's barrel and the big wooden gate in front of it snapped like a twig. When the smoke cleared before it, a gaping ten-foot hole could be seen in the lower half of the giant gate.

The horses harnessed to the flatbed wagon bolted at the sudden thunderous blast. They reared on their hind legs and took flight, galloping off into the alley-ways of Cuzco, leaving the damaged gate wide open.

The three horses I had been charged with procuring reared too. One of them bolted and ran off, but the other two calmed quickly as I held them firmly by their reins.

The Spanish soldiers were still firing blindly up into the shadowy rooftops. I looked up into the dark-ness. Renco and Bassario were nowhere to be seen—

'Monk!' someone called suddenly from behind me.

I turned and saw Bassario come running up with his longbow in his hand.

'Well, you couldn't have fouled this up any more, could you, monk?' said he with a smile as he leapt up into the saddle of one of my horses. 'All you had to do was scare the horses.'

'Where is Renco?' I inquired.

'He is coming,' said Bassario.

Just then a series of shrill, angry screams swept across the plaza and I turned instantly—and saw the row of manacled Incan prisoners charge as one at the Spaniards in the plaza. The Incans were free, no longer joined together by the long length of black rope!

Then suddenly, I heard a death scream and saw Renco up on one of the rooftops—standing over a fallen conquistador, hurriedly taking the fallen man's pistol, while six more Spaniards hustled up the stairs on the side of the building, chasing after him.

Renco looked down at me and cried, 'Alberto! Bassario! The gate! Go for the gate!'

'What about you!' I called.

'I'll be right behind you!' Renco called back as he ducked under a musket shot. 'Just go! Go!'

I leapt up into the saddle of the second horse.

'Come on!' Bassario cried, kicking his horse.

I spurred my own steed and shot off the mark, turning the beast sharply so that it charged toward the gate.

It was then that I turned in my saddle and saw a most amazing sight.

I saw an arrow—a pointed arrow, not a flaming one—soar across the plaza from one of the rooftops. Trailing behind it, wobbling like the undulating body of a snake, was a long length of rope—black rope—the rope that had bound the row of Incan prisoners together!

The arrow shot over my head and, with a firm smacking sound, lodged in the intact upper half of the big wooden gate. No sooner had the arrow hit the gate than I saw the entire length of rope behind it go taut.

And then I saw Renco at the other end of the rope—up on one of the rooftops standing with his legs splayed wide, with his newfound satchel draped over his right shoulder—saw him lash the leather belt of his Spanish pantaloons over it, and grab hold of the belt with one hand. Then I saw him leap off the roof and swing—no, slide—down the length of the rope, *over the entire plaza*, hanging onto the belt with one hand.

Some Spanish soldiers opened fire on him, but the dashing young prince just used his free hand to pull his pistol from his waistband and fire it at them while he slid at incredible speed down the rope!

I spurred my steed on, increased her speed, and pulled her in at a full gallop *under* Renco's rope just as he reached the end of his slide. He released his grip on the belt and dropped down perfectly onto the rump of my horse.

In front of us, Bassario leapt like a seasoned horseman through the enormous hole in the wooden gate. Renco and I followed close behind him, riding double, vaulting through the gate amid a hail of wild gunshots.

We burst out into the cold night air—riding hard across the massive stone slab that formed a bridge over the city's northern moat—and the first thing I heard as I raced across that bridge was a roar of total and utter jubilation from the hordes of Incan warriors in the valley before me.

'How's it going?' a voice said suddenly.

Race glanced up from the manuscript and for a moment was disoriented. He looked out through the small window to his right and saw a sea of snow-capped mountains and an endless expanse of clear blue sky.

He shook his head. He'd been so absorbed in the story that he'd forgotten he was on board the Army cargo plane.

Troy Copeland stood in front of him. He was one of Nash's DARPA people, the hawk-faced nuclear physicist.

'So, how's it going?' Copeland said, nodding at the bundle of paper in Race's lap. 'Found the location of the idol yet?'

'Well, I've found the idol,' Race said, flipping through the remainder of the manuscript. He was about two-thirds of the way through it. 'I think I'm about to find out where they took it.'

'Good,' Copeland said, turning. 'Keep us posted.'

'Hey,' Race said. 'Before you go, can I ask you something?'

'Sure.'

'What is thyrium-261 used for?'

Copeland frowned at the question.

'I think I have a right to know,' Race said.

Copeland nodded slowly. 'Yes . . . yes, I guess you do.' He took a breath. 'As I think you were told before, thyrium-261 is not indigenous to Earth. It comes from a binary star system called the Pleiades, a system not far from our own.

'Now, as you can probably imagine, planets in binary star systems are affected by all sorts of forces because of their twin suns—photosynthesis is doubled; gravitational effects, as well as *resistance* to gravity, are enormous. As such, elements found on planets in binary systems are usually heavier and denser than similar elements found here on Earth. Thyrium-261 is just such an element.

'It was first found in petrified form in the walls of a meteor crater in Arizona in 1972. And even though the specimen there had been inert for millions of years, its potential sent shockwaves throughout the physics community.'

'Why?'

'Well, you see, on a molecular level, thyrium bears a striking resemblance to the terrestrial elements uranium and plutonium. But thyrium *outweighs* both of these earthly elements by an order of magnitude. It is *denser* than our two most potent nuclear elements combined. Which means it is infinitely more powerful.'

Race began to feel a sense of dread crawling up his spine. Where was Copeland going with this?

'But like I said, thyrium has only ever been found on Earth in petrified form. Since 1972, two other samples have been discovered, but again both of those specimens were at least 40 million years old. Which is of no use to anyone since petrified thyrium is inert, chemically dead.

'What we have been waiting for for the past twenty-seven years is the discovery of a specimen of "live" thyrium, a specimen that is still active on a molecular level. And now we think we've found it, in a meteorite that crash-landed in the jungles of Peru five hundred years ago.'

'So what does thyrium do?' Race asked.

'A lot,' Copeland said. 'A *whole* lot. For one thing, its potential as a power source is astronomical. Conservative estimates predict that a properly constituted thyrium reactor would generate electrical energy at a rate *six hundred times* greater than all the nuclear power plants in the United States combined.

'But there's an added bonus. Unlike our terrestrial nuclear elements, when thyrium is used as the core element of a fusion reactor, it decomposes with one hundred per cent efficiency. In other words, it leaves no contaminated waste byproducts. As such, it is unlike any power source on this earth. Uranium waste must be discarded in radioactive rods. Hell, even gasoline produces carbon monoxide. But thyrium is *clean*. It is a perfectly efficient power source. Perfect. It is so internally pure that, based on our modelling, a raw sample of it would emit only microscopic quantities of passive radiation.'

Race held up his hand. 'All right, all right. That all sounds great, but last I heard, DARPA wasn't in the business of providing America with power stations. What *else* does thyrium do?'

Copeland smiled, caught.

'Professor, for the last ten years, DARPA's Tactical Technology Office has been working on a new weapon, a weapon unlike anything this world has ever seen. It is a device codenamed "Supernova".'

As soon as Copeland said the word, something

twigged in the back of Race's mind. He recalled a conversation he'd overheard between Copeland and Nash soon after he had boarded the plane. A conversation in which they had mentioned a break-in at Fairfax Drive and the theft of a device called a Supernova.

'What exactly is this Supernova?'

'Put simply,' Copeland said, 'the Supernova is the most powerful weapon ever devised in the history of mankind. It's what we call a planet killer.'

'A *what*?'

'A planet killer. A nuclear device so powerful that when detonated, it would completely destroy nearly a third of the Earth's mass. With a third of its mass gone, the Earth's orbit around the sun would be corrupted. Our planet would spin out of control, out into space, further and further away from the sun. Within minutes the Earth's surface—what was left of it—would be too cold to sustain human life. The Supernova, Professor Race, is the first man-made device that is capable of ending life as we know it on this planet. Hence its namesake, the name we give to an exploding star.'

Race swallowed. In fact, he felt positively weak.

A million questions flooded his mind.

Like, why would someone build such a device? What possible reason could there be for creating a weapon that could kill everyone on the planet, including its own creators? And all that considered, why was *his* country building it?

Copeland continued, 'The thing is, Professor, the Supernova that we have at present is a prototype, a workable shell. That device—the device that was stolen from DARPA headquarters last night—is useless. For the simple reason that the operation of the Supernova requires the addition of one thing. Thyrium.'

Oh, great . . . Race thought.

'In this regard,' Copeland said, 'the Supernova is not all that dissimilar to a neutron bomb. It is a fission device—which means it operates on the principle of splitting the thyrium atom. Two conventional thermonuclear warheads are used to split a subcritical mass of thyrium, unleashing the mega-explosion.'

'Okay, wait a second,' Race said. 'Let me get this straight. You guys have built a weapon—a weapon that is capable of *destroying the planet*—that is dependent upon an element that you don't even have yet?'

'That's correct,' Copeland said.

'But why? Why is America building a weapon that can do all this?'

Copeland nodded. 'That's always a difficult question to answer. I mean—'

'There are two reasons,' a deeper voice said suddenly from behind Race.

It was Frank Nash.

Nash nodded at the manuscript in Race's lap. 'Have you found the location of the idol yet?'

'Not yet.'

'Then I'll make this quick so you can get back to work. First of all, what I am about to tell you is of the utmost secrecy. There are sixteen people in the country who know what am I about to tell you and five of them are on this plane. If you mention any of this to anyone after the completion of this mission, you'll spend the next seventy-five years in jail. Do you understand me, Professor?'

'Uh-huh.'

'Good. The justification for the construction of the Supernova is twofold. The first reason is this. About eighteen months ago, it was discovered that state-funded scientists in Germany had begun the secret construction of a Supernova. Our response was simple: if they were going to build one, so were we.'

'That's great logic,' Race said.

'It's exactly the same logic Oppenheimer used to justify building the atomic bomb.'

'Geez, you're standing on the backs of giants there, Colonel,' Race said drily. 'And the second reason?'

Nash said, 'Professor, have you ever heard of a man named Dietrich von Choltitz?'

'No.'

'Commanding-General Dietrich von Choltitz was the Nazi general in charge of the German forces in Paris at the time of the Nazis' withdrawal from France in August of 1944. After it became apparent that the Allies were going to retake Paris, Hitler sent Choltitz a communique. It ordered Choltitz to set thousands of incendiary devices all over the city before he left . . . and then, after he was gone, to blow Paris sky-high.

'Now, to von Choltitz's credit, he disobeyed the order. He didn't want to go down in history as the man who destroyed Paris. But what is important here is the logic behind Hitler's order. If *he* couldn't have Paris, no-one could.'

'So what are you saying?' Race said warily.

'Professor, the Supernova is but one evolutionary step in a high-level strategic plan that has existed in U.S. foreign policy for the last fifty years. That plan is called the Choltitz Plan.'

'What do you mean?'

'What I mean is this. Did you know that throughout the Cold War, the U.S. Navy had standing orders to ensure that at any given time there were a number of nuclear ballistic missile submarines stationed at certain strategic locations around the world? Do you know what those submarines were there for?'

'What?'

'The orders those subs had were very simple. Should the Soviet Union in any way defeat the United States in any sudden or unforeseen engagement, those boomers had orders to launch a rain of nuclear missiles not just on Soviet targets, but on *every major city on the European and U.S. mainlands*.'

'What!'

'The Choltitz Plan, Professor Race. If we can't have it, *no-one* can.'

'But this is on a global scale . . .' Race said in disbelief.

'That's right. That's exactly right. And therein lies the reason for the creation of the Supernova. The United States is the most dominant nation on this earth. Should any nation seek to alter that situation, we will inform them of our possession of a workable Supernova. If they take further steps and a conflict ensues and the United States is beaten—or worse, crippled—then we will detonate the device.'

Race felt a knot tighten in his stomach.

Was this for real? Was this *policy*? If America could not control the world, it would destroy it?

'How can you build something like that?'

'Professor Race, what if China decided to wage war against the United States? What if they *won*? Would you have the American people under the rule of a Chinese regime?'

'But you'd rather die?'

'Yes.'

'And take the rest of the world with you,' Race said. 'You guys must be the sorest losers of all time.'

'Be that as it may,' Nash said, changing his tone, 'the law of unintended consequences has taken its effect on this situation. News of the creation of a device with the potential to destroy the planet has brought other parties out of the woodwork, parties who would see such a weapon as a powerful bargaining chip in their own crusades.'

'What kind of parties?'

'Certain terrorist groups. People who if they got their hands on a workable Supernova would hold the world to ransom.'

'Right,' Race said, 'and now your Supernova's been stolen, probably by terrorists.'

'That's correct.'

'You opened Pandora's box, didn't you, Doctor Nash.'

'Yes. Yes, I'm afraid we did. And that's why it is imperative that we get hold of that idol before anyone else does.'

With that, Nash and Copeland left Race alone with the manuscript once again.

Race took a moment to gather his thoughts. His mind was swirling. Supernovas. Global destruction. Terrorist groups. He found it difficult to concentrate.

He shook it all away, forced himself to focus, found his place in the manuscript again—the part where Renco and Alberto Santiago had just blasted their way out of the besieged city of Cuzco.

Then Race took a deep breath, adjusted his glasses and entered the world of the Incas once again.

SECOND READING

We raced through the night, Renco, Bassario and myself, spurring our horses on, making them gallop faster than they had ever done so before. For behind us, close behind us, were the Spaniards—Hernando and his legion of mounted troops, galloping across the countryside, hunting us like dogs.

After departing through the northern gates of the Cuzco valley we veered right, heading to the northeast. We came to the Urubamba River—the same river that had held Renco's prison hulk—and crossed it not far from the town of Pisac.

And thus began our journey, our desperate escape through the wilderness.

I will not trouble you, dear reader, with every trifling incident of our arduous journey, for it went for many days and the incidents that took place during it were far too numerous. Rather, I shall mention only those occurrences which are pertinent to my grander tale.

We were headed for a village named Vilcafor—so Renco informed me—of which his uncle was the chieftain. This village was to be found in the foothills of the great mountains far to the north, at the point where those mountains met the great rainforest to the east.

Apparently, Vilcafor was a secret citadel town—heavily fortified and well defended—that was maintained by the Incan nobility for use in times of crisis. Its location was a carefully guarded secret, and it could be found only by following a series of stone totems placed at certain intervals in the rainforest, and then only when one knew the code to find the totems. But to get to the rainforest, first we had to traverse the mountains.

And so we entered the mountains—the stupendous rocky monoliths that dominate New Spain. It cannot be overstated just how magnificent the mountains of this country are. Their steep rocky bluffs and high pointed summits—capped with snow all year round—can be seen for hundreds of miles, even from the dense rainforests of the lowlands.

After a few days of travel, we discarded our horses, preferring to navigate the delicate mountain trails on foot. Carefully, we walked along slippery narrow paths cut into the sides of steep mountain gorges. Gingerly, we crossed long sagging rope bridges suspended high above raging mountain rivers.

And all the while, echoing through the maze of narrow gorges behind us, were the shouts and marching footsteps of the Spaniards.

We came to several Incan villages, situated in the navels of the splendid mountain valleys. Each village was named after its chieftain—Rumac, Sipo and Huanco.

At these villages we were supplied with food, guides and llamas. The generosity of these people was incredible. It was as if every single villager knew of Renco and his mission and they could not have moved faster to help us. When we had time, Renco would show them the black stone idol and they would all bow before it and fall silent.

But we rarely had such time.

The Spaniards pursued us doggedly.

On one occasion, as we left the town of Ocuyu—a village situated at the base of a wide mountain valley—no sooner had we surmounted the crest of the nearest hill than I heard the reports of heavy musket fire from behind us. I turned to gaze back down the valley.

What I saw filled me with horror.

I saw Hernando and his troops—a whole gigantic column of at least one hundred men—marching on foot at the far end of the valley. Mounted troops flanked the enormous body of foot soldiers, riding ahead of them into the town that we had only just left, firing their muskets at the unarmed Incans.

Later, Hernando would divide his hundred-man legion into three thirty-man divisions. Then he staggered their marching times, so that while one division marched, the other two rested. The rested divisions would then march later, overtaking the first group in their turn, and the cycle would continue. The result was a constantly moving mass of men, a mass that was always moving forward, always closing in on us.

And all this while Renco, Bassario and myself stumbled ever forward, struggling through the rocky wilderness, fighting fatigue every moment of the way.

Of one thing I was certain: the Spaniards would catch us. The only question was when.

Yet still we toiled on.

Now at one point on our journey—and I must say, at a time when my countrymen were so close behind us that we could hear their voices echoing off the canyons to our rear—we stopped at a village named Colco, which is situated on the banks of a mountain river known as the Paucartambo.

It was in this town that I obtained a clue as to why Renco had brought the criminal Bassario along on our journey.

For in the village of Colco there is a quarry. Now, as I have said before, these Indians are masterful stonemasons. All of their buildings are constructed of the most finely cut stones, some of which can be as tall as six men and weigh more than a hundred tons. Such stones are harvested in the massive quarries of towns like Colco.

After speaking quickly with the town's chieftain, Renco was escorted to the quarry—a monumental hole that had been dug into the side of a mountain. He returned a short while later with a goat-skin sack in his hand. The sides of the sack bulged with sharp, rocky corners. Renco handed the sack to Bassario and we rode on.

I did not know what was in that sack, but on the nights when we stopped to rest, Bassario would slink away to a corner of the camp and light his own fire. Then he would sit crosslegged and work over the sack with his back to Renco and myself.

After eleven days of this most brutal travel, we emerged from the mountains and beheld a most momentous sight, a vista like none I have ever witnessed.

We saw the rainforest spread out before us, a seamless carpet of green stretching out to the distant horizon. The only breaks in the carpet were the tablelands—the wide, flat step-like formations in the landscape that marked the gradual transition from rugged mountain range to verdant river basin—and the wide bands of brown that snaked their way through the dense jungle, the mighty rivers of the rainforest.

And so we plunged into the jungle.

It was like Hell on earth.

For days we travelled through the eternal shade of the rainforest. It was wet and it was damp and Lord, how it was dangerous. Obscenely fat snakes hung from the trees, small rodents scurried about under our feet, and on one night—I was certain of it—I saw the veiled outline of a panther, a shadow superimposed on the darkness, slinking silently on padded paws across a nearby branch.

And then, of course, there were the rivers, in which there lurked the greatest danger of all.

Alligators.

Their craggy triangular heads alone were enough to make a man's blood turn to ice, and their bodies, black and heavy and armoured, were at least six paces in length. Their eyes always watched us—unblinking, reptilian, repulsive.

We travelled down the rivers on reed canoes donated to us by the river villages of Paxu, Tupra and Roya—boats which seemed pathetically small when compared to the inordinately large reptiles in the water all around us—and we climbed down the steep cliffs of the tablelands with the aid of skilled Incan guides.

In the evenings, by the light of the fire, Renco would instruct me in his language, Quechuan. In return, I would teach him the finer points of swordsmanship with the two glistening Spanish sabres we had pilfered on our way out of Cuzco.

While Renco and I fenced, if he wasn't toiling away in some corner of the camp Bassario would often practise his archery. Apparently, before he was imprisoned (for what I knew not), Bassario had been one of the finest archers in all of the Incan empire. I believed it. One evening I saw him throw a rainforest fruit high into the air and pierce it with an arrow a moment later, such was his skill.

After a time, however, it became apparent to us that the harsh terrain of the rainforest had slowed our pursuers somewhat. The sounds of Hernando and his men hacking at the branches of the forest behind us grew progressively more faint. Indeed, at one time I thought that perhaps Hernando had given up on his pursuit.

But no. Every day, runners from the various villages we had passed through would catch us up and inform us of the sacking of their town. Hernando and his men were still coming.

And so we toiled on.

And then one day, not long after we had left the village of Roya, at a time when I was walking at the head of our expedition, I pushed aside a large branch and found myself staring into the eyes of a snarling cat-like creature.

I fell backwards with a shout, dropping with a loud splat in the mud.

The next thing I heard was Bassario chuckling softly.

I looked up and saw that I had revealed a large stone totem of some sort. The snarling cat that I had seen was nothing but a stone *carving* of a great, cat-like creature. But the carving was covered in a veil of trickling water, giving the unwary traveller—me—the impression that it was well and truly alive.

As I looked at it more closely, however, I noticed that the stone carving on the totem was not dissimilar to that of the idol that was the cause of our frenetic journey. It was a jaguar of some kind, possessed of large feline fangs, snarling—no, roaring—at the incautious explorer who happened to stumble upon it.

I have wondered more than once at these Incans' fascination with the great cats.

They idolise these creatures, treat them as gods. In fact, warriors who show feline co-ordination in their movements are most revered in their armies—it is seen as a great skill to be able to land on one's feet and pounce immediately back into the fray. Such a warrior is said to be possessed of the *jinga*.

Why, the very evening before I stumbled so embarrassingly upon the stone totem, Renco had been telling me that the most feared creature in their mythology is a great black cat known as the *titi* in Agmara, or the *rapa* in Quechuan. Apparently, this creature is as black as the night and almost as tall as a man even when standing on all four legs. And it kills with unparalleled ferocity. Indeed, Renco said, it is that most feared variety of wild animal—the kind that kills for no other reason than for the pleasure of killing.

'Well done, Brother Alberto,' said Renco as I lay in the mud, staring up at the totem. 'You've found the first of the totems that will lead us to Vilcafor.'

'How will they lead us there?' I inquired as I rose to my feet.

Said Renco, 'There is a code, known only to the most senior of Incan nobles—'

'But if he tells you, he'll have to kill you,' Bassario interjected with a rude grin.

Renco smiled indulgently at Bassario. 'True,' said he. 'But in the event that I should die, I shall need someone to continue my mission. And to do that, that someone will have to know the code to the totems.' Renco turned to face me. 'I was hoping that you would be willing to bear that responsibility, Alberto.'

'Me?' said I, swallowing.

'Yes, you,' said Renco. 'Alberto, I see the qualities of a hero in you, even if you do not. You possess honour and courage in far greater quantities than the average soul. I would have no hesitation in entrusting my people's fate to you should the worst befall me, if you would allow it.'

I bowed my head and nodded, acceding to his wish.

'Good,' Renco smiled. 'You, on the other hand,' he said, grinning wryly at Bassario, 'would give me considerable hesitation. Now go stand over there.'

Once Bassario had moved to stand some paces away from us, Renco leaned close to me and indicated the stone carving of the rapa in front of us. 'The code is simple: follow the rapa's tail.'

'Follow the rapa's tail . . .' said I, looking at the totem. Sure enough, out of the back of the carving extended a thin snaking feline tail, pointing to the north.

'But,' Renco suddenly held up his finger, 'not every totem is to be followed in this way. It is this rule that only the most senior nobles know. Indeed, I was only told of it by the high priestess of the Coricancha when we arrived there to get the idol.'

'What is the rule, then?' I inquired.

'After the first totem every second totem is to be distrusted. In those cases, one is to follow the totem in the direction of the Mark of the Sun.'

'The Mark of the Sun?'

'A mark not unlike this one,' Renco said, indicating the small triangular birthmark below his left eye, the dark brown blemish of skin that looked like an inverted mountain.

'At every second totem after the first one,' he said, 'we are not to follow the rapa's tail, but rather to go in the direction of the Mark of the Sun.'

'What will happen if one continues to follow the rapa's tail?' I inquired. 'Won't our enemies ultimately realise that they are travelling in the wrong direction when they find no more totems?'

Renco smiled at me. 'Oh, no, Alberto. There are more totems to be found, even if one goes in the wrong direction. But they only lead the bamboozled adventurer farther and farther away from the citadel.'

And so we followed the totems through the rainforest.

They were spaced at varying intervals—some were but a few hundred paces from their predecessors, others were some miles overland—so we had to be careful that we travelled in direct lines. Often we were aided by the river system, since at times the totems had been carefully placed along the riverbanks.

Following the totems, we travelled in a northerly direction, crossing the wide rainforest basin until we came to a new tableland that led up to the mountains.

This tableland stretched from the north to the south for as far as the eye could see—a giant jungle-covered plateau—a single step that Our Lord had built to aid him in stepping up from the rainforest to the mountain foothills. It was dotted with waterfalls all along its length. It was a truly magnificent sight.

We climbed the tableland's cliff-like eastern face, hauling with us our reed canoes and paddles. It was then that we came to a final totem which directed us upriver, toward the gigantic snow-capped mountains that loomed above the rainforest.

We rowed against the gentle current of the river in the pouring afternoon rain. After a while, however, the rain stopped and in the mist that followed it the jungle took on an eerie quality. The world fell oddly silent and, strangely, the sounds of the rainforest abruptly vanished.

No birds chirped. No rodents rustled in the under-brush.

I felt a rush of dread flood through my body.

Something was not right here.

Renco and Bassario must have felt it, too, for they paddled more slowly now, dipping their oars silently into the glassy surface of the water, as if not daring to break the unnatural silence.

And then we rounded a bend in the river and suddenly we saw a town on the riverbank, nestled up against the base of the enormous mountain range. An imposing stone structure stood proudly in the centre of a cluster of small huts, while a wide moat-like ditch surrounded the entire enclave.

The citadel of Vilcafor.

But none of us had much care for the great citadel. Nor did we take much notice of the village around it that lay in smouldering ruins.

No. We only had eyes for the bodies, the scores of bodies that lay crumpled on the main street of the town, covered in blood.

SECOND MACHINATION

Monday, January 4, 1540 hours

Race turned the page, looking for the next chapter, but it wasn't there. This, it seemed, was the last page of the manuscript.

Damn it, he thought.

He peered out the window of the Hercules and saw the engines mounted on the green-painted wing outside, saw the snow-capped peaks of the Andes gliding by beneath them.

He looked over at Nash sitting on the other side of the aisle, working on a laptop computer.

'Is this all there is?' he asked.

'I'm sorry?' Nash frowned.

'The manuscript. Is this all we have?'

'You mean you've finished translating it already?'

'Uh-huh.'

'Did you find the location of the idol?'

'Well, kind of,' Race said, looking down at the notes he'd taken as he'd translated the manuscript. They read:

- LEAVE CUZCO→ENTER MTNS.
- VILLAGES: <u>RUMAC, SIPO, HUANCO, OCUYU</u>.
- <u>COLCO</u>—PAUCARTAMBO RIVER—QUARRY THERE.
- 11 DAYS—COME TO RAINFOREST.

- RIVER VILLAGES: <u>PAXU, TUPRA, ROYA</u>.
- STONE TOTEMS—CARVED IN SHAPE OF CAT-LIKE CREATURE—
  LEAD TO <u>CITADEL AT VILCAFOR</u>.
- <u>TOTEM CODE</u>—FOLLOW THE RAPA'S TAIL FOR FIRST TOTEM.
- AT EVERY SECOND TOTEM AFTER THAT, FOLLOW THE 'MARK OF
  THE SUN'.
- FOLLOWED TOTEMS NORTH ACROSS RAINFOREST BASIN—CAME
  TO TABLELAND LEADING UP TO MOUNTAIN FOOTHILLS.
- AT FINAL TOTEM WENT UPRIVER TOWARD MTNS—FOUND CITADEL
  IN RUINS.

'What do you mean you've *kind* of found it?' Nash asked.

'Well, that's the thing,' Race said. 'The manuscript virtually ends in mid-sentence when they reach the town of Vilcafor. There's obviously more to be read, but it isn't here.' He didn't add that he was beginning to find the story kind of interesting and actually *wanted* to read more of it. 'You're sure this is all we have?'

'I'm afraid so,' Nash said. 'Remember, this isn't the original manuscript, but rather a half-finished *copy* of it, transcribed by another monk many years after Santiago wrote the original. This is all there is, this is all that the other monk managed to copy from the original.'

He frowned. 'I was hoping we'd get the exact location of the idol from it, but if it doesn't give us that, then what I need to know are the generalities: where to look, where to start looking. We've got the technology to pinpoint the location of the idol *if* we know where to begin our search. And by the sound of things, from what you've read so far, it appears that you have enough there to tell me where to start looking. So tell me what you know.'

Race showed Nash his notes, told him the story of Renco Capac and his flight from Cuzco. He then explained that from what he'd read, Renco had made it to his intended destination—a citadel-town at the base of the Andes known as Vilcafor. He also told Nash that, so long as they knew one particular fact, the manuscript detailed how to get to that town.

'And what fact is that?' Nash said.

'Assuming the stone totems are still there,' Race said, 'you have to know what the "Mark of the Sun" is. If you don't know what it is, then you can't read the totems.'

Nash frowned and turned to Walter Chambers, the anthropologist and Incan expert, sitting a few seats away. 'Walter. Do you know anything about a "Mark of the Sun" in Incan culture?'

'The Mark of the Sun? Why, yes, of course.'

'What is it?'

Chambers shrugged, came over. 'It's just a birth-mark, really. Kind of like Professor Race's there.' He nodded with his chin at Race's glasses, indicating the dark triangular blemish on the skin under his left eye. Race cringed. Ever since he was a kid, he'd hated that birthmark. He thought it looked like a smudged coffee stain on his face.

'The Incans thought birthmarks were signs of dis-tinction,' Chambers said. 'Signs sent from the gods themselves. The Mark of the Sun was a special kind of birthmark—a blemish on the face, just below the left eye. It was special because the Incans believed that it was a mark sent from their most powerful god, the Sun God. To have a child with such a mark was regarded as a great honour. The Mark of the Sun indicated that that particular child was special, in some way destined for greatness.'

Race said, 'So if someone instructed us to follow a

statue in the direction of the Mark of the Sun, they would be telling us to go to the statue's left?'

'That would be correct,' Chambers said, hesitating. 'I *think*.'

'What do you mean, you *think*?' Nash said.

'Well, you see, over the past ten years, there's been substantial debate among anthropologists as to whether or not the Mark of the Sun was found on the left-hand side of the face or the right-hand side. Incan carvings and pictographs universally depict the Mark of the Sun—whether on pictures of humans or animals or whatever—under the carving's left eye. Problems arise, however, when one reads *Spanish* texts like the *Relación* and the *Royal Commentaries* which talk of people like Renco Capac and Tupac Amaru, both of whom were said to have borne the Mark. The problem is, those books say that Renco and Amaru had the mark under their *right* eyes. And as soon as something like that arises, confusion reigns supreme.'

'So what do *you* think?'

'Left-hand side, definitely.'

'And we should be able to find our way to the citadel?' Nash said, worried.

'You can trust my judgement on this one, Colonel,' Chambers said confidently. 'If we follow each statue to the left, we'll find that citadel.'

Just then, a sing-song little bell rang from somewhere nearby.

Race turned. It had come from Nash's laptop—an e-mail message must have just come through. Nash went back to his seat to get it.

Chambers turned to Race. 'It's all very exciting, isn't it?'

'Exciting isn't exactly the word I would use,' Race said. He was just glad that he'd finished translating the manuscript before they had landed in Cuzco. If Nash was going to venture into the jungle after the idol, he didn't want to be a part of it.

He glanced at his watch.

It was 4:35 pm. It was getting late.

Just then, Nash appeared next to him.

'Professor,' he said. 'If you're up to it, I'd like you to come along with us to Vilcafor.'

There was something in his tone that made Race pause. This was a command, not a question.

'I thought you said if I translated the manuscript before we landed I wouldn't even have to get off the plane.'

'I said that that *might* be the case. You'll recall that I also said that if you *did* have to leave the plane, you'd have a team of Green Berets looking after you. That is the circumstance now.'

'Why?' Race asked.

'I've arranged for a pair of helicopters to meet us at Cuzco,' Nash said. 'We'll be using them to follow Santiago's trail from the air. Unfortunately, I thought the manuscript would be more detailed in its description of the location of the idol, more precise. But now we're going to need you for the trip to Vilcafor, in case there are any ambiguities between the text and the terrain.'

Race didn't like the sound of this. He felt that he had fulfilled his part of the deal, and the idea of going into the Amazon rainforest made him decidedly uneasy.

On top of that, the *tone* of Nash's request made him even more apprehensive. He got the feeling that now that Nash had him on board the Hercules and bound for Cuzco, his options—and his ability to say no—were

117

extremely limited. He felt trapped, railroaded into going somewhere he didn't want to go. This wasn't part of the deal at all.

'Couldn't I just stay in Cuzco?' he offered lamely. 'Keep in contact with you from there?'

'No,' Nash said. 'Definitely not. We're arriving through Cuzco, but we won't be leaving that way. This plane and all the U.S. Army personnel waiting for us in Cuzco will be leaving the city shortly after we head off into the jungle in the choppers. I'm sorry, Professor, but I *need* you. I need you to help me get to Vilcafor.'

Race bit his lip. *Christ* . . .

'Well . . . all right,' he said reluctantly.

'Good,' Nash said, standing. 'Very good. Now, did I hear you say earlier that you had some less formal clothes in that bag of yours?'

'Yeah.'

'Well, I suggest you get changed into them. You're going to the jungle now.'

The Hercules flew over the mountains.

Race emerged from the lavatory in the plane's lower cargo deck, now dressed in a white T-shirt, blue jeans and a pair of black sneakers—the clothes that he'd packed for his lunchtime baseball game. He was also wearing a cap—a battered, navy-blue New York Yankees baseball cap.

He saw the Green Berets on the deck in front of him, preparing and cleaning their weapons for the mission ahead. One of the commandos—a red-headed older corporal named Jake 'Buzz' Cochrane—was talking animatedly as he cleaned the firing mechanism of his M-16.

'I tell you, boys, it was fucking apples,' he was saying. 'Apples. Sweet sixteen with cheap Doreen. Gentlemen, mark my words, she is without a doubt, the most bang-for-your-buck whore in all of South Carolina—'

At that moment, Cochrane caught sight of Race standing—listening—at the lavatory door and he cut himself off.

All of the other Green Berets spun around and Race felt instantly self-conscious.

He felt like an outsider. Someone who wasn't part of the brotherhood. Someone who didn't belong.

He saw his bodyguard—the tall sergeant, Van Lewen—hovering at the perimeter of the circle, and he smiled. 'Hey.'

Van Lewen smiled back. 'How's it going?'

'Good. Really good,' Race said lamely.

He walked past the now silent band of rugged Green Berets, reached the steep flight of steps that led back up to the main passenger deck.

As he climbed the stairs, however, he heard the Green Beret named Cochrane mutter something from the cargo bay.

He knew he wasn't supposed to have heard it, but he heard it anyway.

Cochrane had said, 'Fucking pansy.'

A voice came over the PA system as Race walked back down the centre aisle of the passenger compartment. 'Commencing our descent now. ETA Cuzco, twenty minutes.'

On his way to his seat, Race passed Walter Chambers. The bespectacled little scientist was holding Race's notes alongside another sheet of paper. It was a map of some sort, marked with a felt-tip pen.

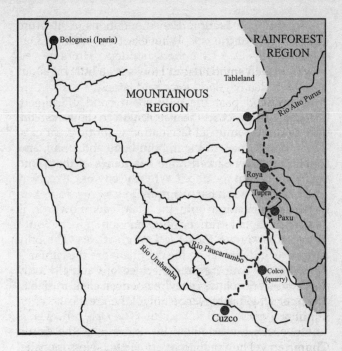

Chambers looked up at Race.

'Ah, Professor,' he said. 'Just the man I was looking for. A point of clarification. These notes here, "Paxu, Tupra and Roya",' he pointed to Race's notes. 'These are *in order*, aren't they? I mean, in the order Renco visited them.'

'They're in the same order as they appear in the manuscript.'

'Okay, good.'

'Hey, Walter,' Race said, sitting down next to Chambers. 'There was something I was hoping I could ask you.'

'Yes?'

'In the manuscript, Renco mentions a creature called the *titi* or the *rapa*. What exactly is that?'

'Ah, the *rapa*,' Chambers nodded. 'Hmmm, yes, yes. Not really my field, but I do know a little bit about it.'

'And?'

'Like many other South American cultures, the Incans had an unusual fascination with the great cats. They built statues to them, both large and small, and sometimes they carved huge bas reliefs of them into entire mountain rockfaces. Why, the city of Cuzco was even *built* in the shape of a puma.

'This fascination with the great cats, however, is really quite a strange phenomenon, since South America is known for its *lack* of great cats. The only large cats indigenous to the continent are the jaguar— or panther—and the puma, which are actually only medium-sized felines. They're not even close in size to the tiger which is the largest of all the great cats.'

Chambers shifted in his seat. 'The *rapa*, however, is another story altogether. It's more like the South American version of Bigfoot or the Loch Ness monster. It's a legendary creature, a great big black cat.

'As with Bigfoot and Nessie, you hear of sightings every couple of years—farmers in Brazil complain about cattle mutilations; tourists on the Inca Trail in Peru claim to see big cats running around at night; and occasionally, local men are found brutally killed in the lowlands of Colombia. But no-one ever gets proof. There are a couple of photos, but they've all been discredited—just blurry, out-of-focus shots that could be anything from an ordinary old panther to a spectacled bear.'

'So it's a myth,' Race said. 'A giant-cat myth.'

'Don't dismiss giant-cat myths so quickly, Professor Race,' Chambers said. 'They are quite common

122

throughout the world. India. South Africa. Siberia. Why, it might surprise you to learn that the most vehement beliefs in giant-cat myths come from England.'

'England?'

'The Beast of Exmoor, the Beast of Bahn. Giant cats that prowl the moors late at night. Never caught. Never photographed. But their prints are often found in the mud. Goodness, if the sightings are true, chances are that the Hound of the Baskervilles was not a dog, but actually a giant *cat*.'

Race snuffed a laugh at that and left Chambers to his work. He returned to his seat. No sooner had he sat down, however, than he felt someone sit down next to him. It was Lauren.

'Ah, the lucky cap,' she said, looking at Race's battered blue Yankees cap. 'I don't know if I ever told you this, but I always hated that damned cap.'

'You told me,' Race said.

'But you still wore it.'

'It's a good cap.'

Lauren's eyes wandered appraisingly over his T-shirt, jeans and Nikes. Race noticed that she was dressed in a thick khaki shirt rolled up at the sleeves, khaki trousers and a sturdy-looking pair of hiking boots.

'Nice outfit,' she said, before he could say exactly the same thing.

'What can I say?' he replied. 'When I packed for work today I wasn't expecting to go to the jungle.'

Lauren threw her head back and laughed. It was the same laugh Race remembered from the old days. Totally theatrical and of utterly dubious sincerity.

'I'd forgotten how *dry* you were,' she said.

Race smiled weakly, bowed his head.

'How have you been, Will?' she asked gently.

'Good,' he lied. 'And you? You've obviously done well for yourself. I mean, geez, DARPA . . .'

'Life is good,' she said. 'Life is very good. Listen, Will . . .' And there it was. The transition. Lauren had always been good at getting down to business. '. . . I just wanted to talk with you before we landed. I just wanted to say that I don't want what happened between us to get in the way of what we're doing here. I never meant to hurt you—'

'You didn't hurt me,' Race said, perhaps a little too quickly. He looked down at his shoelaces. 'Well, nothing that didn't mend after a while.'

Not exactly true.

It had taken him a lot more than a while to get over Lauren O'Connor.

Their relationship had been a classic sort of affair: the all-American college mismatch. Race was smart, but had no money. Lauren was brilliant, and her family had money to burn. Race went to USC on a half sports scholarship. In return for playing football for them, they paid half his tuition. He'd scraped together the other half by working nights behind the bar at a local nightclub. Lauren's parents had paid all her fees in full, in one up-front payment.

They were together for two years. The footballer with decent but not spectacular grades in languages, and the tall, beautiful science major who was acing everything.

Race had loved it. Lauren was all he'd ever wanted in a companion—intelligent, outgoing, acidly funny. At football parties, she'd stand out like the sun on a cloudy day. And when she'd search the room for him and find him and smile, he'd melt.

He fell in love with her.

And then Lauren won a scholarship to study at MIT for a year, doing theoretical physics or something like that. She went. He waited. Now it was the classic long-distance relationship. Love over the phone. Race was faithful. He lived for their weekly phone call.

And then she came back.

He was at the airport, waiting for her. He had the ring in his pocket. He'd practised the speech a thousand times, got it just right so that he'd drop to one knee at precisely the right moment and ask her.

But when she came through the Arrivals gate that day, she already had a diamond ring on her ring finger.

'Will. I'm sorry,' she'd said. 'But . . . well . . . I've met someone else.'

Race never even got the ring out of his pocket.

And so he'd spent the rest of his time in college nose-down in the books, resolutely single and unimaginably miserable.

He'd graduated fourth in his class in ancient languages and, to his complete surprise, got an offer to teach at NYU. With nothing else he wanted to do—except maybe slashing his wrists—he took it.

And now, now he was a humble language professor working out of an old clapboard office in New York City while she was a theoretical physicist working at the cutting edge of the United States military's most esteemed high-technology weapons department. Hmmm.

Race had never expected to see her again. Nor, he thought, did I *want* to. But then, when Frank Nash had mentioned her name earlier that morning, something inside of him had clicked. He'd wanted to see what she had made of herself.

Well, he had seen that now and what he saw was

clear—she'd made a hell of a lot more out of herself than he had.

Race blinked, snapped out of it.

He came back to the present and found that he was staring at her wedding ring.

Jesus, get a grip, he thought to himself.

'Frank said you did a good job with the manuscript,' Lauren said.

Race coughed, clearing his throat as well as his mind. 'As much as I could do. I mean, hey, it isn't theoretical physics, but, it's . . . well, it's what I do.'

'You should be proud of what you do,' she said. And then she smiled at him. 'It's good to see you again, Will.'

Race smiled back as best he could.

Then she stood and looked about herself. 'Well, anyway, I'd better be getting back. Looks like we're about to land.'

It was late in the afternoon when the Hercules landed heavily on a dusty private airstrip at the edge of the Cuzco valley.

The team disembarked the plane on board the troop truck that had made the journey to South America in the big plane's belly. The massive truck rumbled out of the rear loading ramp and immediately headed north along a badly-paved road toward the Urubamba River.

It was a bouncy ride. Race sat in the back of the truck next to his bodyguard, Sergeant Van Lewen.

The other members of the team—the three DARPA people, Nash, Lauren and the hawk-faced physicist, Copeland; Chambers, the anthropologist; and Gaby Lopez, a striking young Latin-American woman who was the team's archaeologist—all sat with their own Green Beret bodyguards.

At one point in the trip, the truck drove along a rise and Race was able to see down the length of the Cuzco valley.

On the left-hand side of the valley, situated on a grassy green hill, lay the ruins of Sacsayhuaman, the mighty fortress he had so recently read about. Its three gargantuan tiers were still discernible, but time and weather had robbed them of their majesty. What four hundred years ago had been a magnificent and imposing fortress fit for the eyes of kings was now a crumbling ruin fit only for the eyes of tourists.

To the right, Race saw a sea of terracotta roofs—the modern-day city of Cuzco, its surrounding wall having long since been removed. Beyond the rooftops lay the barren southern mountains of Peru—brown and harsh, as desolate as the snow-capped peaks of the Andes to the north were spectacular.

Ten minutes later, the truck arrived at the Urubamba River, where it was met by a thirtysomething man dressed in a white linen suit and a cream Panama hat. His name was Nathan Sebastian and he was a lieutenant in the United States Army.

Behind Sebastian, floating lazily in the river alongside a long T-shaped jetty, were two military helicopters.

They were Bell Textron UH-1Ns—'Hueys'. But these two Hueys had been modified slightly. Their long thin landing struts had been removed and replaced with longer pod-like pontoons that floated on the surface of the river. One of the choppers, Race saw, had a complex-looking array of electronic devices suspended beneath its frog-like nose.

The troop truck skidded to a halt near the jetty and Race and the others piled out of it.

Lieutenant Sebastian walked straight up to Nash. 'Choppers are all set, Colonel, just as you requested.'

'Well done, Lieutenant,' Nash said. 'What about our competitors?'

'A SAT-SN scan was conducted ten minutes ago, sir. Romano and his team are currently flying over Colombia, en route to Cuzco.'

'Jesus, they're already over Colombia,' Nash said, biting his lip. 'They're gaining on us.'

'Their estimated time of arrival in Cuzco is three hours, sir,' Sebastian said.

Nash looked at his watch. It was 5:00 pm exactly.

'Then we don't have much time,' he said. 'Let's get these choppers loaded and into the air.'

Even as Nash said it, the Green Berets were already loading six large Samsonite trunks onto the two Hueys. Once they were stowed, the twelve team members split up into two teams of six and climbed aboard.

The two choppers took off from the river, leaving Nathan Sebastian standing on the jetty, holding onto his stupid hat.

The two Hueys soared over the snow-capped mountain peaks.

Race sat in the back of the second chopper, staring in awe at the spectacular mountain gorges that raced by beneath them.

'All right, everyone,' Nash's voice said over their headsets. *'I figure we've got about two hours of daylight left. And I'd like to do as much of this as I can in the light. The first thing we have to do is find that first totem. Walter? Gaby?'*

Nash had Chambers and Gaby Lopez with him in the lead chopper. The two Hueys were heading out over the mountains, past the Paucartambo River, in the general direction of the three river villages mentioned in the Santiago Manuscript: Paxu, Tupra and Roya.

According to the manuscript, they would find the first totem near the last-mentioned town, Roya. Now it was up to Chambers and Lopez, the anthropologist and the archaeologist, to deduce the exact modern-day location of that riverside town.

And so, Race mused, what had taken Renco Capac

and Alberto Santiago eleven days to accomplish, they did in fifty minutes. After soaring over the jagged pointed peaks of the Andes for almost an hour, suddenly—gloriously—the mountains slid away beneath them and Race saw a spectacular expanse of flat green foliage stretching away from him for as far as he could see. It was an amazing sight. The beginning of the vast Amazon River Basin.

They flew north-east, low over the rainforest, the rotor blades of the two helicopters thumping loudly in the silent afternoon air.

They flew over some rivers, long fat brown lines that snaked their way through the impenetrable forest. At times, they would see the remains of old villages on the riverbanks, some of them with stone ruins in the centre of their town squares, others just overgrown with weeds.

At one point in their journey, Race saw the faint yellow glow of electric lights peeking up over the darkening horizon.

'The *Madre de Dios* goldmine,' Lauren said, leaning over him to look at the glow herself. 'One of the largest open-cut mines in the world, also one of the most remote. It's the closest thing we'll get to civilisation around here. Just a great big earthen cone sunk into the earth. I'd heard it was abandoned sometime last year. Guess it's been re-op—'

At that moment, there came a flurry of excited voices over the radio. Chambers and Lopez were speaking animatedly, saying something about the village immediately beneath the two Hueys.

The next voice Race heard belonged to Frank Nash. He was ordering the choppers to land.

The two Hueys landed in a deserted clearing by a riverbank, flattening the long grass with their downdrafts. Nash, Chambers and Lopez all stepped out of their chopper.

Several moss-covered stone monuments stood in the middle of the grassy clearing. After a few minutes of examining the monuments and comparing them to their notebooks, Chambers and Lopez agreed that this was almost certainly the site of the village of Roya.

After the identity of the village was confirmed, Race and the rest of the team disembarked their choppers and a search of the surrounding jungle ensued. Ten minutes later, Lauren found the first stone totem about five hundred metres to the north-east of the town.

Race stared at the giant stone totem in awe.

It was infinitely more frightening in real life than he had imagined it to be.

It was about nine feet high and completely made of stone. And it was covered in vandalism—crucifixes and Christian symbols that had been scratched into it by God-fearing conquistadors four hundred years ago.

The stone carving of the rapa, however, was like nothing he had ever seen. It was absolutely terrifying.

It was covered in moisture, *dripping* with it. And this layer of wetness had a truly strange effect on the carving—it really made it seem as if the stone carving was *alive*.

Race swallowed hard as he stood before the decrepit old totem.

Jesus.

With the first totem found, the team hurried back to their choppers and lifted off quickly.

Nash's chopper led the way, flying low over the jungle, in the direction of the rapa's tail.

Over his headset, Race heard Nash's voice: '—*fire up the magnetometer. Once we get a reading on the next totem, we'll revert to spotlights*—'

'*Got it*—'

Race frowned. He wanted to ask someone what a magnetometer was, but he didn't want to look any more ignorant in front of Lauren than he already did.

'It's a device used by archaeologists to detect relics buried underground,' Lauren said, smiling wryly at him.

Damn it, he thought.

'They're also used commercially by resource exploration companies to detect subterranean reserves of oil and uranium ore,' she added.

'How do they work?'

'A caesium magnetometer like the one we're using here detects minute variations in the earth's magnetic field—variations that are caused by objects interrupting the upward flow of that magnetic field. Archaeologists in Mexico have been using magnetometers for years to find buried Aztec ruins. We're using ours to find the next stone totem.'

'But the totems are on the surface,' Race said. 'Wouldn't there be a problem with the magnetometer picking up trees and animals?'

'It can be a problem,' Lauren said. 'But not here. Nash will have set his reader to detect only objects of a certain density and depth. Trees have a density of only a few thousand megabars, and animals, since they're made of flesh and bone, are even less than that. Incan stone, however, is about five times as dense as the thickest tree in the rainforest—'

'*All right, people,*' Nash's voice said suddenly. '*I've got a reading. Dead ahead. Corporal, the spotlight.*'

And so it went.

For the next hour, as the light faded and the shadows from the mountains grew longer and colder, Race listened as Nash and Chambers and Lopez spotted totem after totem. After the magnetometer found each totem, they would hover their Huey over it and illuminate it with the chopper's blinding white spotlight. Then, depending on which totem they had spotted, they would either go in the direction of the rapa's tail or to the creature's left, in the direction of the Mark of the Sun.

The two helicopters flew north, alongside the massive step-like tableland that separated the mountains from the rainforest.

Just as dusk was setting in, Race heard Nash's voice again.

'*All right, we're coming up on the tableland,*' he said. '*I can see a large waterfall flowing over it . . .*'

Race got up from his seat and moved forward, looked out through the forward windshield of his helicopter. He saw Nash's Huey rise up over a magnificent waterfall that marked the edge of the tableland.

'*All right . . . Following the river now . . .*'

The day grew darker and soon all Race could see were the red tail-lights of Nash's helicopter in front of him, banking and tilting as the Huey followed the path of the wide, black river beneath them, the beam of its spotlight playing over the wavelets on the water's surface. They were heading west now, toward the wall of mountains that towered above the rainforest.

And then abruptly Race saw Nash's chopper bank sharply to the right and round a thickly-forested bend in the river.

'*Wait a second,*' Nash's voice said.

Race peered forward through the windshield. Nash's chopper began to hover above the riverbank to his right.

'Wait now . . . I see a clearing. It seems to be covered over with grass and moss but . . . Wait, there it is. Okay, people, I can see it. I can just make out the ruins of a large pyramid-shaped building . . . Looks like the citadel. All right, stand by. Stand by for landing.'

At the very same moment that Nash's Hueys were landing at the town of Vilcafor, three other—much larger—military aircraft were arriving at Cuzco airport.

They were aeroplanes—one giant C-17 Globemaster III cargo plane and two small F-14 fighters, the big cargo plane's escorts. The three planes taxied quickly to a halt at the end of the landing strip, where they were met by a cluster of other aircraft that had arrived at Cuzco only minutes earlier.

Three massive CH-53E Super Stallion helicopters stood at the end of the runway, waiting for the Globemaster. The Super Stallions made for an imposing sight—big and strong, they were the fastest and most powerful heavy-lift helicopters in the world.

The transfer was made quickly.

Three shadowy figures immediately leapt out of the Globemaster and ran across the tarmac toward the choppers. One of them—he was smaller than the other two and black, and he wore a pair of gold-framed spectacles—carried something under his arm, an object that looked like a large leather-bound book.

The three of them leapt aboard one of the Super Stallions. No sooner were they on board than all three choppers lifted off the tarmac and headed north.

But they did not leave unobserved.

Standing at a distance from the airport, watching the choppers through a pair of high-powered binoculars, was a man dressed in a white linen suit and a cream Panama hat.

Lieutenant Nathan Sebastian.

Frank Nash's two Hueys landed gently on the river beside the ruins of Vilcafor in the fading light of dusk, in a downpour of torrential rain.

After they came to rest on the river's surface, the two pilots manoeuvred their birds around so that their pontoons ran aground on the soft mud of the riverbank.

The Green Berets leapt out onto the shore first, their M-16s up and ready. The civilian members of the team stepped up onto the mud after them. Race came out last of all and stood at the river's edge—gunless—staring in awe at the ruins of the citadel town of Vilcafor.

The village was essentially comprised of a grass-covered central street that ran for about a hundred yards away from the river. It was lined on both sides by roofless stone huts that were overgrown with weeds and moss. The whole town, in fact, was covered in foliage—it was as if the rainforest surrounding it had come alive and consumed it whole.

At Race's end of the street was the river and the rickety remains of an old wooden jetty. At the other end of the street—looking down over the little town like some kind of protective god—were the ruins of the great pyramid-like citadel.

In truth, the citadel was no bigger than a two-storey suburban house. But it was made of some of the most solid-looking stones Race had ever seen. It was that same precise Incan masonry he had read about in the manuscript. Giant square-shaped boulders that had been pounded into shape by Incan stonemasons and then set perfectly in place alongside other, similarly fashioned boulders. No mortar was necessary and none had been used.

The citadel was made up of two tiers, both of them circular in shape—the upper level a smaller concentric circle that rested atop the larger lower one.

The whole structure, however, looked weathered and worn, beaten and decrepit. The once intimidating stone walls were now laced with green vines and a network of forked cracks. The whole upper level was broken and crumbling. The lower level was still largely intact, but completely overgrown with weeds. A large doorstone sat at an odd angle inside the building's main entranceway.

Aside from the citadel, there was one other dominant feature of the village.

The town of Vilcafor was surrounded by a huge dried-up moat—an enormous horseshoe-shaped ditch that ran around the entire town, starting at the riverbank and ending at the riverbank. Two great stone dikes prevented the water in the river from rushing into the moat.

It must have been at least fifteen feet across and just as deep. Tangled thorny thickets of brush snaked their way along its waterless base. Two old wooden logbridges spanned its width on either side of the village. Like the rest of the town, they too had been overcome by the encroaching rainforest. Their wooden beams were laced with sprawling green vines.

Race stood motionless at the end of the old Incan street, the pouring rain running off the brim of his cap.

He felt like he was entering another world.

An ancient world.

A dangerous world.

'Don't stay near the water too long,' Lauren said as she strode past him.

Race turned, not understanding. Lauren clicked on her flashlight and pointed it at the river behind him.

It was as if someone had just flicked on a light switch.

Race saw them instantly. Glinting in the light of Lauren's flashlight.

Eyes.

No less than *fifty* pairs of eyes, protruding from the inky black water, stared back at him from the rain-spattered surface of the river.

He turned quickly to Lauren. 'Alligators?'

'No,' Walter Chambers said, coming over. '*Melanosuchus niger*. Black caimans. Largest crocodilian on the continent. Some say, the largest in the world. They're bigger than any alligator, and in biology more like a crocodile. In fact, the black caiman is a close relative of *Crocodylus porosus*, the giant Australian saltwater crocodile.'

'How big are they?' Race asked. He could only see the eerie constellation of eyes before him. He couldn't tell how big the reptiles in the water actually were.

'About twenty-two feet,' Chambers said cheerfully.

'*Twenty-two feet.*' Race did the calculations in his head. Twenty-two feet equalled seven metres.

'How much do they weigh?' he asked.

'About 2300 pounds. What's that, about a thousand kilograms.'

A thousand kilograms, Race thought. *A metric ton.*
Wonderful.

The caimans in the darkened river began to rise in the water and Race saw their armoured crocodilian backs, saw the pointed plates of their tails.

They looked like dark mounds just hovering in the water. Great big *massive* mounds.

'They're not going to come out of the water, are they?'

'They might,' Chambers said. 'But probably not. Most crocodilians prefer to grab their victims by surprise at the water's edge, from the cover of the water itself. And although black caimans are night hunters, they rarely stray out of the water in the evening, for the simple reason that it's too cold. Like all reptiles they have to watch their body temperature.'

Race stepped away from the water's edge.

'Black caimans,' he said. 'Great.'

Frank Nash stood at the end of the main street of Vilcafor with his arms folded across his chest, alone. He just stared intently at the decrepit old village before him.

Troy Copeland appeared at his side. 'Sebastian just called from Cuzco. Romano just went through the airport there. He arrived in a Globemaster under Tomcat escort. He then liaised with a few choppers and headed off in this direction.'

'What sort of choppers?'

'Super Stallions. Three of them.'

'Christ,' Nash said. A fully-loaded CH-53E Super Stallion could carry up to 55 fully-armed troops. And they had *three* of them. So, Romano had brought firepower, too.

'How long did it take us to get here from Cuzco?' Nash asked quickly.

'About two hours and forty minutes,' Copeland said.

Nash looked at his watch.

It was 7:45 pm.

'They'll be quicker in Stallions,' he said, '*if* they follow the totems correctly. We have to move fast. I'd say we've got about two hours before they get here.'

The six Green Berets began hauling the Samsonite trunks out of the choppers and onto the main street of Vilcafor.

Nash, Lauren and Copeland started opening them up at once, revealing a cache of high-tech equipment inside—Hexium laptop computers, infra-red telescopic lenses and some very futuristic-looking stainless-steel canisters.

The two academics, Chambers and Lopez, were off in the village proper, eagerly examining the citadel and its surrounding structures.

Race—now cloaked in a green Army parka to protect him against the rain—went over to help the Green Berets unload the choppers.

He got to the riverbank to find Buzz Cochrane addressing the youngest member of their team, a fresh-faced corporal named Douglas Kennedy. Sergeant Van Lewen and the Green Berets' leader, Captain Scott, were nowhere to be seen.

'I mean, honestly, Doogie, could she *be* any more out of your league?' Cochrane was saying.

'I don't know about that, Buzz,' one of the other commandos said. 'I reckon he *should* ask her out.'

'What a great idea,' Cochrane said, turning to Kennedy.

'Shut up, you guys,' Doug Kennedy said in a broad Southern accent.

'No, seriously, Doogs, why don't you just walk on up to her and ask her out?'

140

'I said, shut up,' Kennedy said as he heaved a Samsonite container out of one of the Hueys.

Douglas Kennedy was twenty-three, lean, and handsome in a boyish kind of way, with earnest green eyes and fully shaved head. He was also about as green as they came. His nickname 'Doogie' was a reference to the clean-cut and honest nature of the lead character in the old TV show, *Doogie Howser MD*, with whom it was said Doogie shared many characteristics. It was also a 'clumsy' kind of name, suggesting some sort of innocence, which made it all the more appropriate for Doogie. He was particularly shy—and especially clumsy—when it came to women.

'What's going on?' Race said as he arrived next to them.

Cochrane turned—looked Race up and down instantly—then turned away as he said, 'Oh, we just caught Doogie here staring at that pretty young archaeologist over there, and we was just giving him a friendly ribbing.'

Race spun and saw Gaby Lopez, the team's archaeologist, standing over by the citadel with Walter Chambers.

She was certainly very pretty. She had dark hair, a beautiful Latin complexion and a compact curvaceous body. At twenty-seven, so Race had heard, she was the youngest Associate Professor in the Department of Archaeology at Princeton. Gaby Lopez was a very intelligent young woman.

Race shrugged inwardly. Doogie Kennedy could do a lot worse.

Cochrane slapped Doogie heartily hard on the back, spat out a gob of tobacco.

'Don't you worry, son. We'll make a man out of you yet. I mean, take a look at young Chucky over there,'

Cochrane said, indicating the next-youngest member of the unit, a beefy moon-faced 23-year-old corporal named Charles 'Chucky' Wilson. 'Why, only last week Chucky became a fully fledged member of the 80s Club.'

'What's the 80s Club?' Doogie asked, perplexed.

'It's tasty, that's what it is,' Cochrane said, licking his lips. 'Ain't that right, Chucky?'

'Sure is, Buzz.'

'Apples, man,' Cochrane grinned.

'Apples,' Chucky replied, smiling.

As the two soldiers laughed, Race eyed Cochrane cautiously, mindful of what the Green Beret had said on the plane when he had thought Race was out of earshot.

Corporal Buzz Cochrane appeared to be in his late thirties. He had red hair and eyebrows, a thickly creased face and a rough unshaven chin. He was also a big man—bulky across the chest—with thick, powerful arms.

Just from the look of him, Race didn't like him.

There just seemed to be something mean-spirited about him—the not-so-intelligent school bully who by the sheer virtue of his size had had it over the other kids. The kind of brute who had joined the Army because it was a place where people like him thrived. It was no wonder he was almost forty and still a corporal.

'Say, Doogie,' Cochrane said suddenly, 'what do you say I go over there and tell that cute little archae-ologist that we got ourselves a dumb young soldier over here who'd like to ask her out for a burger and a movie—'

'*No!*' Doogie exclaimed, genuinely alarmed.

The other Green Berets burst out laughing.

Doogie went red in the face of their laughter.

'And don't call me dumb,' he muttered. 'I ain't *dumb*.'

Just then, Van Lewen and Scott returned from the other chopper. The soldiers' laughter stopped immediately.

Race saw Van Lewen look warily from Doogie to the others, in the way a big brother would glare at his little brother's tormentors. He got the impression that it was more because of Van Lewen's presence than Captain Scott's that the laughter had ceased.

'How're things progressing here?' Scott said to Cochrane.

'Not a problem in the world, sir,' Cochrane said.

'Then grab your gear and head on into the village,' Scott said. 'They're about to do the test.'

Race and the soldiers came into the village proper. It was still pouring with rain.

As he walked down the muddy street, Race saw Lauren standing with Troy Copeland over by the largest of all the Samsonite trunks.

It was a great big black case, at least five feet tall, and Copeland was unfolding its side panels, transforming it into a portable workbench of some sort.

The lean scientist flipped open the lid of the trunk, revealing a waist-high console made up of some dials, a keyboard and a computer screen. Beside him, Lauren was attaching a silver rod-like object that looked like a boom microphone onto the top of the console.

'Ready?' Lauren asked.

'Ready,' Copeland said.

Lauren flicked a switch on the side of the Samsonite trunk and instantly green and red lights lit up all over the console. Copeland immediately set to work typing on the unit's all-weather keyboard.

'It's called a nucleotide resonance imager, or NRI,' Lauren told Race before he could ask. 'It can tell us the location of any nuclear substance in the surrounding area by measuring the resonance in the air around that substance.'

'Say what?' Race said.

Lauren sighed and then said, 'Any radioactive substance—be it uranium, plutonium or thyrium—reacts with oxygen at a molecular level. Basically, the radioactive substance causes the air *around* it to vibrate, or resonate. This device detects that resonance in the air, and hence gives us the location of the radioactive substance.'

A moment later, Copeland finished typing. He turned to Nash. 'NRI's ready.'

'Do it,' Nash said.

Copeland hit a key on the keyboard and immediately the silver rod mounted on top of the machine began to rotate. It moved slowly, in a steady, measured circle.

As it did so, Race looked about himself and noticed that Lopez and Chambers had returned from their exploring. Now they were staring intently at the machine. Race looked at the rest of the team around him—*everyone* was staring intently at the nucleotide resonance imager.

And then suddenly it dawned on him.

This was what everything depended on.

If the imager didn't detect the idol somewhere in the immediate vicinity, then they had all wasted their time coming here—

The rod on top of the imager stopped turning.

'We have a reading,' Lauren said suddenly, her eyes locked on the console's screen.

Race saw Nash let out the breath he'd been holding. 'Where?'

'One second . . .' Lauren typed something on the keyboard.

The rod on the imager was now pointing upriver—toward the mountains—toward the area where the trees of the rainforest met the sheer face of the nearest rocky plateau.

Lauren said, 'The signal's weak because the angle's not right. But I'm picking up *something*. Let me see if I can adjust the vector some . . .'

She hit some more keys and the rod on top of the unit slowly began to tilt upwards. It had reached an angle of about thirty degrees when suddenly Lauren's eyes lit up.

'All right,' she said. 'Strong signal. Very high frequency resonance. Bearing 270 degrees—due west. Vertical angle is 29 degrees, 58 minutes. Range . . . 793 metres.'

Lauren looked up at the dark rocky mountain face that rose above the trees to the west. It looked like a plateau of some sort. Slanting sheets of rain whipped across its face.

'It's somewhere in there,' she said. 'Somewhere up in the mountains.'

Nash turned to Scott. 'Get on the radio to Panama. Tell them that the preliminary team has verified the existence of the substance. But also say that we have intel on hostile forces en route to our location as we speak. Tell them to send in a full protective force for extraction as soon as they can.'

Nash spun to face the rest of the assembled group. 'All right, folks, saddle up. Let's go get that idol.'

Everyone started getting ready.

The Green Berets readied their M-16s. The DARPA

scientists grabbed compasses and various computer equipment to take with them.

Race saw Lauren and Troy Copeland head inside one of the Hueys, presumably to grab some gear of their own. He hurried after them to see if he could help—and while he was at it, maybe also to ask Lauren what Nash had meant when he'd said that hostile forces were on their way to Vilcafor.

'Hey—' Race said as he arrived in the doorway of the chopper. 'Oh . . .'

He'd caught the two of them in a clinch—kissing like a pair of teenagers—hands through each other's hair, tongues in each other's mouths. Hot to trot.

Upon Race's unexpected arrival, the two scientists separated instantly. Lauren blushed. Copeland scowled.

'I'm . . . really sorry,' Race said. 'I didn't mean to—'

'It's okay,' Lauren said, pushing her hair back into place. 'This is just a very exciting moment for us.'

Race nodded, turned away, headed back into the village.

Obviously.

What he couldn't help thinking about, however, as he walked back to join the others in the village, was the image of Lauren running her fingers through Copeland's hair as she kissed him. He had seen her wedding ring clearly.

Copeland, on the other hand, hadn't been wearing one.

146

The group walked along the remains of a muddy path that ran along the edge of the riverbank. They were heading toward the base of the rocky mountain-plateau, the sounds of the night-time forest loud in their ears. The sea of leaves around them rippled under the weight of the steady rain.

It was dark now and the beams of their flashlights played across the forest. As he walked, Race noticed some gaps in the dark storm clouds above them—gaps which allowed the odd shaft of brilliant blue moon-light to illuminate the river beside them. Occasionally in the distance he would see the strobe-like flash of lightning. A storm was coming.

Lauren and Copeland led the way. Lauren held a digital compass out in front of her. Walking alongside her, his M-16 held across his chest, was her bodyguard, Buzz Cochrane.

Nash, Chambers, Lopez and Race followed close behind them. Scott, Van Lewen and a fourth soldier—the chunky corporal named Chucky Wilson—brought up the rear.

The last two Green Berets—Doogie Kennedy and the final soldier in the unit, another corporal named

George 'Tex' Reichart—had been left back at the village as rearguards.

Race found himself walking next to Nash.

'Why didn't the Army send a full protective force here to begin with?' he asked. 'If this idol is so important, why did they only send a preliminary team in to get it?'

Nash shrugged as he walked. 'There were some people high up who thought this was a pretty speculative mission—following a four-hundred-year-old manuscript to find a thyrium idol. So they stopped short of giving us a full offensive unit and made it a force-on-discovery mission. But now that we know it's here, they'll send in the cavalry. Now, if you'll excuse me.'

With that, Nash went forward and joined Lauren and Copeland up front.

Race was left walking at the rear of the line, alone, feeling more than ever like a fifth wheel—a stranger who had no reason at all to be there.

As he walked along the riverside path he kept one eye on the surface of the river beside him. He noticed that some of the caimans were swimming alongside the path, keeping pace with his party.

After a while Lauren and Copeland came to the base of the rocky plateau—an immense wall of vertical wet rock that stretched away to the north and to the south. Race guessed they had come about six hundred yards from the town.

Off to the left—on the other side of the river—he saw a surging waterfall pouring out of the rockface, feeding the river.

On his own side of the river, he saw a narrow, vertical fissure slicing into the face of the massive wall of rock.

The fissure was barely eight feet wide but it was

148

tall—unbelievably tall—at least three hundred feet, and its walls were perfectly vertical. It disappeared into the mountainside. A trickle of ankle-deep water flowed out from it into a small rock-strewn pool that, in turn, overflowed into the river.

It was a natural passageway in the rockface. The product, Race guessed, of a minor earthquake in the past that had shunted the north–south-running rockface slightly east–west.

Lauren, Copeland and Nash stepped into the rocky pool at the mouth of the passageway.

As they did so, Race turned and saw that the caimans in the river had stopped their shadowing of the party. They now hung back a good fifty yards away, hovering menacingly in the deeper waters of the river.

Fine by me, Race thought.

And then, suddenly, he paused and spun around where he stood.

Something wasn't right here.

And not just the behaviour of the caimans. Something about the *whole area* around the passageway was wrong . . .

And then Race realised what it was.

The sounds of the forest had disappeared.

Except for the pattering of the rain on the leaves, it was perfectly silent here. No droning of cicadas, no chirping of birds, no rustling of branches.

Nothing.

It was as if they had entered an area where the sounds of the jungle just ceased. An area where the jungle animals feared to tread.

Lauren, Copeland and Nash didn't seem to notice the silence. They just shone their flashlights into the passageway in the rockface and peered inside it.

'Seems to go all the way through,' Copeland said.

Lauren turned to Nash. 'It's going in the right direction.'

'Let's do it,' Nash said.

The ten adventurers made their way along the narrow rocky passageway, their footfalls splashing in the ankle-deep water. They walked in single file, Buzz Cochrane in the lead, the small flashlight attached to the barrel of his M-16 illuminating the way ahead of them.

The passageway was basically straight, with a slight zigzag in the middle, and it seemed to cut through the plateau for about two hundred feet.

Race looked up as he walked behind the others. The rock walls on both sides of the narrow fissure soared into the sky above him. For a fissure that was so narrow, it was unbelievably tall. As Race looked upwards, a light rain fell on his face.

And then suddenly he emerged from the passageway and stepped out into wide-open space.

What he saw took his breath away.

He was standing at the base of a massive rocky canyon of some sort—a wide, cylindrical crater that was at least three hundred feet in diameter.

A glistening expanse of water stretched away from him, rippling silver in a stray shaft of moonlight, bounded on every side by the circular wall of the enormous crater. The fissure that they had just come through, it seemed, was the only entrance to this massive cylindrical chasm. A thin waterfall fell in a steady sheet on the far side of the crater, plunging fully four hundred feet into the shallow lake at the bottom of the wide, circular canyon.

But it was what stood in the centre of the canyon that commanded everyone's immediate attention.

Rising up out of the body of water—in the exact centre of the cylindrical crater—was an enormous rock formation.

It was about eighty feet wide and at least three hundred feet tall, a gigantic natural rock tower—easily the size of a medium-rise skyscraper—that soared up out of the glistening moonlit lake into the night sky. Against the backdrop of the light evening rain, the massive black monolith looked absolutely magnificent.

The ten of them just stood there gazing up at the enormous rock tower in awe.

'Jesus Christ . . .' Buzz Cochrane said.

Lauren showed Nash the reading on her digital compass. 'We've come exactly 600 metres from the village. If we take into account the elevation, I'd say it's a definite possibility that our idol is sitting right on top of that rock tower.'

'Hey,' Copeland said from the left.

Everyone turned. Copeland was standing in front of a path of some sort that had been cut into the curved outer wall of the canyon.

The path appeared to rise steeply, winding its way up the canyon's circular outer wall in a spiral-like fashion, hugging the circumference of the cylinder—encircling the giant rock tower in the centre of the crater, but separated from it by an enormous moat of empty space at least one hundred feet wide.

Lauren and Nash went first, stepping up out of the ankle-deep water at the base of the crater and onto the path.

The group made its way up the path.

The rain was lighter here, the clouds above the great canyon thinner, allowing shafts of blue moonlight to penetrate them more easily.

Up and up they went, following the narrow curving path, all of them staring in a kind of silent awe at the magnificent rock tower in the centre of the crater.

The sheer size of the tower was incredible. It was enormous. But it was curiously shaped: it was slightly wider at the top than it was at the bottom. The whole formation gradually tapered inward to the point where it met the lake at the bottom of the crater.

As they climbed higher and higher up the crater's spiralling pathway, Race began to make out the peak of the rock tower. It was rounded in shape—dome-like—and it was completely covered in dense green foliage. Gnarled, waterlogged branches leaned out from its edges, unfazed by the vertiginous three-hundred-foot drop beneath them.

The group was nearing the top of the crater when they came to a bridge—or rather the *makings* of a bridge that connected the outer, spiralling path to the rock tower.

It was situated just below the lip of the canyon, not far from the thin waterfall that cascaded out over the rim and plummeted down the western wall of the canyon.

Two flat stone ledges faced each other on opposite sides of the chasm, a hundred feet apart. On each ledge sat a pair of stone buttresses, presumably the foundations from which a rope bridge of some kind once hung.

The two buttresses on Race's side of the chasm were pitted and worn but they looked sturdy beyond belief. And they looked *old*. Really, really old. Race had no doubt that they easily dated back to Incan times.

It was then that he saw the rope bridge itself.

It was hanging from the ledge on the *other* side of the chasm, the tower side. It hung vertically from the two buttresses on the far ledge so that it fell flat against the tower's rocky wall. Attached to the bottom end of the rope bridge, however, was a long length of frayed yellow rope that drooped in a wide arc *across* the chasm, over to Race's ledge, where it had been tied to one of the buttresses.

Walter Chambers examined the frayed yellow rope. 'Dried grass rope. Interlocking braid formation. This is classic Incan rope construction. It was said that a whole Incan town, working together, could build an entire rope bridge in three days. The women picked the grass and braided it into long thin lengths of string. Then the men braided those lengths of string into thicker, more sturdy segments of rope like this.'

'But a rope bridge couldn't possibly survive the elements for four hundred years,' Race said.

'No . . . No, it couldn't,' Chambers said.

'Which means somebody else built this bridge,' Lauren said. 'And recently, too.'

'But why the elaborate set-up?' Race said, indicating the length of rope that stretched out across the ravine to the lowest point of the rope bridge. 'Why attach a rope to this end of the bridge and drop the whole thing down on the other side?'

'I don't know,' Chambers said. 'You'd only do something like that if you wanted to keep something trapped on the tower top . . .'

Nash turned to Lauren. 'What do you think?'

Lauren peered over at the tower, partially obscured by the veil of lightly falling rain.

'It's high enough to match the angle on the NRI,' she looked at her digital compass. 'And we're exactly

632 metres horizontally from the village. Factoring in the elevation, I'd say it's a good bet the idol's over there.'

Van Lewen and Cochrane hauled the rope bridge up and looped its ends around the two stone buttresses on their side of the ravine. Now the great swooping rope bridge spanned the chasm, linking the skyscraper-like rock tower to the spiralling path that ran around it.

The rain continued to fall.

Jagged forks of brilliant white lightning began to illuminate the sky.

'Sergeant,' Captain Scott said. 'Safety rope.'

Van Lewen immediately brought a strange-looking object out from his backpack. It was a shiny silver grappling hook of some sort. Attached to it was a coil of black nylon rope.

The tall sergeant quickly jammed the shaft of the grappling hook into the M-203 grenade launcher attached to the barrel of his M-16. Then he aimed his gun across the chasm and fired.

With a gaseous *shoosh!* the grappling hook shot out from Van Lewen's grenade launcher and arced gracefully over the chasm, its sharp silver claws snapping out into position as it flew, its black rope wobbling through the air behind it.

The hook landed on the tower top on the other side of the chasm and dug its claws into the base of a thick tree there. Van Lewen then secured his end of the rope to one of the stone buttresses on their side of the chasm so that now the nylon rope spanned the gorge just above the drooping suspension bridge.

'All right, everyone,' Scott said, 'keep one hand on the safety rope as you cross the bridge. If the bridge drops from under you, the rope will keep you from falling.'

Van Lewen must have seen Race go pale. 'You'll be all right. Just keep a hold of that rope and you'll make it.'

The Green Berets went first, one at a time.

The narrow rope bridge rocked and swayed beneath their weight as they walked, but it held. The rest of the group followed behind them, holding onto the nylon safety rope as they crossed the long swooping suspension bridge in the constant subtropical rain.

Race crossed the rope bridge last of all, holding onto the safety rope so hard his knuckles went white. As such, he crossed the bridge more slowly than the others, so by the time he stepped onto the ledge on the other side, they had already gone on ahead and all he saw was a damp stone stairway leading up into the foliage. He hurried up it after them.

Dripping green leaves crowded in on either side of him. Wet fern fronds slapped against his face as he climbed the watersoaked stone slabs after the others. After about thirty seconds of climbing, he burst through a large set of branches and found himself standing in a small clearing of some sort.

Everyone else was already there. But they just stood there, motionless. At first Race didn't know what had made them stop, but then he saw that they all had their flashlights pointed up and to the left.

His gaze followed their flashlight beams and he saw it.

'Holy *Christ*,' he breathed.

There, situated on the highest point of the rock tower—covered in hard-packed mud and moss, concealed by weeds all around it, and glistening wet in the ever-falling rain—stood an ominous stone structure.

It was cloaked in shadow and wetness, but it was clear that this was a structure that had been *designed* to exude menace and power. A structure that could have had no other purpose than to inspire fear, idolatry and worship.

It was a temple.

Race stared at the dark stone temple and swallowed hard.

It looked *evil*.

Cold and cruel and evil.

It wasn't a very big structure. In fact, it was barely even one storey tall. But Race knew that wasn't really the case.

He guessed what they were seeing was only the very top of the temple—the tip of the iceberg—because the ruined section of it that they now saw finished too abruptly. It just disappeared into the mud beneath their feet.

Race presumed that the rest of the enormous structure lay buried in the mud beneath them, consumed by four hundred years of accumulated wet earth.

What he saw, however, was frightening enough.

The temple was roughly pyramidal in shape—two wide stone steps led up to a small cube-like structure that was no larger than the average garage. He had an idea what the cube-shaped structure was—it was a tabernacle of some sort, a holy chamber not unlike those found atop Aztec or Mayan pyramids.

A series of gruesome pictographs had been carved into the walls of the tabernacle—snarling cat-like monsters wielding scythe-like claws; dying humans screaming in agony. Cracks of age littered the stone walls of the temple. The unending subtropical rain ran in rivulets down its carved stone walls, giving life to the characters in the horrific scenes on the walls—generating the same effect that running water had produced on the stone totem earlier.

In the centre of the tabernacle, however, lay the most intriguing aspect of the whole structure—an entrance of some kind. A square-shaped portal.

But this portal had been stopped up. At some time in the distant past someone had wedged an enormous boulder into it, blocking it. The boulder was absolutely huge. Race guessed that it must have taken at least ten men to move it into place.

'Definitely pre-Incan,' Chambers said, as he examined the carvings.

'Yes, absolutely,' Lopez said.

'How do you know?' Nash asked.

'Pictographs are too closely spaced,' Chambers said.

'And much too detailed,' Lopez said.

Nash turned to Captain Scott. 'Check on Reichart back at the village.'

'Yes, sir.' Scott stepped away from the circle and pulled a portable radio from his pack.

Lopez and Chambers were still talking shop.

'What do you think?' Lopez said. 'Chachapoyan?'

'Possibly,' Chambers said. 'Could be Moche. Look at the feline images.'

Gaby Lopez cocked her head doubtfully. 'It could be, but that would make it nearly a thousand years old.'

'Then what about the spiralling path around the crater and the stairs here on the tower?' Chambers said.

'Yes . . . yes, I know. Very peculiar.'

Nash cut in. 'I'm glad you both find it so fascinating, but what the hell are you talking about?'

'Well,' Chambers said, 'it appears that we have a slight anomaly here, Colonel.'

'What do you mean?'

'Well, you see, the spiralling path that runs around this crater and the steps on this tower were without a doubt constructed by *Incan* engineers. The Incans built all sorts of tracks and trails through the Andes and their construction methods are well documented. These two examples bear all the hallmarks of Incan trail construction.'

'Meaning?'

'Meaning that the path and the steps were constructed roughly four hundred years ago. This temple, on the other hand, was built long before then.'

'*So*?' Nash said irritably.

'So, that's the anomaly,' Chambers said. 'Why would the Incans construct a pathway to a temple that they didn't even build?'

'And don't forget the rope bridge,' Lopez said.

'No,' Chambers said. 'Quite right. Quite right.' The bookish little scientist looked up fearfully at the rim of the crater. 'I would suggest we hurry.'

'Why?' Nash said.

'Because, Colonel, it is highly likely that there exists in this area a tribe of natives who will probably not take too kindly to the fact that we have intruded upon their sacred site.'

'How do you know that?' Nash said quickly. 'How do you know that there are natives around here?'

'Because,' Chambers said, 'they are the ones who built the rope bridge.'

'As Professor Race pointed out earlier,' Chambers explained, 'suspension bridges made out of rope decay very quickly over time. A grass-based rope bridge will disintegrate, say, within a few years of its being built. The bridge that we crossed to get to this temple *could not* have existed four hundred years ago. It was built recently, by someone knowledgeable in Incan bridge-building methods, in all likelihood a primitive tribe of some sort through whom this knowledge has been passed down through the generations.'

Nash groaned audibly.

'A primitive tribe,' Race said flatly. 'Here. Now?'

'It's not that improbable,' Gaby Lopez said. 'Lost tribes are discovered all the time in the Amazon Basin. As recently as 1987, the Villas Boas brothers made contact with the lost Kreen Akrore tribe in the Brazilian rainforests. Hell, the Brazilian government even has a policy of sending explorers into the jungle to make contact with Stone Age tribes.

'As you can imagine, though, a lot of those primitive tribes are extremely hostile to Europeans. It is not unknown for state-sponsored explorers to come home in pieces. Some, like the famous Peruvian anthropologist Dr Miguel Moros Marquez, don't come back at all—'

'*Hey*!' Lauren said suddenly from over by the portal.

Everyone turned. Lauren was standing in front of the boulder that was wedged inside the square-shaped doorway. 'There's something written on this.'

Race and the others came over to where she was standing. Lauren brushed away some chunks of mud that clung to the boulder and Race saw what she was looking at.

Something was engraved in the surface of the great stone.

Lauren scraped away some more mud, revealing something that looked like a letter from the alphabet.

It was an 'N'.

'What the hell . . . ?' Nash said.

Words began to take shape.

No entrare . . .

Race recognised them.

'*No entrare*' was Spanish for 'Do not enter'.

Lauren scraped away some more mud and a whole sentence appeared in the centre of the boulder, crudely scratched into the surface of the stone. It read:

> *No entre por ningún motivo!*
> *La muerte espera por dentro.*

AS

Race translated the words in his head. Then he swallowed hard.

'What does it say?' Nash said.

Race turned to face him. At first, he didn't say anything. Then at last he said, 'It says, "Do not enter at any cost. Death lies within."'

'What does "AS" mean?' Lauren said.

'I would guess,' Race said, 'that "AS" stands for Alberto Santiago.'

Back in the village, Doogie Kennedy kicked away a loose rock restlessly. It was dark now and the rain was still falling and he was pissed at having been left back in the village when he really wanted to be up in the mountains with the others.

'What's the matter, Doogs?' Corporal George 'Tex' Reichart asked from over by the moat on the eastern side of the village. Reichart was a tall, lanky beanpole of a man. He hailed from Austin and was a genuine, grass-chewing cowboy—hence his nickname. 'Not gettin' enough action?'

'I'm awright,' Doogie said. 'I'd just rather be up there in them mountains findin' whatever it is we're here to find, than down here babysitting a goddamned village.'

Reichart chuckled softly to himself. Doogie was good value. A bit on the dim side, but keen—keen as mustard.

What Tex Reichart didn't know, however, was that behind his small-town Southern drawl, Doogie Kennedy was in fact an exceptionally intelligent young man.

Preliminary testing at Fort Benning had revealed that Doogie had an IQ of 161—which was odd, because he had only just barely graduated high school.

It was soon discovered that, throughout his school years in Little Rock, Arkansas, young Douglas Kennedy's quiet, God-fearing accountant father had beaten him senseless every evening with a leather strap.

Kennedy Snr had also refused to buy school books for his son and on most nights he would make the boy stand in a dark, three-by-four-foot closet as punishment for serious misdemeanours such as slamming the door too loudly or overcooking his father's steak. Homework never got done and young Doogie only managed to complete high school through his extraordinary ability to take in mentally what was said in class.

He joined the Army the day he graduated and he would never return home. What school administrators had seen as just another shy young kid scraping through high school, one sharp old recruiting sergeant had seen as the mark of a determined and brilliant mind.

Doogie was still shy, but given his intelligence, his willpower and the support network of the Army, he soon became a hell of a soldier. He swiftly made Ranger grade, majoring in sniping. The Green Berets and Fort Bragg had followed soon after.

'Guess I'm just itchin' for some action,' Doogie said, as he came over to where Reichart was laying an AC-7V 'Eagle Eye' sensor by the eastern moat.

'I wouldn't go getting your hopes up,' Reichart said, flicking on the Eagle Eye's motion-activated thermal-imaging system. 'I don't think there's gonna be much excitement on this trip—'

There came a loud *beep* from the motion sensor.

Doogie and Reichart exchanged a quick look.

Then both of them snapped around to scan the dense section of rainforest in front of the motion sensor.

There was nothing there.

Just a tangle of criss-crossing fern fronds and empty forest. Somewhere nearby a bird whistled.

Doogie snatched up his M-16 and cautiously stepped over the log-bridge that spanned the eastern section of the moat. He moved slowly forward, toward the suspect section of jungle.

He reached the edge of the rainforest, flicked on his barrel-mounted flashlight—

—and he saw it.

Saw the glistening, speckled body of the largest snake he had ever seen in his life! It was a thirty-foot anaconda, a monster of a snake, slinking lazily around the gnarled branches of an Amazonian tree.

It was so large, Doogie figured, that its movement must have set off the motion sensor.

'What is it?' Reichart said, coming alongside him.

'It's nothing,' Doogie said. 'Just a sna—'

And then abruptly, Doogie whirled back around to face the snake.

The snake couldn't have set off the motion sensor. It was cold-blooded and the motion sensor operated on a thermal-imaging system. It relied on picking up heat signatures—

Doogie whipped his gun up again and played his flashlight beam over the forest floor in front of him.

And he froze.

A man lay in the wet brush in front of him.

He was lying flat on his belly—looking up at Doogie through a black porcelain hockey mask—*not ten yards away*. So good was his camouflage, he was barely distinguishable from the dark foliage around him.

But Doogie hardly noticed the man's camouflage.

His eyes were locked on the silenced MP-5 sub-machine-gun that the man held, aimed right at the bridge of Doogie's nose.

Slowly, the camouflaged man raised his index finger to his masked lips, miming the word '*Shhh*', and as he did so, Doogie noticed a second man—identically dressed—lying in the brush alongside him, and then a third, and a fourth, and a fifth.

A whole team of black wraiths lay in the underbrush all around him.

'What the fuck—' Reichart said as he caught sight of the commandos on the forest floor in front of them. He immediately reached for his gun, but a series of loud *clicks*—the sound of about twenty safeties being released in the darkness—made him think again.

Doogie shut his eyes in disgust.

There must have been at least twenty men hidden in the brush in front of them.

He shook his head sadly.

He and Reichart had just lost the village.

'Death lies within.' Nash frowned as he looked at the boulder wedged inside the temple's portal.

Race stood beside him, staring at the graphic images carved into the stone walls of the temple—the horrific scenes of the monstrous cats and the dying people.

'Actually, it's more literal than that,' he said, turning. '*Asomarse* literally means "looms", "Death *looms* within."'

'And Santiago wrote it?' Nash said.

'It looks that way.'

At that moment, Captain Scott returned to Nash's side. 'Sir, we have a problem. I can't get through to Reichart.'

Nash didn't turn when he spoke, he just continued to gaze at the portal. 'Interference from the mountains?'

'The signal's fine, sir. Reichart's not picking up. Something's wrong.'

A frown creased Nash's face. 'They're *here* . . .' he breathed.

'Romano?' Scott said.

'Damn it,' Nash said. 'How did they get here so fast?'

'What do we do?'

166

'If they're in the village, then they know we're here.' Nash turned quickly to face Scott. 'Call the base at Panama,' he said. 'Tell them we had to go to Plan B and had to head into the mountains. Tell them to radio the air support team and instruct the pilots to home in on our portable beacons. Come on. We have to move fast.'

Lauren, Copeland and a couple of the Green Berets hurriedly began to attach some wads of Composition-2 explosive to the boulder lodged in the portal.

C-2 is a soft-detonating brand of plastique explosive used by archaeologists around the world to blast away obstructions in ancient structures without destroying the buildings themselves.

While the others went quickly about their work, Nash decided to investigate the area behind the temple, in case it revealed another way in. With nothing else to do, Race took off after him.

The two of them walked around behind the squat cube-like structure, sticking to a flat stone path that skirted its way around the tabernacle like a rail-less balcony.

They came to the rear of the building and immediately saw a steep muddy embankment that sloped sharply away from them, down to the very edge of the tower top.

As he stood at the top of the muddy hill, Race looked down at the tightly-packed arrangement of rectangular blocks that made up the path beneath him.

Amid all the sharply cornered, square-shaped blocks he saw a very odd-looking stone.

It was a *round* stone.

Nash saw it, too, and the two of them bent to examine it more closely.

It was about two-and-a-half feet in diameter—about the width of a broadshouldered man—and it lay flush against the surface of the path. Indeed, it looked to Race as if it had been slotted perfectly into a cylindrical hole *within* the path itself, a hole that had been carved *into* the square-shaped blocks around it.

'I wonder what it was used for,' Nash said.

'Who is Romano?' Race asked, catching Nash completely off guard.

Race remembered Nash telling him earlier about the team of German assassins who had slaughtered those monks in their monastery in the Pyrenees—remembered the picture Nash had shown him of the leader of that group of assassins, a man named Heinrich Anistaze.

But Nash had never mentioned anyone named Romano. Who was he and what was he doing down in the village? More importantly, why was Nash running from him?

Nash looked up sharply at Race, his expression darkening.

'Professor, please . . .'

'*Who is Romano?*'

'Excuse me,' Nash said, brushing roughly past him, heading back toward the front of the temple.

Race just shook his head and followed at a distance. He came back around to the front of the temple and sat down on its wide stone steps.

He was so tired, his mind was feeling like mush. It was just after nine now, and after travelling for nearly twelve hours, he was feeling absolutely exhausted.

He leaned back against the steps of the temple and pulled his Army parka close around himself. A sudden, overwhelming fatigue had come over him. He rested his head on the cold stone steps and shut his eyes.

As he did so, however, he heard a noise.

It was a strange noise. A sharp *scratching* sound.

It was quick, insistent—almost impatient—but oddly muffled. It seemed to be coming from *within* the stone steps beneath his head.

Race frowned.

It sounded like claws scraping against stone.

He sat up instantly and looked over at Nash and the others.

He thought about saying something to them about the scratching noise but he didn't get the chance to, because at that moment—at that precise moment—two hawk-like attack helicopters exploded through the veil of rain above the rock tower with their rotors roaring and their guns blazing, illuminating the tower top with powerful beams from their spotlights.

At exactly the same instant, deafening automatic gunfire rang out all around Race and a series of bullet holes smacked into the stone wall inches above his head.

Race dived for cover behind the corner of the temple and looked back just in time to see a small army of shadowy figures burst out from the treeline at the edge of the clearing, long tongues of fire spewing forth from the muzzles of their guns, dark wraiths in the night.

THIRD MACHINATION

Monday, January 4, 2110 hours

VILCAFOR AND SURROUNDS

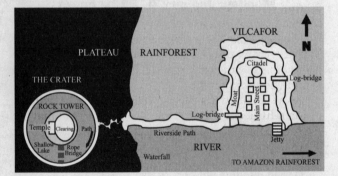

Race covered his head as another volley of automatic gunfire slammed into the stone wall next to him.

And then suddenly—shockingly—another source of gunfire exploded out from somewhere right above his head. Somewhere very, very close.

Race opened his eyes and looked up and found himself staring directly into the spotlight of one of the choppers. He squeezed his eyes shut, saw spots, reeled from the blinding light.

As he shielded his eyes with his forearm, slowly his vision returned and it was then that he realised that the source of this new gunfire was someone standing over his own prone body, firing up at the light.

It was Van Lewen. His bodyguard.

Defending him with his M-16.

Just then, one of the attack helicopters roared by overhead—its rotor blades thumping loudly, its white spotlight playing over the tower's peak—and pummelled the muddy ground in front of Van Lewen with a burst from its side-mounted cannons, the incredible noise of the cannons drowning out the clatter of automatic gunfire on the tower top.

Frantic voices shouted over Race's earpiece:

'—*Can't see where they*—'

'—*too many of them!*'

And then suddenly he heard Nash's voice: '*Van Lewen! Cease fire! Cease fire!*'

A second later, Van Lewen's fire stopped and with it the gun battle, and in the eerie stillness that followed—bathed as it was in the harsh white light of the two attack choppers circling the tower top—Race saw that he and his companions were completely surrounded by at least twenty men, all of them dressed in black and armed with submachine-guns.

The two attack helicopters began to hover above the clearing in front of the temple, illuminating it with their powerful spotlights. They were American-made AH-64 'Apache' assault choppers—skinny, evil-looking attack birds.

Slowly, the group of shadowy figures began to emerge from the foliage at the edge of the clearing.

All of them were heavily armed. Some held compact German-made MP-5s, others carried extremely high-tech Steyr-AUG assault rifles.

Race was surprised at himself, surprised at his knowledge of the range of weapons before him.

It was all Marty's fault, really.

Apart from being a design engineer at DARPA and the world's most annoying Elvis Presley fan (all of his PIN numbers and computer passwords were the same number—53310761—the King's Army serial number), Race's brother Marty was also a walking encyclopaedia on guns.

Ever since they were kids, right up to the last time Race had seen him nine years ago, whenever they visited a sporting goods store, Marty would be able to identify for his younger brother every make, model and manufacturer of the guns in the firearms section. The strange thing was that now, thanks to Marty's incessant observations, Race suddenly found that he, too, could identify them all.

He blinked, came back to the present, resumed his view of the phalanx of armed commandos gathered in front of him.

They were all dressed in black—jet-black combat fatigues, jet-black webbing, jet-black gloves and boots.

But by far the most striking feature of their uniforms was on their faces. Each soldier wore a charcoal-coloured porcelain hockey mask over his face—a solid black featureless mask that covered everything but its wearer's eyes. The masks made the soldiers in front of Race look cold, inhuman, almost robotic.

Just then one of the masked commandos hurried over to where Van Lewen was standing and snatched his M-16 away from him, hastily relieved him of his other weapons.

Then the black-clad man leaned down toward Race and smiled through his menacing black mask.

'*Guten abend*,' he said wryly before yanking Race roughly to his feet.

The rain continued to fall.

Nash, Copeland and Lauren stood by the portal, their hands clasped tightly behind their heads. The Green Berets stood next to them, disarmed.

Walter Chambers stared wide-eyed and stunned at the squad of masked commandos surrounding them. Gaby Lopez just eyed them all coolly.

Van Lewen and Race were shoved alongside the others.

Race gazed fearfully at the black-clad soldiers, stared at their cold black hockey masks. He had seen masks like that before. South American riot police wore them during extremely violent protests, to protect their faces against rocks and other hurled objects.

He counted about twenty soldiers in total.

Standing in the darkness behind the circle of commandos, however, was another group of people—men and women. This new group of people were not dressed in uniforms or masks. They wore civilian clothes, hiking clothes not unlike Lauren's.

Scientists, Race thought. *German scientists who had come here in search of the thyrium idol.*

He glanced over at the portal, at the huge boulder wedged inside its doorway. Wires protruded from every side of it—the soft-detonating C-2 explosives.

Just then, one of the commandos stepped forward and reached up to remove his black hockey mask.

Race tensed with anticipation—waited to see the cold hard features of Heinrich Anistaze, the former Stasi agent who had led the squad of German assassins in the bloody slaughter at that monastery.

The commando removed his mask.

Race frowned. He didn't recognise him.

It wasn't Anistaze.

Rather, he was a stout, older man, with a round, creased face and a bushy grey moustache.

Race wasn't sure whether to be relieved or terrified.

The German leader didn't say a word as he brushed roughly past Race and crouched down in front of the portal.

He examined the assorted wires leading out from the boulder and snorted. Then he dropped the cables and walked over to Frank Nash.

He stared imperiously down his nose at the retired Army colonel, evaluating him, appraising him.

And then suddenly he spun around and barked an order to his troops. '*Feldwebel Dietrich, bringen Sie sie in das Dorf und sperren Sie sie ein! Hauptmann von Dirksen, bereiten Sie alles vor um den Tempel zu offnen.*'

Race translated the words in his head: 'Sergeant Dietrich, take them to the village and lock them up. Captain von Dirksen, prepare to open the temple.'

Led by a German sergeant named Dietrich and surrounded by six of the masked German commandos, the ten Americans were marched unceremoniously back across the rope bridge and down the spiralling pathway.

When they came to the bottom of the path, they were directed through the narrow fissure in the plateau that led back to the riverside path. After about twenty minutes of walking, they arrived back at the village.

But the village had changed.

Two enormous halogen floodlights illuminated the main street, bathing it in artificial light. The two Apache helicopters that Race had seen up on the tower top now sat at rest in the middle of the street. About a dozen German troops stood at the river's edge, staring out at the river.

Race followed their gaze and saw his team's battered Hueys resting up against the edge of the riverbank. When seen alongside the two sleek Apaches, Frank Nash's Hueys seemed old and clunky.

It was then that Race saw what the German commandos were really looking at.

It lay beyond the two Hueys, resting on the river's surface, cloaked in the steadily falling night rain.

A seaplane.

But this was no ordinary seaplane. It must have had a wingspan of at least two hundred feet. And its underbelly—that part of it that rested majestically in the water—was absolutely *enormous*, easily larger than the main body of the Hercules that had flown Race and the others into Peru. Four turbojet engines were slung underneath its massive wings, while two bulbous pontoons stretched down from each wing, touching the water's surface, stabilising the aircraft.

It was an Antonov An-111 *Albatross*, the largest air-capable seaplane in the world.

The big plane was rotating slowly on the river's surface as Race and the others emerged from the riverside path led by the German sergeant, Dietrich. It was reversing in toward the riverbank.

No sooner had it run aground in the soft mud than a loading ramp began to lower from its hindquarters.

As soon as the ramp touched dry land, two vehicles rumbled out from within the giant plane—one eight-wheeled all-terrain vehicle that looked like a tank on wheels, and one hard-topped Humvee.

The two armoured vehicles skidded to a stop in the middle of the main street. Race and the others were led toward them. As they arrived at the two cars, Race saw two more German commandos shoving Tex Reichart and Doogie Kennedy down the street toward them.

'Gentlemen,' Dietrich said to the other commandos in German. 'Put the soldiers and the government men in the ATV under restraints. Throw the others in the Humvee. Lock them inside, and then disable both vehicles.'

Nash, Copeland and the six Green Berets were all put inside the big tank-like all-terrain vehicle. Race, Lauren, Lopez and Chambers were shoved inside the Humvee.

The Humvee was kind of like an oversized jeep, only a lot wider and with a solid reinforced metal roof. It also had Lexan glass windows which, at the moment, were rolled up.

After they were put inside the Humvee, one of the German commandos lifted up the bonnet and leaned over the big vehicle's engine. He flicked a switch underneath the radiator and immediately—*thwack!*—all the doors and windows of the Humvee were instantly locked into place.

A portable prison, Race thought.

Wonderful.

Meanwhile, the tower top was a hive of activity.

The German soldiers up there were all from the *Fallschirmjäger*—the crack rapid-response unit of the German Army—and they moved as such, quickly and efficiently.

The leader of their squad, General Gunther C.

Kolb—the grey-mustachioed man who had coldly appraised Frank Nash earlier—was barking orders at them in German: *'Move! Move! Move!* Come on! We do not have much time!'

As his men dashed about in every direction, Kolb surveyed the scene around him.

The C-2 explosives around the boulder in the temple's doorway had been removed and were now being replaced by ropes, the entry team was ready to go, and a digital video camera had been set up in front of the portal to document the opening of the temple.

Kolb nodded to himself, satisfied.

They were ready.

It was time to go in.

Rain drummed loudly on the roof of the Humvee.

Race sat slumped in the driver's seat. Walter Chambers sat beside him in the passenger seat. Lauren and Gaby Lopez were in the back.

Through the car's rain-spattered windshield, Race saw that the German soldiers in the village were crowded around a single monitor, watching it intently.

Race frowned.

Then he saw that there was a small television screen on the central console of his Humvee's dashboard—in the place where the radio would be in a regular car. He wondered if the shutdown of the Humvee's engine affected its electrical systems. He pressed the power on the little television to find out.

Slowly, a picture came to life on the screen.

On it, he saw the Germans up at the temple, gathered around the portal. He heard their voices come in over the television's speakers:

'Ich kann nicht glauben, dass sie Sprengstoff verwenden

wollten. Es konnte das gesammte Gebaude zum Einsturz gebracht haben. Machen Sie die Seile fest—'

'What are they saying?' Lauren asked.

'They're removing the explosives you set around the boulder,' Race said. 'They think the C-2'll bring down the whole structure. They're going to use ropes instead.'

A woman's voice came over the speakers, speaking rapidly in German.

Race translated for the others: 'See if you can get in touch with headquarters. Tell them we've arrived at the temple, and that we have encountered and subdued members of the United States Army. Awaiting instructions—'

Then the woman on the speakers said something else.

'—Was ist mit dem anderen amerikanischen Team? Wo sind die jetzt?'

What the hell? Race thought.

Das anderen amerikanischen Team?

At first he thought he mustn't have heard her right. But he had. He was sure of it.

But that just didn't make—

Race frowned inwardly and *didn't* translate the sentence for the others.

On the screen, ropes were being looped around the boulder in the portal.

'Alles klar, macht Euch fertig—'

'All right. Get ready.'

The men on the screen lifted the ropes.

'Zieht an!'

'And . . . heave!'

Up on the tower top, the ropes went taut and the boulder lodged in the portal slowly began to move, grinding loudly against the stone floor of the doorway.

Eight German commandos were pulling on the ropes, hauling the giant boulder from its four-hundred-year-old resting place.

Slowly—very slowly—the boulder came away from the portal, revealing an inky black interior.

Once it was clear, Gunther Kolb stepped forward, peered down into the darkened interior of the temple.

He saw a set of wide stone stairs descending into the darkness beneath him, into the belly of the great subterranean structure.

'All right,' he said in German. 'Entry team. Your turn.'

In the Humvee, Race turned to Lauren.

'They're going in.'

Up on the tower top, five fully-loaded German commandos stepped forward. The entry team.

Led by a wiry young captain named Kurt von Dirksen, they met Kolb at the entrance to the temple, guns in hand.

'Keep it simple,' Kolb said to the young captain. 'Find that idol and then get the hell—'

At that moment, without warning, a series of sharp whistling noises cut through the air all around them.

Thwat-thwat-thwat-thwat-thwat-thwat!

And then—*smack!*—something long and sharp lodged itself in a clump of moss on the wall of the temple *right next to Kolb's head!*

Kolb stared at the object in amazement.

It was an arrow.

Voices began to shout out from the Humvee's little television screen as a hailstorm of arrows rained down on the German troops gathered around the temple.

'*Was zum Teufel!*'

'*Duckt Euch! Duckt Euch!*'

'What's going on?' Lauren said, leaning forward from the back seat.

Race turned to her, amazed. 'It looks like they're being attacked.'

The deafening roar of submachine-gun fire engulfed the tower top once again as the German commandos raised their MP-5s and Steyr-AUGs and fired hard.

They all stood around the temple's open portal, facing outwards, aiming up at the source of the lethal arrows—the rim of the massive crater.

From the cover of the portal's walls, Gunther Kolb peered up into the darkness, searching for his enemy.

And he saw them.

Saw a collection of shadowy figures gathered up on the rim of the canyon.

There were maybe fifty of them in total—thin human shapes loosing a barrage of primitive wooden arrows at the German commandos on the tower top.

What the hell—? Kolb thought.

Race listened in stunned amazement to the German voices coming in over the little television's speakers.

'*Temple team! What's going on up there?*'

'*We're under attack! I repeat, we are under attack!*'

'*Who is attacking you?*'

'*They look like Indians! Repeat. Indians. Natives. They're firing down on us from the upper rim of the crater!*

But we seem to be pushing them back—wait. No, wait a minute. They're pulling back. They're pulling back.'

A moment later, the roar of automatic gunfire ceased and there was a long silence.

Nothing.

More silence.

The Germans on the screen looked cautiously around themselves, their guns smoking.

In the Humvee, Race exchanged a look with Chambers.

'A tribe of natives in the area,' Race said.

Gunther Kolb was shouting orders.

'Horgen! Vell! Take a squad up there and form a perimeter around the rim of the crater!' He turned to face von Dirksen and his entry team. 'All right, Captain. You may enter the temple.'

The five members of the entry team gathered in front of the open portal.

It yawned before them, dark and menacing.

Captain von Dirksen stepped cautiously forward—gun in hand—and stood at the threshold of the portal, at the top of the set of wide stone steps that led down into the bowels of the temple.

'All right,' he said formally into his throat mike as he took his first step downward. 'I can see some stone stairs in front of me. Descending—'

'—*the stairs now*—' von Dirksen's voice said over the Humvee's speakers.

Race stared intently at the image of the five commandos as they walked slowly into the portal until finally the last soldier's head disappeared below the floorline and he saw nothing but the empty stone doorway.

'Captain, report,' Kolb's voice said inside Kurt von Dirksen's headset as the young German captain reached the bottom of the damp stone steps, the beam of his flashlight slicing through the darkness.

He was now standing in a narrow stone-walled tunnel. It stretched away from him, bending around and down to the right in a smooth curve. It sloped steeply downwards, spiralling down into the gloom of the temple's core. Small indented alcoves lined its walls.

'We've reached the base of the stairs,' he said. 'I see a curved tunnel ahead of me. Moving toward it.'

The entry team spaced themselves out as they began to move cautiously down the steeply graded tunnel. The beams of their flashlights played over its glistening wet walls. An echoing, dripping sound could be heard from somewhere deep within the temple.

Von Dirksen said, 'Team, this is One. Call in.'

The rest of the entry team responded quickly:

'This is Two.'

'Three.'

'Four.'

'Five.'

They ventured further down the tunnel.

Race and the others watched the Humvee's television screen in tense silence, listened to the hushed voices of the German entry team. Race translated.

'—so wet in here, water everywhere—'

'—*stay sharp. Watch your step*—'

Just then, a loud burst of static screeched out from the television's speakers.

'*What was that?*' von Dirksen said quickly. '*Team, call in.*'

'This is Two.'

'Three.'

'Four.'

And then nothing.

Race waited expectantly for the final soldier to call in. But his call never came.

No 'Five'.

Inside the temple, von Dirksen spun around.

'Friedrich,' he hissed as he walked back up the passageway, past the others.

They had come a short way down the steep spiralling tunnel and now they stood in pitch darkness, the only light the beams of their flashlights.

Behind them, up the slope, they could see a wash of blue moonlight bending around the tunnel's gentle curve, indicating the way back to the surface.

Von Dirksen peered back up the tunnel.

'Friedrich!' he whispered into the darkness. '*Friedrich!* Where are you?'

At that moment, von Dirksen heard a loud *whump* from somewhere behind him.

He spun.

And now saw only *two* of his men standing behind him. The third was nowhere to be seen.

Von Dirksen turned back to face the entrance and was about to say something into his microphone when suddenly he saw an unusually large shadow slink around the bend in the tunnel above him and, in that instant, he completely lost the ability to speak.

It was silhouetted by the moonlight behind it.

And it looked absolutely terrifying.

The soft blue light of the moon glistened off its muscly black flanks. The beam of von Dirksen's flashlight glinted off its long razor-sharp teeth.

The German captain just stared at the creature before him in stunned silence.

It was *huge*.

And then suddenly it was joined by a second, identical creature, stepping out from behind it.

They must have been hiding inside the alcoves, von Dirksen thought.

Lying in wait. Waiting for him and his men to walk past them, so that they could now cut off their retreat.

And then in a flash the first creature pounced. Von Dirksen never had a chance. It moved incredibly fast for an animal of its size and in a second its slashing jaws filled his field of vision and in that moment all Kurt von Dirksen could do was scream.

Shouts and screams burst out from the television's speakers.

Race and the others stared at the screen in horror.

The screams of the last three members of the entry team being attacked echoed across the airwaves. Briefly, Race heard gunfire, but it only lasted for a second before abruptly both it and the screaming cut off together and there was silence.

Long silence.

Race stared at the television screen, at the picture of the open mouth of the temple.

'Von Dirksen, Friedrich, Nielson. Report.'

There was no reply from the men inside the temple.

Race swapped a glance with Lauren.

And then suddenly a new voice came in over the speakers.

It was a breathless voice, panting and afraid.

'Sir! This is Nielson! Repeat, this is Nielson! Oh God . . . God help us. Get out of here, sir! Get out of here while you still—'

Smack!

It sounded like a collision of some sort.

Like the sound of something big slamming into the man named Nielson.

Sounds of a scuffle ensued and then, abruptly, Race heard a blood-curdling scream and then—*over* the scream—he heard another, infinitely more terrifying, sound.

It was a *roar*—an ungodly roar—loud and deep like that of a lion.

Only fuller, more resonant, *fiercer*.

Race's eyes flashed back to the television screen and suddenly he froze.

He saw it.

Saw *it* emerge from the shadowy darkness of the portal.

And as he watched the giant black creature step out from the mouth of the temple, Race felt a deep sickness in the pit of his stomach.

Because he knew then, in that moment, that despite all their technology, all their guns, and all of their selfish desires to find a new and fantastic power source, the men on that rock tower had just violated a far, far simpler rule of human evolution.

Some doors are meant to remain unopened.

Gunther Kolb and the other dozen or so Germans on the tower top just stared at the animal standing in the portal in awe.

It was magnificent.

It was fully five feet tall, even while standing on all four legs, and it was completely black in colour, jet-black from head to toe.

It looked like a jaguar of some sort.

A *giant* black jaguar.

The massive cat's eyes glinted yellow in the moon-light, and with its furrowed angry brows, hunched muscular shoulders and dagger-like teeth, it truly looked like the Devil incarnate.

And then, abruptly, the soft blue moonlight that illu-minated the temple's portal was replaced by a harsh strobe-like flash of lightning and in the deafening crash of thunder that followed, the great animal roared.

It might as well have been a signal.

Because at that moment—at that precise moment—over a dozen *other* giant black cats burst forth from the darkness of the temple and attacked the Germans on the tower top.

Despite the fact that they were armed with assault rifles and submachine-guns, the members of the German expedition never stood a chance.

The cats were too fast. Too agile. Too powerful. They slammed into the stunned crowd of soldiers and scientists with shocking ferocity—bowling them over, leaping onto them, mauling them alive.

A few of the soldiers managed to get some shots off and one of the cats went crashing to the ground, spasming violently.

But it didn't matter, the other cats barely seemed to notice the bullets whizzing around them and within seconds they were all over those soldiers, too—tearing into their flesh, biting into their throats, suffocating them with their powerful clamp-like jaws.

Hideous screams filled the night air.

General Gunther Kolb ran.

Wet fern fronds slapped hard against his face as he hurried down the stone stairway that led back to the suspension bridge.

If he could just make it to the bridge, he thought, and untie it from the buttresses on the far side, then the cats would be trapped on the rock tower.

Kolb bolted down the wet stone slabs, the sound of his own breathing loud in his ears, the sound of something large crashing through the foliage behind him even louder. More fern fronds smacked against his face, but he didn't care. He was almost—

There!

He saw it.

The rope bridge!

He even saw a few of his men bouncing across its length, fleeing from the carnage on the tower top.

Kolb flew down the last few steps and ran out onto the ledge.

He'd made it!

It was then that a tremendous weight thudded into him from behind and the German general went sprawling forward.

He landed hard—face-first—on the cold wet surface of the ledge. He scratched about desperately with his hands, trying to get to his feet again when suddenly a giant black paw slammed down hard on his wrist, pinning it to the ground.

Kolb looked up in horror.

It was one of the cats.

It was standing on top of him!

The demonic black cat peered down at him intently, curiously examining this strange little creature that had foolishly attempted to outrun it.

Kolb stared fearfully up into its evil yellow eyes. And then with a loud blood-curdling roar, the big animal's head came rushing down at him and Kolb shut his eyes and waited for the end.

Down in the village, there was silence.

The twelve German commandos gathered around the monitor just stared at each other in astonishment.

On their screen, they saw their comrades up on the tower top running about in every direction. Occasionally, they would see one of them dash across the screen and open fire with an MP-5 only to be violently smacked out of the frame a second later by a large feline shape.

'Hasseldorf, Krieger,' the sergeant named Dietrich said sharply. 'Dismantle the western log-bridge.' Two of the German soldiers immediately broke out of the circle.

Dietrich turned to face his young radio operator. 'Have you been able to get through to anyone up there?'

'I'm getting through, sir, but no-one's answering,' the radio man said.

'*Keep trying.*'

Through the rainspattered windows of the Humvee, Race was watching Dietrich and the German commandos assembled around their monitor when suddenly he heard a shout.

He snapped around instantly.

And saw one of the German commandos from the tower top come charging out from the riverside path.

The commando was waving his arms wildly, yelling, '*Schnell, zum Flugzeug! Schnell, zum Flugzeug! Sie kommen!*'

He was shouting: '*Get to the plane! Get to the plane! They're coming!*'

Just then a flare of lightning illuminated the path behind the running man and Race caught a glimpse of something bounding along the path behind him.

'*Oh, my God . . .*'

It was one of the giant cat-like creatures—just like the one he had seen stepping out of the temple only minutes earlier.

But the image he had seen on the Humvee's tiny television screen hadn't done the creature justice at all.

It was absolutely terrifying.

It ran with its head held low and its pointed ears pinned back, its powerful muscular shoulders driving it forward after its fleeing human prey.

It moved beautifully, with fluid feline grace—that

striking combination of balance, power and speed common to cats the world over.

The German commando was running hard but there was no way he was going to outrun the massive animal behind him. He tried to swerve as he ran, to dodge in behind some trees next to the path. But the cat was too agile. It looked like a cheetah in full flight—its powerful legs adjusting perfectly as it ran, copying the movements of its prey, ducking to the left, veering to the right, keeping its centre of gravity low, never once losing its footing.

It loomed above the hapless German, got closer and closer, and then, when it was near enough, the great cat leapt forward and—

Abruptly, the lightning flash vanished and the path was plunged into complete darkness.

Darkness.

Silence.

And Race heard a scream.

Then suddenly another flash of lightning lit up the riverbank, and as he registered the image before him, Race felt his blood run completely cold.

The immense black cat was standing astride the body of the commando, its massive head bent over the fallen man's neck area. Abruptly, the cat jerked its jaws upward and with a sickening ripping sound, wrenched the dead commando's throat clear from his body.

And in another glaring flash of lightning, the giant black cat roared in triumph.

For a whole minute, no-one in the Humvee said anything.

Walter Chambers broke the silence. 'We are in so much trouble.'

And he was right. For at that moment, at that terrible moment, all of the *other* black cats burst out from the foliage near the riverbank and attacked every living thing in sight.

The cats stormed the village from every side, catching Dietrich and his men—gathered foolishly around the monitor in the centre of the town—completely by surprise.

The cats bounded into the main street like bats out of hell—crash-tackling the German commandos where they stood, bowling them off their feet before they could grab their guns, slamming them to the ground, biting into their throats.

Race wasn't sure how many of the cats there were. At first he counted ten, then twelve, then fifteen.

Jesus.

Then suddenly he heard gunfire and he snapped around to see the two German soldiers Dietrich had sent to raise the western log-bridge—Hasseldorf and Krieger—firing desperately at the onslaught of charging cats.

The two commandos managed to hit a couple of the fearsome animals—they pitched wildly forward, crashed down into the mud—before the other cats simply leapt over their bodies and overwhelmed the two humans with their numbers.

One cat leapt onto Hasseldorf's back and immediately ripped out his spine. Another just clamped its massive jaws around Krieger's throat, breaking his neck with a nauseating *crrrrunch!*

The rest of the village looked like a riot zone, with German soldiers running in every direction—toward the two Apache helicopters, toward the huts, toward the river—in a desperate bid to escape the rampaging cats.

'*Get to the choppers!*' someone yelled. '*Get to the—*'

Just then, Race heard an engine turn over and he spun in his seat to see the rotor blades of both of the Apache attack helicopters slowly begin to rotate.

German soldiers ran desperately for the two choppers, but they were small and skinny—each only had room for a single pilot and a gunner.

The first Apache began to lift off just as a terrified trooper leapt up onto its landing strut and yanked open the cockpit door. But before he could even try to climb inside, one of the cats bounded up onto the strut after him, shoving him roughly out of the way before it slithered in through the cockpit door, its long slashing tail whipping over the side as it did so.

A second later, the interior of the cockpit windows was splattered with blood and the chopper—hovering ten feet off the ground—went wild.

It yawed sharply to the right, its rotor blades a speeding blur of movement, *toward* the other Apache, just as the six-barrelled rotary cannon under its nose blasted wildly to life, assaulting the entire village with supermachine-gun fire.

Tracer bullets sprayed everywhere.

The windshield of Race's Humvee exploded into a spiderweb of cracks as the storm of bullets slammed into it.

Race ducked away from the impacts instinctively. As he did so, however, he saw a series of orange impact sparks flare out all over the tail section of one of the Hueys moored on the riverbank nearby.

Then suddenly, like fireworks shooting into the sky on the fourth of July, two Hellfire missiles shot out from the flailing Apache's missile pods.

One of the missiles slammed into a nearby stone hut, blasted it to rubble, while the other just shot straight down the main street of Vilcafor, heading directly for the massive Antonov seaplane parked at the riverbank, before—*shoom!*—it whizzed in through the open loading ramp of the plane and disappeared inside its cargo bay.

There was about a second's delay.

And then the giant seaplane exploded. It was a monstrous explosion, momentous in its force. The Antonov's walls just blew out in an instant and the whole plane immediately listed dramatically to the left and began to sink into the river and drift slowly downstream.

In the meantime, the Apache that was causing all this damage was still lurching wildly toward its twin. The second helicopter tried desperately to get out of its way, but it was too late. The rotor blades of the first Apache struck the rapidly-spinning blades of the second helicopter and a shrill metal-on-metal shriek filled the air.

Then suddenly, shockingly, the blades of the first chopper ruptured the fuel tanks of the second and the two Apaches exploded in a massive orange fireball that fanned out along the main street of Vilcafor.

Race turned away from the fiery scene, glanced at Walter Chambers in the front seat beside him.

'Jesus Christ, Walter,' he said.'Did you see that?'

Chambers didn't answer him.

Race frowned. 'Walter? What's the—?'

Purrrrrrr.

Race froze at the sound.

Then he looked at Chambers' face more closely. The bookish anthropologist's eyes were as wide as saucers and he seemed to be holding his breath.

He was also looking directly over Race's shoulder.

Slowly—very, very slowly—William Race turned around.

One of the cats was standing at the window.

Right at the window!

Its black head was absolutely massive. It took up the entire window. The gigantic creature just stared in at Race with narrowed yellow eyes.

It purred again. A deep, resonating growl.

Purrrrrrr.

Race saw its chest rising and falling, saw its long white fangs protruding over its lower lip. Then abruptly the animal snorted and he almost jumped out of his skin and then—*whump!*—all of a sudden, the whole Humvee jolted beneath him.

He spun to look forward.

Another cat had just leapt onto the bonnet of the Humvee!

It stood with its muscular forelimbs splayed wide on the bonnet of the car, its angry yellow eyes staring down at Race and Chambers, boring into their very souls.

Race touched his throat mike. 'Ah, Van Lewen. You out there?'

No response.

Screeeeeeeeeech!

The black cat on the bonnet took a slow, ominous step forward, its claws scraping against the steel hood as it did so. At the same time, the cat to Race's left nudged the Humvee's door roughly with its nose, testing it.

Race began tapping his throat mike repeatedly. 'Van Lewen!'

Van Lewen's voice came in over his earpiece. *'I see you, Professor. I see you.'*

Race looked over and saw the all-terrain vehicle sitting motionless on the muddy street not far from the Humvee.

'Now would be a good time to do some of that bodyguard stuff,' Race said.

'Take it easy, Professor. You're safe while you're inside the Humvee.'

It was at that precise moment that the black cat on the bonnet of the Humvee slammed its left forepaw *right through* the cracked forward windshield of the vehicle!

Glass showered everywhere as the cat's huge fist-like claw exploded through the windscreen and came to a jolting halt two inches away from the brim of Race's Yankees cap.

'Van Lewen!'

'All right! All right! Quickly! Look under the dashboard!' Van Lewen said. *'Down near the gas pedal. Look for a black rubber button on the underside of the steering column!'*

Race looked there.

Found it.

'What's it do?'

'Just press it!'

Race pressed the rubber button and the Humvee's engine immediately roared to life.

It wasn't disabled anymore! Race didn't know why, didn't care. So long as it was working.

He quickly came back up from under the steering

wheel—and found himself staring into the wide-open jaws of the black cat on the bonnet!

The cat snarled at him—a wild, angry hiss. It was so close, Race could feel its hot rancid breath washing all over his face. The big cat writhed and squirmed as it tried desperately to squeeze in through the hole it had punched in the windshield and get to the human flesh inside.

Race leaned back in his seat, away from the frenzied animal's teeth, pushing himself up against the driver's side window—where he turned and saw the *other* cat's enormous jaws come rushing toward him at frightening speed!

The second cat slammed into the window. The Humvee rocked on its suspension, bounced under the weight of the cat's stunning impact. A series of lightning-shaped cracks spontaneously appeared all over the driver's side window.

But the car's engine was still running, and that was all that mattered. Jolted into action by the ramming, Race grabbed hold of the gearstick, crunched the gears, found one—didn't care which one—and slammed the gas pedal to the floor.

The Humvee shot backwards through the muddy main street of Vilcafor.

Jesus! He'd found reverse!

The cat on the bonnet seemed oblivious to the Humvee's momentum as the oversized jeep-like vehicle bounced wildly over the uneven ground of the village. The demonic animal just yanked its head out of the windshield and began reaching in through the shattered glass with its foreclaw, trying to get at Race.

For his part, Race just leaned back as far as he could, keeping his body clear of the slashing claw, pressing his foot down harder on the gas pedal.

The Humvee hit a pothole, shot into the air for a moment, thumped back down to earth. The cat was still on the bonnet, still clutching maniacally at Race as the armoured vehicle careered down the rain-soaked street in reverse, totally out of control.

'Will! Look out!' Lauren yelled.

'What?' Race called.

'Behind us!'

But Race wasn't looking behind them.

He was looking at the vision from Hell that was reaching in through the forward windshield of the car trying to rip open his chest.

'Will! Stop! *We're heading for the river!*'

Race's head snapped up.

Did she just say 'river'?

He shot a look at the rear-view mirror and caught a glimpse of the black river behind them—approaching quickly—caught a glimpse of one of the American Hueys resting in the shallows, *directly in their path!*

Race grappled with the steering wheel, but it was no use. In his panic to get away from the cat on the bonnet, he'd long since lost control of the backward-speeding Humvee.

He yanked hard on the wheel, slammed his foot down on the brakes, but the wheels just locked and in an instant the big Humvee lost all its traction. It just skidded in the mud, aquaplaning wildly out of control. And then suddenly, sickeningly, before Race even knew what was happening, the big vehicle launched itself off the edge of the bank, out into the air, out over the river.

The Humvee flew through the air, soaring out over the riverbank, flying in a high graceful arc. And then it smashed—*hard*, tail-first—into the glass bubble of the Huey sitting in the shallows.

The inertia of the crash was so great that it sent both car and helicopter floating out into the river proper. It also sent the cat on the Humvee's bonnet shooting off the hood of the car and completely over the Huey too! The big cat landed way out in the middle of the river, hitting the water with a great ungainly splash.

Within seconds, the crocodile-like caimans were all over it.

Shrieking wildly, the cat put up a hell of a fight, until finally it succumbed to their numbers and went under.

What remained near the shore was a bizarre-looking Humvee-Huey hybrid that sat half-submerged in the water about twenty feet out from the riverbank.

The whole forward bubble of the Huey had been crushed inwards by the Humvee, and now the wide jeep-like vehicle stuck out awkwardly from the chopper's crushed front section. The Huey's rotor housing and tail section, however, had not been damaged by the impact. Its two rotor blades just sat high above the whole ghastly contraption, immobile but intact.

Inside the Humvee, Race tried desperately to stay calm.

Slimy green water lapped against the window to his left while powerful mini-jets of spray shot in through the network of cracks in it. Looking out through the window itself was like looking into one of those aquariums where you can see both above and below the waterline.

Only this was the aquarium from Hell.

Through the window, Race saw the underbellies of no less than five gigantic caimans, all of them making a beeline right for him, their tails slinking back and forth behind them, driving their bodies toward the Humvee.

To make matters worse, a torrent of water was gushing in through the large hole in the windshield in front of him, splashing all over his jeans, creating a deep sloshing puddle at his feet.

Walter Chambers began to hyperventilate. '*Oh my God! Oh my God! Oh my God!*' Behind Chambers, Race saw that Gaby Lopez now had a deep bloody gash above her left eye. She must have hit her head when the Humvee had impacted against the chopper.

'We have to get out of here!' Lauren yelled.

'You think!' Race shouted, as a large silver fish with big teeth was carried in through the windshield in front of him and landed in his lap.

Just then there came a loud *whump!* from somewhere to his left and Race was almost jolted out of his seat as the whole Humvee rocked wildly sideways.

He turned and saw the enormous shape of a black caiman hovering at the window beside him, staring in through the cracked glass, gazing hungrily at him!

'Oh, man,' he said.

Then he saw the massive reptile draw back from the glass.

'Oh, man . . .'

'What? *What?*' Walter Chambers said from beside him.

'It's going to ram us!' Race yelled as he hastily began climbing over into the back seat. '*Move*, Walter! *Move now!*'

Chambers immediately started to scramble over into the back seat, too, just as the caiman outside surged forward. A split second later, the driver's side window of the Humvee exploded inwards in a spectacular shower of glass.

The sudden rain of glass was quickly followed by the massive scaly body of the caiman as it slithered in through the window into the front section of the Humvee, riding a wave of water as it cascaded into the car.

The caiman rushed across the front seat of the Humvee, its giant body taking up all of the tiny space. Race yanked his feet into the back seat a nanosecond before its slashing jaws shot past them.

Walter Chambers wasn't so lucky. He didn't get his legs out of the way in time and the caiman smashed into them hard, driving them into the passenger side door, pinning them there.

Chambers screamed. The caiman bucked and snorted as it tried to get a better grip on him.

From the back seat, all Race could see was the creature's enormous armoured back and its long plated tail, slashing viciously back and forth.

Then, abruptly, *violently*—and so quickly that it made Race gasp in horror—the giant caiman wrenched Chambers out through the window through which it had come.

'*Nooooo!*' Chambers screamed as he disappeared out the window and was taken under the surface outside.

Race exchanged a horrified look with Lauren.

'What are we going to do now!' she yelled.

How the hell should I know? he thought as he looked at the situation around him.

The front seat of the vehicle was filling up with water fast, causing the Humvee to tilt sharply to the left and drop lower in the water.

'We've got to get out of here before this car sinks!' he yelled. 'Quickly! Open your window! We should be able to open them now!'

Water began to flow over the front seat and into the back as Lauren began to unwind her window. The car was higher over on her side, and when at last she opened the window fully, she revealed only the cold night air.

Then suddenly another giant caiman came surging in through the driver's side window of the Humvee and splashed down into the pool of water in the front half of the vehicle.

'*Go!*' Race yelled. 'Get onto the roof!'

Lauren moved fast. In a second she was out of the Humvee, climbing up onto its roof. The dazed Gaby went next—she shuffled quickly across the back seat and reached out through the window. Lauren immediately began to pull her out from up on the roof, while Race pushed her from below.

The caiman in the driver's seat bucked and snorted, searching for its prey.

Water was now *rushing* over the front seat in a thick steady stream. It was almost waist-deep in the back.

Just then another caiman rammed into the rear-left window of the Humvee, causing the entire vehicle to jolt. Race spun at the impact and saw that *the whole left-hand side of the Humvee* was now completely underwater!

Gaby Lopez was halfway out the right-side window. Race was the last one left.

It was then, however, as he pushed on Gaby's feet, that he heard a sickening metallic groan from somewhere within the Humvee.

Abruptly the whole car lurched dramatically to the right.

At first he thought it was another ramming from one of the caimans. But it wasn't. No, this time *the whole car* had shifted laterally. It was moving. Moving . . .

Downstream.

Oh, God, Race thought.

They were being carried downstream by the current of the river!

'This is not happening,' he said.

At that moment there came another, more familiar jolt as one of the caimans rammed the left-hand window again.

'Come *on*, Gaby!' he yelled at Lopez's feet as they dangled inside the right-hand window in front of him.

By this time, the caiman in the front seat seemed to have realised where Race and the others were and it began to shuffle clumsily backwards so that it could leap over into the back seat.

Race saw it move.

'Gaby!'

'Almost there . . .' Lopez called back.

'*Hurry up!*'

Then suddenly, Gaby's feet disappeared out the window and Lauren yelled, 'She's clear, Will!' and Race leapt for the window, poked his head out through it and saw Lauren and Gaby standing on the roof above him.

The two women quickly reached down and grabbed his hands and hauled him out of the car not a second before the caiman in the front seat clambered over into the back and snapped angrily at his outward-moving feet, missing them by millimetres.

Back in the village, Nash, Copeland and the six American soldiers were all sitting—handcuffed—in the safety of the all-terrain vehicle, watching the nightmare outside unfold, when suddenly the sliding side door of their armoured vehicle was wrenched open from the outside and a blast of rain and wind swirled into the interior of the ATV.

Two soaking Germans hurried in through the door, their mudsoaked feet clanging on the floor of the vehicle. They shut the great steel door behind them and abruptly there was silence inside the ATV once again.

Nash and the others just stared at their new companions.

A man and a woman.

Both were sopping wet, and both were completely covered in mud. They wore civilian clothes—blue jeans and white T-shirts—but with a twist: both wore black Gore-Tex holsters and compact Glock-18 pistols on their hips. They both also wore navy blue bulletproof vests. Their appearance screamed: *undercover cops.*

The man was burly, strong-looking and barrel-chested. The woman small but athletic, with short peroxide-blonde hair.

The man didn't waste any time. He walked straight over to the Americans and began unlocking their handcuffs.

'You're not prisoners anymore,' he said in English. 'We are all in this together now. Come, we must save as many of the others as we can.'

Race, Lauren and Lopez were standing—stranded—on the roof of the Humvee, as the whole Humvee-Huey combination drifted awkwardly downriver, caught in the current.

Just then Race saw the rickety wooden jetty about ten yards away from them, downstream. It looked like they would float right by it.

That was their chance.

The Humvee-Huey lurched again, sank lower in the water. At the moment, the *Humvee's* roof was about a foot above the river's surface, while the *Huey's* was a little higher. But for every yard that the two vehicles moved downriver, they both seemed to drop a couple of inches.

It was going to be close.

Very close.

They edged another yard downstream.

The caimans began to circle.

Eight yards to the jetty and water began to seep onto the roof of the Humvee and under their feet. The three of them stepped up onto the rotor housing of the Huey.

Five yards away.

Sinking fast.

From atop the Huey's rotor housing, Race looked out over the floodlit village.

It was deserted now, the only movement the

occasional feline shadow that darted across the main street. There was no sign of human life. None at all.

It was then that Race noticed it.

The all-terrain vehicle was gone.

The eight-wheeled tank-like ATV that had been holding Nash, Copeland and the Green Berets was nowhere to be seen.

Race spoke into his throat mike. 'Van Lewen! Where are you?'

'*I'm here, Professor.*'

'Where?'

'*Couple of the Germans opened up the ATV and unlocked our cuffs. We're doing a circuit of the village now, picking up anybody we can find.*'

'While you're at it, why don't you swing by the jetty in about thirty seconds.'

'*Ten-four, Professor. We'll be there.*'

Three yards from the jetty, and the Humvee's roof went completely under.

Race bit his lip.

Although they were now standing on the exposed rotor housing of the Huey, they were still going to have to step across the *submerged* Humvee's roof to get to the jetty.

'Come on, baby, stay afloat,' he said.

Two yards.

The Humvee's roof went six inches under.

One yard.

A whole foot under.

Lauren looped an arm underneath the dazed Gaby's shoulders.

'Okay, kids,' she said. 'Listen up. I'll take Gaby first. Will, you bring up the rear. Got it?'

'Got it.'

The Humvee-Huey came alongside the jetty.

As it did so, Lauren and Gaby leapt off the rotor housing of the Huey and splashed down onto the submerged roof of the Humvee—their legs dropping knee-deep into the water.

They took two sloshing strides forward before Lauren threw Gaby up onto the jetty. Then she leapt up onto it herself, pulling her feet up just as two massive crocodilian shapes lunged through the water behind her, snapping their jaws ferociously.

'Will! *Come on!*' she called from the jetty.

Race readied himself to jump down onto the submerged roof of the Humvee. He couldn't imagine how it must have looked—him, in his jeans, T-shirt and baseball cap standing atop a submerged Army helicopter in the middle of a caiman-infested Amazonian river.

How the hell did I get into this? he thought.

Then, without warning, the whole Humvee-Huey contraption lurched dramatically, dropped another foot in the water.

Race lost his balance, almost fell off, but recovered quickly. Then he looked up to see that things had just gotten seriously worse.

The Humvee's roof was now at least *three feet* underwater.

Even if he *could* jump onto it, his mobility would be shot. The caimans would get him for sure.

The Huey's situation wasn't much better.

Even though he was standing on the chopper's rotor housing, it, too, was now submerged underneath an inch of water.

Race looked frantically about himself—saw that the only part of the Huey still above the water were its two rotor blades.

He glanced quickly over at the jetty and saw the

ATV skid to a stop at its base—saw the sliding door on the big eight-wheeler's side whip open to reveal Van Lewen and Scott inside it—saw Lauren drag Gaby over toward it.

Lauren yelled over her shoulder. 'Will! *Come on!* Jump!'

The Huey lurched again and Race's sneakers went fully under the surface.

He looked at the sinking chopper around him, looked at its rotor blades hovering above the surface.

The rotor blades . . . he thought.

Maybe he could . . .

No.

He'd be too heavy, they'd sag underneath his weight.

He spun back round to look at the jetty. Three large caimans now hovered, half-submerged, in the water *between* him and the old wooden wharf.

Maybe . . .

Race quickly reached out and grabbed hold of one of the rotor blades. Then he heaved on it as hard as he could, turning the thirty-foot blade around on its pivot.

The sunken Huey was still drifting slowly downstream with the current.

The rotor blade came round, its forward tip almost touching the jetty, so that it now looked like a narrow bridge stretched out low over the river, connecting the Huey to the wharf.

The Huey rocked again, sank another two inches, just as an enormous black shape exploded out of the water next to Race and on a reflex he spread his legs as far apart as he could and the caiman shot right through them—brushing against the insides of his calves—and off the other side of the Huey.

That was too close! his mind screamed. *Move!*

Race took a final look up at his passage to free-dom—the rotor blade, a plank of steel ten inches wide, hanging a foot above the surface of the river.

Do it!

And so he did.

Race jumped up onto the rotor blade and ran out across its length.

Three steps forward and he saw the jetty twenty feet in front of him. The jetty, safety, salvation—

—halfway across and he felt the rotor blade sag beneath him, and lower itself toward the waterline and—

—*come to rest on the backs of the three caimans in the water between the helicopter and the jetty!*

Race danced across the narrow bridge, now supported by the bodies of the three caimans!

He reached the end of the rotor blade at a full stride and launched himself off it, diving through the air, slamming chest-first into the edge of the jetty.

Get your feet out of the water! his mind screamed as he felt his feet splash down into the inky black liquid beneath him.

He quickly yanked his feet up out of the water and rolled up onto the safety of the jetty.

He swallowed, breathless. He couldn't believe it.

He was—

'*Professor! Come on!*' Van Lewen's tinny voice yelled suddenly in his ear.

Race looked up immediately and saw the ATV parked at the end of the jetty, its sliding side door open.

Just then, however, some movement *above* the ATV caught his eye and he glanced up just in time to see one of the massive black cats leap clear over the all-terrain vehicle with its claws extended and its jaws bared wide.

The giant animal landed on the jetty barely five feet in front of him. It just stood there before him, crouching low, its ears pinned back, its lips curling, its muscles tensing for the final pounce . . .

And then suddenly the rickety jetty fell away beneath it.

There was no creak. No warning sound.

The old wooden jetty just gave way beneath the cat and with a bewildered *screech* the big black creature dropped into the water beneath it.

'It's about time I had some luck,' Race said.

The caimans moved in quickly.

Two big bulls charged in toward the fallen cat and soon the water around the big animal became a seething, frothing mess.

Race seized the opportunity and leapt across the newly created gap in the jetty and bolted for the ATV.

As he stepped inside the ATV and Van Lewen slid the heavy steel door shut behind him, he looked back out at the river through a narrow rectangular slit in the door.

What he saw was completely unexpected.

He saw the cat—the same black cat that had accosted him only moments before—climb slowly up out of the water and back up onto the jetty. Blood dripped from its claws, ragged chunks of flesh hung from its jaws, water dripped from its glistening flanks.

The animal's chest heaved. It seemed absolutely exhausted from the battle it had just fought.

But it was alive.

It had won.

It had just survived an encounter with two bull caimans!

Race slumped down on the floor of the ATV, totally exhausted. He let his head fall against the cold metal wall behind him and allowed his eyes to close.

As he did so, however, he heard noises.

He heard the grunts and snorts of the cats outside— close, loud, large.

He heard their paws splashing in puddles. Heard the crunch of breaking bones as they feasted on the bodies of the dead German commandos. He even heard the sound of someone crying out in agony in the near distance.

Soon Race would fall asleep, but before he did he would have one final, terrifying thought.

How the hell am I going to get out of here alive?

FOURTH MACHINATION

Tuesday, January 5, 0930 hours

Special Agent John-Paul Demonaco walked slowly down the white-lit corridor, careful not to step on the bodybags.

It was 9:30 in the morning, January 5, and Demonaco had just arrived at 3701 North Fairfax Drive in response to an order from the Director of the FBI himself.

Like the rest of the world, Demonaco knew nothing of the break-in at DARPA headquarters the day before. All he knew was that the Director had received a phone call at 3:30 that morning from a four-star admiral standing in the Oval Office asking for him to send his best domestic anti-terrorist man down to Fairfax Drive as soon as humanly possible.

His best man was John-Paul Demonaco.

'J.P.' Demonaco was fifty-two years old, divorced, and a little loose around the waistline. He had thinning brown hair and wore a pair of horn-rimmed glasses. His rumpled grey polyester suit had been bought from J.C. Penney for a hundred dollars in 1994, while the Versace tie that he wore with it had been bought for three hundred dollars only last year. It had been a birthday gift from his youngest daughter—apparently it was trendy.

Despite his dress sense, Demonaco was Special Agent in Charge of the FBI's Anti-Terrorist Unit (Domestic), a position he had occupied for four years now, principally because he knew more about American terrorism than anybody else alive.

Walking down the white-lit hallway, Demonaco saw another bodybag lying on the floor in front of him. A star of blood smeared the wall above it. He added the bag to his tally. That made ten already.

What on earth had happened here?

He turned a corner and immediately saw a small crowd of people standing at the entrance to a laboratory at the end of the corridor.

Most of the members of the crowd, he saw, were dressed in perfectly starched, dark blue U.S. Navy uniforms.

A twentysomething lieutenant met him halfway down the corridor.

'Special Agent Demonaco?'

Demonaco flashed his ID in response.

'This way, please. Commander Mitchell is expecting you.'

The young lieutenant led him into the laboratory. As he entered the lab, Demonaco silently took in the wall-mounted security cameras, the thick hydraulic doors, the alpha-numeric locks.

Jesus, it was a goddamn vault.

'Special Agent Demonaco?' a voice said from behind him. Demonaco turned to see a handsome young officer standing before him. The man was about thirty-six years old, tall, with blue eyes and short sandy-blond hair—a Navy poster boy. And for some reason that Demonaco couldn't quite pin down, he looked oddly familiar.

'Yeah, I'm Demonaco.'

'Commander Tom Mitchell. Naval Criminal Investigative Service.'

NCIS, Demonaco thought. *Interesting*.

When he had arrived at Fairfax Drive, Demonaco had barely even noticed the Navy servicemen guarding the entrance to the building. It wasn't unusual in the DC area to have certain federal buildings guarded by specific branches of the armed forces. For example, Fort Meade, the headquarters of the NSA, was actually an Army compound. The White House, on the other hand, was guarded by members of the United States Marine Corps. It would have come as no surprise to Demonaco to learn that DARPA was protected by the U.S. Navy. Which would have explained all the Navy suits here now.

But no. If the NCIS was here, that meant something else entirely. Something that went beyond merely failing to protect a federal building. Something internal . . .

'I don't know if you remember me,' Mitchell said, 'but I took your seminar at Quantico about six months ago. "The Second Amendment and the Rise of the Militia Groups".'

So that was where he had seen Mitchell before.

Every three months, Demonaco gave a seminar at Quantico on domestic terrorist organisations in the United States. In his lectures, he basically outlined the make-up, methods and philosophies of the more organised militia groups in the country—groups like the Patriots, the White Aryan Resistance or the Republican Army of Texas.

After the Oklahoma City bombing and the bloody siege at the Coltex nuclear weapons facility in Amarillo, Texas, Demonaco's seminars had been in high demand. Especially among the armed forces, since their bases—and the buildings they protected—were often the targets of domestic terrorist acts.

'What can I do for you, Commander Mitchell?' Demonaco said.

'Well, first of all, as you will no doubt appreciate, everything you see or hear in this room is strictly classifi—'

'What is it you want me to do?' Demonaco was famous for his inability to put up with bullshit.

Mitchell took a deep breath. 'As you can see, we had something of an . . . incident . . . here yesterday morning. Seventeen security staff killed and a weapon of immense importance stolen. We have reason to believe that a domestic terrorist organisation was involved, which is why you were called in—'

'Is that him? *Is that him?*' a rough-sounding voice said from somewhere nearby.

Demonaco turned and saw a severe-looking captain with a grey moustache and a matching grey crew-cut striding quickly toward him and Commander Mitchell.

The captain glared at Mitchell. 'I told you this was a mistake, Tom. This is an internal matter. We don't need to involve the FBI in this.'

'Special Agent Demonaco,' Mitchell said, 'this is Captain Vernon Aaronson. Captain Aaronson has overall responsibility for this investigation—'

'But Commander Mitchell here, it seems, has the ear of those who would like to see this puzzle solved more slowly than it has to be,' Aaronson quipped.

Demonaco judged Vernon Aaronson to be a couple of years older—and at least a decade more bitter—than his subordinate, Commander Mitchell.

'I had no choice, sir,' Mitchell said. 'The President insisted—'

'The President insisted . . .' Aaronson snorted.

'He didn't want to see a repeat of the Baltimore freeway incident.'

Ah, Demonaco thought. *So that was it.*

On Christmas Day 1997, an unmarked DARPA transport truck travelling from New York to Virginia was hijacked as it travelled along the Baltimore beltway. Stolen from the truck were sixteen J-7 jet packs and forty-eight prototype explosive charges—small chrome-and-plastic tubes that looked like glass laboratory vials.

But these were no ordinary explosive charges. Officially, they were called M-22 isotopic charges, but around DARPA they were known as 'Pocket Dynamos'.

Put simply, the Pocket Dynamo was an evolutionary step forward in high-temperature liquid chemical technology. The result of thirteen years' concerted labour by the United States Army and DARPA's Advanced Ordnance Division, the M-22 utilised laboratory-created isotopes of the element chlorine to deliver a concentrated blast wave of such savage intensity that it literally *vaporised* anything within a two-hundred-yard radius of the detonation point. It was designed for use by small incursionary units on sabotage or search-and-destroy missions—where the mission objective was to leave absolutely *nothing* behind. The isotopic explosion of an M-22 charge was second only in intensity to a thermonuclear blast, but without the attendant radio-active after-effects.

What Demonaco also knew about the Baltimore freeway incident, however, was that the Army had handled the investigation into the theft themselves.

Two days after the daring robbery, the Army investigators received a tip-off regarding the location of the stolen weapons and without so much as consulting with the FBI or the CIA, a squad of Green Berets was ordered to storm the headquarters of an underground militia group in northern Idaho. Ten people were killed, twelve were wounded. It turned out to be the wrong group. In fact, more than that, it turned out to be one of the more benign paramilitary groups around, more like a gun club than a terrorist cell. No isotopic explosives were found on their premises. The ACLU and the NRA had had a field day.

The jet packs and the M-22s were never recovered.

Quite obviously, Demonaco thought, the President didn't want another such embarrassment here. Which was why he had been called in.

'So what is it you want me to look at?' he said.

'This,' Mitchell said, pulling something from his pocket and handing it to Demonaco.

It was a clear plastic evidence bag.

In it was a blood-stained bullet.

Demonaco sat down at a nearby table to examine the blood-smeared bullet.

'Where was this taken from, one of the security personnel?'

'No,' Mitchell said. 'The driver of the delivery van they used to get in. He was the only one they killed with a pistol.'

Captain Aaronson added, 'After they used him to get past the garage guards, they popped him in the head at point-blank range.'

'A calling card,' Demonaco said.

'Uh-huh.'

'Looks like a tungsten core . . .' Demonaco said, perusing the spent projectile.

'That's what we thought, too,' Aaronson said. 'And

as far as we know, only one terrorist organisation in the United States is known to use tungsten-based ammunition. The Oklahoma Freedom Fighters.'

Demonaco didn't look up from the bullet in his hands. 'That's true, but the Freedom Fighters—'

'—are known to operate like this,' Aaronson cut in. 'Special forces-type entry, double-taps to their victims' heads, the theft of cutting-edge military technology.'

'It would appear that you've been to one of my seminars, too, Captain Aaronson,' Demonaco said.

'Yes, I have,' Aaronson said, 'but I also consider myself to be a specialist in this field, too. I've studied these groups extensively as part of ongoing Naval security updates. We have to keep an eye on these people, too, you know.'

'Then you'd know that the Freedom Fighters are in the middle of a turf war with the Texans,' Demonaco said.

Aaronson bit his lip, frowned. He obviously hadn't known that. He glared at Demonaco, stung by the veiled retort.

Demonaco looked up at the two Naval officers through his horn-rimmed glasses. There was something they weren't telling him.

'Gentlemen. What happened here?'

Aaronson and Mitchell exchanged a look.

'What do you mean?' Mitchell asked.

'I can't help you if I don't know the full story of what happened here. Like, for starters, what it was that was stolen.'

Aaronson grimaced. Then he said, 'They were after a device called the Supernova. They knew where it was and how to get it. They knew all the codes and had all the cardkeys. They moved with precision and speed, like a well-oiled commando unit.'

Demonaco said, 'The Freedom Fighters' strike team is good but it isn't big enough to take down a place this size. It's too small, maybe two or three men at the most. That's why they only attack soft targets—computer labs, low-level government offices—places from which they can steal technical data like electrical schematics or satellite overpass times. But most importantly, they only attack sites that are lightly guarded. Not fortresses like this. They're first and foremost techno-nuts, not a full-frontal assault squad.'

'But they *are* the only group known to use tungsten-based ammunition,' Aaronson said.

'That's true.'

'So maybe they've stepped up their operations,' Aaronson said smugly. 'Maybe they're trying to make the leap into the big leagues.'

'Possible.'

'It's possible,' Aaronson snorted. 'Special Agent Demonaco, perhaps I haven't made something clear. The device that was stolen from this facility is of the utmost importance to the future defence of the United States. In the wrong hands, its use could be catastrophic. Now, I have SEAL teams standing by right now to take out three suspected Freedom Fighter locations. But my bosses need to know that this is clean—they don't want another Baltimore. All we need from you is an acknowledgment that this robbery could *only* have been done by them.'

'Well . . .' Demonaco began.

It all depended on the tungsten bullets, really. But for some reason that Demonaco couldn't quite put his finger on, their use here troubled him . . .

'Agent Demonaco,' Aaronson said, 'let me make this simpler. To the best of your knowledge, is there any paramilitary group in the United States *other* than the Oklahoma Freedom Fighters that uses tungsten-cored ammunition?'

'No,' Demonaco said.

'Good. Thank you.'

And with that, Aaronson gave Demonaco and Mitchell a withering glare and stalked away to a nearby telephone where he dialled a short number and said, 'This is Aaronson. Assault operations are go. Repeat. Assault operations are go. Take the bastards down.'

Daylight came to the rainforest.

Race awoke to find himself propped up against the wall of the ATV. His head ached and his clothes were still damp.

The sliding side door of the ATV lay open. He heard voices outside.

'—what are you doing here?'

'—my name is Marc Graf, and I am a lieutenant in the *Fallschirmjäger*—'

Race got up and went outside.

It was morning and a low fog had descended upon the village. The ATV was now parked in the centre of the main street, and as he stepped out of the big armoured vehicle, it took him a moment to adjust his eyes to the wall of grey all around him. Slowly, however, the main street of Vilcafor began to take shape.

Race froze.

The street was completely deserted.

All the bodies from the previous night's slaughter were gone. Indeed all that remained in their place were large pools of mud and water, peppered by the falling rain.

The cats, he saw, were also gone.

He saw Nash, Lauren and Copeland standing off to his left, over by the citadel. With them stood the six Green Berets and Gaby Lopez.

Before them, however, stood five other people.

Four men and one woman.

The surviving Germans, he guessed.

Race also noticed that only two of the Germans wore military fatigues—soldiers. All the others wore civilian clothing, including two—a man and a woman—who looked like undercover cops. All of them had been disarmed.

Sergeant Van Lewen caught sight of Race, came over.

'How's the head?' he said.

'Awful,' Race said. 'What's happening here?'

Van Lewen indicated the five Germans. 'They're the only ones who survived the night. Two of them jumped inside the ATV during the battle and uncuffed us. We managed to pick up the other three just before we got you at the jetty.'

Race nodded.

Then he turned suddenly to face his bodyguard. 'Say, I have a question for you.'

'Yes?'

'How did you know about that rubber button inside the Humvee—the one that started it after the Germans had shut it down?'

Van Lewen smiled at him. 'If I tell you I'll have to kill you.'

'Fine, go ahead.'

Van Lewen grinned at that. Then he said, 'It's fairly standard practice in armed forces around the world to use field vehicles like Humvees and ATVs as portable prisons. You lock the prisoners in the car and then you disable it.

'The United States, however, is the leading *supplier* of field vehicles worldwide. Humvees, for example, are made by the AM General Company in South Bend, Indiana.

'The thing is—and this is something that *not* everyone knows—all American-made field vehicles are fitted with a safety release button, a button that allows the vehicle to be restarted in the event that it is shut down. The theory is that no U.S. vehicle will ever be used as a prison to hold U.S. personnel. Hence, only U.S. military personnel are informed of the whereabouts of those safety buttons. It's a trapdoor, known only to American soldiers.'

With that, Van Lewen smiled and headed off to join the others over by the citadel. Race hurried after him.

He and Van Lewen joined the others at the citadel.

They arrived there to find Frank Nash interrogating one of the disarmed German commandos—the man Race had heard identify himself as Marc Graf, a lieutenant in the *Fallschirmjäger*.

'So are you here for the idol too?' Nash demanded.

Graf shook his head.

'I do not know the details,' he said in English. 'I am only a lieutenant, I do not have clearance to know the full extent of the mission.'

He nodded with his chin at one of the other Germans, the burly-looking man wearing jeans and a holster. 'I think it would be better if you asked my associate here, Mr Karl Schroeder. Mr Schroeder is a special agent with the *Bundes Kriminal Amt*. The *Bundeswehr* is working in conjunction with the BKA on this mission.'

'The BKA?' Nash said, perplexed.

Race knew what he was thinking.

The *Bundes Kriminal Amt* was the German equivalent of the FBI. Its reputation was legendary. It was often said to be the finest federal investigative bureau in the world. But still, it was essentially a police force, which was why Nash was confused. It had no reason to be in Peru looking for an idol.

'What does the BKA want with a lost Incan idol?' he asked.

Schroeder paused a moment, as if he were contemplating just how much he should reveal to Nash. And then he sighed—like it would matter now after the previous night's slaughter.

'It is not what you think,' he said.

'What do you mean?'

'We do not want the idol to make a weapon,' Schroeder said simply. 'In fact, contrary to what you probably believe, my country does not even possess a Supernova.'

'Then what do you want the idol for?'

'What we want it for is simple,' Schroeder said. 'We want to get it before somebody else does.'

'*Who?*' Nash said.

'The same people who were responsible for the massacre of those monks in the Pyrenees,' Schroeder said. 'The same people who were responsible for the kidnap and murder of the academic Albert Mueller after he published that article about the meteor crater in Peru late last year.'

'So who are they?'

'A terrorist organisation who call themselves the *Schutz Staffel Totenkopfverbände*—the Death's Head Detachment of the SS. They are named after the most

231

brutal unit of Hitler's SS, the soldiers who ran the Nazi concentration camps in World War II. They call themselves the "Stormtroopers".'

'The Stormtroopers?' Lauren said.

'They are an elite paramilitary force of expatriate Germans, based in a heavily fortified Nazi retreat in Chile called Colonia Alemania. They were formed at the end of the Second World War by an ex-Auschwitz lieutenant named Odilo Ehrhardt.

'According to Auschwitz survivors, Ehrhardt was a psychopath—an ox of a man who relished the sheer act of killing. Apparently, Rudolph Höss, the Commandant of Auschwitz, took a liking to him, and during the latter years of the war groomed him as his protégé. At twenty-two, Ehrhardt was elevated to the SS rank of *Obersturmführer*, or lieutenant. After that, if Höss pointed at you, a second later you would find yourself looking down the barrel of Ehrhardt's P-38.'

Race swallowed.

Schroeder went on. 'According to our records, Ehrhardt would now be seventy-five years of age. But within the Stormtrooper organisation, his word is law. He goes by the supreme SS rank of *Oberstgruppenführer*, General.

'The Stormtroopers are a singularly repulsive organisation,' Schroeder said. 'They advocate the forcible incarceration and execution of all Negroes and Jews, the destruction of democratic government worldwide and, most importantly, the restoration of a Nazi government to the unified Germany and the establishment of the *Herrenvolk*—the "master race"—as the ruling elite on earth.'

'The restoration of a Nazi government in Germany? The establishment of the master race as the ruling elite on earth?' Copeland said in disbelief.

'Wait a second,' Race said. 'You're talking about *Nazis*. In the *nineties*.'

'Yes,' Schroeder said. 'Nazis. Modern-day Nazis.'

Frank Nash said, 'Colonia Alemania has long been believed to be a safe haven for former Nazi officers. Eisler stayed there for a short time in the sixties. Eichmann, too.'

Schroeder nodded. 'Colonia Alemania consists of pastures and lakes and Bavarian-style houses, all of which are surrounded by barbed wire fences and guard towers that are patrolled by armed guards and Doberman Pinschers twenty-four hours a day.

'It was said that during the Pinochet regime, in exchange for protection from the government, Ehrhardt allowed Colonia Alemania to be used by the dictatorship as an unofficial torture centre. It was a place where people were sent to "disappear". And with the protection of the military regime, Ehrhardt and his Nazi colony remained immune from search by foreign agencies like the BKA.'

'All right, then,' Nash said, 'so how do they come into this equation?'

'You see, Herr Nash, that is the problem,' Schroeder said. 'It is the Stormtroopers who have a Supernova.'

'The Stormtroopers have a Supernova?' Nash said flatly.

'Yes.'

'Jesus . . .'

'Herr Nash, please. You must understand. In twenty years of counter-terrorist work, I have never encountered a group like the Stormtroopers. It is well financed, well organised, strictly hierarchical, and totally and utterly ruthless.

'It is made up of two types of person—soldiers and scientists. The Stormtroopers recruit mainly experienced soldiers, often men who have been dishonourably discharged from the former East German Army or the *Bundeswehr* for their predilections for using excessive force. Men like Heinrich Anistaze, men trained in the arts of terror, torture and assassination.'

'Anistaze is a *Stormtrooper*?' Nash said. 'I was under the impression he was working for German intellig—'

'Not anymore,' Schroeder said bitterly. 'After the Eastern Bloc collapsed, Anistaze was hired by the German government on a contract basis only—to take care of certain "problems". But it appears our leash wasn't short enough.

'Anistaze is a mercenary, a killer for hire. It wasn't

long before someone offered him *more* than we were paying him, and he betrayed two of his case officers and turned them over to the enemy.

'It came as no surprise to us when, not long after that incident, his rather distinctive methods of persuasion started showing up in Stormtrooper-related incidents. Apparently, Anistaze's rise through the Stormtrooper ranks has been swift. We believe he is now an *Obergruppenführer* in their ranking system. A lieutenant-general. Second only to Ehrhardt himself.'

'Son of a bitch . . .'

'As for scientists,' Schroeder shrugged, 'the same principles apply. The Stormtroopers lure many highly educated men and women who are working on projects that are not seen as keeping with modern Germany's collective guilt.

'For example, when the Wall came down, certain East German scientists developing NA grenades—grenades filled with nitric acid, designed to inflict horrific injuries but not to kill their victims—soon found themselves out of a job. The Stormtroopers, on the other hand, are *always* on the lookout for those kinds of people, and they are willing to pay handsomely for their services.'

'How?' Copeland asked. 'How can they afford all this?'

'Doctor Copeland. The modern Nazi movement has never been short of cash. In 1994, an illegal BKA trace of a suspected Nazi account in a Swiss bank estimated the Stormtroopers' total cash reserves at more than half a billion dollars—the proceeds of the sale of priceless artefacts stolen during World War II.'

'Half a *billion* dollars,' Race breathed.

'Gentlemen,' Schroeder said, 'the Stormtroopers, they do not hijack aeroplanes. They do not murder federal officials or blow up federal buildings. They look for greater victories—victories that will overthrow the *entire* world order.'

'And now you think they have a Supernova?' Nash said.

'Up until about three days ago, all we had were unprovable suspicions,' Schroeder said. 'But now we are certain of it. Six months ago, BKA surveillance agents in Chile photographed a man strolling around the grounds of Colonia Alemania with Odilo Ehrhardt himself. He was later identified as Doctor Fritz Weber. Herr Nash, I imagine that you would know who Doctor Weber is.'

'Yes, but . . .' Nash paused, frowning. 'Fritz Weber was a German scientist during the Second World War, nuclear physicist, borderline genius, but also a borderline sociopath. He was one of the first people to state that the creation of a planet-destroying device was possible. In 1944, when he was only thirty, he worked on the Nazis' atomic bomb project. But before that, it was said that Weber worked on the infamous Nazi torture experiments—they would put a man in freezing water and monitor how long it took for him to die. But I thought Weber was executed after the war . . .'

Schroeder nodded. 'He was. Doctor Fritz Weber stood trial at Nuremberg for crimes against humanity in October 1945. He was found guilty and sentenced to death. He was officially executed on 22 November 1945 at Karlsburg prison. Whether it was actually *Weber* who was executed has been disputed for many years. There have been numerous sightings of him over the decades by people who claim to have been tortured by him—in Ireland, in Brazil, in Russia.'

Schroeder said seriously, 'We believe that the Soviets spirited Weber out of Karlsburg the night before he was to be executed and replaced him with an impostor. In return for saving his life, the Soviets used Weber's considerable skills to advance their own nuclear weapons program. But when the Soviet Union collapsed in 1991, and the BKA went looking for Weber, there was no sign of him at all. He had disappeared off the face of the earth.'

'Only to turn up eight years later at the headquarters of a Nazi terrorist organisation,' Nash added.

'Correct. So at that stage, we were thinking that the Nazis were constructing a conventional nuclear device. But the Stormtroopers raided that monastery in France after it was discovered to possess the legendary Santiago Manuscript,' Schroeder said. 'When one pieced together the murder of Albert Mueller and his discovery of a meteorite crater in Peru and the supposed tale in the Santiago Manuscript of an idol with rather strange properties, suddenly our suspicions took on a whole new reality. Maybe, under Weber's tutelage, the Stormtroopers were doing more than just building a regular nuclear bomb, maybe they had succeeded in creating a Supernova and were now on the hunt for thyrium.

'And then, three days ago—the same day as the raid on the French monastery—our surveillance team in Chile picked up this.'

Schroeder pulled out a folded sheet of paper from his breast pocket and handed it to Nash.

'It's a transcript of a telephone conversation that was made from a cellular phone somewhere in Peru to the main laboratory at Colonia Alemania three days ago,' Schroeder said.

Nash showed the German transcript to Race, who translated it aloud.

VOICE 1:	---ase of operations has been established--- rest of the---will be---mine---
VOICE 2:	---about the device?---ready?
VOICE 1:	---have adopted hourglass formation based on the American model---two thermonuclear detonators mounted above and below a titanium-alloy inner chamber. Field tests indicate that---device---operational. All we need now---the thyrium.
VOICE 2:	---don't worry, Anistaze's taking care of that---
VOICE 1:	What about the message?
VOICE 2:	---will go out as soon as we get the idol--- to every Prime Minister and President in the EU---plus the President of the United States via internal emergency hotline--- ransom will be one hundred billion dollars U.S.---or else we detonate the device . . .

Nash stared at the transcript in shock.

Everyone else was silent.

Race gazed at the words: *one hundred billion dollars U.S., or else we detonate the device.*

Jesus H. Christ.

Nash turned to Schroeder. 'So what have you done about all this?'

'We have executed a two-pronged plan,' the German said. 'Two separate missions, each designed to reinforce the other should either of them fail.

'Mission One was to get the thyrium idol before the Nazis did. To do that, we obtained a copy of the Santiago Manuscript and used it to find our way here. And as it happened, we beat the Stormtroopers—but we never expected to find those *things* inside the temple.'

As he listened to Schroeder speak, something twigged in the back of Race's mind, something about what the German agent had just said. Something that wasn't quite right.

He shook it off, put it to the back of his mind.

'And the second part of the mission?' Nash said.

'Take out Colonia Alemania,' Schroeder said. 'After we intercepted that telephone conversation three days ago, we opened entreaties with the new Chilean government for a warrant that would allow BKA agents to search Colonia Alemania in co-ordination with Chilean authorities.'

'And?'

'We got it. If everything has gone according to plan, BKA agents and the Chilean National Guard are right this minute storming the grounds of Colonia Alemania and seizing the Stormtroopers' Supernova. I'm hoping to receive a radio update from them any minute now.'

At that very same moment six hundred miles away, a ten-ton truck owned by the Chilean National Guard exploded through the gates of Colonia Alemania.

A stream of olive-skinned Chilean soldiers rushed through the gates behind the rampaging truck. A dozen German agents dressed in blue assault helmets and SWAT gear hurried into the compound after them.

Colonia Alemania was a large estate, easily twenty hectares in size. Its grassy green pastures contrasted sharply with Chile's barren brown hills. Its Bavarian-style cottages and idyllic blue lakes were an oddly peaceful sight in what was an otherwise harsh and dry land.

Doors were smashed open and windows exploded inwards as the National Guardsmen entered every building in the estate. Their main target was the Barracks Hall—a large, hangar-like building in the centre of the compound.

Minutes later, the doors to the Barracks Hall were blasted open and a horde of National Guardsmen and BKA agents rushed into the building.

And then they stopped.

Row upon row of empty bunk beds stretched away from them for the length of the enormous hall. Each bed was crisply made and perfectly aligned with the bunk next to it. It looked like an army barracks.

The only problem was, it was empty.

Reports came in quickly from the rest of the compound.

The whole compound was empty.

Colonia Alemania was completely deserted.

In one of the laboratory buildings adjoining the Barracks Hall, two German tech agents waved small Geiger counter wands in front of them, measuring the radioactivity in the air. Their small detection units clattered loudly.

The two agents entered the compound's main laboratory and their Geiger counters instantly went into the red.

'All units, this is Lab Team, we are detecting high trace quantities of uranium and plutonium in the primary laboratory—'

The first agent came to a door that opened onto a glass-walled office of some kind.

He pointed his wand at the closed door—

—and his Geiger counter went off the charts.

He exchanged a quick look with his partner. Then he pushed open the door, tripping the wire.

The explosion that ripped through Colonia Alemania was absolutely devastating.

It rocked the world.

A pulse of blinding white light shot out laterally in every direction, obliterating everything in its path— whole barns blew out instantly into a billion matchsticks, concrete silos were shattered in a millisecond, everything within a five-hundred-yard radius of the Barracks Hall was vaporised—including the one hundred and fifty Chilean National Guardsmen and the twelve BKA agents.

When they were interviewed about it in the days to come, the inhabitants of the surrounding villages would say that it had looked like a sudden flare of lightning on the horizon, followed by an enormous plume of black smoke that rose high into the sky in the shape of a gigantic mushroom.

But they were simple folk, peasants.

They didn't know that they were describing a thermonuclear explosion.

Back in Vilcafor, Nash ordered the Green Berets to bring the German team's radio satellite equipment out onto the main street.

'Let's see what your people in Chile have got to say,' he said to Schroeder.

Schroeder popped the lid on the portable radio console and began typing something quickly on its all-weather keyboard. Nash, Scott and the Green Berets crowded around him, watching the console's screen intently.

Race stood outside the circle, excluded yet again.

'How are you feeling?' a woman's voice said suddenly from behind him.

He turned, half-expecting to see Lauren, but instead found himself looking into the dazzling blue eyes of the German woman.

She was small, petite—and seriously cute. She stood with her hands resting lazily on her hips and a smile that disarmed Race completely.

She had a small button nose and short blonde hair, and liberal doses of mud splotched all over her face, T-shirt and jeans. She wore a bulletproof vest over her white T-shirt and a black Gore-Tex holster on her hip—identical to the one Schroeder wore. Like Schroeder's, her holster was now empty.

'How is your head feeling?' she asked. She had a slight German accent. Race liked it.

'It hurts,' he said.

'It should,' she said, coming over and touching his brow. 'I think you suffered a minor concussion when your Humvee crashed into that helicopter. All of your subsequent acts of derring-do on top of the chopper must have been the work of pure adrenalin.'

'You mean I'm not a hero?' Race said. 'You're saying it was just the adrenalin talking?'

She smiled at him, a beautiful smile. 'Wait here,' she said, 'I have some codeine in my medicine pack. It'll help your headache.'

She moved off toward the ATV.

'Hey . . .' Race said. 'What's your name?'

She smiled at him again. That cute, nymph-like smile.

'My name is Renée Becker. I am a special agent with the BKA.'

'I've got it,' Schroeder said suddenly from over by the portable radio.

Race went over to the small group gathered around the radio console.

Looking over Nash's shoulder, he saw a list printed on the screen in German. He translated it in his head. It read:

COMMUNICATIONS SATELLITE TRANSMISSION LOG 44-76/BKA32

NO.	DATE	TIME	SOURCE	SUMMARY
1	4.1.99	1930	BKAHQ	PERU TEAM REPORT STATUS
2	4.1.99	1950	EXT SOURCE	SIGNATURE UHF SIGNAL
3	4.1.99	2230	BKAHQ	PERU TEAM REPORT STATUS

4	5.1.99	0130	BKAHQ	PERU TEAM REPORT STATUS
5	5.1.99	0430	BKAHQ	PERU TEAM REPORT STATUS
6	5.1.99	0716	FIELD (CHILE)	ARRIVED SANTIAGO, HEADING FOR COLONIA ALEMANIA
7	5.1.99	0730	BKAHQ	PERU TEAM REPORT STATUS
8	5.1.99	0958	FIELD (CHILE)	HAVE ARRIVED COLONIA ALEMANIA; BEGINNING SURVEILLANCE
9	5.1.99	1030	BKAHQ	PERU TEAM REPORT STATUS
10	5.1.99	1037	FIELD (CHILE)	CHILE TEAM URGENT SIGNAL; CHILE TEAM URGENT SIGNAL
11	5.1.99	1051	BKAHQ	PERU TEAM REPORT IMMEDIATELY

Race frowned.

It was a list of every communication signal that had been picked up by the BKA's Peruvian field team.

By the looks of it, they had received 'status update' requests from BKA headquarters every three hours from 7:30 last night, plus a few intermittent messages from the other BKA team in Chile.

The tenth message, however—one of the messages from the other team in Chile—seized Race's attention. It screamed with the German word *dringendes*— 'urgent'.

Schroeder saw it, too.

He quickly tabbed down to the tenth message and hit 'ENTER'.

A full-screen message came up. Race saw the words in German, translated them:

MESSAGE NO:	050199-010
DATED:	5 JANUARY 1999
RECEIVED AT:	1037 (LOCAL TIME—PERU)
RECEIVED FROM:	FIELD TEAM (CHILE)

SUBJECT: CHILE TEAM URGENT SIGNAL;
                  CHILE TEAM URGENT SIGNAL

MESSAGE IS AS FOLLOWS:

<u>ATTENTION PERU TEAM. ATTENTION PERU TEAM.</u>

THIS IS CHILE SECOND UNIT. REPEAT. THIS IS CHILE SECOND UNIT.
FIRST UNIT IS DOWN. REPEAT. FIRST UNIT IS DOWN.

15 MINUTES AGO FIRST UNIT ENTERED COLONIA ALEMANIA IN
CONCERT WITH CHILEAN NATIONAL GUARD. REPORTED ENTIRE
COMPOUND DESERTED. REPEAT. FIRST UNIT REPORTED ENTIRE
COMPOUND DESERTED.

PRELIMINARY TESTING REVEALED HIGH TRACE LEVELS OF URANIUM
AND PLUTONIUM ORE, BUT BEFORE FURTHER DATA COULD BE
OBTAINED A DETONATION OCCURRED INSIDE THE COMPOUND.

DETONATION APPEARS TO HAVE BEEN NUCLEAR. REPEAT.
DETONATION APPEARS TO HAVE BEEN NUCLEAR.

ENTIRE FIRST UNIT HAS BEEN LOST. REPEAT. ENTIRE FIRST UNIT HAS
BEEN LOST.

MUST ASSUME STORMTROOPERS ARE ALREADY EN ROUTE TO PERU.

Race looked up from the message in horror.

Colonia Alemania had been empty at the time the BKA team had arrived. It had also been booby-trapped, set to explode as soon as someone set foot on it.

A sliver of ice ran down Race's spine as he looked at the final line of the message again:

MUST ASSUME STORMTROOPERS ARE ALREADY EN ROUTE TO PERU.

Race looked at his watch.

It was 11:05 am.

'How long till they get here?' Nash asked Schroeder.

'It's impossible to say,' Schroeder said. 'There's no knowing how long ago they left the compound. They could have left it two hours ago or two days ago. Either way, the trip from Chile to here is not a long one. We must assume that they are very close.'

Nash turned to Scott. 'Captain, I want you to get on the horn to Panama and find out when that damned extraction team is going to get here. We need firepower and we need it now.'

'Got it.' Scott nodded to Doogie who dashed off toward the radio unit.

'Cochrane,' Nash said. 'How's the situation with the surviving Huey?'

Buzz Cochrane shook his head. 'It's shot. It took a hammering when that Apache went wild during the cats' attack. Stray gunfire damaged both the tail rotor and the ignition ports.'

'How long will it take to fix?'

'With the tools we've got here, we can fix the ignition ports, but it'll take time. As for the tail rotor, well, you can't fly without it, and it's a bitch to repair. I guess we could strip some of the secondary systems and use them, but what we really need are brand-new axles and rotary switches, and we ain't gonna find them here.'

'Sergeant. Get that Huey ready to fly again. Whatever it takes,' Nash said.

'Yes, sir.'

Cochrane left the circle, taking Tex Reichart with him.

There was a long silence.

'So we're stuck here . . .' Lauren said.

'With a group of *terrorists* on their way . . .' Gaby Lopez added.

'Unless we decide to trek out of here on foot,' Race suggested.

Captain Scott turned to Nash. 'If we stay, we die.'

'And if we leave, the Nazis get the idol,' Copeland said.

'*And* a workable Supernova,' Lauren said.

'Not an option,' Nash said firmly. 'No, there's only one thing we can do.'

'What's that?'

'We get the idol before the Nazis get here.'

The three soldiers made their way cautiously up the riverside path in the pounding subtropical rain.

Captain Scott and Corporal Chucky Wilson led the way, their M-16s trained warily on the dense foliage to their right. The lone German paratrooper, Graf, now armed with an American M-16, walked along the path behind them, bringing up the rear.

Each man wore a tiny fibre-optic camera attached to the side of his helmet which sent images back to the others in the village.

After a while, the three soldiers came to the fissure in the mountainside—the fissure that led to the rock tower and the temple.

Scott nodded to Wilson and the young corporal entered the narrow stone passageway, gun-first.

Back in the village, Race and the others watched on a monitor as Scott, Wilson and Graf made their way through the fissure. The images being sent back from the three commandos were depicted in separate rectangles on the screen, in ghostly black-and-white.

The plan was simple.

While Scott, Wilson and Graf entered the temple

249

and seized the idol inside it, the remaining Green Berets and the other German paratrooper—a private named Molke—would get to work repairing the remaining Huey. Once the idol was obtained, they would all fly out of Vilcafor before the Nazi terrorists arrived.

'Ah, aren't we forgetting something?' Race said.

'Like what?' Nash said.

'Like the cats. Aren't they the reason we're in this mess in the first place? Where are they?'

'The cats retreated from the village with the onset of daylight,' a voice said from behind Race in perfect clipped English.

Race turned to see the fourth and last German man standing behind him, smiling.

He couldn't have been more different from the other three German males—Schroeder, Graf and Molke. While they were all visibly strong and fit, this man was older—much older, at least in his fifties—and quite obviously *un*athletic. His most dominant feature was a long grey beard. Race disliked him on sight. His whole stance and posture reeked of pomposity and arrogance.

'At dawn, the cats departed in the direction of the plateau,' the man said uppishly. 'I presume that they returned to their nest inside the temple.' He smiled wryly. 'I imagine that since the last few generations of their species have spent almost four hundred years in pitch darkness, their kind are not very comfortable in daylight.'

The bearded man extended his hand in an abrupt German way. 'I am Doctor Johann Krauss, zoologist and cryptozoologist from the University of Hamburg. I have been brought along on this mission to advise on certain *animal* issues raised in the manuscript.'

'What's a cryptozoologist?' Race asked.

'One who studies mythical animals,' Krauss said.

'Mythical animals . . .'

'Yes. Bigfoot, the Loch Ness monster, the yeti, the great cats of the English moors, and of course,' he added, 'the South American *rapa*.'

'You know about these cats?' Race said.

'Only what I have learned from unverified sightings, local legends and ambiguous hieroglyphs. But such is the beauty of cryptozoology, it is the study of animals that cannot be studied, because no-one can actually prove they exist.'

'So you think we were attacked by a pack of mythical animals,' Race said. 'They didn't look very mythical to me.'

Krauss said, 'Every fifty years or so, there is a spate of unusual deaths in this part of the Amazon rainforest. At those times, local men who embark on night-time trips between villages are known to just, well, disappear. On rare occasions, their remains are found in the morning. At those times, men are found with their throats wrenched from their bodies or their spines ripped out.

'The local people have a name for the beast that comes in the night to kill without mercy, a name which has been passed down from generation to generation. They call it the *rapa*.'

Krauss looked at Race closely. 'We should heed this local folklore very carefully, because it can be of great use to us in evaluating our enemy.'

'How?'

'Well, for one thing, we can use it to discern certain things about our feline antagonists.'

'Like what?'

'Well, first of all, we can safely assume that the rapa is nocturnal. The remains of local men are found only in the morning. And we know from our own experience that these cats flee from the morning light. Ergo, they are nocturnal. They hunt only at night and retire for the main part of the day.'

'If they've been shut up inside that temple for generations,' Race said, 'how could they have survived? What have they been eating?'

'That I do not know,' Krauss said, frowning seriously, as if he were pondering a troublesome mathematical equation.

Race looked up at the mountain-plateau that housed the mysterious temple. A veil of slanting rain covered its rocky eastern face.

'So what are they doing now?' he said.

'Sleeping, I imagine,' Krauss said, 'in the safety of their temple. Which is why now is the best time to send our men in to get that idol.'

Scott, Wilson and Graf emerged from the narrow passageway and stepped out into the pool of shallow water at the base of the magnificent crater.

It was unusually dark in the canyon. Any light that there was had been blocked out by the thick rain clouds in the sky and the dense canopy of trees that overhung the crater's rim. Every fissure and crack in the canyon's walls was cloaked in shadow.

Scott and Wilson walked in front. Thin beams of light shot out from the small flashlights attached to the barrels of their M-16s.

'All right—' Scott said into his throat mike.

'—*we're heading up the path now,*' his voice said over the monitor's speakers.

Race watched tensely as, on the screen, Scott, Wilson and Graf stepped up out of the water and onto the narrow pathway that was cut into the crater's outer wall.

Johann Krauss said, 'What we must also remember about our enemy, however, is that they are, first and foremost, *cats*. They cannot change what they are. They think like cats, they act like cats.'

'Meaning?'

'Meaning that only one species of great cat—the cheetah—catches its prey by chasing after it.'

'How do other great cats catch their prey?'

'There are several strategies. Tigers in India are known to lie in wait covered in leaves, sometimes for hours at a time, waiting for their prey to arrive on the scene. Once their prey comes close enough, they pounce.

'On the other hand, lions in Africa employ quite sophisticated pack-hunting methods—one such technique involves a lioness parading around in front of a herd of gazelles while her colleagues sneak up on the gazelles from behind. It's quite ingenious really, and very effective. But it is also very unusual.'

'Why?' Race asked.

'Because it implies the existence of some kind of *communication* between the lions.'

Race turned back to face the monitor.

The three soldiers had made it a short way up the spiralling path, so that they were now about ten feet above the wide body of water that covered the base of the crater.

Race was watching Corporal Wilson's camera view as it panned out over the flat expanse of water when suddenly he saw a flicker of movement on the water's surface.

It had been a ripple of some sort—from something just *underneath* the water's surface.

'What was that?' he said.

'What was what?'

'Wilson,' Race said, leaning close to the microphone. 'Look to your right for a second, at the water.'

Graf and Scott must have heard Race's question too because, at that moment, *all three* camera views panned right, out over the glistening expanse of water that encircled the base of the rock tower.

'*I don't see anything . . .*' Scott said.

'There!' Race said, pointing at another ripple in the water. It seemed to have been made by the whiplash of an animal's tail. An animal that seemed to be travelling in the direction of the three soldiers.

'What the hell . . . ?' Scott said as he looked out over the wide body of water before him.

A small bow-wave of water seemed to be cutting across the lake at an unusually quick speed—coming *right toward* him and his men.

Scott frowned. Then he took a cautious step forward, toward the edge of the path and the ten-foot drop down to the water's surface.

He peered out over the edge.

And saw three black cats clawing their way up the sheer stone wall beneath him!

Scott quickly raised his M-16 but at that exact moment an enormous black shape burst out from a dark fissure in the rock wall behind him and slammed into his back, sending him flying off the edge of the pathway and down into the water below, where a whole cluster of other black shapes converged on him in an instant.

Race stared at the monitor in stunned awe as he watched the whole horrific scene *from Scott's point of view*. All he saw was the blur of slashing razor-like teeth and flailing human arms, all overlaid with Scott's own gasps and futile screams.

Then, not a moment later, the camera went under the surface and the screen cut to hash and abruptly there was silence.

In the crater, a roar of gunfire shattered the unnatural stillness as the German soldier Graf jammed down on the trigger of his M-16.

But no sooner had a flaring tongue of fire spewed out from the muzzle of his gun than—*smack!*—Graf was pounced upon from above, by a cat that had been lurking on the rock wall high above him!

Further down the path, Chucky Wilson spun instantly to see the struggle between Graf and the cat, saw that the German paratrooper was putting up one hell of a fight.

And then suddenly—*riiiiippppp!*—Graf's throat came clear of his neck and his body fell instantly limp.

Wilson blanched. 'Oh, *fuck.*'

And at that moment the cat standing over Graf's body slowly looked up at him and stared into his eyes.

Wilson froze. The big cat stepped ominously forward, over Graf's immobile body, toward him.

Wilson spun.

Only to see another massive black cat standing on the path behind him, cutting off his retreat.

Nowhere to run.

Nowhere to hide.

Wilson turned again and saw the fissures and crevices in the rock wall and for a second thought there might be an escape there. He looked into one of the shadowy fissures in the rockface—

—and found himself staring at the smiling face of one of the cats.

And then with a suddenness that was nothing short of horrifying, the big cat's jaws rushed toward him at phenomenal speed and in an instant there was nothing.

Everyone just stared at the monitor in silence.

'*Oh my God*,' Gaby Lopez breathed.

'Shit,' Lauren said.

The four remaining Green Berets just gazed at the monitor, speechless.

Race turned to the German zoologist, Krauss. 'They only come out at night, do they?'

'Well,' Krauss said, bristling. 'Quite obviously, the darkness at the base of the crater allows them to spend the greater part of the day there—'

'Kennedy,' Nash said sharply, 'what's the status on that extraction team?'

'I'm still trying to get through to Panama, sir,' Doogie said from over by the radio pack. 'Signal keeps dropping out.'

'Keep trying.' Nash looked at his watch.

It was 11:30 am.

'*Shit*,' he said.

He wondered what had happened to Romano and his team. Last he heard, they'd taken off from Cuzco at 7:45 pm last night. They should have been here by now. What had happened to them? Could the Nazis have shot them down? Or had they just misread the totems and gotten hopelessly lost?

Whatever the case, if they were still alive, one thing was certain: they would find the village eventually.

Which meant he now had *two* hostile groups on their way to Vilcafor.

'*Shit*,' he said again.

Doogie came over.

'The extraction team took off from Panama one hour ago—three choppers: two Comanches, one Black Hawk. They estimate that they'll be here by late afternoon, at approximately 1700 hours. I put up a UHF signal, so they can home in on that and extract us.'

As Doogie reported his news to Nash, a strange thought hit Race: *Why wasn't the Army extracting them via Cuzco? Why were they sending choppers down from Panama?*

Surely the easiest way out of here was to go back the same way they had come.

It was at that moment that a sentence from the Santiago Manuscript popped into his head.

A thief never uses the same entrance twice.

Nash turned to Van Lewen. 'Do we have access to the SAT-SN network?' He said it 'Sat-sun'—'the Sat-sun network'.

'Yes, sir, we do.'

'Patch us in. Set a tracking pattern over central-eastern Peru. I want to know exactly where those Nazi bastards are. Cochrane.'

'Yes, sir.'

'Get me satellite imagery of Vilcafor. We have to set up a defensive position.'

'Yes, sir.'

'What's SAT-SN?' Gaby Lopez asked.

Troy Copeland answered. 'SAT-SN is the acronym for the Satellite Aerospace Tracking and Surveillance Network. It's the aerial equivalent of SOSUS, the array of hydrophones that the U.S. Navy has stretched across the north Atlantic to detect enemy submarines.

'Put simply, SAT-SN is an array of fifty-six geosynchronous satellites in near-earth orbit that monitor the world's airspace, airplane by airplane.'

'If that's the *simple* explanation,' Race said drily, 'I'd hate to hear the complex one.'

Copeland ignored him. 'Any aircraft has seven different types of observable characteristics—radar, infra-red, visual, contrails, engine smoke, acoustics and electromagnetic emissions. The SAT-SN satellites use all seven of these characteristics to record the signature and location of individual aircraft all over the world—military and civilian.

'What Colonel Nash wants now is a snapshot of central-eastern Peru so that he can spot every airplane over it—in particular, those planes *outside* regular commercial air corridors. From those pictures, we'll be able to see where our Nazi friends are and hopefully calculate how long we've got till they get here.'

Race looked over at Nash.

He appeared to be deep in thought—as one would expect from a leader who had just lost three of his best fighting men.

'What are you thinking?' Race asked.

'We have to get that idol,' Nash said, 'and soon. Those Nazis will be here any second now. But there's no way past those cats. There's no way of *knowing* how to get past them.'

Race cocked his head.

Then he said, 'There was someone who knew.'

'Who?'

'Alberto Santiago.'

'What?'

'Remember the boulder that was wedged in the doorway to the temple?'

'Yeah . . .'

'On it was a warning: "*Do not enter at any cost. Death looms within.*" That warning had the initials "*A.S.*" written underneath it. Now I haven't read enough of the manuscript yet, but I can only assume that Santiago and Renco stumbled onto the same problem we have now—before they arrived at Vilcafor, someone opened up that temple and let the rapas loose.

'But *somehow*,' Race said, 'Santiago figured out a way to get those cats back inside the temple. Then he carved a warning into that boulder for anyone who would think to open it up again.

'Now, we used the manuscript to find this village and we figured that was *all* it was good for—but the copy I read was only partially completed. I'll bet my life that the key to getting past those cats lies in the rest of the Santiago Manuscript.'

'But we don't have any more of the manuscript,' Nash said.

'I'll bet they do,' Race nodded at the four remaining Germans.

Schroeder nodded with his eyes.

'And I'll bet you didn't translate it beyond the part where it revealed the location of Vilcafor, did you?' Race said.

'No,' Schroeder said. 'We did not.'

A new look of purpose came over Nash's face. He turned to Schroeder.

'Get your copy of the manuscript,' he said. 'Get it *now*.'

A few minutes later, Schroeder handed Race a fat stack of paper wedged inside a worn cardboard folder. The stack of paper was a lot thicker than Race's earlier pile had been.

The complete manuscript.

'I don't suppose any of you four are your team's translator?' Nash asked the BKA man.

Schroeder shook his head. 'No. Our language expert was killed during the cats' attack on the rock tower.'

Nash turned to Race. 'Then it looks like you're it, Professor. Lucky I insisted on bringing you along.'

Race retired to the ATV to read the new copy of the manuscript.

Once he was safely ensconced inside the big armoured vehicle, he opened the folder surrounding the new manuscript. He was met by a Xeroxed cover sheet.

It was an odd cover sheet—markedly different from the overly elaborate one he had seen on the earlier copy. The main difference being that this cover sheet was remarkably, almost deliberately, *plain*.

The title, *The True Relation of a Monk in the Land of the Incas*, was written in a very rough handwritten scrawl. One thing was for sure—elegance and majesty had been the last thing on the mind of whoever had written this.

And then it hit Race.

This was a photocopy of the actual, *original* Santiago Manuscript.

A Xerox of the document that had been written *by Alberto Santiago himself*.

Race leafed through the text. Page after page of Santiago's scratchy handwriting unfolded before him.

He scanned the words, and soon he found the place

where his last reading had stopped so abruptly—the part where Renco, Santiago and the criminal Bassario had landed at Vilcafor only to find it in ruins, only to find its people scattered all along the main street, bathed in blood . . .

THIRD READING

Renco, Bassario and I walked up the deserted main street of Vilcafor.

The silence around us filled my heart with dread. Never before had I heard the rainforest so mute.

I stepped over a blood-stained body. The head had been ripped clean from its trunk.

I saw other bodies, saw horrified faces with their eyes open in abject terror. Some had had their arms and legs wrenched from their sockets. Many, I saw, had had their throats removed by some violent external force.

'Hernando?' I whispered to Renco.

'Impossible,' my brave companion said. 'There is no way he could have arrived here before we did.'

As we progressed down the main street of the town, I saw the giant dry moat that encircled the village. Two flat wooden bridges—constructed of several tree trunks laid down side by side—spanned its breadth on either side of the village. They looked like bridges that could be withdrawn at a moment's notice, the bridges of a citadel town. Quite obviously, whoever had attacked Vilcafor had taken it by surprise.

We arrived at the citadel. It was a great two-tiered stone building, pyramidal in shape, but round, not square.

Renco hammered on the large stone door set into its base. He called Vilcafor's name and proclaimed that it was he, Renco, arrived with the idol.

After a time, the stone slab was rolled aside from within and some warriors appeared, followed by Vilcafor himself, an old man with grey hair and hollow eyes. He was dressed in a red cape but he looked about as regal as a beggar on the streets of Madrid.

'Renco!' the old man exclaimed when he saw my companion.

'Uncle,' said Renco.

It was at that moment that Vilcafor saw me.

I suppose I expected a look of surprise to cross his face—at the sight of a *Spaniard* accompanying his nephew on his heroic mission—but none did. Rather Vilcafor just turned to Renco and said, 'Is this the gold-eater my messengers have told me so much about? The one who helped you escape from your confinement, the one who rode out of Cuzco by your side?'

'He is, Uncle,' Renco replied.

They spoke in Quechuan, but by now Renco had improved my fledgling knowledge of this most peculiar language and I was able to understand most of what they said.

Vilcafor grunted. 'A noble gold-eater . . . humph . . . I did not know such an animal existed. But if he is a friend of yours, my nephew, he is welcome here.'

The chieftain turned again, and this time he saw the criminal Bassario standing behind Renco with an impish grin spread across his face. Vilcafor recognised him instantly.

He shot an enraged look at Renco. 'What is he doing here—?'

'He travels with me, Uncle. For a reason,' said

Renco. He paused before he spoke again. 'Uncle. What happened here? Was it the Span—?'

'No, my nephew. It was not the gold-eaters. No, it was an evil a thousand times worse than that.'

'What happened?'

Vilcafor bowed his head. 'My nephew, this is not a safe place for you to seek refuge . . .'

'Why?'

'No . . . no, not safe at all.'

'Uncle,' said Renco and sharply. 'What—have—you—done?'

Vilcafor looked up at Renco, then his eyes darted to the great rocky plateau that towered over the little town.

'Nephew, quickly, come inside the citadel. It will be nightfall soon and they come out with the dusk or at times of darkness. Come, you will be safe inside the fortress.'

'Uncle, what is going on here?'

'It is my fault, my nephew. It is all my fault.'

The weighty stone door to the citadel rolled shut behind us with a resounding thud.

The interior of the two-storey pyramid was dark, illuminated only by the light of a few hand-held torches. I saw a dozen frightened faces huddled in the darkness before me—women holding children, men bearing injuries or wounds. I guessed that they were all Vilcafor's kin, those fortunate enough to have been inside the citadel when the slaughter had occurred.

I also noticed a square-shaped hole in the stone floor—into and out of which some of the men climbed every few moments. There seemed to be a tunnel of some kind down there.

'It is a quenko,' Bassario whispered in my ear.

'What is that?' I inquired.

'A labyrinth. A maze. A network of tunnels carved into the rock underneath a town. There is a famous one not far outside Cuzco. Originally, quenkos were designed as escape tunnels for the ruling elite—only the royal family of a given town would know the code that would enable them to navigate the labyrinth's confusing array of tunnels.

'Now, however, quenkos are mainly used for sport and gambling at festival time. Two warriors are placed inside the maze, along with five adult jaguars. The warrior who successfully navigates the quenko—and evades the jaguars—and finds the exit first, wins. It is very popular to gamble on the result. I would imagine, however, that the quenko in this town is used more for its original purpose—as a tunnel through which royalty can beat a hasty retreat.'

Now it happened that Vilcafor guided us to a corner of the citadel where there was a fire. He begged us to sit in some hay. Some servants arrived and gave us water.

'So, Renco. You have the idol?' said Vilcafor.

'I do.' Renco pulled the idol—still cloaked in its magnificent silken cloth—from his leather satchel. He uncovered the glistening black-and-purple carving and the small group gathered in the corner of the citadel gasped as one.

If it were at all possible, I do believe that in the flickering orange light of the citadel the idol's snarling feline features attained a new level of malevolence.

'You are truly the Chosen One, my nephew,' said Vilcafor. 'The one destined to save our idol from those who would take it away from us. I am proud of you.'

'And I you, Uncle,' said Renco, although I gathered

from the inflection in his voice that he was anything but. 'Tell me what happened here.'

Vilcafor nodded.

Then he spoke thusly: 'I have heard of the inroads the gold-eaters have been making into our country. They have penetrated villages both in the mountains and in the wetland forests. I have long believed that it is only a matter of time before they find this secret encampment.

'With this in mind, two moons ago I ordered a new path be constructed, a path that would lead deep into the mountains, away from these gold-lusting barbarians. But this path would be a special path—once it was used it could be destroyed. Then, owing to the terrain in these parts, there would be no other entrance into the mountains within twenty days' travel from here. Any pursuer would lose weeks trying to follow us, by which time we would be long gone.'

'Go on,' said Renco.

'My engineers found the perfect place for this path, a most wondrous canyon not far from here. It is a wide circular canyon with an enormous finger of rock protruding up through the middle of it.

'As it happened, the walls of this canyon were perfect for our new path and I ordered the commencement of building work immediately. All went well until the day my engineers arrived at the summit of the canyon. For on that day, as they looked down on the canyon beneath them, they saw it.'

'What did they see, Uncle?'

'They saw a building of some kind—a building made by man—situated on top of the enormous finger of stone.'

Renco cast a worried glance in my direction.

'I immediately ordered the construction of a rope

bridge, and then, accompanied by my engineers, I crossed that bridge and examined the structure on top of it.'

Renco listened in silence.

'Whatever it was, it was not built by Incan hands. It looked like a religious structure of some sort, a temple or shrine not unlike others which have been found elsewhere in these forests. Temples built by the mysterious empire that inhabited these lands many years before our own.

'But there was something very strange about this particular temple. It had been sealed by a great boulder. And on this boulder were inscribed many pictures and markings which not even our most holy men could decipher.'

'What happened then, Uncle?' said Renco.

Vilcafor lowered his eyes. 'Someone suggested that perhaps this was the fabled Temple of Solon, and if it was, then in it there would be a most fabulous treasure of emeralds and jade.'

'*What did you do*, Uncle?' said Renco seriously.

'I ordered that the temple be opened,' said Vilcafor, bowing his head. 'And in doing so, I unleashed an evil like none I have ever seen. I unleashed the rapa.'

Night fell and Renco and I repaired to the roof of the citadel to keep watch over the town and look for this animal that they call the rapa.

Unsurprisingly, Bassario went off to a shadowy corner of the great stone fortress and sat with his back to the room, doing whatever it was that he did.

From the roof of the citadel, I looked out over the village.

Now, it must be said that after our journey through the forests, I had become accustomed to the sounds of the night-time jungle. The croaking of frogs, the droning of insects, the rustling of the high branches as monkeys scampered among them.

But there were no such sounds here.

The forest surrounding the village of Vilcafor was absolutely silent.

No animal made a sound. Not a living thing stirred.

I looked down at the bodies that lay strewn all over the main street.

'What happened here?' I inquired of Renco softly.

At first he did not reply. Then at last he said, 'A great evil has been unleashed, my friend. A great evil.'

'What did your uncle mean when he said that the temple they found might have been "the Temple of

Solon"? Who or what is Solon?'

Said Renco, 'For thousands of years, many great empires have inhabited these lands. We do not know much about these empires, except what we have learned from the buildings they left behind and the stories that have been passed down through the local tribes.

'One popular tale among the tribes of this region pertains to a strange empire of men who called themselves the Moxe, or Moche. The Moxe were prolific builders, and according to the local natives, they worshipped the rapa. Some say that they even tamed the rapa, but this is disputed.

'Anyway, the fable that the local tribes most like to tell about the Moxe concerns a man named Solon. According to legend, Solon was a man of remarkable intellect, a great thinker, and as such, he soon became chief adviser to the supreme Moxe emperor.

'When Solon reached old age, as a reward for his years of loyal service, the emperor presented him with a hoard of fabulous riches and bequeathed to him a temple to be built in his honour. The emperor said that Solon could have the temple built at any location he desired, in whatever shape or form. Whatever he wanted, the emperor's best engineers would build.'

Renco stared out into the darkness.

'It is said that Solon requested his temple be built at a secret location and that all his riches be placed inside it. Then he instructed the emperor's most able huntsmen to capture a pack of rapas and place them inside the temple with his treasure.'

'He put a pack of rapas inside the temple?' said I incredulously.

'That is so,' said Renco. 'But to understand why he did that, you must understand what Solon wanted to achieve. He wanted his temple to be the ultimate test of human conduct.'

'What do you mean?'

'Solon knew that word of the immense treasure inside his temple would spread quickly. He knew that greed and avarice would drive adventurers to seek it out and plunder its riches.

'And so he made his temple a test. A test of the choice between fabulous wealth and certain death. A test designed to see if man could control his own wanton greed.'

Renco looked at me. 'The man who conquers his greed and chooses not to open the temple lives. The man who succumbs to temptation and opens the temple in search of fabulous wealth will be killed by the rapas.'

I took this in silently.

'This temple that Vilcafor has spoken of,' said I, 'the one situated atop a giant finger of stone. Do you think it is Solon's temple?'

Renco sighed. 'If it is, then it saddens me.'

'Why?'

'Because it means that we have come a long way to die.'

I stayed with Renco a while on the roof of the citadel, staring out into the rain.

An hour passed.

Nothing emerged from the forest.

Another hour. Still nothing.

At which time, Renco instructed me to repair to the citadel and sleep. I happily obeyed his command, so fatigued was I from our long journey.

And so I retired to the main body of the citadel,

where I lay down on a mound of grass. A couple of small fires burned in the corners of the room.

I rested my head in the hay, but no sooner had my eyelids touched than I felt an insistent tapping on my shoulder. I opened my eyes and found myself looking at the ugliest face I have ever seen in my entire life.

An old man stood crouched in front of me, smiling at me with a toothless grin. He had horrid tufts of grey hair sticking out from his eyebrows, nose and ears.

'Greetings, gold-eater,' said the ancient fellow. 'I have heard of what you did for young Prince Renco—aiding his escape from his cage—and I wanted to express my profound gratitude to you.'

I looked around the citadel. The fires were now out, the people who had previously been huddled about the room were now silent, sleeping. I must have actually fallen asleep, at least for a short time.

'Oh,' said I. 'Well, you . . . you are welcome.'

The old man pointed a bony finger at my chest and nodded knowingly. 'Take heed, gold-eater. Renco is not the only one whose destiny lies with that idol, you know.'

'I do not understand.'

'What I mean is Renco's role as guardian of the Spirit of the People comes directly from the mouth of the Oracle at Pachacámac.' The old man smiled that same toothless grin. 'And so does yours.'

I had heard of the Oracle at Pachacámac. She was the venerable old woman who kept watch over the temple-shrine there. The traditional keeper of the Spirit of the People.

'Why?' said I. 'What has the Oracle said of me?'

'Soon after the gold-eaters arrived on our shores, the Oracle announced that our empire would be crushed. But she also foretold that so long as the Spirit

of the People stayed out of the hands of our con-
querors, our soul would live on. But she made it very
clear that only one man—and one man only—could
keep the idol safe.'

'Renco.'

'Correct. But what she said in full was this:

"There will come a time when he will come,
A man, a hero, beholden of the Mark of the Sun.
He will have the courage to do battle with great lizards,
He will have the jinga,
He will enjoy the aid of bravehearted men,
Men who would give of their lives, in honour of his noble
cause,
And he will fall from the sky in order to save our spirit.
He is the Chosen One."'

'The Chosen One?' said I.

'That is right.'

I began to wonder whether I fell into the category
of a 'bravehearted man' who would give of his life to
help Renco. I decided that I didn't.

Then I mused on the Oracle's use of the word *jinga*.
I recalled that it was a quality most revered in Incan
culture. It was that rare combination of poise, balance
and speed—the ability of a man to move like a cat.

I recalled our daring escape from Cuzco and the
way Renco had leapt lightly from rooftop to rooftop,
and how he had slid down the rope to land on the back
of my horse. Did he move with the surefooted grace of
a cat? Without a doubt.

'What do you mean when you say he will have the
courage to do battle with great lizards?' I inquired.

The old man said, 'When Renco was a boy of thirteen, his mother was taken by an alligator as she was

retrieving water from the banks of her local stream. Young Renco was with her at the time, and when he saw the monster drag his mother into the river, he dived into the water after her and wrestled with the ugly beast until it released her from its grip. Not many men would leap into a stream to do battle with such a fearsome creature. Not least a boy of thirteen.'

I swallowed.

I had not known of this tremendous act of courage that Renco had performed as a boy. I knew he was a brave man, but this? Well. I could never do something like that.

The old man must have read my thoughts. He tapped my chest again with his long bony finger.

'Don't dismiss your own brave heart, young gold-eater,' said he. 'You yourself displayed enormous courage when you helped our young prince escape from his Spanish cage. Indeed, some would say that you showed the greatest courage of all—the courage to do what was right.'

I bowed my head in modesty.

The old man leaned close to me. 'I do not believe such acts of courage should go unrewarded either. No, as a reward for your bravery, I would like to present you with this.'

He held up a bladder which had evidently been taken from the body of a small animal. It appeared to be filled with some variety of liquid.

I took the bladder. It had an opening at one extremity, through which I surmised the bladder's holder could pour out its contents.

'What is it?' I inquired.

'It is monkey urine,' said the old man keenly.

'Monkey urine,' said I and flatly.

'It will protect you against the rapa,' said the old

man. 'Remember, the rapa is a cat, and like all cats, it is a most vain creature. According to the tribes of this region, there are some liquids that the rapa despises with a fury. Liquids which, if smeared all over one's body, will frighten off the rapa.'

I smiled weakly at the old man. It was, after all, the first time I had ever been given the excrement of a jungle animal as a token of appreciation.

'Thank you,' said I. 'Such a . . . wonderful . . . gift.'

The old man seemed terribly pleased by my response and so he said, 'Then I should like to provide you with another.'

I endeavoured to beg off his generosity—lest he give me *another* variety of animal discharge. But his second gift was not of the physical kind.

'I would like to share with you a secret,' said he.

'And what secret is that?'

'If ever you need to escape from this village, enter the quenko and take the third tunnel on the right-hand side. From there, alternate left then right, taking the first tunnel you see every time, but make sure you go to the left first. The quenko will take you to the waterfall overlooking the vast wetland forests. The secret to the labyrinth is simple, one only has to know where to begin. Trust me, young gold-eater, and mark these gifts. They could save your life.'

Refreshed by my slumber, I wandered up onto the roof of the citadel once again.

There I found Renco, nobly keeping his vigil. He must have been supremely fatigued, but he did not betray any such weariness. He just stared vigilantly out over the main street of the town, oblivious to the veil of rain that landed lightly on the crown of his head. I arrived at his side wordlessly and followed his gaze out over the village.

Aside from the rain, nothing moved.

Nay, nothing made a sound.

The eerie stillness of the village was haunting.

When he spoke, Renco didn't turn to face me. 'Vilcafor says he opened the temple in daylight. Then he sent five of his finest warriors into it to find Solon's treasure. They never returned. It was only with the onset of night that the rapas emerged from within the temple.'

'Are they out there now?' I inquired fearfully.

'If they are, then I have been unable to see them.'

I looked at Renco. His eyes were red and he had large bags beneath both of them.

'My friend,' I said gently, 'you must sleep. You have to retain your strength, especially if my countrymen find this town. Sleep now, I shall keep the vigil, and I shall wake you if I see anything.'

Renco nodded slowly. 'As usual, you are right, Alberto. Thank you.'

And with that he went inside and I found myself standing alone on the roof of the citadel, alone in the night.

Nothing stirred in the village below me.

It happened about an hour into my watch.

I had been watching the tiny wavelets of the river, glistening silver in the moonlight, when suddenly a small raft floated into view. I spied three figures standing on the deck of the small vessel, dark shadows in the night.

My blood ran cold.

Hernando's men . . .

I was about to run to get Renco when the raft pulled alongside the village's small wooden jetty and its passengers stepped up onto the wharf and I garnered a better look at them.

My shoulders sank with relief.

They were not conquistadors.

They were Incans.

A man—dressed in the traditional attire of an Incan warrior—and a woman with a small child, all of them covered against the rain by hoods and cloaks.

The three figures walked slowly up the main street, staring in awe at the carnage that littered the muddy road around them.

And then I saw it.

At first I thought it was just the shadow of a swaying branch cast onto the side of one of the huts that lined the street. But then the branch's shadow swayed away from the hut's wall and another shadow remained in its place.

I saw the dark outline of a large cat—saw the black feline head, the upturn of the nose, the tips of its high-pointed ears. Saw its mouth open in silent anticipation of the kill.

At first I couldn't believe its size. Whatever this animal was, it was enormous—

And then suddenly the animal was gone and all I saw was the hut's wall, bare and empty, illuminated by the moon's rays.

The three Incans were now about twenty paces from the citadel.

I whispered loudly to them in Quechuan. 'Over here! Come quickly! Come quickly!'

At first they didn't seem to understand what I was saying.

And then the first animal stepped slowly out into the main street behind them.

'Run!' I called. 'They're behind you!'

The man of the group turned and saw the giant cat standing in the mud behind them.

The animal moved slowly, with precision and calculation. It looked like a panther. A massive black panther. Cold yellow eyes looked down a tapered black snout—eyes that stared with the unblinking coolness of the cat.

At that moment, a second animal joined the first and the two rapas stared intently at the small group before them.

Then they both lowered their heads and tensed their bodies like two tightly wound springs waiting to burst into action.

'Run!' I cried. 'Run!'

The man and the woman broke into a run and hastened toward the citadel.

The two cats in the street leapt after them in pursuit.

I ran to the open doorway that led from the roof of the citadel down into the main body of the structure. 'Renco! Someone! Anyone! Open the main door! There are people out there!'

I hastened back to the edge of the roof and arrived there just in time to see the woman reach the base of the citadel, carrying the child in her arms. The man arrived right behind her.

The cats bounded down the street.

No-one downstairs had opened the door.

The woman looked up at me with frightened eyes—and for the shortest of moments I found myself entranced by her beauty. She was the most striking woman I had ever—

I made my decision.

I ripped my cloak from my body and, holding onto one end of it, hurled the other end out over the edge of the roof.

'Grab my cloak!' I called. 'I will pull you up!'

The man snatched the other end of my garment and handed it to the woman.

'Go!' he cried. 'Go!'

The woman took hold of my cloak and I pulled on it with all my strength, hauling her—and the child in her arms—up toward the roof of the citadel.

No sooner was she off the ground than I saw the warrior beneath her get pummelled by one of the rapas. The man's body made a sickening sound as it was thrown against the outer wall of the citadel. He screamed as the rapa began to eat him alive.

With all my strength I heaved on my cloak, lifting the woman and the child to safety.

They reached the rim of the roof, and in the light falling rain the woman grabbed hold of the stone battlements, while at the same time she attempted to hand her child over to me. He was a small boy, with large, frightened brown eyes.

I struggled to hold onto three things at once—the woman, the boy, my cloak—and I looked out in horror to see that several other rapas had slunk out into the main street of Vilcafor to view the commotion.

Just then, one of the cats beneath us leapt up from the mud and tried to snap its jaws around the woman's dangling feet. But the woman was too alert. She lifted her toes at the very last moment and the cat's jaws closed on nothing but air.

'Help me,' she pleaded, her eyes frantic.

'I will,' said I, as the rain beat down on my face.

Whence the cat in the mud beneath her leapt again, this time reaching out for her with its huge scythe-like claws, and this time it caught the hem of her cloak and to my absolute horror I saw the entire cloak go taut under its weight.

'*No!*' the woman cried as she felt the weight of the cat begin to pull her down.

'Oh, Lord,' I breathed.

At which moment the cat yanked down hard on the woman's cloak and she tightened her grip on my wet hand, but it was no use, the great cat was too heavy, too strong.

With a final scream, the woman slipped out of my grasp and, with her child in her arms, she fell off the rim of the roof and out of my sight.

It was then that I did the unthinkable.

I leapt out over the rim after her.

To this day, I don't know why I did it.

Maybe it was the way she had held onto her son that made me do it. Or maybe it was the look of pure fear on her beautiful face.

Or maybe it was just her beautiful face.

I don't know.

I landed rather unheroically in a pool of mud that lay in front of the citadel. As I did so, a spray of brown wetness splattered all over my face, blinding me.

I wiped the mud away from my eyes.

And immediately saw no less than seven rapas standing in a close semicircle around me, staring at me with their cold yellow eyes.

My heart was pounding loudly inside my head. What I intended to do now, I surely did not know.

The woman and the boy were right beside me. I stepped in front of them and yelled fiercely at the phalanx of monsters before us.

'Be gone, I say! Be gone!'

I extracted an arrow from the quiver on my back and slashed it back and forth in front of the giant cats' faces.

The rapas didn't seem to care for my pathetic act of bravado.

They closed in around us.

Now truly, it must be said that if these fiendish creatures had looked large from the roof of the citadel, up close they looked positively massive. Dark, black and powerful.

Then, and abruptly, the rapa standing nearest to me lashed out with its forepaw and snapped the sharpened point of my arrow clean off. The big creature then lowered its head and snarled at me, tensed itself to launch and then—

Something dropped with a loud splash into a muddy puddle of water to my right.

I turned to see what it was. And I frowned.

It was the idol.

It was Renco's idol.

My mind spun like a windmill. What was Renco's idol doing down here? Why would anyone throw it down into the mud at a time like this!

Whence I looked up and saw Renco himself leaning out over the edge of the citadel's roof. It was he who had just thrown the idol down to me.

And then it happened.

I froze.

The noise was like nothing I had ever heard in my life.

It was only a soft sound, but it was utterly pervasive. It cut through the air like a knife, piercing even the sound of the falling rain.

It was similar to the sound a chime makes when it is struck. A kind of high-pitched hum.

Mmmmmmmm.

The rapas heard it too. Indeed, the one which had only moments before been readying itself to attack now just stood there in front of us, staring in a kind of dumbstruck wonderment at the idol which now lay half-submerged in the brown puddle beside me.

It was then that the strangest thing of all happened.

The pack of rapas around us slowly began to move backwards. The rapas were stepping away from the idol.

'Alberto,' Renco whispered. 'Move very slowly, do you hear. Very slowly. Pick up the idol and go to the door. I'll have someone let you back inside.'

I obeyed his command to the letter.

With the woman and child beside me, I scooped up the wet idol in my hands, and with our backs pressed firmly against the wall of the citadel, we slowly made our way around its circular outer wall until we were at the doorway.

For their part, the rapas just followed us at a careful distance, entranced by the melodious song of the wet idol.

But at no stage did they attack.

And then all at once the large stone slab that acted as a door to the citadel was rolled aside and we all slid in through it, and as I came in last of all and the great doorstone was rolled back into place behind me, I fell to the floor, breathless and soaking and shaking, and totally and utterly amazed that I was still alive.

Renco came hurrying down from the roof to meet us.

'Lena!' said he, recognising the woman. 'And Mani!' he cried, taking the boy up in his arms.

I just lay exhausted on the floor to the side of all this happiness.

I am ashamed to say it now, but in that moment I actually felt a pang of jealousy toward my friend Renco. No doubt this astonishingly beautiful woman was his wife—as one would expect of so dashing a character as Renco.

'Uncle Renco!' the boy exclaimed as Renco held him high.

Uncle?

My eyes snapped up.

'Brother Alberto,' said Renco, coming over. 'I don't know what it was you were planning to do out there, but my people have a saying. "It is not so much the gift as the intention behind it that matters." Thank you. Thank you for rescuing my sister and her son.'

'Your sister?' said I, staring at the woman as she removed her waterlogged cloak and revealed a minuscule tunic-like undergarment that was itself soaked through to the skin.

What I saw made me swallow.

She was far more beautiful than I had at first per-
ceived—if indeed such a thing were possible. She was
perhaps twenty years of age, with soft brown eyes,
smooth olive skin and flowing dark hair. She had long
slender legs and smoothly muscled shoulders, and
through her saturated undergarment I could see her
ample bosom and—much to my embarrassment—her
erect nipples.

She was radiant.

Renco wrapped her in a dry blanket and she smiled
at me and I truly felt weak at the knees.

'Brother Alberto Santiago,' said Renco formally.
'May I present to you my sister, Lena, first princess of
the Incan empire.'

Lena stepped forward and took my hand in hers. 'It
is a pleasure to make your acquaintance,' said she with
a smile. 'And thank you for your most brave act.'

'Oh, it was . . . nothing,' said I, blushing.

'And thank you also for rescuing my errant brother
from his prison cell,' said she.

Seeing my surprise, she added, 'Oh, rest assured,
my hero, word of your noble deed has spread throughout the empire.'

I bowed my head modestly. I liked the way she
called me 'my hero'.

Just then something occurred to me and I turned to
Renco. 'Say, how did you know the idol would have
that effect on the rapas?'

Renco gave me a crooked smile.

'As a matter of fact, I didn't know it would do that.'

'What!' I cried.

Renco laughed. 'Alberto, I am not the one who
jumped off a perfectly safe roof to rescue a woman and
child I didn't even know!'

He put an arm around my shoulders. 'It has been

said that the Spirit of the People has the ability to soothe savage beasts. This I have never seen, but I have heard that when it is immersed in water, the idol will calm even the most enraged animal. When I was awoken by your shouts and I saw the three of you surrounded by the rapas, I surmised that this was as good a time as any to test that theory.'

I shook my head in wonderment.

'Renco,' said Lena, stepping forward, 'I hate to disturb your revelry, but I have come with a message.'

'What?'

'The Spaniards have taken Roya. But they cannot decipher the totems. So whenever they reach one, they have Chanca trackers scour the surrounding area until they pick up your trail. After the gold-eaters sacked Paxu and Tupra, I was sent here to tell you of their progress since I am one of the few who know the code to the totems. I have since learned that they have burned Roya to the ground. They have picked up your scent, Renco. And they are on their way here.'

'How long?' said Renco.

Lena's face darkened.

'They move fast, brother. Very fast. At their current rate of travel, I estimate that they will be here by daybreak.'

'Found anything?' Frank Nash said suddenly from behind Race.

Race looked up from the manuscript to find Nash, Lauren, Gaby and Krauss standing in the doorway to the ATV, looking at him expectantly. It was late in the afternoon, and owing to the storm clouds overhead, the sky behind them had already begun to darken considerably.

Race looked at his watch.

4:55 pm.

Damn.

He hadn't realised he'd been reading so long.

Night would fall soon. And with it would come the rapas.

'So? Have you found anything yet?' Nash asked.

'Er . . .' Race began. He'd become so engrossed in the manuscript that he'd almost forgotten why he was reading it—to find out anything he could about defeating the rapas and getting them back inside the temple.

'Well . . . ?' Nash said.

'It says that they only come out at night, or at times of unusual darkness.'

Krauss said, 'Which explains why they were active in the crater earlier. It was so dark in there, even during the day, that they were—'

'It also looks like the rapas know that this town is a good food source,' Race said, cutting Krauss off before he could justify his earlier error—an error that had resulted in the deaths of three good soldiers. 'They attacked it twice in the manuscript.'

'Does it say how they came to be inside the temple?'

'Yes. It says that they were put inside the building by a great thinker who wanted to make the temple a test of human greed.' Race looked up at Nash pointedly. 'Guess we failed that one.'

'*Solon's temple . . .*' Gaby Lopez breathed.

'Did it say anything about how we can fight them?' Nash asked.

'It did say something about that, two things actually. One, monkey urine. Apparently all cats hate it. Douse yourself in it and the rapas will steer well clear of you.'

'And the second thing?' Lauren said.

'Well, it was very strange,' Race said. 'At one point in the story, just when the cats were about to attack Santiago, the Incan prince threw the idol down into a puddle of water. Once the idol came into contact with the water, it emitted a strange kind of humming noise that seemed to stop the cats from attacking.'

Nash frowned at that.

'It was very peculiar,' Race said. 'Santiago described it as sounding like a chime being struck, and it seemed to operate on the same principle as a dog whistle—some kind of high-frequency vibration that seemed to affect the cats but not the humans.

'The really strange thing,' Race added, 'was that the Incans seemed to know about this. On a couple of occasions in the manuscript it's said that the Incans believed that their idol, when immersed in water, could soothe even the most savage beast.'

Nash glanced at Lauren.

'Could be resonance,' she said. 'Contact with the concentrated oxygen molecules in water would cause the thyrium to resonate, the same way other nuclear substances react with oxygen in the air.'

'But this would be on a much larger scale—' Nash said.

'Which is probably why the monk also heard the humming sound,' Lauren said. 'Human beings can't hear the resonant hum caused by the contact of, say, plutonium with oxygen—the frequency is too low. But since thyrium is a whole order of magnitude denser than plutonium, it's possible that when *it* comes into contact with water, the resonance is so great it can be heard by humans.'

'And if the monk heard it, then it must have been twice as bad for the cats,' Krauss added pointedly.

Everyone turned to face Krauss.

'Remember, cats have a hearing capability approximately ten times that of human beings. They hear things that we *physically* cannot, and they communicate on a frequency that is beyond our auditory range.'

'They communicate?' Lauren said flatly.

'Yes,' Krauss said. 'It has long been accepted that the great cats communicate via grunts and guttural vibrations that are well beyond the aural perception of humans. The point, however, is this: whatever that monk heard was probably only one-tenth of what the cats heard. That humming sound must have driven them crazy, hence the pause it gave them.'

'The manuscript went even further than that,' Race said. 'It didn't just make them pause. The cats seemed to follow the idol after it had been dropped in the water. It was as if they were *drawn* to it or something, hypnotised even.'

Nash said, 'Did the manuscript say anything about how the idol came to be inside the temple?'

'No,' Race said. 'Not yet, at least. Who knows, maybe Renco and Santiago wet the idol and used it to lead the cats back inside the temple. Whatever they did, somehow they managed to lure the cats back inside the temple and at the same time put the idol inside it.' Race paused. 'It's not entirely inappropriate, really. By placing the idol inside the temple, they merely made it another part of Solon's test of human greed.'

'These cats,' Nash said. 'The manuscript says they're nocturnal, right?'

'It says that they like any kind of *darkness*—night-time or otherwise. I guess that would make them nocturnal and then some.'

'But it says that they came down to the village each night to hunt for food?'

'Yes.'

Nash's eyes narrowed. 'Can we assume, then, that they leave the crater to forage for food *every* night?'

'Judging from the manuscript, that would appear to be a safe assumption.'

'Good,' Nash said, turning.

'Why?'

'Because,' he said, 'when those cats come out tonight, we're going to go inside the temple and get that idol.'

The day grew darker by the minute.

Black storm clouds rolled in overhead, and with the cool air of the late afternoon, a thick grey fog settled over the village. A light rain fell.

Race sat next to Lauren as she packed some

equipment to take over to the citadel in anticipation of their night-time activities.

'So how has married life been to you?' he asked as casually as he could.

Lauren smiled wryly to herself. 'Depends which one you're talking about.'

'There's more than one?'

'My first marriage didn't exactly work out. Turned out he didn't share my career ambitions. We got divorced about five years ago.'

'Oh.'

'But I've recently remarried,' Lauren said. 'And it's been great. Real nice guy. Just like you, in fact. Lot of potential, too.'

'How long?'

'About eighteen months now.'

'That's great,' Race said politely. In truth, he was thinking about the incident he had witnessed earlier— Lauren and Troy Copeland kissing passionately in the back of the Huey. He recalled how Copeland hadn't been wearing a wedding ring. Was Lauren having an affair with him? Or maybe Copeland just didn't wear his ring . . .

'Did you ever get married, Will?' Lauren asked, yanking him from his thoughts.

'No,' Race said softly. 'No, I didn't.'

'SAT-SN report is coming through,' Van Lewen said from a computer terminal on the wall of the ATV.

He, Cochrane, Reichart, Nash and Race were now standing with the two German BKA agents— Schroeder and the blonde woman, Renée Becker—inside the eight-wheeled all-terrain vehicle. It was parked close to the river, not far from the western

293

log-bridge and the muddy path that led up to the fissure, in anticipation of their night-time assault on the temple.

Lauren had already left the ATV for the citadel, with Johann Krauss in tow behind her.

Just then, Buzz Cochrane returned to the ATV with a handful of sloppy light-brown mush. The smell of it in the confined space of the vehicle was putrid.

'There ain't a single monkey out there that I could catch to get its piss,' Cochrane said. 'Guess they get out of here before nightfall.' He held up the brown mush in his hand. 'I was able to get this, though. Monkey shit. I figured it'd be just as good.'

Race winced at the smell of it.

Cochrane saw him. 'What? Don't want to smear yourself in shit, Professor?' He looked over at Renée and smiled. 'Guess we're lucky it ain't the professor who's going in there, then, ain't we?'

Cochrane began to apply the monkey excrement to the exterior of his fatigues. Reichart and Van Lewen did the same. They also applied it to the rims of the narrow slit-like windows of the ATV.

While Race had been reading the manuscript earlier, Nash had got the other civilians to set up a base of operations inside the citadel. While they had been doing that, the four remaining Green Berets had been hard at work trying to fix the surviving Huey. Unfortunately, they'd only managed to repair the chopper's ignition ports. Repairing its damaged tail rotor had been more difficult than Cochrane had at first anticipated. Complications had arisen and it still wouldn't turn over and the Huey couldn't fly without it.

Then, with the onset of dusk, Nash decided that the retrieval of the idol had to take priority. The Green Berets had been taken away from the chopper and brought over to the ATV, where Race had briefed them on the wet idol incident in the manuscript.

As Race did exactly that, Nash ordered Gaby, Copeland, Doogie and the young German private, Molke, to remain in the citadel.

He had said that it was a necessary part of his plan for seizing the idol to have most of the team stationed inside the citadel when the cats arrived in the village—while he and a few of the Green Berets remained in the ATV, closer to the riverside path that led up to the temple.

Race—who had only just finished briefing the Green Berets on the wet idol incident—was to join them in the citadel immediately.

'SAT-SN is in,' Van Lewen said from the computer terminal. 'Satellite imagery should be coming through any minute now, too.'

'What's it say?' Nash said.

'Take a look,' Van Lewen said, stepping aside.

Nash stared at the screen in front of him. The image on it showed the northern half of South America:

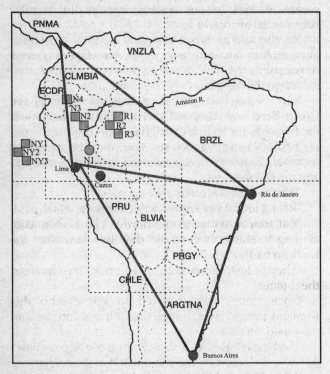

'What the hell—?' Nash frowned.

'At least the immediate area is all clear . . .' Van Lewen said.

'What's it all mean?' Race asked.

Van Lewen said, 'The straight lines represent the

five main commercial air corridors in South America. Basically, Panama acts as a gateway to the continent, with commercial flights usually going direct from there to Lima and Rio de Janeiro and then from those two cities down to Buenos Aires. The grey squares represent aircraft in our quarter *outside* the regular commercial air corridors.'

Race looked at the screen—saw the three clusters of grey squares hovering over the north-western quarter of the continent.

'What do the letters and numbers mean?'

Van Lewen said, 'The grey circle just above Cuzco—the one with "N1" written underneath it—is us. It stands for "Nash-One", our team here at the village. N2, N3 and N4 are our air support choppers, en route to Vilcafor from Panama. But it looks like they're still a good way out.'

'What about the other grey squares?'

'R1, R2 and R3 are Romano's choppers,' Nash said.

'But they're so far to the north,' Van Lewen said, turning to Nash. 'How could they have overshot the mark so badly?'

'They're lost,' Nash said. 'They must have misread the totems.'

Once again, Race wanted to know who this Romano person was, but he just bit his tongue and remained silent.

'And these?' Renée said, indicating the three squares out over the ocean on the extreme left of the screen.

'NY1, NY2 and NY3 are U.S. Navy signatures,' Van Lewen said. 'The Navy must have a carrier out there somewhere.'

'No sign of the Stormtroopers?' Schroeder asked.

'No,' Nash said sombrely.

Race's watch ticked over to five o'clock. With the harsh black storm clouds rolling in overhead, the late afternoon sky had become unusually dark. It might as well have been night.

Nash turned to Van Lewen. 'How are we for vision?'

'Satellite imagery will be with us in about sixty seconds.'

'Delayed or real-time?'

'Real-time infra-red.'

'Good,' Nash said. 'We should be able to get a clear picture of those cats as they come out of the crater and head into the village. You all set?'

Van Lewen stood up. Beside him, Buzz Cochrane and Tex Reichart hefted their M-16s across their chests.

'Yes, sir,' Cochrane said, casting a sideways wink at Renée. 'Cocked, locked and ready to rock.'

Race cringed.

Cochrane leered at the petite German woman with a bully's confidence. It was as if his gun—dripping with its laser sights, M-203 grenade/grappling hook launcher and barrel-mounted flashlight—and his combat uniform somehow made him Mr Irresistible.

Race hated him for it.

'Satellite imagery is coming through,' Van Lewen said.

At that moment, another computer screen on the wall of the ATV glowed to life.

The image on it was in grainy black-and-white, and at first Race couldn't tell what it was.

The extreme left-hand side of the screen was completely black. To the right of that was a section of blurry grey hash, and next to that was something that looked like an inverted horseshoe—in the centre of which was a series of small square dots and one large round dot near the apex of the horseshoe.

At the base of the screen was a wide band of darker grey. Next to the wide band of dark grey was a small dark box-like object. Two tiny white blobs moved away from the small box toward the large round dot at the apex of the horseshoe.

And then it hit him.

He was looking at the village of Vilcafor.

The horseshoe shape was the gigantic moat that encircled the village, the dots inside it the huts and the citadel. The large section of blackness on the left was the rocky plateau that housed the temple. The blurry grey hash—the rainforest *between* the plateau and the village. And the band of dark grey at the base of the screen—the river itself.

The small dark box beside the river, Race realised, was the ATV in which he now sat, parked alongside the western log-bridge.

He looked at the two blobs on the screen hurrying from the ATV to the citadel. Then he spun around and looked out through the door and saw Lauren and Krauss trotting quickly through the fog toward the citadel.

Oh—my—God, he thought.

This was a picture of Vilcafor taken from a satellite hundreds of miles above the earth—in real-time.

This was *now*.

Nash spoke into his throat mike. 'Lauren, we're all set over here. You in yet?'

'Just a second,' Lauren's voice replied over their intercoms.

On the viewscreen, Race saw the two white blobs that were Lauren and Krauss disappear inside the round dot that was the citadel.

'*All right. We're in,*' Lauren said. '*You sending Will over?*'

'Right now,' Nash said. 'Professor Race, you better get on over to the citadel, before it gets fully dark.'

'Right,' Race said, moving for the door.

'*Hold it a second . . .*' Van Lewen said suddenly.

Everybody froze.

'What is it?' Nash said.

'We got company.'

Van Lewen nodded at the viewscreen.

Race turned, and on the harsh black-and-white viewscreen saw the dark blob that was the mountain-plateau and the horseshoe-shaped village.

And then he saw them.

They were in the section of blurry grey hash to the left of the horseshoe—the rainforest in between the village and the plateau.

About sixteen of them.

All coming from the direction of the plateau.

Sixteen ominous white blurs—each one possessed of a long slinking tail—stealthily making their way through the foliage toward the village.

The rapas.

The thick steel door of the ATV slid along its rail and slammed with a loud thud.

'They're early,' Nash said.

'*It's the storm clouds*,' Krauss's voice said over the speakers. '*Nocturnal animals don't use clocks, Doctor Nash, only the level of ambient light around them. If it's dark enough, they emerge from their hiding holes—*'

'Whatever,' Nash said. 'So long as they're out, that's all that matters.' He turned to face Race. 'Sorry, Professor. Looks like you're staying with us. Lauren, seal up the citadel.'

Over at the citadel, Lauren and Copeland grabbed hold of the fortress's big six-foot doorstone and rolled it into a groove that had been cut into the floor of the structure's doorway.

The doorstone was roughly rectangular in shape, but with a curving rounded base that allowed it to be rocked easily in and out of its groove inside the door-frame. The fact that it was set in a groove on the *inside* of the fortress's walls meant that any external enemies couldn't hope to budge the great stone from the outside.

The stone rolled into place—although Lauren and

Copeland deliberately left a small crack of air between it and the doorframe. It was important to the plan that the cats be able to detect them inside the citadel.

After all, they were the bait.

Inside the ATV, everyone stared intently at the live satellite image on the viewscreen.

The cats came in two distinct 'teams'—one team coming directly from the plateau to the west, the other swinging up and around from the north.

Race felt a chill as he watched their bodies—glowing white on the infra-red—their tails curling and uncurling slowly behind them.

It was disturbing, he thought. Disturbingly co-ordinated behaviour for a pack of animals.

The cats crossed the moat at various locations. Some went over the western log-bridge, others just leapt softly onto the fallen tree trunks that littered the dry moat-bed and then hopped effortlessly up onto the other side.

They entered the village.

Most of the rapas, Race saw, headed straight for the citadel and the scent of the people inside it.

Just then, however, he saw a lone, white blob on the screen appear alongside the stationary ATV.

Race spun instantly to his right—and saw the enormous black whiskers of one of the cats *right outside* the slit-like window next to him!

The rapa snorted once, registered the foul-smelling monkey excrement that had been smeared on the sill of the slit. Then it ambled off to join the others at the citadel.

'Okay,' Nash said. 'All of the cats appear to be converging on the citadel. Lauren, what's happening over there?'

'They're all over here. They want to get in, but the citadel's sealed tight. We're safe in here for the moment. You can send the boys out now.'

Nash turned to the three Green Berets beside him. 'You ready?'

The three soldiers nodded.

'Then get to it.'

And with that, Nash pushed opened a pop-up hatch in the rear of the ATV and Cochrane, Van Lewen and Reichart—their helmets and clothes smeared all over with the putrid brown monkey shit—climbed up and out through it. As soon as they were out, Nash quickly shut the hatch behind them.

'Kennedy,' he said into his mike. 'Anything on the SAT-SN?'

'There's nothing within a hundred miles of here, sir,' Doogie's voice came in from the citadel.

As Nash talked, Race stared intently at the satellite image of the village.

He saw the pack of cats gathered around the citadel. Saw their slithering tails, their cautious, inquisitive movements. At the same time, however, on the bottom of the screen, he saw three new blobs sneak out from the ATV and race westward, across the western log-bridge and *away* from the village, toward the dark mountain-plateau.

Cochrane, Van Lewen and Reichart.

Going after the idol.

The three Green Berets burst through the veil of mist that covered the riverside path and raced toward the fissure. They were running fast, breathing hard. All three of them wore helmet-mounted cameras.

They came to the fissure.

It too was cloaked in a thick grey mist. The three soldiers didn't miss a step. They dashed into it at full speed.

In the ATV, Nash, Schroeder and Renée were all watching the video monitors intently, watching the feed coming in from the three soldiers.

On the monitors, they saw the walls of the fissure streaking by at phenomenal speed. On the wall-mounted speakers, they heard the three soldiers' heavy panting breaths.

Race stood a few paces away from the video monitors. He didn't want to get in the way.

It was then, however, that he noticed that Nash and the two Germans were now watching *only* the pictures coming from the three helmet cameras. Their interest in the soldiers' mission was paramount, and as such, they were completely ignoring the satellite image screen.

Race turned to look at the satellite picture.

And then he frowned.

'Hey,' he said. 'What the hell is that?'

Nash glanced around idly at Race and the satellite monitor. But when he saw the image on the satellite screen, he suddenly stood bolt upright.

'What the *fuck*—?'

On the far *right*-hand side of the satellite image—on the eastern side of the village—was another cluster of blurry grey hash that represented more rainforest, the forest that led to the edge of the tableland and the greater Amazon Basin.

Nobody had paid it much attention before because nothing had been in it.

But there was something in it now.

The section of blurry grey hash of the right-hand side of the village was now *littered* with tiny white blobs—easily thirty of them in total—all of them converging quickly on the village.

Race felt his blood run cold.

Each blob was distinctly human in shape, and every single one of them was carrying what appeared to be a gun.

They came out of the rainforest silently, with their machine-guns pressed firmly against their shoulders, ready to fire but not firing yet.

Race and the others were now watching them intently through the ATV's slit-like windows.

The intruders were all dressed in black ceramic body armour, and they moved with precision and speed, covering each other smoothly as they leapfrogged forward in perfect, silent unison.

The rapas gathered around the citadel turned as one as they caught sight of their new enemy. They tensed to attack and then they—

Didn't move.

For some reason, the rapas didn't attack these new intruders. Rather, they just stopped where they stood and stared at them.

And then—just then—one of the intruders opened fire on the rapas with an assault rifle that looked to Race like something out of a *Star Wars* movie.

An unbelievable amount of bullets flared out from the gun's rectangular muzzle and ripped one of the cats' heads to shreds. One second the cat's head was there, the next it just erupted in an ugly splash of exploding flesh and blood.

The cats scattered in an instant just as another one of their number was torn to pieces by the savage hail of gunfire.

Race peered out through his window, tried to get a better look at the gun in the intruder's hands.

It looked remarkable, space-age even.

It was completely rectangular in shape, with no apparent gunbarrel. Indeed, the barrel must have been concealed somewhere *within* the gun's long rectangular body.

Race had seen these guns before, but only in pictures, never in real life.

They were Heckler & Koch G-11s.

According to Race's brother Marty, the Heckler & Koch G-11 was the most advanced assault rifle ever built.

Designed and built in 1989, even now—ten years on—it was still twenty years ahead of its time. It was the Holy Grail of firearms as far as Marty had been concerned.

It was the only production weapon in history to fire a caseless cartridge. Indeed, it was the only hand-held firearm in the world known to contain a microprocessor—principally because it was the only firearm in the world *complex* enough to require one.

Due to the fact that it fired a caseless bullet, the G-11 was not only able to fire at the unimaginable rate of 2300 rounds per minute, it was also able to store *in its body* some 150 rounds—five times the number of bullets held in the clip of a regular assault rifle like the M-16. And even then it was only half the size of an M-16.

Truth be told, the only thing that had stopped the G-11 was money. In late 1989, political considerations forced the German government to rescind its deal with Heckler & Koch to use the G-11 in the *Bundeswehr*.

As a result, only four hundred G-11s were ever made. Strangely, however, in an audit of the company during its takeover by Britain's Royal Ordnance only ten of that original batch were accounted for.

The other three hundred and ninety guns had disappeared.

I think we just found them, Race thought as he watched the rapas take flight in the face of the barrage of supermachine-gun fire coming out of the guns.

'It's the Stormtroopers,' Schroeder said from beside him.

The hailstorm of gunfire outside continued.

Two more cats fell, squealing and shrieking, as a couple of the Stormtroopers pummelled the village with their devastating rain of supermachine-gun fire.

The remainder of the cats took refuge in the rainforest surrounding the town, and soon the main street was filled only with the heavily-armed Stormtroopers.

'How the hell did they get here without us seeing them on the SAT-SN?' Nash demanded.

'And why aren't the cats attacking them?' Race said.

Up until now, the cats had been merciless in their assaults, but for some reason they had neither sensed nor attacked these new soldiers.

It was then that the distinct smell of ammonia wafted in through the windows of the ATV. The smell of urine. Monkey urine. The Nazis had read the manuscript, too.

Suddenly Van Lewen's voice came in over their speakers. *'We're coming to the rope bridge now.'*

Race and Nash spun together to face the monitor

that displayed the views of the three soldiers up in the crater.

On the monitor they saw Van Lewen's point of view as he bounced across the rope bridge that led to the temple.

'Cochrane! Van Lewen! *Hurry!*' Nash said into his radio. 'We've got hostil—'

Just then a shrill, ear-piercing shriek warbled out from the ATV's speakers and Nash's radio went dead.

'They've engaged electronic countermeasures,' Schroeder said.

'What?' Race said.

'They're jamming us,' Nash said.

'What do we do?' Renée asked.

Nash said, 'We've got to tell Van Lewen, Reichart and Cochrane that they can't come back down here. They've got to get that idol and get it as far away from here as possible. Then, somehow, they have to get in touch with the air support team and get the choppers to pick them up from somewhere in the mountains.'

'But how are you going to do that if they're jamming our radios?' Race said.

'One of us is going to have to go up to that temple and tell them,' Nash said.

A short silence followed.

Then Schroeder said, 'I'll go.'

Good idea, Race thought. After the Green Berets, Schroeder was easily the most 'soldierly' of the group.

'No,' Nash said decisively. 'You can handle a gun. We need you down here. You also know these Nazi guys better than any of us.'

That left Nash, Renée . . . or Race.

Oh, man, Race thought.

And so he said, 'I'll do it.'

'*But . . . ?*' Schroeder began.

'I was the fastest guy in the football team back in college,' Race said. 'I can make it.'

'But what about the rapas?' Renée said.

'*I can make it.*'

'All right, then, Race is elected,' Nash said, heading for the pop-up hatch in the rear of the ATV.

'Here, take this,' he said, handing Race an M-16 complete with all the extras. 'Might stop you becoming cat food. Now go. Go!'

Race took a step toward the hatch, inhaled a slow, deep breath. He took a final look at Nash, Schroeder and Renée.

Then he let out the breath he was holding and pushed up through the hatch—

—and entered another world.

Supermachine-gun fire echoed out all around him, smacked into the leaves nearby, splintered their trunks. It seemed so much louder out here, so much more real. So much more lethal.

Race's heart thumped loudly inside his head.

What the hell am I doing out here with this gun in my hand?

You're trying to be a hero, that's what you're doing, you stupid schmuck!

He took another breath.

All right . . .

Race leapt off the back of the ATV, landed on the western log-bridge and took off down the riverside path beyond it. He was surrounded by impenetrable grey fog. It lined the path around him. Gnarled tree branches jutted out through it like daggers.

The M-16 felt heavy in his hands and he held it awkwardly across his chest as he ran, kicking up water with every step.

Then, without warning, a rapa slid out from the mist to his right and rose to its full height in front of him and—

Blam!

The rapa's head exploded and the giant cat dropped like a stone, began flopping wildly in the mud.

Race didn't miss a beat, he just hurdled the fallen cat. Once he was over it, he turned to see Schroeder—with an M-16 pressed against his shoulder—sticking out from the hatch at the back of the ATV.

Race ran.

A minute later, the fissure in the mountainside emerged from the fog. Just as he caught sight of it, he heard voices behind him, shouting in German.

'Achtung!'

'Schnell! Schnell!'

Then suddenly he heard Nash's voice shouting from somewhere in the mist behind him: *'Race, hurry! They're behind you! They're heading for the temple!'*

Race bolted into the fissure.

Its damp stone walls flashed past him on either side as he raced down its length.

Then all of a sudden he burst out into the massive canyon that housed the skyscraper-like rock tower. The fog was thick here too. The base of the rock tower was cloaked in a spooky grey mist.

Race didn't care. He saw the spiralling path to his left, jumped up onto it, took off up its steep curving length.

Back in the village, Renée Becker stared fearfully out through the narrow windows of the ATV.

About thirty Nazi troops were massing in the village now. They were dressed in state-of-the-art combat attire—ceramic body armour, lightweight kevlar tactical helmets and, of course, black ski masks—and they moved with purpose, like a well-trained, well-prepared raiding party.

Renée saw one of the Nazis step out into the middle of the main street and remove his helmet. The man then peeled off his black ski mask and surveyed the area around him.

Renée's eyes went wide.

Although she had seen his picture a thousand times before on all manner of 'MOST WANTED' posters, seeing him here, *now*, in the flesh, made her skin crawl.

She immediately recognised the forward-brushed hair and the narrow slit-like eyes. And the left hand that was possessed of only four fingers.

She was looking at Heinrich Anistaze.

Without saying a word, Anistaze made a 'V' with his fingers and pointed in the direction of the ATV.

Already a dozen of his G-11-armed men had dashed past the all-terrain vehicle, heading up the riverside path toward the fissure and the temple.

Now six more hustled over to the ATV, while the remaining twelve took up defensive positions around the perimeter of the village.

Two men, however, stood off to one side, guarding the Nazis' radio-jamming device.

It was a small backpack-sized unit—called a pulse generator that corrupted enemy radio signals by emitting a controlled electromagnetic pulse, or EMP.

It was a rather unique device. Ordinarily, an electromagnetic pulse will affect anything with a CPU in it—computers, televisions, communications systems. Such a pulse is called an 'uncontrolled' EMP. By *controlling* the frequency of their pulse, however, and by ensuring that their own radios were set on frequencies above it, the Nazis were able to jam their enemies' radio systems while still maintaining their own communications.

As they were doing right now.

The six Nazis arrived at the ATV's side to find every window shutter closed and every hatch bolted.

Inside the big vehicle, Nash, Schroeder and Renée sat huddled in its various corners, holding their collective breaths.

The Stormtroopers didn't waste any time.

They immediately crouched underneath the big armoured vehicle and began planting the explosives.

Race ran.

Up and up, round and round, following the long, curving bend of the spiralling path.

Legs pumping. Heart pounding.

He came to the rope bridge. Bounced across it. Hurried up the stone steps that led to the temple.

Race burst through the encroaching fern leaves and abruptly found himself standing in the clearing in front of the portal.

The clearing was completely deserted.

No animal—neither man nor cat—was in sight.

The temple's portal yawned open before him, looming out of the fog. The downward-leading steps inside it were cloaked in shadow.

Do not enter at any cost.

Death looms within.

Race held his M-16 out in front of him, flicked on its barrel-mounted flashlight, cautiously stepped toward the portal. He stood inside the great stone doorway—

surrounded by the horrific carvings of the rapas and the screaming humans—and peered down into the blackness.

'Van Lewen!' he hissed. 'Van Lewen! Are you in there?'

No reply.

He took a step down into the temple, holding his gun awkwardly out in front of him.

It was then that he heard the reply.

A long, slow growl from somewhere deep inside the temple.

Uh-oh.

Race gripped his gun a little more tightly, held his breath, took another step down into the temple.

Ten more steps and he was standing in a dark stone passageway that spiralled down and around to his right in a wide gentle curve.

He saw a small alcove sunk into its wall, turned the beam of his flashlight into it.

A horribly mangled skeleton stared back at him.

Its skull had been smashed inwards at the back and one of its arms was missing, and its mouth was open in a horrified frozen scream. It was also wearing an ancient leather vest.

Race took a horrified step back from the filthy skeletal figure.

And then he noticed the object looped around its neck. He only just saw it, hidden as it was in the folds of the dirty old skeleton's vertebrae. He leaned forward to get a better look at whatever it was.

It was a leather necklace of some sort.

Race touched the thin leather strap, worked it round the filthy skeleton's neck. A few seconds later, a dazzling green emerald appeared from behind the skeleton's bony neck, attached to the leather necklace.

Race's heart skipped a beat. He knew of this emerald pendant. Indeed, he had read about it only recently.

It was Renco's necklace.

The necklace that the high priestess in the Coricancha had given to him the night he had spirited the idol out of Cuzco.

Race looked at the skeleton again in horror.

Renco.

Race lifted the necklace off the skeleton's head and held it in his hands.

He thought of Renco for a moment—and then suddenly he recalled something that he himself had said to Frank Nash not long ago.

Somehow Renco and Santiago managed to lure the cats back inside the temple, and at the same time put the idol inside it.

Race swallowed hard. Had Renco—while carrying the wet idol with him—led the cats back inside the temple?

He stared down at the mangled skeleton in horror.

So this was what had become of Renco.

This was what happened to heroes.

He placed the emerald necklace solemnly around his own neck. 'Take care, Renco,' he said aloud.

Just then harsh white light illuminated Race's face and he turned—eyes wide, like an animal caught in the headlights of a car—and found himself staring at the faces of Cochrane, Van Lewen and Reichart as they emerged from the darkness of the temple's inner depths.

Reichart was holding something wrapped inside a tattered purple cloth.

Cochrane brushed roughly past Race, pushing his M-16 aside as he did so. 'Why don't you put that fucking thing down before you kill somebody.'

Tex Reichart stopped in front of Race and smiled as he held up the object in his hands, the object wrapped inside the purple cloth.

'We got it,' he said.

Reichart quickly unwrapped the cloth parcel and for the first time, Race saw it.

The Incan idol.

The Spirit of the People.

Like the stone totem he had seen in the rainforest earlier, the Spirit of the People looked infinitely more sinister in real life than it had in his imagination.

It was about a foot tall, and roughly the size and shape of a shoebox. The front section of the rectangular stone, however, had been carved into the shape of a rapa's head—the angriest, *fiercest* rapa Race had ever seen.

It was snarling ferociously, its jaws bared wide, its sharp pointed teeth ready to slash and maim and kill.

What struck Race most about the carving, though, was how *alive* it looked. Through a combination of skilled craftsmanship and the unusual nature of the stone itself, it seemed as if the rapa had somehow been imprisoned *inside* the lustrous black-and-purple stone and was now trying—maniacally, ferociously, rabidly—to force its way out of it.

The stone, Race thought as he gazed at the thin veins of purple that snaked their way down the snarling rapa's face, giving it an extra level of anger and malevolence.

Thyrium.

If only the Incas had known what they were starting when they carved this idol, he thought.

Reichart quickly replaced the cloth over the idol and the four of them hurried back up to the temple's entrance.

'What the fuck are you doing up here?' Cochrane growled as they came to the open portal.

'Nash sent me to tell you guys that the Nazis are down in the village. They jammed our radios so we lost contact with you. They're sending men up here now. Nash said to tell you *not* to come back down to the village, but rather to get out of here some other way and get in contact with the air support team and get them to pick you up from somewhere in the mountains—'

At that moment, a burst of supermachine-gun fire raked the stone walls of the portal all around them. The four of them ducked quickly as a devastating line of bullets strafed the portal's frame, shredding its solid stone walls as if they were made of plaster.

Race snapped round instantly and saw about twelve Nazi commandos in the trees at the edge of the clearing, firing hard with their G-11s.

Cochrane returned fire from the cover of the portal. Van Lewen did the same. The *crack* of their M-16s sounded almost pathetic alongside the relentless droning *whirrrrr* of the ultra-high-tech G-11s.

Race also tried to return the Nazis' fire, but when he pulled the trigger of his M-16, nothing happened.

Cochrane saw him, reached out and yanked back on a T-shaped handle on Race's rifle.

'Christ, you're about as useless as a priest in a whorehouse,' Cochrane barked.

Race pulled the trigger again and, this time, a stream of bullets erupted from his M-16, almost dislocating his shoulder with the force of the recoil.

'What the hell are we gonna do!' Reichart yelled above their gunfire.

'We can't stay here!' Van Lewen yelled. 'We have to get back to the rope—'

At that moment there came a sudden, resounding *voooom*! from somewhere above their heads.

Race looked up just in time to see a black MD-500 'Mosquito' light-attack helicopter explode out from the fog above them and roar over the tower top.

The Mosquito was a nimble little attack chopper— much smaller than any Apache or Comanche—but what it lacked in grunt and firepower, it more than made up for in speed and manoeuvrability.

Its nickname came from its resemblance to certain members of the insect world. It had a round split-glass bubble that resembled the wide hemispherical eyes of a bee, and two long spindly landing struts that looked like the elongated legs of a mosquito.

The Mosquito above the tower top loosed a burst of gunfire from its two side-mounted cannons, chewing up a pair of long unbroken lines in the mud in front of the temple.

'This is getting worse!' Race yelled.

Down in the village, the explosives that the Nazis had placed underneath the ATV went off.

A billowing fireball erupted beneath the big eight-wheeled vehicle—lifting it fully ten feet off the ground, flipping it in mid-air—and the massive ATV came crashing down on its side.

Inside it, the world went crazy.

As soon as they had heard the Nazis attaching their explosives to the bottom of the vehicle, Nash, Renée and Schroeder had strapped themselves into some seats and braced themselves for the explosion.

Now they hung perpendicular to the ground, still strapped into their seats, their world turned completely sideways.

But the important thing was that the ATV had held.

For the moment.

Doogie Kennedy peered out fearfully from the roof of the citadel.

He saw the village laid out before him, shrouded in mist and fog—saw about a dozen Nazi commandos standing at regular intervals in the cloudy grey soup, their G-11s pointed outwards.

He had just seen the ATV get blasted and he thanked God that the Nazis hadn't realised that there were more members of Nash's team inside the citadel. Its walls wouldn't be able to survive such a ferocious blast.

And then suddenly he heard a shout—someone barking orders in German.

Doogie didn't know much German, so nearly all of the words meant nothing to him. But then, strangely, amid all the gabble, he heard two words that he *did* know: '*das Sprengkommando*'.

Doogie froze when he heard the words. Then he snapped around in horror as he saw four Nazi commandos hurry off in the direction of the river in response to the command.

He didn't know much German, but a stint at a NATO missile facility outside of Hamburg had provided him with at least a basic vocabulary of commonly used German military terms.

'*Das Sprengkommando*' was one of those terms.

It was German for 'demolition team'.

From the cover of the portal, Van Lewen fired a grenade from his M-203 launcher. A second later, an explosion blew out from the trees near the Nazi positions, showering the area with mud and leaves.

'Sergeant!' Cochrane yelled.

'What!'

'We're fucked if we keep this up! They've got too much firepower! They'll just stay out of sight until we run out of ammo and then we'll be trapped inside this fucking temple! We have to get off this rock!'

'I'm open to suggestions!' Van Lewen yelled.

'*You're* the sarge, Sarge,' Cochrane shouted back.

'All right, then,' Van Lewen frowned. He thought for a moment, then said, 'The only way off this tower is the rope bridge, right?'

'Right,' Reichart replied.

'So somehow we have to get back to that bridge, right?'

'Right.'

Van Lewen said, 'I say we skirt round the back of this temple and go down to the edge of the tower top. Then we hack our way through the foliage back to the rope bridge. We cross the bridge and then we drop it behind us, trapping these assholes on the tower.'

'Sounds like a plan,' Reichart yelled.

'Then let's do it,' Van Lewen said decisively.

The Green Berets readied themselves for the dash out of the temple's doorway. Race just tried to stay close to them—whatever the hell they did.

'Okay . . .' Van Lewen said. '*Now!*'

And with that the four of them burst out from the entrance to the temple, their guns blazing, and raced out into the rain.

Their guns roared.

The Nazis in the treeline ducked.

Van Lewen and Reichart turned the corner first, headed towards the rear of the temple.

Seconds later, they rounded the rear corner—so that they were now shaded by the temple from the Nazis' fire—and found themselves standing on the flat stone path at the peak of the muddy slope that Race had seen earlier, the path that contained the unusual circular stone.

The slope beneath them was completely covered in mud and it stretched steeply down and away from them for about fifteen metres, ending at a small rocky ledge that formed the very edge of the tower top—a ledge that overlooked a sheer three-hundred-foot drop. To the left of the ledge, however, was a stand of thick trees and foliage—foliage that led back to the rope bridge.

Cochrane and Race rounded the corner behind the others. They both saw the steep muddy slope instantly.

'I think this is gonna be harder than we expected,' Cochrane said to Van Lewen.

Just then, like a shark rising from the depths of the ocean, the Mosquito attack helicopter burst up out of the fog beneath the ledge and hovered right in front of the four Americans, its side-mounted cannons spewing forth a devastating wave of gunfire.

Everyone dived for the ground.

Tex Reichart moved too slowly. The fusillade of bullets ripped into his body mercilessly—one after the other after the other—keeping him upright long after he was dead. With every shot that went into him, star-shaped explosions of blood sprayed out onto the wet stone wall behind him.

Buzz Cochrane took two hits to the leg, shouted in agony. Race hit the mud hard—unscathed—covered his ears against the roar of the helicopter's fire. Van

Lewen just fired fearlessly back at the Mosquito with his M-16 until finally in the face of his relentless fire, the helicopter banked away and Reichart's body—released from its grip—fell face-down into the mud with a loud splat.

Unfortunately, Reichart had been holding the idol.

As his body hit the ground, the idol in his hand was instantly dislodged. It bounced to the ground and immediately began to slide down the steep muddy embankment . . . toward the edge.

Race saw it first.

'No!' he yelled, diving forward, landing on his belly, sliding quickly down the muddy slope after it.

Van Lewen yelled, 'Professor! *Wait, no—!*'

But Race was already sliding fast through the mud, M-16 and all, heading straight for the idol.

Eight feet away.

Five feet.

Three feet.

And then suddenly the Mosquito returned and let fly with another burst of machine-gun fire and a line of exploding impact craters shredded the mud *in between* Race and the idol.

Race reacted quickly. He reeled away from the bullet impacts, shielding his eyes from the flying mud—and abandoned his dive for the idol, shifting his weight so that he was now sliding down the slope, away from the ragged line of impact craters.

He saw the ledge at the bottom of the embankment rapidly approaching him—saw the sheer drop beyond it, saw the black Mosquito hovering above it—but he was sliding too fast, too quickly, and then suddenly, before he even knew what was happening, he was shooting out over the edge of the rock tower into clear open space three hundred feet above the bottom of the canyon.

As he went over, Race shot out a hand and caught the lip of the ledge.

He came to a jarring halt as he hung one-handed from the edge of the ledge, three hundred feet above the bottom of the crater!

The roaring downdraft of the Mosquito helicopter above him blasted against the top of his Yankees cap as he threw his spare hand—the hand still holding his M-16—up onto the ledge and began to haul himself up.

Whatever you do, Will, don't look down.

He looked down.

The sheer side of the rock tower stretched away from him into darkness. The rain just seemed to fall away into it, disappearing into the impenetrable grey mist.

With a heaving grunt, Race got his elbows up onto the ledge and hauled himself onto it and looked up just in time to see Van Lewen—with Cochrane draped over his shoulder—hurrying off into the stand of trees to his right.

He also saw the Nazis—all twelve of them, all armed with G-11s—as they came swarming around the temple from both sides in perfect unison.

They saw the idol instantly, sitting on its side halfway down the steep muddy slope.

They fanned out quickly, taking up covering positions while a single man cautiously sidestepped his way down the embankment to retrieve the idol from its resting place.

The Nazi arrived at the idol. Grabbed it.

Race could have sworn.

But he never got the chance to, because at that precise moment one of the Nazis looked up and saw him—hanging half-off the ledge, staring up at them with wide frightened eyes.

The Nazis brought their G-11s up as one, all aimed squarely at Race's forehead, and as they all reached for their triggers, Race did the only thing he could think to do.

He let himself fall.

Race fell.

Fast.

Down the side of the rock tower.

He saw the uneven surface of the tower's wall rushing past him at phenomenal speed. He looked up and saw the ledge that he had fallen off receding into the grey sky even faster.

His mind reeled.

I can't believe I just did that! Stay calm, stay calm, you did it because you knew you could get out of this.

Right.

As he fell, Race quickly brought his M-16 round in his hands.

You are not going to die.

You are not going to die.

He tried to recall how Van Lewen had fired his grappling hook across the chasm earlier. Now how had he done it? He had pulled a *second* trigger on his gun to fire the hook, a trigger that had been situated underneath his M-16's barrel.

Still falling.

Race peered frantically at his weapon, searched for the second—

There!

He immediately raised his M-16 and aimed it at the rapidly receding tower top above him. Then he jammed his finger down on the second trigger.

With a loud, puncture-like *whump!* the silver grappling hook shot out from the grenade launcher of his gun, its silver claws opening in mid-air with a sharp *snick-snick!*

Race fell downwards.

The grappling hook shot upwards, its nylon rope wobbling through the air behind it.

Still falling.

The hook flew over the edge of the tower top.

Still falling.

Race held his M-16 tightly. Then he just shut his eyes and waited—waited for the jolt of his rope or the impact with the lake, whichever came first.

The jolt came first.

In an instant, the grappling hook's rope went taut and Race came to a sudden, jarring halt.

It felt as if his arms had just been wrenched out of their sockets, but somehow he managed to keep hold of the M-16.

Race opened his eyes.

And found himself hanging from the rope about a hundred feet below the edge of the tower top.

He hung there in silence for a full thirty seconds, breathing hard, shaking his head. No Nazis appeared on the ledge high above him. They must have left the embankment as soon as they had seen him fall.

Race sighed deeply with relief. Then he set about the task of hauling himself back up to the tower's peak.

Up on the tower top, Van Lewen was hacking his way through the foliage, using his Bowie knife as a machete.

Moments earlier, he had also seen the Nazis get the idol, and now he was trying desperately to get back to the rope bridge before they did.

It was at the extreme southern edge of the tower's peak, and now he and the wounded Cochrane were making their way toward it, forging a path through the brush on the tower's south-western flank.

The Nazis were taking the more direct route, heading back to the bridge via the clearing and the stone stairway.

Van Lewen hacked away a final branch and abruptly he and Cochrane were met by the sight of the rope bridge, majestically spanning the chasm between the tower top and the outer path.

The great swooping bridge was about fifteen yards away from them—and right now, the dozen or so Nazi troops who had assailed them at the portal were crossing it, arriving at the path on the other side.

Damn it, Van Lewen thought, *they'd beaten him to the bridge!*

Van Lewen stared at one of the Nazis as he stepped up onto solid ground on the other side of the ravine. He was holding something cradled in his arms—something covered in a ragged purple cloth.

The idol.

Shit.

It was then that the Nazis on the other side of the ravine did the one thing that Van Lewen feared the most—the one thing he had intended to do himself if he had reached the rope bridge first.

They unlooped the bridge from its foundations and they let it fall.

The great bridge fell down into the ravine. It was still attached to its foundations on the tower side of the chasm, so it didn't fall all the way down to the bottom, rather it just ended up falling flat against the side of the rock tower, its retrieval rope trailing down into the impenetrable fog beneath it.

Van Lewen stared in a kind of helpless frustration at the squad of Nazis hustling down the path on the other side of the chasm, carrying the idol in their midst.

They had the idol.

While he was now stranded on the rock tower.

Heinrich Anistaze stood in the centre of Vilcafor with his hands on his hips. He was pleased with the way the assault on the village had gone.

The pulse generator had worked perfectly, cutting off any radio communication between the enemy. The Americans in the ATV had been neutralised with ease. And now he had just heard that his assault squad had successfully retrieved the idol from the Americans up at the temple.

Things were going very well indeed.

There came a shout and Anistaze turned to see the tower squad come charging out from the riverside path.

The leader of the squad immediately came up to him and presented him with a cloth-enwrapped object.

'Herr Obergruppenführer,' the man said formally. 'The idol.'

Anistaze smiled.

Once he had managed to climb back up his grappling hook's rope, Race dashed across the now-deserted clearing in front of the temple, searching for the Green Berets, if any of them were still alive.

He found Van Lewen and Cochrane at the ledge which had once held up the rope bridge.

'Son of a bitch,' he said as he saw the yawning chasm in front of them. 'They cut the bridge.'

'There's no way off this thing,' Van Lewen said. 'We're stuck here.'

Just then the black Mosquito helicopter came roaring past them again, its side-mounted cannons blazing. The Nazis must have left it behind to finish the job.

Race and the others immediately dived for cover in the brush. Leaves exploded above their heads, tree trunks shattered into splinters.

'Fuck a duck!' Cochrane yelled over the roar of the gunfire.

Race peered out at the Mosquito chopper as it hovered above the chasm, long tongues of fire spewing out from its guns, its long spindly landing skids dangling beneath its body.

The landing skids . . . he thought.

And at that moment, something inside Race clicked—a kind of fierce determination that he had never known he possessed.

'Van Lewen!' he called suddenly.

'What!'

'Give me some cover fire!'

'What for?'

'Just get that chopper to hover a little higher, will you! But don't scare it off!'

'What are you doing?'

'I'm getting us off this rock!'

That was good enough for Van Lewen. A second later, he snapped out from behind the foliage and loosed a volley of fire at the hovering black chopper.

The Mosquito responded by rising a little higher in the air and firing back.

Meanwhile, Race was working feverishly with his grappling hook, unspooling its rope. He looked out at the chopper.

'Get it higher!' he yelled. 'Higher! It's too low!'

Race gauged the distance between him and the chopper.

It was too close to *fire* the grappling hook from its launcher. He was going to have to throw it.

He unspooled the rope a little more, keeping it loose so that when he did throw it, it wouldn't get all tangled up.

'Cochrane!' he shouted. 'Can you swing with that busted leg of yours?'

'What do you think, Einstein?'

'Then you're no good to me!' Race said fiercely. 'You're staying here. Van Lewen! Give me cover!'

Then, as Van Lewen loosed another burst at the chopper, Race quickly leapt out of the foliage with the grappling hook hanging from his hand, and in one fluid motion he threw it, underhanded, out at the Mosquito's left-hand landing skid.

He knew as soon as he did it that he'd weighted the throw perfectly.

The grappling hook sailed through the air toward the hovering helicopter, reaching the zenith of its arc just as it arrived at the Mosquito's left landing skid, and then—with a sharp *clink-clink*—the hook swung *over* the landing strut and looped itself around it twice, clinging to it.

'All right, Van Lewen! Let's go!'

Van Lewen let off a final burst of fire at the chopper before he ran over and joined Race at the edge of the ledge.

'Grab on,' Race offered Van Lewen his M-16. The gun was tied to the end of the grappling hook's rope.

Van Lewen took it and gave Race a look. 'You know, you're a lot braver than most people would give you credit for.'

'Thanks.'

And with that, Race and Van Lewen pushed themselves off the ledge and swung—together—across the wide one-hundred-foot chasm, in a wonderful graceful arc, suspended from the landing skid of the hovering attack helicopter!

'*Motherfucker . . .*' Buzz Cochrane said as he watched the two of them swing away from him across the bottomless ravine.

Race and Van Lewen swung up onto the path on the other side of the chasm, onto their feet. Once they were up, Race quickly disengaged the grappling hook's rope from his M-16 and let it go.

The chopper above them didn't seem to know where they had gone—it just wheeled around wildly above the gorge, firing its guns in frustration, shooting at anything and nothing, while Race and Van Lewen took off down the spiralling path, heading back toward the village.

Heinrich Anistaze held the cloth-enclosed package in his hands, held his breath as he unwrapped it.

'Yes,' he said as he revealed the glistening black idol beneath the cloth. '*Yes . . .*'

Then abruptly he spun on his heel and began walking toward the eastern log-bridge.

'Demolition team,' he called in German as he walked, 'are those chlorine charges set yet?'

'Three more minutes, Herr Obergruppenführer,' a man called from over near the battered ATV.

'Then you've taken three minutes too long,' Anistaze barked. 'Finish laying them and then meet us at the river.'

'Yes, Obergruppenführer.'

Anistaze keyed his radio. 'Herr Oberstgruppenführer? Do you read me?' *Oberstgruppenführer* was the highest of all the SS ranks—General.

'*Yes,*' came the reply.

'We have it.'

'*Bring it to me.*'

'Yes, Oberstgruppenführer. At once,' Anistaze said as he strode across the eastern log-bridge and plunged into the rainforest.

Race and Van Lewen ran down the spiralling path.

They came to the bottom of the crater, hit the fissure, bolted down its length. Then along the riverside path, guns up. Mist everywhere.

As Race ran down the path, his radio earpiece suddenly burst to life:

'—*an Lewen, report. Repeat. Cochrane, Reichart, Van Lewen, report*—'

It was Nash. Their radios were working again. The Nazis must have turned off their jamming system, or at least taken it out of range.

Van Lewen spoke as he ran. 'Colonel, this is Van Lewen. We've lost Reichart and Cochrane is wounded. But the Nazis have the idol. Repeat. *The Nazis have the idol.* I have Professor Race with me now. We're on our way back to the village.'

'*You lost the idol?*'

'Yes.'

'*Get it back,*' was all Nash said.

Race and Van Lewen came to the western log-bridge. They stepped cautiously over it, guns up.

The village was deserted, cloaked in fog. No Nazis in sight. No rapas either.

Immediately in front of them, they saw the dark shape of the ATV turned up on its side. To their left, they could see the shadows of the various buildings of Vilcafor rising out of the fog.

Van Lewen took a step toward the ATV.

'Colonel . . . ?' he said.

He was answered by gunfire—G-11 gunfire from the three-man Nazi demolition squad who had been left behind in the village to plant Anistaze's chlorine charges.

Race dived left, Van Lewen dived right, both of them raising their M-16s, but it was no use. They couldn't see a thing in this mist.

Race clambered back to his feet just as he saw a Nazi commando burst around the side of the ATV, his G-11 raised and ready.

Then suddenly—*bam!*—a loud, single gunshot rang out from somewhere behind Race and the Nazi's head just snapped backwards in a spray of blood and all Race could do was stare in stunned awe as his assailant fell to the ground, dead.

'What the—' he turned in the direction of the gunshot.

Suddenly a rapa burst out of the fog right in front of him, bared its teeth and leapt at his throat—

Bam!

The rapa jolted sideways in mid-flight as it was hit in the side of the head by another speeding bullet—killed instantly. The big animal's carcass slid to a halt inches away from Race's feet.

What the hell was going on!

'Professor!' Doogie's voice cut through the mist. 'Over here! Come on! I've got you covered!'

Squinting through the fog, Race caught a glimpse of the roof of the citadel, and there—perched on top of it with a sniper rifle pressed against his shoulder—he saw the silhouette of Doogie Kennedy.

From his position on the roof of the great stone fortress, Doogie had a great view of the village.

Through the thermal sights of his M-82A1A sniper rifle, he could see everyone in the town as if it were daytime. Each figure appeared on his scope as a multi-coloured blob—from the vaguely human-shaped blobs

337

of Race, Van Lewen and the two remaining members of the German demolition team, to the trapezoidal but heatless shape of the ATV; to the ominous, four-legged shapes of the cats.

The cats.

With the disappearance of the Nazi troops and their weaponry, the cats were now free to move throughout the village again.

They were back. And they were looking for blood.

Race spun where he stood, saw Van Lewen standing over by the upturned ATV.

'Professor, get out of here!' the Green Beret sergeant yelled. 'Doogie'll cover you! I've got to get this thing upright again!'

Race didn't have to be told twice. He immediately hurried off through the village, surrounded by fog. As soon as he did so, however, he heard quick muddy footsteps splashing through the greyness behind him.

Getting closer, gaining on him.

And then suddenly—*bam-smack-splat*.

It was the sound of another of Doogie's gunshots—*bam*—followed by the sound of the bullet smacking into one of the Nazis—*smack*—followed by the sound of the Nazi hitting the ground—*splat*.

Another rapa slid out in front of him, prepared to pounce—*bam!*—its head just exploded, nailed by Doogie. The rapa's body began to convulse. *Bam! Bam! Bam! Bam! Bam!* The body went still.

Race couldn't believe it.

It was like navigating your way through a fog-enshrouded maze while being protected by a guardian angel. All he could do was just keep running—keep moving forward—while Doogie took care of the dangers all around him, dangers which he himself couldn't see.

He heard more muddy footsteps—heavier this time—the four-legged variety.

Bam.

Smack.

Splat.

Up on the citadel, Doogie swore.

That last hit had run him dry. He was out of ammo. He ducked behind the parapet and frantically began to reload.

Over by the river, Van Lewen hung from the underside of the upturned ATV, heaving on it with all his weight, conscious of the fact that there were rapas out there in the mist behind him.

'Get your weight up higher!' he called to Nash and the others inside the vehicle. 'We've got to tip it over!'

They moved instantly and almost immediately the ATV—already precariously balanced on its side—began to tip over.

Van Lewen quickly scurried out of its way, just as—*whump*—the big eight-wheeler landed on its tyres and he hurried for the door on its side.

Race was still running hard through the mist when suddenly, like a curtain being drawn to reveal a stage, the veil of fog before him parted and he beheld the citadel.

It was then that he heard the *clack-clack* of a safety being released on a G-11 somewhere nearby and he froze—and slowly turned—and saw the last Nazi commando standing in the fog behind him, his G-11 aimed squarely at Race's head.

Race waited for the now-familiar report of Doogie's sniper rifle. But it never came.

Why wasn't he firing anymore?

And then abruptly there came an almighty roar, which Race translated as the roar of one of the cats.

But it wasn't the roar of a cat.

It was the roar of an *engine*.

The next instant, the ATV came exploding out of the mist and slammed into the Nazi commando's back.

The Nazi fell, crushed beneath the big all-terrain vehicle, and even Race himself had to dive out of the way as the ATV rumbled past him and skidded to a halt in front of the citadel—stopping right in front of the fortress's entrance, aligning itself so that its sliding left-hand door opened flush onto the citadel's doorway.

A second later, Race saw the rear hatch of the ATV pop open and Van Lewen's head appear.

'Hey, Professor, you coming or what?'

Race leapt up onto the back of the vehicle and dived head-first into its hatch. No sooner was he inside than Van Lewen slammed the steel hatch shut behind him with a loud resounding thud.

'They got the idol,' Van Lewen said, sitting on the floor of the citadel, surrounded by the others, in the half-light of their flashlights. The open door of the ATV was behind him, completely filling the wide stone doorway of the citadel.

'*Fuck*,' Lauren said. 'If they get that thyrium to a workable Supernova we're screwed . . .'

'What are we going to do?' Johann Krauss said.

'We're going to get it back,' Nash said flatly.

'But how?' Troy Copeland said.

'We have to go after them now,' Van Lewen said. 'They're at their most vulnerable *right now*. They came here to grab the idol and then, presumably, take it back to wherever it is they're keeping their Supernova. But on a snatch-and-grab mission like the one they just pulled, you're at your most vulnerable when you're in transit from the target objective.'

'So where is their home base?'

'It has to be close,' Race said firmly, surprising everyone with his conviction, including himself. 'Judging by the way they got here.'

'And how exactly did they get here, Professor?' Copeland said disbelievingly.

'I don't know for sure,' Race said, 'but I think I can

make a pretty good guess. *One*, they got here using a method of transport that avoided detection by your fancy SAT-SN network, so they didn't fly. *Two*, aside from flying and travelling on foot, what's the quickest and easiest way to get a force of about thirty men through the rainforest?'

'Oh, *damn*, why didn't I think of that . . .' Lauren said.

'What?' Copeland said irritably.

'The rivers,' she said.

'Exactly,' Race said. 'They came here by boat. Which means their base of operations can't be too far aw—' He cut himself off.

'So where is it?' Nash said. 'Where is their base of operations?'

But Race wasn't listening. Something had just clicked in the back of his mind.

Base of operations . . .

Where had he heard those words before?

'Professor Race?' Nash said.

No, wait. He hadn't *heard* them at all.

He had *seen* them.

And then suddenly it hit him.

'Lauren, do we still have that telephone transcript here? The one with the Nazis' ransom demand on it. The telephone conversation that the BKA intercepted between a cellular phone somewhere in Peru and Colonia Alemania.'

Lauren spun and immediately began rummaging through the equipment in the darkened citadel.

'Got it.' She handed a sheet of paper to him.

Race looked at the transcript that he'd seen earlier.

VOICE 1:   ---ase of operations has been established---
             rest of the---will be---mine---

VOICE 2: ---about the device?---ready?

VOICE 1: ---have adopted hourglass formation based on the American model---two thermonuclear detonators mounted above and below a titanium-alloy inner chamber. Field tests indicate that---device---operational. All we need now---the thyrium.

VOICE 2: ---don't worry, Anistaze's taking care of that---

VOICE 1: What about the message?

VOICE 2: ---will go out as soon as we get the idol---to every Prime Minister and President in the EU---plus the President of the United States via internal emergency hotline---ransom will be one hundred billion dollars U.S.---or else we detonate the device . . .

Race's eyes zeroed in on the first two lines of the transcript.

VOICE 1: ---ase of operations has been established---rest of the---will be---mine---

'Will be mine . . .' Race said aloud. 'Mine . . . the mine.'

He turned to Lauren. 'What was the name of that abandoned goldmine we saw from the Huey on our way here? The one that was all lit up? The one that didn't look all that abandoned anymore.'

'The *Madre de Dios* goldmine,' Lauren said.

'Is it situated on a river?'

'Yes, on the Alto Purus. Nearly all the open-cut mines in the Amazon are situated on rivers, because seaplanes and boats are the only way to get the gold out of here.'

343

'How far away is it from here?'

'I don't know. Sixty, seventy miles.'

Race turned to Nash. 'That's where they're going, Colonel. The *Madre de Dios* goldmine. By boat.'

Heinrich Anistaze crashed through the undergrowth, forging his way eastward until at last he pushed aside the final branch and was confronted by a truly spectacular sight.

The Amazon rainforest spread out before him like a lush green carpet running all the way to the horizon.

Anistaze was standing at the edge of the tableland—at the top of a sheer, foliage-covered cliff that overlooked the rainforest. To his immediate right was a magnificent two-hundred-foot waterfall that flowed out over the tableland, the end product of the caiman-infested river that ran alongside Vilcafor.

Anistaze ignored the waterfall.

Of more importance to him was what lay at its base, in the wide section of river down there.

He smiled at the sight.

Yes . . .

Then, with the idol under his arm, he quickly began to climb down the set of ropes that snaked their way up the cliff-face, heading down to the river.

'All right, then,' Copeland said, 'so how are we going to catch these bastards? They've got a fifteen-minute head-start on us and just in case anyone has forgotten, there are rapas out there—'

'If their boats are where I think they are, then there's another way to get to them,' Race said. 'A route that avoids having to go past the cats.'

344

'What route?' Nash asked.

Race immediately dropped to his knees and began sweeping his hands across the earthen floor of the citadel.

'What are you doing?'

'I'm looking for something.'

'What?'

Race searched the floor for it. According to the manuscript, it should be here somewhere. The only question was whether or not the Incas had used the same symbol to mark it—

'*This,*' he said suddenly, as he swept his hand across the earthen floor and revealed a stone slab beneath the thin layer of mud and dirt.

Inscribed in the corner of the slab was a symbol—a circle with a double 'V' in it.

'Here, help me,' he said.

Van Lewen and Doogie came over, got a hold of the slab and heaved on it.

The slab rumbled against its neighbours as it slowly slid out of its resting place—revealing an inky black hole beneath it.

'It's the quenko,' Race said.

'The what?' Nash said.

'I read about it in the manuscript. It was a maze dug into the rock beneath the village, an escape route, a tunnel system that leads to the waterfall at the edge of the tableland—if you know the key to the maze.'

'And you know that key?'

'Yes, I do.'

'How?' Troy Copeland asked mockingly.

'Because I've read the manuscript,' Race said.

'So who goes?' Lauren said.

'Van Lewen and Kennedy,' Nash said. 'And anyone else who can carry a gun,' he added, looking at the two

BKA agents and the German paratrooper, Molke. Renée, Schroeder and Molke all nodded.

Nash turned to Copeland. 'What about you, Troy?'

'I've never held a gun in my life,' Copeland said.

'All right, then. Looks like it's just you five—'

'I can handle a gun,' Race said.

'What?' Lauren said.

'*You?*' Copeland said.

'Well,' Race shrugged, 'some guns. My brother used to bring them home all the time. I'm not all that good at it, but—'

'Professor Race can run with me any time,' Van Lewen said, stepping forward—exchanging a look with Race—and handing him a spare SIG-Sauer pistol. 'Judging from what he did up on the rock tower.'

He turned to Nash. 'Is that it then, sir?'

Nash nodded. 'Do whatever you have to do, *just get that idol*. Our air support should be here any minute now. As soon as they get here, I'll send them after you. If you can somehow get your hands on that idol and keep those Nazi bastards at bay for a while, the air support team should be able to get you out of there. You got that?'

'Got it,' Van Lewen said, grabbing his M-16. 'Then let's go.'

Van Lewen led the way, charging through one of the narrow stone passageways of the quenko beneath Vilcafor.

He held his M-16 pressed against his shoulder, illuminating the cramped tunnel in front of them with the tiny flashlight that was attached to its barrel.

Race, Doogie, Molke and the two BKA agents hurried along the dark stone passageway behind him. Doogie and the three Germans held M-16s in their hands. Race just carried the silver SIG-Sauer.

Although he didn't want to say it, Race was scared out of his mind. But he was where he wanted to be—with Van Lewen and Doogie and the Germans, going after the idol, going after the Nazis. *Doing* something.

The quenko, however, didn't help ease his mind.

It was like some horrific kind of dungeon—a nightmarish subterranean maze with close stone walls and slippery muddy floors.

Enormous hairy spiders scuttled away into dark crevices as the six of them hustled past, while obscenely fat snakes slithered through the stagnant mud on the tunnel floor, almost tripping them over. And it was claustrophobic—claustrophobic as hell—each slimy passageway that he saw was barely three feet wide.

Van Lewen ran quickly in the lead.

'Take the third tunnel on the right,' Race said from behind him. 'And then zigzag, starting with the left.'

At exactly the same time as Race and the others were dashing through the underground maze, Heinrich Anistaze was reaching the bottom of the tableland's cliff-face.

He strode over to the riverbank where he stepped straight into a rubber Zodiac speedboat.

He keyed his radio mike. 'Demolition team. Report.'

He received no reply.

Through the quenko they ran.

Running hard, running fast, ducking left, cutting right, bursting through spiderwebs, tripping over forty-foot snakes, stumbling through the slick moss-covered tunnels of the ghastly subterranean maze.

'Hey, Van Lewen,' Race said in between breaths as they jogged down a long section of tunnel.

'Yeah?' Van Lewen replied.

'What's the 80s Club?'

'The 80s Club?'

'Cochrane mentioned it last night while you guys were unpacking the choppers, but he wouldn't say what it was. I'd like to know what it is before I die.'

Van Lewen snorted as he ran. 'I can tell you, but it's pretty, uh, *unrefined*.'

'Try me.'

'Okay . . .' Van Lewen said. 'It goes like this. To become a member of the 80s Club, you must have had sex with a girl who was born in the 1980s.'

'Oh, *man!*' Race said, cringing.

'I told you it was unrefined,' Van Lewen said.

They ran on.

The six of them had been running for about seven minutes through the quenko when—abruptly—Van Lewen turned a corner and slammed into a solid stone wall.

Only it wasn't a wall at all.

It was a doorstone.

In fact, it was a doorstone not unlike the one in the doorway of the citadel itself—a square-shaped boulder with a rounded base that could be easily rolled open from the inside, but which was impregnable from without.

Race and Van Lewen rolled the boulder aside—

—and they were instantly assailed by the roar of a mighty waterfall.

A light spray of water hit their faces as they were confronted by the sight of a curtain of falling water not ten feet in front of them.

Race scanned the area around them.

They were standing on a path—an Incan path—carved into the rockwall *behind* the waterfall.

They were at the edge of the tableland already.

The roar of the surging waterfall above them was incredible. It drowned out all other sound. Van Lewen had to shout over it to be heard.

'This way!' he yelled, hurrying left.

The rocky path was wet and slippery, but Race and the others managed to keep their footing as they hustled along its length behind the falling curtain of water.

Even though they moved quickly, it still took them a full minute to reach the edge of the curtain—the waterfall above them was wide, and they had emerged from the quenko at its very centre.

Van Lewen came out onto solid ground first, skidded to a halt on the muddy riverbank. 'Holy shit,' he said.

'What is it?' Race asked as he came alongside him and looked out at the river.

The first thing he saw was Heinrich Anistaze's little Zodiac speedboat, cutting a ribbon of wash as it sped away from them into the wider waters of the river proper.

'What are you talking about?' he asked.

And then he saw the other boats.

'*Holy* shit.'

It looked like a veritable armada.

There must have been at least twenty boats out there on the wide brown river at the base of the water-fall. Boats of all shapes and sizes.

Five long-bodied shallow-draught assault boats sped around the perimeter of the fleet. They were Rigid Raiders—sleek, open-topped aluminium-hulled attack craft commonly used by the SAS for high-speed raiding.

Four Vietnam-era military patrol boats known as 'Pibbers' cruised casually alongside some of the larger boats near the centre of the armada. Pibbers were superfast 35-foot gunboats fitted with armour plating, turret-mounted 20mm machine-guns and side-mounted torpedo pods. Their name was a serviceman's abbreviation of their official designation PBR (Patrol Boat River), and although the Pibber was already well known for its exploits in Vietnam, it had been immortalised in the Hollywood movie *Apocalypse Now*.

Three massive helicopter landing barges surged along the river inside the circle of attack boats. On the helipads of two of the barges sat Mosquito light-attack helicopters. The chopper that had been up on the tower top earlier was in the process of landing on the third barge's helipad right now.

Trailing behind the middle helipad barge, however—and looking remarkably out of place alongside the three ultra-high-tech Mosquitos—was a rather battered-looking little seaplane.

It was a Grumman JRF-5 'Goose', a compact twin-propellered riverplane that dated back to the Second World War.

The Grumman Goose was a very distinctive little plane, classic in its design. From the side, its bow was roughly the same shape as a labrador's snout—short and flat-topped but rounded at the waterline. It sat in the water on its belly with two stabilising pontoons hanging down from its outstretched wings. Notably, the Goose had two methods of entry, a side door and a pop-up hatch in the nose.

This Goose, however, also packed a punch—a light-weight twin-barrelled 20mm Gatling gun had been affixed to its left-hand flank.

In the centre of the Nazi fleet sat the armada's focal point—and the destination of Anistaze's Zodiac—an enormous white catamaran.

The command boat.

It looked magnificent, sleek in the extreme, at least 150 feet long. Its two massive hulls were painted pristine white while its sharply slanting windows were tinted jet black. Sonar arrays rotated atop its roof. A dazzling white Bell Jet Ranger helicopter sat on the helipad that made up the stern of the giant craft.

In addition to the helicopter, rocking in the water alongside the big catamaran, tied to it, was the meanest-looking speedboat Race had ever seen. It, too, was painted white, the same colour as the command boat and the helicopter—a matching set. It sat low in the water and it had an ultra-long hull that tapered sharply to a point at the bow. A backward-slanting spoiler arched over the driver's seat—an aerodynamic precaution designed to prevent the high-powered speedboat from being lifted off the river's surface while it flew across the water at top speed. Race saw the word 'SCARAB' painted across its side.

Scooting around the whole motley fleet—cutting thin ribbons of white wash behind them—were about six Jet Raiders: small one-man assault vehicles not unlike regular jet-skis.

But they were longer than normal jet-skis—maybe nine feet from tip to tail. And they were sleeker, meaner, *faster*. They had saddle-like seats and bullet-shaped noses, and they all sat high in the water as they moved, with only the back half of their hulls touching the water's surface as they skimmed lightly across it, whipping around the larger boats.

Race and the others watched as Anistaze's Zodiac reached the command boat and the notorious Nazi field commander climbed aboard. Immediately, the big white catamaran began to power up. As it did so, the rest of the fleet began to move out.

'They're leaving!' Doogie shouted.

'*There!*' Van Lewen said, spotting three abandoned Jet Raiders lying on the riverbank not far from the waterfall—left there, no doubt, by the members of the Nazi demolition team.

'Come on,' Van Lewen said.

The six of them raced for the three Jet Raiders.

The river's surface raced by beneath them.

The three stolen Jet Raiders kicked up spectacular sprays of white behind them as they raced side by side across the water in pursuit of the Nazi armada.

Race rode double with Van Lewen. He drove while the Green Beret sat behind him like a pillion passenger on a motorcycle, with one hand wrapped around Race's waist, the other holding his M-16 ready to fire.

Doogie Kennedy skimmed across the water to their right, riding double with the German paratrooper Molke, while Renée and Schroeder shot along the river's surface to their left—Renée driving, Schroeder riding shotgun.

The Nazi armada was about three hundred yards ahead of them, powering quickly along the wide brown river—looking a lot like a carrier battle group, with the big command boat in the centre, surrounded by Rigid Raiders and Pibbers.

The three helipad barges trailed behind the other boats, bringing up the rear, while the little Jet Raiders just ducked and weaved madly in between all the larger boats like flies around a rubbish heap.

Race rode hard, wind and water pounding against his face. Out of the corner of his eye he saw the trees along the river's edge racing past him in a blur of green, saw the odd stray log floating on the surface next to him.

Don't hit the logs, Will. Don't hit the logs . . .

And then he realised.

They weren't logs.

They were caimans.

Don't hit the caimans, Will. Don't hit the caimans . . .

'Van Lewen!' he yelled above the roaring wind. 'What's the plan?'

'Easy! We take the command boat, we get the idol, then we hold the boat until the air support arrives!'

'We take the command boat . . .'

'Once we get it, we can hold it.'

'Whatever you say,' Race yelled.

Up ahead, the Nazi armada rounded a bend in the river and disappeared from Race's view. From above, the Alto Purus River looked like the undulating body of a snake, a neverending series of twisting bends and turns.

'All right, everybody,' Van Lewen said into his throat mike. 'See those trees up ahead. That's where we're going.'

Race looked forward and saw that the bend in the river that the Nazis had just rounded was comprised of a thick outcropping of trees. As he looked at the outcropping more closely, however, he noticed something odd about it—there was no dirt or soil at the base of the trees situated there. It looked as if the trees simply rose up out of the water.

Then he realised. It was the rainy season, and with the advent of the annual rains, the water levels of the rivers in the Amazon Basin rose dramatically. The land upon which that outcropping of trees stood was deeply submerged—a flooded forest.

Which meant that someone travelling on a small rivercraft like a Jet Raider might be able to wend their way *through* the trees, rather than going *around* the natural bend in the river.

Doogie's Jet Raider shot into the treeline—Race's right behind it—Renée's close behind.

Tree trunks whipped past them on either side, blurring with motion.

The three Jet Raiders shot through the maze of thick dark trees—banking left, leaning right, skimming lightly across the waves, their long flat hulls barely even touching the surface—while off to their left, through the flashing wall of tree trunks, they could make out the Nazi armada as it powered *around* the bend in the river.

Race tried desperately to concentrate as he drove. The speed at which they were travelling was utterly frightening.

It was so fast. So incredibly, *incredibly* fast!

Tree trunks whooshed past him at phenomenal speed. Wavelets streaked underneath the bow of his riverbike. So quickly were they travelling—so lightly and smoothly on the surface of the water—that he barely had to touch the handlebars of his bike in order to bank it left or right.

Race was sitting high in the saddle of his Jet Raider as he sped along behind Doogie's riverbike when suddenly he saw Doogie and Molke duck for apparently no reason. And then abruptly he saw why and he yelled, 'Van Lewen! *Duck!*' and the two of them yanked their bodies down just as a low-hanging branch whistled by over their heads.

'Thanks!' Van Lewen yelled.

'No problem!'

And then through the lattice of dark tree trunks

ahead of him he saw daylight. Heavy, grey, late-afternoon daylight.

'All right, everyone,' Van Lewen said. 'Arrowhead formation. Doogie and Molke, you take the lead. Agents Schroeder and Becker, you've got the left. Professor Race and I will cover the right. Okay, you all ready?' The big Green Beret raised his M-16 in one hand while he held onto Race with the other.

Up ahead, Race saw Doogie and Molke lift their own M-16s.

'*Ready,*' Doogie's voice came back.

The three Germans called in. '*Ready-Ready-Ready.*'

'Professor?'

'As ready as I'll ever be,' Race said.

'Then let's rock,' Van Lewen said.

The three American–German Jet Raiders burst out from the treeline in a perfect arrowhead formation *right alongside the Nazi armada* and in an instant Race found himself shooting across the water in the midst of four Nazi Jet Raiders!

The four Nazis turned as one to see the three American riverbikes, total surprise in their eyes. They reached for their guns just as Van Lewen called, 'Doogie! Take left!' and the two Green Berets let fly in *both* directions with simultaneous bursts of M-16 gunfire. The four Nazis were blasted off their riverbikes in an instant as the three stolen Jet Raiders whipped past them.

As he shot by the fallen Nazis, Race turned in his seat to see several sets of ripples cut a beeline through the water toward them.

The caimans . . .

And then suddenly a line of 20mm bullet holes raked the water on either side of his speeding Jet Raider and he was instantly snapped out of his trance.

He spun quickly and saw two attack boats—one Rigid Raider and one Pibber patrol boat—swing in quickly behind them, the Pibber firing wildly with its turret-mounted 20mm cannon.

Race gunned the accelerator and his riverbike surged forward. Behind him, Van Lewen swivelled around on the saddle so that he was now facing backwards, levelled his M-16 and opened fire on their pursuers.

His volley of machine-gun fire strafed both boats, cracking the windshield of the Pibber and nailing three of the four men on board the Rigid Raider.

Then, abruptly, the whole fleet veered left as it rounded another bend in the river.

'Everybody! Bank hard left!' Van Lewen yelled.

'*Left?*' Race shouted, confused.

'Through the trees again! We've got to get to that command boat!'

At that moment, more gunfire rang out all around them as two Nazi riverbikes swung in behind them.

Bullets flew everywhere, whizzed over Race's head, and then suddenly—*sprack!*—Race saw a hideous gout of blood splash out from Doogie's left shoulder as the young Green Beret was hit.

'*Arrrggghhh!*' Doogie's voice roared over the radio, but somehow he managed to keep up his speed.

Voom-voom-voom. The three American riverbikes shot into the treeline—Renée and Schroeder first, Doogie and Molke second, Race and Van Lewen last of all.

They were followed a split second later by the two Nazi bikes.

Bullets smacked against the tree trunks just above Race's head as he flew by them at phenomenal speed. Low-hanging branches rushed at him. Each time he saw one approaching, he yelled at Van Lewen—still facing backwards—and ordered him to duck.

Van Lewen was firing hard with his M-16 at the two Nazi riverbikes close behind them, but the Nazis found cover behind the trees, and after an extended burst of fire Van Lewen suddenly went dry.

Seeing the chance, the two Nazi Jet Raiders closed in.

One of them pulled up quickly alongside Race and Van Lewen's riverbike, sped along the water on their right-hand side, and the Nazi rider immediately drew a Glock from his saddlebag. With nothing else to call on, Van Lewen swung his empty M-16 like a baseball bat, hitting the Nazi's pistol clean out of his hand—just as the trees all around the two speeding Jet Raiders splintered violently under the weight of a burst of G-11 gunfire!

Van Lewen and Race ducked instantly as the second Nazi Jet Raider roared out of the trees to their *left* and slammed into the side of their riverbike.

Race was almost jolted out of his seat by the impact, but somehow he managed to hold on. He kept his speed up, banked quickly to avoid an onrushing tree. Then he glanced left, tried to get a look at his new assailant—

—and found himself staring into the barrel of a G-11 supermachine-gun.

Race looked up from the barrel and saw the face of its holder, grinning evilly, smiling with delight.

And then—*SMACK!*—the Nazi was crunched out of sight as his Jet Raider slammed at full speed into the centre of a thick black tree trunk and his riverbike exploded into a great billowing fireball.

Race's head whipped around.

It had happened so fast!

It was as if the tree had just swooped past them and collected the Nazi on its way by.

The other Nazi—the one immediately to their right—snapped round to look at the explosion too. Van

Lewen caught him looking and in one swift movement, M-16 in hand, he jumped across *onto the man's speeding Jet Raider*, landing on its saddle, right behind him!

The Nazi rider turned in surprise. As he did so, however, Van Lewen looked forward at the river ahead of them—and his eyes widened—and then with the reflexes of a cat he ducked, just as the Nazi turned to look forward and caught the full force of a speeding branch whipping by at head-height.

The branch ploughed into the bridge of his nose, drilled itself into the back of his brain, killing the man in an instant, and the Nazi toppled backwards, over Van Lewen's bent-over body and off the back of the riverbike.

A few seconds later, Van Lewen and Race—now on separate Jet Raiders—pulled alongside Doogie and Molke's speeding riverbike. Renée and Schroeder were up ahead of them, racing along in the safety of the trees.

'Doogie! You okay?' Van Lewen said into his throat mike.

'I'll be okay. The bullet went right through,' Doogie's voice came back.

While Van Lewen checked on Doogie, Race kept watch for more Nazis. There were no more coming through the trees behind them. But through the flashing rush of tree trunks to his right, he could see a couple of the silver Rigid Raider assault boats racing across the river's surface parallel to them. Armed Nazi commandos lined their decks, peering into the flooded forest, searching for them, waiting for them to emerge again.

Van Lewen said. 'All right, everybody, listen up. Doogie's taken a hit, but he's okay to keep going. Here's the plan. We want that command boat, okay. The way we're going to get it is this: you two BKA guys'—he nodded at Renée and Schroeder—'I want you two to grab one of those Pibbers. If we're gonna hold that cruiser we're gonna need some heavy fire support and that means getting our hands on one of those 20mm turrets. Think you can manage that?'

'*We can try,*' Schroeder said.

'Good. Doogie. You, me and Molke are gonna go for the command boat, you up for that?'

'*I can handle it,*' Doogie grimaced.

'What about me?' Race asked.

'I got a special job for you, Professor,' Van Lewen said. 'Owing to your lack of special forces training, I kinda figured you wouldn't want to go storming any boats.'

'Good thinking.'

'So I thought that, instead, you could run decoy for us.'

'Decoy?'

'I want you to scoot around in front of those Nazi gunboats as fast as you can and draw their fire while we take the command boat and a Pibber. Once we've got those two boats, we'll bring you aboard the main cruiser.'

Race swallowed. 'Okay . . .'

As he said it, he glanced left and caught Renée's eye. She must have seen the apprehension on his face and nodded reassuringly.

'*You'll be all right,*' she said softly over his earpiece.

'Thanks,' he said.

Then he looked forward and saw that their tree-lined sanctuary ended about a hundred yards ahead of them at a stand of half-submerged trees.

Beyond the stand of trees, he could see grey daylight and the river proper.

In the river, would be the Nazis.

'All right, everybody,' Van Lewen said. 'Speed up and stay sharp. You know what you have to do.'

Race felt his blood rush. He couldn't begin to imagine what lay beyond those trees.

But he didn't have long to dwell on it, because a second later, the six of them hit the edge of the trees at full throttle and burst out into daylight.

The Nazis were waiting for them.

No sooner had Race and the others blasted out of the treeline than a wave of supermachine-gun fire erupted all around them.

'Look out!' Doogie yelled, ducking, but Molke was too slow. A thunderous barrage of bullets whizzed over Doogie's head and slammed into the young German soldier's body, ripping his chest open, causing Molke to convulse violently before he was thrown off the back of the speeding riverbike.

Race's eyes went wide as saucers as he saw Molke get shot to bits right alongside him. They went wider still when he beheld the sight before him.

Two of the three Mosquito choppers that had previously been resting on the helipad barges now hovered in the air above the water *right in front of* him and his team, while the rest of the Nazi fleet powered up the river behind them!

Damn it!

A spray of deadly 20mm machine-gun fire spewed out from the helicopters' side-mounted cannons, raking the tree trunks behind Race, strafing the water all around him.

'*Split up! Split up!*' Van Lewen yelled.

The four American–German Jet Raiders split up instantly—two going left, two going right—and suddenly Race found himself racing across the water alongside Doogie Kennedy, who was now sitting alone on his river-bike, his wounded left shoulder caked in blood.

Van Lewen and Renée and Schroeder shot off in the other direction, whipping out of sight behind the flotilla of riverboats.

Race and Doogie sliced in between the Nazi boats, ducking and weaving. One of the Mosquitos wheeled around in the air above them, came roaring in toward them with its cannons blazing.

In the face of the onslaught, Race banked away to the left and sped in between two of the helipad barges. The line of gunfire behind him pummelled the side of the nearer barge, kicking up sparks along its length.

Race shot along the alleyway of water between the two barges, then abruptly he burst out into open space in front of them and cut right, taking air as he leapt across the bow-wave of the right-hand barge.

He was met with the sight of Doogie's Jet Raider racing alongside him at exactly the same speed—but underneath the hovering Mosquito helicopter and alongside one of the speeding Nazi Pibbers.

'*Professor! Quickly!*' Doogie yelled as he drew his SIG-Sauer pistol with his blood-smeared left hand. '*Give me cover! I'm going to board that Pibber!*'

'What about the command boat!' Race yelled into his throat mike. 'What about the plan!'

'*The plan went to hell as soon as we came outta the trees! Come on!*'

'All right!'

With that, Race quickly drew his own SIG and opened fire on the two Nazi crew members standing on the stern platform of the Pibber.

As he fired, they ducked for cover, and as they did so Doogie quickly pulled his Jet Raider alongside the speeding Pib and leapt up onto its elevated foredeck.

Race watched in amazement as Doogie found his footing on the Pibber's roofed forward section and took two bounding steps aft, dancing up onto the roof of the gunboat's wheelhouse and then leaping down onto its open stern platform and blasting the two Nazi crew members to kingdom come with his SIG.

'*Professor! Get over here! I need you to man this gun!*' Doogie jabbed a finger at the Pibber's turret-mounted 20mm cannon.

Race skimmed across the river's surface, heading for the Pibber.

On board the Pibber, Doogie scooped up a G-11 from one of the fallen Nazis and took the wheel, firing up at the Mosquito helicopter above him while still maintaining his furious speed.

Race came alongside the speeding Pibber.

He brought his Jet Raider in close to the fast-moving patrol boat, trying desperately to keep control as the riverbike bounced wildly on the Pib's side wash.

Race rode grimly, trying to keep up with the Pibber, his eyes locked onto the speeding gunboat's side handrail, three feet away.

That was all he wanted. To get his hands on that rail.

Just then a wave of bullet holes cut across the Pib's side—right in front of him.

He spun instantly.

And saw *another* Pibber skipping across the water toward him, with five more Nazis on its deck!

It was coming right for him.

And it wasn't slowing down.

It was going to ram Doogie's Pibber, *whether Race was in the way or not!*

Race turned to look at Doogie's boat again, his eyes zeroing in on the handrail once again.

Do it! his mind screamed.

Race leapt off the Jet Raider, grabbed hold of the handrail, his legs dragging through the water behind him. He quickly swung his legs up and over the rail just as—*crunch!*—the second gunboat slammed into the port-side rail of Doogie's Pibber.

Race rolled across the deck as the entire boat under him jolted wildly.

'Professor! Over here!' Doogie yelled.

Race was still lying flat on his belly on the deck. He looked up quickly, saw Doogie standing in the wheel-house waving him over when suddenly a pair of combat boots thudded down into his field of vision, cutting off his view of Doogie.

At exactly the same moment as the boots landed on the deck—*bam!*—a gun went off and the owner of the boots dropped instantly, his bug-eyed face landing on the deck right in front of Race, a single bullet hole gouged in the middle of his forehead. In the background behind the dead Nazi, Race saw Doogie standing with his G-11 extended in his good right arm.

Christ, Race thought, as he saw the second Pibber barrelling along just beyond the handrail of his own boat—saw the four Nazis arrayed along its deck, readying themselves to board him.

He snapped to look out in the other direction and saw one of the large helipad barges closing in from the other side, cutting off their escape—boxing them in.

'This is not good,' he said to himself.

Doogie was obviously thinking the same thing.

He swung their Pibber left, ramming it into the Nazi boat hard, causing all of the commandos on its stern deck to lose their balance for an instant, buying himself the precious few seconds he needed to raise his G-11 and fire.

But he didn't fire at the deck of the Nazi Pibber, principally because he didn't have enough time to bring his gun that far around. Rather, he trained it at the *bow* of the Nazi boat—where no Nazis were standing.

'What the hell are you doing!' Race yelled.

Doogie's G-11 roared to life.

An extended burst, maybe two dozen shots.

Sparks flew up instantly all around the steel anchor at the bow of the Nazi Pibber.

And then suddenly—*smack!*—the small metal latch securing the Pibber's anchor to its housing was hit by Doogie's fire and the anchor was dislodged from the deck and went plunging off the side of the Pibber's bow and into the rushing water below, its nylon rope shooting rapidly over the side as it did so.

The four Nazis on the Pibber saw their anchor drop, turned back to face Doogie and Race with their G-11s up.

And then it happened.

Whatever it snagged on—a submerged tree root, or maybe just a whole goddamned submerged tree— Race never knew, but whatever it was, that anchor must have snagged on something big.

It was as if some hideously strong monster had just *yanked* on the speeding Pibber's anchor, because in a single shocking instant, the Nazi Pibber went from sixty-five nautical miles an hour to zero—the whole boat just snapping over on itself, ass-over-keel, as its bow was abruptly jerked down into the water.

As the bow went under, the stern shot up out of the waves and the whole boat did a complete floundering cartwheel, flipping over in mid-air and crashing down on the roof of its wheelhouse, smacking down into the water with an enormous explosive splash.

Race spun to see the overturned Nazi boat shrink into the distance behind them, sinking slowly.

Leonardo Van Lewen weaved his Jet Raider in and out of the Nazi armada, zipping lightly across the river's surface as he alternately disappeared and reappeared from behind the various helipad barges, Pibbers and Rigid Raiders.

Angry gunfire rang out all around him as he desperately tried to outrun the Rigid Raider assault boat and the Mosquito attack chopper that were in hot pursuit behind him.

Strangely, there was only one Nazi on board the Rigid Raider behind him. It was the boat that he had assailed with gunfire earlier, killing all its occupants bar one.

Truth be told, though, Van Lewen didn't really care much for the boat or the chopper astern of him. He only had eyes for the vessel looming fifty yards in front of him.

The big white catamaran.

The Nazi command boat.

Twenty yards behind Van Lewen, the lone helmsman of the Rigid Raider fired wildly after the American soldier's riverbike, his bullets spraying all over the place as his long-bodied assault boat bounced madly over the waves.

Then abruptly the helmsman heard a loud *whump!* from somewhere behind him and he turned quickly—

—just in time to see Karl Schroeder's fist come rushing at his face.

Renée Becker rode her Jet Raider hard, flecks of spray assaulting her face like a thousand pin-pricks.

To her immediate left, she saw Schroeder take the wheel of the Rigid Raider he had just jumped onto and give her the thumbs up.

Once she was sure he was in control of the Nazi boat, Renée immediately gunned the engine of her riverbike and swung in front of the Rigid Raider, using it for cover against the helicopter above them as she took off after Van Lewen, joining him in his pursuit of the command boat.

The massive Nazi command boat powered down the river at the head of the fleet.

About a half-dozen Nazis lined its aft rail—standing underneath the rotor blades of the white helicopter that sat on the helipad there—firing on Van Lewen.

But the big Green Beret deftly weaved his speeding Jet Raider left and right, ducking their fire, before suddenly—without warning—he whipped in behind a nearby helipad barge just astern of the command boat.

Under the cover of the barge, Van Lewen picked up the pace, gradually overtaking the bigger boat on his nimble Jet Raider.

In a few seconds, he came to the bow of the barge, where he took a last deep breath.

Then, when he was ready, he yanked his handle-bars hard to the left.

Like a fighter jet swooping in after its prey, his Jet Raider swung in fast across the bow of the helipad barge and in behind the big twin-hulled command boat.

The Nazis on the stern of the massive catamaran immediately opened fire on him, but to Van Lewen's surprise, they were suddenly taken down by Renée—screaming in from the *left* on her own Jet Raider, firing hard with her M-16 as she skipped across the water.

With the Nazis down, the two of them zoomed in *underneath* the bridge-like body of the catamaran, shooting into the shadows in between its one-hun-dred-and-fifty-foot hulls!

The two Jet Raiders shot forward in the darkness beneath the catamaran, quickly came to the bow of the boat.

Van Lewen pulled in close to the right-hand hull. Renée took the left. Then she watched as Van Lewen reached up and grabbed hold of the bow rail above him and hauled himself up onto the command boat's bow, disappearing from her view.

A second later, with a deep breath of her own, she reached up for the left-hand bow rail and began to climb aboard.

Gale-force wind assaulted her face as she emerged from the shadows beneath the catamaran and stood up on its left-hand bow.

She saw Van Lewen on the other bow, about fifty feet away from her, holding his M-16 up and ready.

With the command boat powering along at the head of the fleet, the Nazis obviously hadn't expected anyone to board them from the front, so there were no commandos up here.

Not yet anyway.

Renée took in the catamaran around her. It was big—really big. The superstructure mounted on top of the two enormous hulls was sleek in the extreme, aerodynamic beyond belief. It was made up of two levels, both of which were hidden behind deeply-tinted slanted windows. Wide side passageways ran down both of the big boat's flanks.

'Where to now?' she yelled.

'We take the boat and then we hold it until the choppers get here!' Van Lewen called back.

'What about the idol! If we can't take the boat, we should at least try to get the—'

At that moment two Nazi commandos came charging out from the port-side passageway, their G-11s blazing. But they were shooting from the hip, firing high. Van Lewen just whipped his M-16 around, drew a bead on them and took them down with two brutally accurate shots.

'What did you say!' he yelled to Renée.

'Never mind!' she said. 'Go now! I'll cover you!'

And with that the two of them took off down the starboard passageway.

Race and Doogie raced across the water in their Pibber patrol boat.

One of the Mosquito attack choppers shot low through the air above them—hovering over the top of their speeding boat, occasionally pivoting in mid-air so it flew backwards in front of them and fired on them directly. It even had one of its side doors open—out of which a Nazi commando sat, firing on them with a G-11.

To their right rumbled one of the helipad barges, boxing them in, cutting off any escape in that direction.

As he drove, Doogie fired up at the chopper with his G-11.

He was trying in vain to get up into the forward gun turret of their Pibber, but the blistering suppressing fire from the chopper was keeping him pinned down in the wheelhouse.

'God *damn* it! I can't get to it!' he yelled as the Mosquito whipped by overhead again, the loud roar of its rotors quickly followed by the impact of about a million armour-piercing rounds banging into the roof of the wheelhouse.

'We have to do something about that chopper!' Race shouted.

'I know! I know!' Doogie yelled. 'Professor, quickly! Go down below! See if you can find any grenades or something down there!'

Race obeyed instantly, threw open the hatch at the forward end of the wheelhouse and hurried down into the belly of the gunboat.

He found himself standing in a bare, small room with grey metal walls.

Netting and wooden crates lined its slanted walls. In the centre of the room he saw a grey box-like object. It was about three feet high and three feet wide—roughly the size of a card table—and at first glance he thought it was just another crate, some kind of ammunition container or something.

But it wasn't a container at all. On closer inspection, Race saw that it was *attached* to the floor.

Then he realised. It was a diver's hatch. In Vietnam, Special Forces and the SEALs had preferred to use Pibbers ahead of other river boats because they alone had these special hatches concealed in their hulls.

Using them, frogmen could enter the water without the bad guys knowing where they'd been let off.

Race quickly began searching the various racks and shelves for weapons.

The first thing he found was a small crate of British L2A2 anti-personnel hand grenades. The second thing was a kevlar box with some words stencilled across its side in English:

PROPERTY OF THE UNITED STATES ARMY
ORDNANCE ISSUE K/56-005/C/DARPA
6 X M-22 CHARGES

Race opened the box and saw six futuristic-looking chrome-and-plastic vials sitting snugly inside separate foam-lined pockets. Each vial was quite small—about the size and shape of a tube of lipstick—and they were all filled with a strange kind of lustrous amber liquid.

Race shrugged, grabbed the kevlar box, and carried it and the crate of regular grenades up to Doogie in the wheelhouse.

'Ah, Professor,' Doogie said when he saw the kevlar box. 'I—uh—wouldn't go throwing those babies too quickly if I were you.'

'Why not?'

'Because you'll kill us too.'

'*What?*'

'They're M-22s. High-temperature explosive charges. Serious shit. See the amber liquid inside 'em. Isotopic liquid chlorine. One ounce of that stuff'll vaporise everything within a two-hundred-yard radius, including us. These Nazi assholes must have been the ones who stole that shipment of M-22s from that truck in Baltimore a few years back.'

'Oh,' Race said.

'We won't be needing *that* much firepower,' Doogie smiled, grabbing one of the more conventional L2A2 hand grenades. 'This should be all we need.'

Not a moment later, the Mosquito above them made another pass, pummelling the walls of the Pib with bullet holes.

But this time, as it shot by overhead Doogie pulled the pin on his grenade and threw it baseball-style with his good arm, *up at the chopper's open side door*.

The grenade shot through the air like a missile . . .

. . . and then it disappeared inside the Mosquito's door.

A second later the Mosquito's walls blasted out as one and the little attack chopper pitched wildly forward, crumpling over on itself and bursting into flames, before slamming down nose-first into the speeding water beneath it.

'Nice throw,' Race said.

Van Lewen and Renée raced down the wide starboard side passageway of the command boat, their M-16s pressed firmly against their shoulders.

They moved quickly, sweeping their guns from side to side, until suddenly they burst out into open space— out onto the aft helipad deck of the big catamaran.

Van Lewen immediately saw the white Bell Jet Ranger chopper sitting on the deck before them, with its pilot standing beside it.

The man saw them instantly, reached for his gun. Van Lewen dropped him, turned right—just in time to see a squad of six more Nazi commandos come charging out from the interior of the catamaran, their G-11s up and firing.

Supermachine-gun fire raked the deck all around

them, splintered the wooden handrail behind them.

Van Lewen ducked, saw Renée dive back behind the corner they had come from.

He, however, was too far gone.

He looked back at the Nazis coming towards him—they were about fifteen yards away with their futuristic machine-guns spewing forth a shocking wave of bullets and in the face of their onslaught, with absolutely nothing else to call on, Leo Van Lewen did the only thing he could think to do.

He leapt over the side.

From the helm of his Rigid Raider speeding along the river behind the command boat, Karl Schroeder watched in horror as he saw Van Lewen go sailing off the side of the big catamaran.

But Schroeder didn't have time to gawk.

At that moment, a hailstorm of G-11 fire came his way as two Nazi Rigid Raiders swooped in on him from either side, assailing his boat's flanks with gunfire, forcing him to dive for cover.

He hit the deck hard, and immediately scanned the floor of the boat for something he could use to fight off the two Nazi Rigid Raiders.

The first thing he saw was a G-11, lying on the deck next to a kevlar box of some sort. Good start.

But then, beyond the G-11, he saw something else.

And he frowned.

Van Lewen flew through the air, waited for the impact with the speeding river beneath him.

It never came.

Rather he landed on something hard—something

solid—something that felt like plastic or fibreglass.

He looked about himself and found that he was lying on the deck of the Scarab speedboat that was secured to the rear right-hand rail of the command boat.

Not a second later, three Nazi commandos snapped their G-11s over the command boat's rail and drew a bead on the bridge of his nose and in that moment, as he looked up into their eyes, Van Lewen knew that his battle was over.

The three Nazis jammed down on the triggers of their guns.

At first, Schroeder hadn't realised what it was.

It was an odd-looking, backpack-sized device—roughly rectangular in shape, with a series of digital gauges on it, variously measured in kilohertz, mega-hertz and gigahertz.

Frequency measurements . . .

And then it had dawned on him.

It was the Nazis' jamming device—the device that they had used to neutralise the Americans' communications systems when they had arrived at Vilcafor.

Stuck to the front of the device was a strip of grey electrician's tape, on which was written in German the words:

WARNING!
DO NOT SET EMP LEVELS ABOVE 1.2 gHZ.

Schroeder's eyes had gone wide at the sight of the word: 'EMP'.

Jesus.

A pulse generator.

The Nazis had an electromagnetic pulse generator.

But why would they set a limit on the level of the pulse at 1.2 gigahertz?

And then it had hit him.

Schroeder immediately snatched up the G-11 next to him and looked at the specifications marked on its body.

HECKLER & KOCH, DEUTSCHLAND
- 50 V.3.5 MV: 920 CPU: 1.25 gHz

In the nanoseconds of time in which the mind operates, he quickly recalled the theory of electromagnetic pulses: EMP nullified anything with a microprocessor in it—computers, radio transmitters, televisions.

And also, Schroeder realised, *G-11 assault rifles*, since the G-11 was the only gun in the world to use a microprocessor—the only gun complex enough to require one.

The Nazis didn't want their men to set the levels on their EMP generator too high, because if they did, the electromagnetic pulse would knock out their G-11s.

Schroeder smiled.

And then—at exactly the same moment as Van Lewen looked up into the barrels of the Nazis' G-11 assault rifles from his position on the deck of the Scarab—Karl Schroeder had flicked on the pulse generator and turned the gigahertz dial to '1.3'.

Click. Click. Click.

Van Lewen's look of resignation turned to one of complete bewilderment as each of the three G-11s above him failed to fire.

The Nazis seemed even more bewildered. They didn't know what the hell was going on.

Van Lewen didn't miss a beat.

In a second, he had his M-16 raised in one hand and

his SIG-Sauer in the other. He pulled both triggers at the same time.

Both guns blazed to life.

All three Nazis were hit instantly and they flopped back behind the rail, their heads exploding in identical fountains of blood.

Bullets pinged off the rail itself, ricocheting in every direction, one of them slicing through the rope that held the Scarab to the command boat.

The speedboat immediately fell away from the big catamaran and all the Nazis on the command boat could do was hold their useless G-11s in their hands and stare at the Scarab as it receded into the wash behind them.

On the other side of the river, Doogie Kennedy sat in the swivel chair of his Pibber's forward gun turret, creating all manner of hell with the patrol boat's double-barrelled 20mm cannon.

He spun the turret around and let fly with a hailstorm of fire, turning one of the Rigid Raiders speeding across the river to his left into Swiss cheese.

Then he turned his sights onto one of the helipad barges in front of him—the one with a Mosquito helicopter still on it—and pummelled it with 20mm gunfire, rupturing its fuel tanks, causing the entire boat-and-chopper combination to erupt into a billowing ball of fire.

'That's right! Take that, you Nazi sunzabitches!'

Three yards behind him, in the wheelhouse of the Pibber, Race drove hard, scanning the river as he did so.

Just then the third—and last—Mosquito attack chopper made another low pass, its side-mounted cannons blazing. Race ducked quickly. On the forward deck in front of him, Doogie swung the revolving gun turret around and loosed a deafening burst of 20mm gunfire at the chopper, but the Mosquito just banked away sharply as his red-hot tracers hit only air around it.

At that moment, however, Race saw another Pibber gunboat swing in ominously behind them.

No Nazi gunmen lined its rails, no gunfire spewed forth from its 20mm gun turret.

It just kept its distance, cruising silently, hanging well back behind them, at least three hundred yards away.

And then suddenly Race saw a puff of smoke burst out from the square-shaped pod that hung off its side and abruptly something long and white shot out of the pod and splashed down into the water.

'Is that what I think it is?' he said, at exactly the same moment as another Nazi Rigid Raider swung in behind their boat, *in between* it and the Pibber that had just launched the strange object from its side-mounted pod. Four Nazis stood on the deck of the open-topped Rigid Raider, firing at Race and Doogie with Beretta pistols.

And then suddenly—so suddenly that it made Race jump—the Rigid Raider in between the two Pibbers just exploded.

There was no warning.

No apparent cause.

The long-bodied aluminium assault boat just shot up into the air in a geyser of smoke, water and twisted metal.

No apparent cause, Race thought, except for the object that the other Pibber had just launched into the water from its pod.

The realisation hit him and Doogie at the same time.

'*Torpedoes . . .*' they both said, exchanging a look.

As they said it, another wisp of smoke puffed out from the pod on the side of the Nazi Pibber and a long white torpedo exploded out from it, splashed down into the water, and shot forward at incredible speed, heading directly for their boat.

'Oh, man,' Doogie breathed.

Race pushed forward on the throttle of the Pibber.

The torpedo shot through the water.

Race guided the speeding Pibber away from it, swinging left in the water, toward the rest of the fleet, in the hope that he could put another boat between them and the torpedo.

But it was no use.

The nearest boats to theirs were the two remaining helipad barges—the one with the Grumman JRF-5 Goose seaplane trailing behind it immediately to their right, and another forward and to their left.

Both barges' flight decks were empty—their wide, rail-less helipads bare.

Race gunned the engine.

His Pibber shot forward, hit a stray wave, bounced high into the air and then with a sudden crashing lurch, came down again, hitting the water hard.

The torpedo bore down on them.

'Professor!' Doogie yelled. 'You got about ten seconds to do something!'

Ten seconds, Race thought.

Shit.

He saw the helipad barge to his left, got an idea, swung in toward it.

Eight seconds.

The Pibber shot across the surface about thirty yards to the right of the wide, flat barge.

Race's eyes were glued to the barge. It was little

more than a landing pad on water—just a wide, flat helipad that floated about three feet above the waterline, with a small glass-enclosed wheelhouse at its bow.

Six seconds.

Abruptly, Race yanked his steering wheel hard to port and the Pibber banked left through the water, skipping quickly across the waves, taking air every few metres as it shot at breakneck speed *in toward* the helipad barge.

Five seconds.

The torpedo closed in.

Four seconds.

'What are you doing!' Doogie yelled.

Three.

Race jammed the throttle forward as far as it would go.

Two.

The Pibber skimmed across the water on a collision course with the barge's starboard flank.

Then suddenly the Pibber hit a wave and like a stunt car leaping off a ramp, it shot high into the air.

The speeding gunboat leapt clear out of the water, its propellers spinning in the air behind it—literally flying—and with a bone-jarring *whump!* its hull landed *right on top* of the barge's empty helipad!

But the Pibber was still moving—fast—and with a scraping, shrieking, ear-splitting screech, the patrol boat *skidded* across the empty helipad deck, kicking up sparks as it shot across it until—*shoom!*—the Pibber blasted off the left-hand edge of the barge and splashed down into the water on the other side where its propellers caught hold of water again and it peeled away from the helipad barge, just as the torpedo behind it hit the hapless barge and detonated.

The walls of the barge blew out as one. Jagged lengths of steel, curving pieces of hull and a thousand shards of glass went blasting out into the air as the barge exploded with the impact of the torpedo.

'Wa-hooooo!' Doogie yelled from the gun turret. *'What a goddamn ride!'*

Breathless, Race peered back at the river behind them as pieces of the destroyed barge rained down on the roof of his wheelhouse.

'Whoa,' he said.

Renée Becker slid in through a side door of the command boat, cautiously made her way down a narrow white-lit corridor.

She slipped into an alcove as a door in front of her opened suddenly. Two Nazis emerged and hurried past her, carrying pistols in their hands, one of them saying, 'They're using our own EMP against us!' The two Nazis ran off down the corridor, unaware of her presence.

Renée pressed on. The interior of the catamaran was plush beyond belief—white walls with dark wooden panelling and lush blue carpet.

But she didn't care.

She was only after one thing.

The idol.

After leaping out of the water and dry-skiing across the landing pad of the helipad barge, Race and Doogie's Pibber was now whipping across the river's surface again, with Doogie firing from his turret up at the last Mosquito helicopter as it buzzed wildly about above them.

But the Mosquito was too quick, too nimble. It evaded his fire easily until finally his 20mm cannon ran out of ammo and just started clicking repeatedly.

Doogie frowned. 'Aw, shit.'

He quickly slid out of the turret, snatched up his G-11, and joined Race in the wheelhouse.

'We gotta nail that chopper,' he said. 'While it's still up there, we got no chance of beating these guys.'

'What do you suggest?'

Doogie nodded at the last remaining helipad barge ploughing along the river about fifty yards to their right—the one with the Grumman Goose seaplane being towed along behind it.

'I suggest we get up in the air with it,' he said.

Seconds later, their Pibber swung in alongside the wide, flat helipad barge.

The two boats touched for a moment and as they did so, Doogie leapt across onto the landing deck of the barge.

'Okay, Professor!' he yelled. 'Your turn!'

Race nodded, left the wheel of the Pibber—just as the entire patrol boat jolted wildly under the weight of a stunning impact.

Race fell to the deck, looked up in time to see one of the two remaining Nazi Pibbers ram the left-hand side of his boat again.

On the helipad barge to the right of the two Pibbers, Doogie whipped up his G-11 and pulled the trigger— but for some reason, it wouldn't fire.

'Damn it! *Shit!*' he yelled as he watched Race and the other Pibber drift away from his barge.

Race was in Hell.

Gunfire rang out all around him as the Nazis on the other Pibber opened fire on his wheelhouse with pistols from close range. The forward windshield of his Pib shattered and a storm of shards rained down all over him.

Then suddenly he felt another lurching thump as the second Pibber rubbed up against his port-side rail.

He snapped around and saw the Nazi Pibber looming large alongside his boat—saw four commandos on its stern deck holding Berettas, readying themselves to board his Pib and kill him.

He spun, looked the other way, and saw that the gap between his own boat and the helipad barge with Doogie was now at least thirty feet wide. Too far away.

He was on his own now.

He drew his SIG.

What are your options, Will?

Can't see many.

The first Nazi leaped over onto his Pibber.

Race whirled around instantly and dived forward —through his boat's shattered windshield and up onto the Pibber's elevated foredeck—just as the Nazi opened fire with his pistol, his bullets pinging off the windshield's frame inches above Race's head.

Race went sprawling on the foredeck of the Pibber, out of the line of fire, at least for the moment.

He heard the sounds of the other Nazis landing on the aft deck of his boat.

Shit.

He looked aft and saw the heads of the four Nazi commandos coming forward. He instinctively rolled away from them and abruptly something sharp hit his back.

Race turned.

It was the Pibber's anchor.

The Nazis were still coming forward.

Do something!

All right . . .

Race quickly aimed his SIG-Sauer at the anchor's rope and fired.

The bullet cut the rope just above the anchor and the stainless-steel weight instantly dropped free from it, clattered down onto the deck.

Race then yanked off his Yankees cap and wedged it firmly between his teeth.

The first Nazi appeared in the wheelhouse, raised his Beretta and fired.

Race dived clear of the bullet, scooping up the anchor rope in his hand as he did so, and then, without so much as a second thought, he rolled quickly across the foredeck towards the bow of the boat.

The steel foredeck around him erupted with bullet holes as he rolled but the bullets missed their mark.

For at the exact moment that the four Nazis appeared in the wheelhouse of the Pibber, William Race rolled his body off the bow of the patrol boat and fell down into the speeding water below.

Race hit the water hard—back-first.

He kicked up a spectacular spray of wash as he bounced wildly on the speeding surface, skipping over it at phenomenal speed, trying desperately to keep his grip on the anchor rope. Occasionally his entire body would spring up off a wave and bang against the side of the Pibber's bow as it carved knife-like through the water beside him.

Race bit down firmly on the brim of his cap, held onto the rope as hard as he could.

It was a rough ride—bruising, belting, battering— but he knew if he didn't do one more thing, it was about to get a lot worse.

He heard the heavy *thump-thump-thump* of Nazi boots on the foredeck above him. If they saw him hanging from the bow, he was a dead man for sure. They would shoot him where he hung.

Do it, Will!

All right, he thought. *Let's do it.*

Race steeled himself against the speeding waves beneath him, squeezed his eyes shut against the spray that assaulted his face. Then he adjusted his grip on the anchor rope and stiffened all of his muscles at once.

And then he allowed himself to *sink* into the water, *under the speeding bow of the Pibber!*

His legs went under first.

Then his waist, then his stomach, then his chest.

Slowly, his shoulders edged under, followed by his neck.

Then, with a final, deep breath, Race allowed his head to go under the surface.

The world went eerily silent.

There was no roar of outboard motors, no thumping of choppers, no clatter of automatic gunfire. Just the constant vibrating hum of boat engines echoing across the underwater spectrum.

The steeply-slanted grey hull of the Pibber filled Race's field of vision. Small specks of God-only-knew-what rushed past his face at a million miles an hour, disappearing into the murky green darkness that lay beyond his flailing feet.

Slowly, deliberately, hand over hand, Race lowered himself down the length of the anchor rope, heading aft along the hull of the Pibber, holding his breath for dear life—while still holding onto his cap with his teeth!

He was about a third of the way down the length of the hull when the first reptilian shape materialised from the green darkness around him.

A caiman.

It swooped in alongside the speeding Pibber, opening its mouth *right next to his flailing feet*, and with a rattlesnake-quick snapping motion, lunged viciously at his sneakers.

Race lifted his legs up just as the caiman's jaws

came crunching together, catching nothing but water, and the big reptile, unable to keep up with the speeding Pibber, shrank prizeless into the hazy green darkness behind him.

Race desperately needed air. His lungs burned. He felt bile crawling up the back of his throat.

He quickened his pace down the rope until, finally, he found what he was looking for.

The diver's hatch.

Yes!

Race quickly reached up into the hatch and punched upwards with his fist, knocking its interior lid off. Then he shoved his head up through it.

His head broke the surface—inside the lower cabin of the Pibber!

Race quickly spat his Yankees cap out of his mouth and sucked in every ounce of air that he could.

Then, when he had got his breath back, he hauled himself up through the box-like hatch and fell in a clumsy heap onto the floor of the cabin—battered, bruised and absolutely breathless, but glad as hell to be alive.

Doogie Kennedy ran across the open deck of the last helipad barge with a trail of sparks strafing the deck behind him.

As soon as he had seen Race go under the bow of the Pibber, he had opened fire on the four Nazis in its wheelhouse. Now they were returning his fire as he made a break for the seaplane being towed behind the big helipad barge.

He came to the stern edge of the barge and quickly unlooped the rope that secured the Goose to it.

Then he leapt across onto the bow of the seaplane and yanked open the small entry hatch situated on top of its nose. He dived head-first down into the hatch, rising several seconds later inside the cockpit of the plane.

Doogie punched the ignition switch and the Goose's two wing-mounted propellers immediately kicked into gear, at first rotating slowly, and then abruptly snapping into rapid blurring circles.

The seaplane pulled away from the helipad barge, the Nazis' bullets pinging against its bodywork.

In response, Doogie rotated the Goose on the river's surface so that it pointed at the deck of his recently abandoned Pibber.

Then he jammed down on the trigger of his control stick.

Instantly, a deafening burst of 20mm machine-gun fire spewed out from the Gatling gun mounted on the side of the Goose.

Three of the Nazis on the Pibber dropped immediately—hit square in their chests by the Goose's powerful fire.

The fourth one fell too, but of his own accord, dropping quickly out of the line of fire.

'God, I love these 20-millimetre guns,' Doogie said.

On the Pibber, Race had been standing just behind the small metal doorway that led back up to the wheelhouse when Doogie's gunfire had assailed the boat.

When at last the gunfire stopped, Race peered out the doorway to see that only one of the original four Nazis was still alive—he was lying on the deck of the Pibber, reloading his Beretta.

It was his chance.

Race took a moment to steel his nerves. Then he threw open the door, levelled his SIG-Sauer at the surprised Nazi, and pulled the trigger.

Click!

The SIG's slide was racked back into the empty position.

No bullets!

Race threw the gun down in disgust and then—seeing the Nazi jam a new magazine into the grip of his own pistol—did the only thing he could think to do.

He took three bounding steps forward and hurled himself at the man.

He hit him hard and both men went sliding along the deck of the speeding Pibber, toward the stern.

They got to their feet quickly, and the Nazi swiped at Race backhanded, but Race ducked and the Nazi's fist went sailing over his head.

And then suddenly Race was up in the commando's face, rushing at him with an angry right. The punch connected and the Nazi recoiled at the blow, his head flailing backwards.

Race hit him again, and again—and *again*—yelling with each punch as the Nazi staggered backwards.

'Get—'

Punch.

'—off—'

Punch.

'—my—'

Punch.

'—boat!'

With the final blow the Nazi slammed into the stern railing of the Pibber and tumbled over it, falling off the back of the boat, splashing down into its wake.

Race—his chest heaving, his knuckles bleeding—stared out after the fallen Nazi and swallowed hard. After a few moments, he saw a familiar pack of ripples converge on the soldier and he turned away as the Nazi began to scream.

Renée was creeping cautiously down a narrow corridor of the command boat, leading with her gun, when all of a sudden she heard voices coming from a room to her right.

She stepped forward, peered around the doorframe.

And saw a man she recognised standing in the centre of an ultra-high-tech laboratory. He was an older man, but huge, obese, with a fat bull-like neck and an enormous girth—his white wash-and-wear shirt was stretched tight across his enormous belly.

Renée held her breath as she stared at the old man.

It was Odilo Ehrhardt.

The leader of the Stormtroopers.

One of the most feared Nazis of World War II.

He must have been—what?—seventy-five years old now, but he didn't look a day over fifty. His classically Aryan features were still apparent, if worn with age. His white-blond hair was thinning on top, revealing a series of ugly brown lesions. And his blue eyes sparkled, glistened with madness as he barked orders to his men.

'—then *find* that generator and *turn it off*, you imbecile!' he bellowed into a radio. He jabbed a pudgy finger at one of his commandos. 'You! Hauptsturmführer! Get Anistaze in here right now!'

The laboratory around the Nazi general was a mix of glass and chrome. Cray YMP supercomputers lined its walls, vacuum-sealed chambers sat on work-benches. Lab technicians in white coats ran about in every direction, commandos with pistols hustled out through the main glass doors that led out onto the boat's rear helipad deck.

But Renée only had eyes for the object that Ehrhardt held in his left hand.

An object wrapped inside a ragged purple cloth.

The idol.

At that moment, Heinrich Anistaze charged in from the helipad deck and stood to attention before Ehrhardt.

'You sent for me, sir.'

'What's going on?' Ehrhardt said.

'They're everywhere, Herr Oberstgruppenführer. There must be dozens of them, maybe more. They appear to have split up, taking out different sections of the fleet and causing significant damage.'

'Then we leave,' Ehrhardt said, handing the idol to Anistaze and guiding him back toward the helipad deck. 'Quickly. We will take the idol in the helicopter and get it to the mine that way. Then, if the heads of government haven't responded to our demands by the time we insert the thyrium into the Supernova, we will detonate it.'

From the wheelhouse of his newly-recovered Pibber, Race surveyed the aquatic battlefield around him.

What was left of the fleet still surged forward along the river, but it was a shadow of its former self.

Three Pibbers were still afloat, but one of them belonged to Race. Only one helipad barge remained, along with three of the original five Rigid Raiders—and one of those belonged to Schroeder.

Van Lewen's Scarab sped along in front of the fleet, and of course, there was the last Mosquito chopper—still wreaking havoc from above.

About forty yards behind him, Race saw Doogie's Goose seaplane wheel out of the wash of the helipad barge in front of it. It surged out into the river proper in search of a clear stretch of water from which it could take off.

Race spun to look forward.

About thirty yards ahead and to the left of his Pibber, he saw the massive Nazi command boat powering along the river.

At that moment, however, as he watched the command boat, Race suddenly saw two men burst out onto its rear deck and dash for the white Bell Jet Ranger helicopter sitting on its stern.

He recognised one of them instantly—Anistaze.

The other man was considerably older than Anistaze—fat, with a thick muscular neck and a semi-bald head. Race didn't know who he was, but he guessed that he was the man Schroeder had spoken about earlier—the Stormtroopers' leader, Otto Ehrhardt or something like that.

Anistaze and Ehrhardt leapt into the rear compartment of the Bell Jet Ranger and immediately the rotor blades on top of the chopper began to rotate.

And then it hit Race.

They were taking the idol away . . .

Just then, as he was gazing at the activity on the stern of the command boat, Race saw a flash of movement out of the corner of his eye—the glint of a small shadowy figure hustling down the starboard passage-way of the command boat.

His eyes went wide.

It was Renée.

She was running swiftly down the side passageway, heading aft, holding her M-16 firmly across her chest.

She was going after the idol . . .

By herself!

Race watched in astonishment as Renée rounded the rear corner of the passageway and opened fire on the Nazi chopper with her M-16.

A couple of the Nazi troops standing near the chopper were hit instantly and dropped where they stood, but the others just turned and fired back at Renée with AK-47s.

Renée ducked in the face of their gunfire and fell back behind the corner as the Nazis on the helicopter deck took off after her.

Race could only watch in horror as she stumbled backwards up the starboard-side passageway of the command boat, heading towards the bow.

She fired wildly with her M-16 as she moved—determinedly—keeping the Nazis at the aft end of the passageway pinned down, until at last she was able to hunker down at the forward end of the passageway, holding her attackers at bay at the other end.

It was at that moment that Race saw him.

A lone Nazi commando. Moving slowly across the wide *roof* of the command boat, *toward* Renée's position!

The man held his gun high, and moved with slow deliberate steps, out of Renée's field of vision, sneaking up on her from above.

Renée had no chance of seeing him. No way of knowing he was there.

'Shit,' Race said, looking around himself for an option.

His eyes fell upon Doogie's seaplane skipping quickly over the waves behind his boat, coming alongside it—*in between* his Pibber and the command boat—as it dashed forward through the fleet in search of a clear stretch of water.

Race saw the chance instantly, and without so much as a blink, he quickly leapt out through the shattered forward windshield of the wheelhouse and climbed up onto its roof.

Then, just as Doogie's Goose swept past his Pibber, Race leapt across *onto the wing of the moving seaplane* and danced across its length!

It was an amazing sight. The Goose seaplane, speeding along *in between* the Nazi command boat and the Pibber, with the tiny figure of William Race—in his saturated jeans and T-shirt and his New York Yankees baseball cap—running across its wings, his body bent forward, braced against the battering wind.

Race ran hard, his feet moving quickly but surely across the fifty-foot wingspan of the Goose.

He saw the command boat looming in front of him; saw the world streaking laterally beyond it; saw Renée up near its bow holding off the three Nazis at the other end of the passageway; saw the lone Nazi up on the big catamaran's roof, closing in on her position.

And then, like a racing car overtaking its rival, the Goose came alongside the command boat and Race hit the edge of the left wing at full stride and leapt off it—

—and flew through the air—

—and landed, cat-like, on both feet, on the roof of the command boat, right next to the Nazi who had been sneaking up on Renée!

Race didn't miss a beat. Gunless, he just hurled himself at the man, slammed into him, sending both of them flying forward, *off* the roof of the command boat.

They landed in a heap on the foredeck of the catamaran not far from where Renée was hunkered down at the forward end of the starboard passageway.

Disoriented, Race rolled clear of where they had fallen, and looked up in horror to see that the Nazi was already on his feet.

In a fleeting instant, Race saw the man's face. It was without a doubt one of the ugliest faces he had ever seen—long and lopsided and heavily cratered with pockmarks. It was also the picture of anger—the picture of pure unadulterated fury.

But it was only to be a fleeting glimpse, for in the next flashing instant, his view of the Nazi's hideously ugly face was replaced by the sight of the butt of the man's AK-47 assault rifle rushing toward his face and then—*smack!*—he saw nothing but black.

Renée whirled around just in time to see Race's head snap violently backwards with the blow. His body dropped to the deck, hitting it hard, out cold.

Renée saw the ugly Nazi standing over Race's body—saw him suddenly snap to look up at her.

Then she saw him raise his gun and smile.

The Goose seaplane shot out in front of the command boat, into the open water ahead of the fleet.

Doogie was pushing forward on the throttle, trying to get the little seaplane up to take-off speed, when suddenly there came a loud *bang!* from somewhere to his left. Abruptly he felt the whole plane lurch dramatically and he looked out to see that there was now nothing in the place where his left-hand stabilising pontoon should have been.

Not a second later, a pair of Nazi Rigid Raiders zoomed across his bow from either side, criss-crossing in front of him, the commandos on their decks spattering his windshield with heavy machine-gun fire.

Doogie ducked. His windshield cracked into spiderwebs.

Then he looked up to see one of the Nazis on the right-hand Rigid Raider heft an M-72A2 man-portable rocket launcher onto his shoulder and aim it right at the Goose!

'Oh, man . . .' Doogie breathed.

The Nazi fired.

A puff of smoke issued from the barrel of the rocket launcher at exactly the same moment as Doogie yanked his steering yoke hard to the left.

The Goose banked wildly—so wildly in fact that the tip of its pontoon-less left wing actually *touched* the water, kicking up a spectacular shower of spray!

As a result, the missile from the rocket launcher shot right *underneath* Doogie's elevated right wing, missing it by inches before shooting off into the treeline and blasting an unfortunate tree trunk to hell.

Doogie's little Goose continued to careen across the river's surface—racing along on its belly and its one remaining pontoon.

Just then the last Mosquito attack chopper roared in from out of nowhere, loosing a devastating burst of cannonfire that raked the water all around the little seaplane.

'God damn it!' Doogie yelled as he ducked beneath the dashboard again. 'Could this situation *get* any worse?'

It was then that he heard an ominous, but very familiar, sound.

Poof!

He spun in his seat.

Just in time to see one of the two remaining Nazi Pibbers swing in behind him and launch a torpedo from its side-mounted pod.

The torpedo splashed into the water, shot forward under the surface.

Doogie gunned it.

The two Rigid Raiders were now speeding along on either side of him, off the tips of his wings, boxing him in.

'Shit,' Doogie said. 'Shit-shit-shit.'

The torpedo closed in.

He pushed the Goose's throttle forward.

The little seaplane shot across the water, surrounded by enemy vessels on no less than *four* sides: by the two

Rigid Raiders on both of its flanks, by the Pibber a hundred yards astern of it, and by the black Mosquito attack chopper shooting through the air above it.

Doogie looked about himself desperately. While his little plane struggled to maintain its pace, the two Rigid Raiders sped alongside him easily, their supercharged engines roaring, their crews seeming to take a perverse kind of pleasure in watching him struggle.

'Don't smile too soon, you fascist assholes,' Doogie said aloud. 'It's not over yet.'

The torpedo was within twenty yards of his tail now. Doogie pushed the throttle as far forward as it would go.

Fifteen yards, and he hit eighty knots.

Ten—ninety.

Five—a hundred.

Doogie could see the Nazis on the Rigid Raiders laughing at him as he desperately attempted to outrun the torpedo in his hopelessly outdated Goose.

Two yards—a hundred and ten. Top speed.

The torpedo slid underneath the Goose.

'*No!*' Doogie yelled. 'Come on, baby! *Do it for me!*'

The Goose shot across the river's surface.

The Nazis laughed.

Doogie swore.

And then suddenly, gloriously, the little Goose did what no-one except Doogie thought it was still capable of doing.

It lifted off the surface.

It only lifted slightly off the river's rushing surface—maybe a foot or two at the most—but it was enough.

With its initial target lost, the torpedo in the water immediately began searching for another.

It found it in the Rigid Raider to Doogie's right.

No sooner had the Goose lifted off the surface than that Rigid Raider was blasted out of the water by the shocking detonation of the torpedo.

The Goose touched back down again, kicking up a shower of spray behind it.

The Mosquito above it saw what had happened and it powered forward, ahead of the Goose—turning laterally in the air as it did so—so that it now flew *backwards* in front of the speeding seaplane, unleashing a savage burst of gunfire at it.

Doogie ducked under the dashboard. 'Damn choppers!' he yelled. 'Let's see how you like this!'

And with that he yanked his steering yoke hard to the left.

The Goose banked sharply—the tip of its pontoonless left wing touching the surface again—cutting across the path of the surviving Rigid Raider!

The skipper of the Rigid Raider didn't react fast enough.

Like a missile shooting up into the sky, the Rigid Raider lifted completely out of the water as it rushed *up the steeply-slanted wings of the seaplane*!

The assault boat raced up the reinforced wings of the Goose, its exposed silver hull screeching loudly as it shot along the seaplane's heavily banked wings, using them as a launching ramp, and then—*shoom!*— the Rigid Raider launched itself off the end of the right-hand wing and out into the air beyond it where it *smashed* into the canopy of the Mosquito helicopter that was hovering in front of the sharply-turned Goose!

The Mosquito lurched backwards—reeling like a boxer punched square in the nose—as the Rigid Raider ploughed into its bubble at incredible speed. Its canopy shattered in an instant and a split second later, the whole helicopter exploded into an enormous billowing fireball.

Doogie stared back at the carnage behind him; saw the blackened shell of the torpedoed Rigid Raider sinking slowly into the water; saw the charred remains of the Mosquito and the other Rigid Raider crash down into the river with an enormous splash.

'Eat that, you Nazi bastards,' he said softly.

Dazed, confused and possessed of one hell of a headache, William Race was marched at gunpoint out onto the rear deck of the Nazi command boat.

Renée walked along beside him, shoved forward by the extraordinarily ugly Nazi Race now thought of as 'Craterface'.

No sooner had he and Renée been subdued by Craterface up on the bow than the big Nazi had called upon his comrades at the other end of the starboard passageway to cease their fire. Then he had marched his two captives down the passageway and out onto the rear helipad, where the pristine white Bell Jet Ranger helicopter was on the verge of taking off.

Anistaze saw them instantly, kicked open the side door of the helicopter.

'Bring them to me!' he shouted.

Van Lewen was racing across the river's surface out in front of the fleet.

He sat at the helm of the Scarab, shooting across the river with only the rear third of the boat's bullet-shaped hull touching the water, the sound of its twin 450-horsepower engines thundering in his ears.

He turned in his seat to see the white Bell Jet Ranger helicopter lift off from the stern deck of the command boat.

'Damn it,' he breathed.

Karl Schroeder was in a world of trouble.

His Rigid Raider was near the back of the fleet, shooting across the river's surface in between the last two Nazi Pibbers, being pummelled by their relentless fire.

Schroeder tried desperately to duck their bullets, but they were too close, too fast.

And then suddenly—*smack-smack-smack*—a line of bullet holes raked his Rigid Raider, cutting across his right leg, opening up three jagged red holes in his thigh.

He fell, clenching his teeth, stifling a scream.

Somehow he managed to get up on one knee and keep driving the boat, but it was no use. The Nazi Pibbers were all over him.

He looked forward, caught sight of what was left of the fleet—the command boat, the Scarab, the Goose seaplane and one of the helipad barges—speeding off into the distance a good hundred yards ahead of him.

He also saw the white Bell Jet Ranger helicopter as it flew away from the command boat. Only minutes earlier, he had seen Race and Renée get thrown into it—

At that moment, another wave of gunfire assailed Schroeder's boat, strafing a line of holes across his back, puncturing his bulletproof vest as if it were made of tissue paper. Schroeder roared in agony, fell to the deck.

And in that instant he knew he was going to die.

His wounds burning, his nerve ends screaming, his entire body on the verge of going into shock, Karl Schroeder looked desperately about himself for anything he could use to take as many of the Nazis down with him as he could.

His gaze fell upon the kevlar box that he had seen earlier on the floor of the Rigid Raider. It was only now, however, that he saw that it had words stencilled on its side in English.

Slowly, Schroeder read the markings on the side of the kevlar box.

When he had finished reading them, his eyes went wide.

Schroeder's Rigid Raider drifted further and further behind what was left of the fleet, with the two Nazi Pibbers crowding in on either side of it.

Karl Schroeder now lay on his back on the deck of his assault boat, gazing up at the storm clouds that rolled by overhead, darkening the late-afternoon sky, the life slowly draining from his body.

Abruptly, the face of a rather sinister-looking Nazi cut across his view of the sky and Schroeder realised that one of the Pibbers had come alongside him.

But he didn't care.

Indeed, as the Nazi calmly raised his AK-47 to his shoulder, Schroeder just looked up into the barrel of the man's gun, uninterested, resigned to his fate.

And then, strangely, he smiled.

The Nazi hesitated.

Then he looked slightly to the side—at the kevlar box that lay to Schroeder's left.

The box's lid was open.

Inside it, he saw five small chrome-and-plastic

vials, each filled with a small amount of shiny amber liquid. Each vial sat snugly inside a foam-lined pocket.

The Nazi knew what they were instantly.

M-22 isotopic charges.

But there was a sixth foam-lined pocket in the box. It lay empty.

The Nazi's eyes snapped left to see the last vial sitting in Schroeder's bloodsmeared hand.

Schroeder had already broken the rubber seal on top of the charge, had already uncocked the red safety latch that covered its release mechanism.

Now he had his thumb pressed down on the release button. He held it down as he gazed calmly into space.

The Nazi's eyes went wide with horror. 'Oh, fuck . . .'

Schroeder closed his eyes. It would be up to Renée and the American professor now. He hoped they succeeded. He hoped the two American soldiers were far enough ahead of his boat, out of the blast radius. He hoped . . .

Schroeder sighed a final time, and as he did so he let go of the release button and the M-22 isotopic charge went off in all its glory.

The world shook.

A massive—*massive*—white-hot explosion blasted out from the Rigid Raider and shot out in every direction.

It shot into the trees on either side of the river, incinerating them in an instant, blasting them to nothing.

It shot under the river's surface—a bubbling, frothing wall of heat shooting downwards at unimaginable speed, boiling the water on contact, killing anything in its path as it raced downwards like a speeding comet.

It shot into the sky, high into the sky, flaring white like the flashbulb on a camera, an all-consuming monumental flash that must have been visible from space.

Worst of all, the expanding wall of white-hot light shot along the river's surface, chasing after the remainder of the fleet.

Van Lewen's Scarab and Doogie's Goose skipped across the water at the head of the fleet—out in front of the gargantuan wave of white light eating up the river behind them.

To a certain extent, they'd been lucky. They had been a good three hundred yards ahead of Schroeder's Rigid Raider when the M-22 charge had gone off.

The other boats—the last helipad barge, the two remaining Pibbers and the command boat itself—hadn't.

They had been closer. And now the expanding wall of white-hot light just loomed above them like some immense mythological monster, dwarfing them. And then suddenly, in an instant, the gigantic wall of white *consumed* the helipad barge and the Pibbers, detonating them on contact before swallowing them whole and continuing on its voracious charge forward.

Its next target was the command boat. Like a lumbering rhino trying to outrun a runaway Mack truck, the massive catamaran powered forward in a desperate attempt to get clear of the oncoming wall of searing-hot energy.

But the blast was just too fast, too powerful.

As it had done with the barge and the Pibbers before it, the expanding wall of light just reached out and snatched the command boat in its clutches, yanking it into its mass, obliterating the enormous craft in a single fiery instant.

And then as quickly as it had risen, the massive wall of light began to subside and dissipate. Soon it lost all of its forward momentum and sank back into the distance.

Van Lewen took a final look back at the singed and smoking jungle river behind him. He saw a wispy black smoke cloud rising into the sky above the treetops—but it was broken up quickly by the sheets of subtropical rain that had just begun to fall.

It was then, however, that he looked about himself and realised that his Scarab and Doogie's Goose were the only vessels left on the river.

In fact, the only *other* remnant of the chase just concluded was a small white speck disappearing over the trees ahead of them.

The white Bell Jet Ranger helicopter.

FIFTH MACHINATION

Tuesday, January 5, 1815 hours

THE MADRE DE DIOS GOLDMINE
TOP VIEW

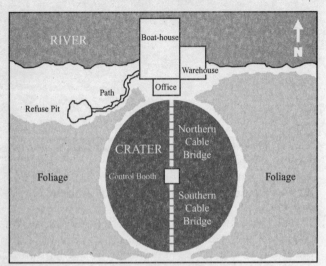

CROSS-SECTION

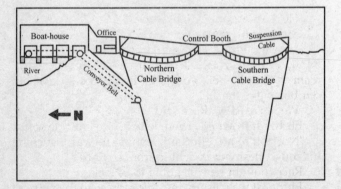

'Who are you!' Odilo Ehrhardt demanded in German, slapping Renée hard across her face.

'I told you!' she yelled back at him. 'My name is Renée Becker and I am a special agent with the *Bundes Kriminal Amt.*'

The white helicopter was now flying low over the river, heading east. Race and Renée sat in the rear compartment, handcuffed. Before them sat Ehrhardt, Anistaze and Craterface. A lone pilot was up front flying the chopper.

Ehrhardt turned to face Race. 'So who, then, are *you*?'

'He's American—' Renée said.

Ehrhardt hit her again. Hard.

'I wasn't addressing you.' He turned back to Race. 'Now, who are you? FBI? Or are you Navy? A SEAL team, perhaps—hell, you must be SEALs to take out our boats like that.'

'We're DARPA,' Race said.

Ehrhardt frowned. Then he began to chuckle softly.

'No, you're not,' he said, leaning forward, sticking his round fleshy face right in front of Race's.

Race thought he was going to be sick.

Ehrhardt was disgusting, *vile*—obese to the point of

being grotesque, reeking of body odour and possessed of an evil moonlike face. A thin string of saliva smacked between his lips when he spoke and his breath smelled like horseshit.

'I'm working with Doctor Frank Nash,' Race said, trying desperately to remain calm. 'He's a retired Army colonel working with the Defense Advanced Research Projects Agency in conjunction with members of the United States Army.'

'Frank Nash, eh?' Ehrhardt said, breathing his foul, rancid breath all over Race's face.

'That's right.'

'And who, then, might you be, Little Man Trying To Be So Brave?' he said, as he lifted Race's Yankees cap off his head.

'My name is William Race,' Race said, grabbing his cap with his cuffed hands. 'I'm a professor of ancient languages at New York University.'

'Ah,' Ehrhardt said, nodding. 'So you are the one they brought along to translate the manuscript. Very good, very good. Before I have you killed, Mister William Race, professor of ancient languages at New York University, I would like to correct a certain misimpression that you appear to possess.'

'And what is that?'

'Frank Nash is not with DARPA.'

'What?' Race said, frowning.

'And he most certainly is not a *retired* Army colonel, either. On the contrary, he is most active indeed. For your information, Colonel Francis K. Nash is the head of the United States Army's Special Projects Unit.'

'*What?*'

Race didn't get it. Why would Nash say he was DARPA when in fact he wasn't?

'Ah-ha!' Ehrhardt cackled, clapping his hands. 'I

love to see the look of betrayal on a man's face just before he is about to die.'

Race was thoroughly confused now.

He didn't know what to think.

Even if Nash *wasn't* with DARPA, what did it matter? The Supernova was an Army project, and Nash was with Army Special Projects.

Unless . . .

Ehrhardt turned to Anistaze. 'So. The American Army is here, too. What do you say about that?'

'There must be another mole,' Anistaze said, ignoring Race and Renée entirely.

'In DARPA?' Ehrhardt said.

Anistaze nodded. 'We know of the link to the American terrorist group, but we didn't know about this—'

'*Bah!*' Ehrhardt waved his hand dismissively. 'It is of no importance now, because it is we who have the idol.'

'What do you hope to achieve by all this?' Renée asked defiantly. 'Do you *want* to destroy the world?'

Ehrhardt smiled at her indulgently. 'I do not want to destroy the world, Fraulein Becker. Far from it. I want to rebuild it. Re-*order* it, the way it should be.'

'With what? One hundred billion dollars. Is that what this is all about? *Money?*'

'My dear Fraulein Becker, is that the limit of your vision? *Money.* This is not about *money*. It is about what money *can do*. One hundred billion dollars—*bah*—it is nothing. It is but a means to an end.'

'And what is the end?'

Ehrhardt's eyes narrowed. 'One hundred billion dollars will buy me a new world.'

'A new world?'

'Brave Fraulein Becker, what do you think I want?

417

A new country, perhaps? To pursue the tired old Nazi goal of establishing an Aryan nation with the Herrenvolk at the head, and the *untermenschen* beneath them? *Bah!'*

'What is it that you want, then? How can you buy yourself a new world?'

'By dumping one hundred billion U.S. dollars on world financial markets at the bargain price of one cent apiece.'

'What?' Renée said.

'The American economy is in a most precarious situation, *the* most precarious situation it has found itself in in fifty years. Accumulated foreign debt stands at approximately eight-hundred and thirty billion dollars, gross budget deficits occur annually. But what the United States depends on through all of this is a robust currency with which it will repay its debts in the future.

'But if the *value* of that currency were to fall dramatically, say, to levels one-quarter of its current strength, then the United States would be unable to repay those debts.

'It would be bankrupt, its dollar worthless. What I intend to do with my hundred billion dollars is cripple the American economy.'

Ehrhardt's eyes gleamed as he raved. 'Since the Second World War this world has been an *American* world—has been force-fed American culture, made to endure American trade dominance and the ruthless policy of economic slavery conducted and condoned by the American government. I have determined that the dumping of one hundred billion U.S. dollars on world markets would be enough to cripple the American dollar beyond recoverable limits. American corporations will be worth *nothing*. The American people will not have the purchasing power to *buy* anything, because their currency will not be worth the paper it's written on. The United States will become the world's beggar and the world will start anew. That is what I am doing, Fraulein Becker. I am buying myself a new world.'

Race couldn't believe what he was hearing.

'You can't possibly be serious—' he said.

'No?' Ehrhardt said. 'Look at George Soros. In 1997, the Prime Minister of Malaysia publicly blamed Soros for causing the Asian economic crisis by dumping vast sums of Asian currencies. And this was one man—*one man*—and he didn't even have a *tenth* of the wealth that I am willing to utilise. But then, of course, I *am* going after a much bigger fish.'

'What if they won't give you the money?' Renée said.

'They will. Because I am the only man on earth who possesses an operational Supernova.'

'But what if they don't?'

'Then I will detonate the device,' Ehrhardt said simply.

The Nazi general turned in his seat and peered out through the forward windshield of the chopper. Race and Renée followed his gaze.

A truly spectacular sight met them.

They saw the Amazon rainforest stretching away to the horizon, a vast blanket of limitless unending green.

In the near distance, however, there was a break in the blanket of green—an enormous brown cone-shaped crater buried in the earth.

It was situated right on the river, and it was absolutely massive—at least half a mile in diameter. Long gently-sloping truck-trails wound their way down to the bottom of the gigantic earthen crater.

Huge floodlights stood on its rim, illuminating it like a football stadium in the dim early-evening light.

In the centre of the crater, suspended high above it by a web of tightly-stretched cables, was a large white box-shaped cabin—a control booth of some sort—possessed of wide oblong windows on all four of its sides.

The only route of access to the control booth was via two long drooping suspension bridges that spanned the crater from opposite ends—from the north and the south. Each bridge was at least four hundred yards long and constructed of thick steel cables.

It was the goldmine.

The *Madre de Dios* goldmine.

The Bell Jet Ranger helicopter landed on a pontoon-mounted helipad that floated on the river's surface not far from the edge of the massive open-cut mine.

The mine itself lay directly to the south of the Alto Purus River, and it was connected to it by a collection of decrepit old buildings—three hulking warehouse-like structures that were dreadfully worn with age.

The largest of the three buildings jutted out over the river, resting on stilts. A series of wide garage-style doors lined its length, enabling boats and seaplanes to be stored inside it. In years gone by, Race guessed, this must have been where the mining company's boats and planes had come to be loaded up with gold.

Today, however, it performed a different task.

It allowed the Nazis to hide their armada of boats, helicopters and seaplanes from the prying eyes of America's spy satellites.

No sooner had the chopper landed on the floating helipad than the pilot hit a switch.

Immediately, the rusty garage door to the helicopter's left opened, and the square pontoon on which the chopper sat began to be pulled across the water toward it by some underwater cable mechanism.

Race looked up as the chopper was pulled slowly inside the big warehouse.

A second later the sky above him abruptly disappeared, replaced by the interior of the warehouse's roof—a complex latticework of rusting steel girders and dark wooden cross-beams.

Race stared at the warehouse all around him.

It was positively huge—an *enormous* enclosed space, about the size of an aeroplane hangar—the whole cavernous space illuminated by cone-shaped halogen lights that were attached to the ceiling's girders.

The 'floor' of the warehouse, however, was quite unusual. It was the river's surface. A long finger-like deckway stretched out over the water, branching out at about a dozen intervals into smaller decks that ran at right angles to it—mooring slots for the boats and planes that came to the mine to load up with gold.

A long, wide conveyor belt ran at ground level for the length of the central deckway. It rose out of a large square hole in the wall at the landward end of the hangar and looped back at the far end of the deckway.

Race guessed that the *landward* end of the conveyor belt was to be found somewhere deep within the cone-shaped mine itself, probably on a loading ledge somewhere, or maybe even at the very bottom of the crater.

The way he figured it, gold was loaded onto the conveyor belt down in the mine, then the conveyor belt lifted it up through the long tunnel cut into the earth, until it appeared here in the warehouse and was loaded onto a boat or plane.

The chopper's slow-moving pontoon came to a halt inside one of the mooring slots, its slowing rotor blades hanging marginally out over the conveyor belt, glinting in the glare of the halogen lights.

From his seat in the back of the chopper, Race saw four men step out from a glass-enclosed office at the landward end of the warehouse.

Three of them wore white lab coats—scientists. The fourth wore combat fatigues and carried a G-11 assault rifle—a soldier.

One of the three scientists, Race saw, was much smaller than the other two, and infinitely older—he was a tiny little man, bent with age, with long silver hair and huge round eyes that were magnified by a pair of thick spectacles. Race guessed that this was Dr Fritz Weber, the brilliant Nazi scientist Schroeder and Nash had talked about earlier.

Apart from the four men standing in front of the glass-walled office, the rest of the warehouse was completely deserted.

There's no-one else here, Race thought.

The Nazis must have taken everyone they had to Vilcafor to get the idol. The four men here—plus Anistaze, Ehrhardt, Craterface and the pilot—were all they had left.

'Unterscharführer,' Ehrhardt said to Craterface as the chopper beneath them jolted to a halt. 'If you would be so kind, please take Agent Becker and Professor Race out to the refuse pit. Then shoot them and bury their remains.'

Race and Renée were shoved down a dirt path that ran westward through the rainforest away from the enormous riverside warehouses.

Behind them, Craterface and the other Nazi soldier—the only other soldier at the mine—marshalled them forward with their G-11s.

'Any idea how we're going to get out of this?' Race asked Renée as they walked.

'None at all,' she replied coolly.

'I thought you might have a plan or something. You know, something hidden up your sleeve.'

'No plan.'

'So we're going to die?'

'It looks that way.'

They rounded a bend in the path and Race winced as an overwhelmingly putrid smell assaulted his senses. A moment later, the four of them came to the end of the path and Race saw a pile of garbage scattered among the trees in front of them. It stretched away for about fifty yards—old tyres, rotting piles of discarded food and waste, gnarled pieces of metal, even a few animal carcasses.

The refuse pit.

'On your knees, both of you,' Craterface growled.

They dropped to their knees.

'Hands on your heads.'

They laced their fingers behind their heads.

Chick-chick!

Race heard the other Nazi release the safety on his G-11. Then he heard him step forward through the mud behind him, *felt* him place the barrel of the assault rifle against the back of his head.

This isn't how it's supposed to happen! his mind screamed. *It's going too fast. Aren't they supposed to dawdle or something? Give you a chance . . . a chance to get—*

Race faced forward, away from the gun, bit his lip and shut his eyes, and gave in to the hopelessness of his situation, waited for the end.

It came quickly.

Blam!

Nothing happened.

Race's eyes were still closed.

The G-11 had gone off, but for some reason—some bizarre reason—his head was still where it was supposed to be.

And then suddenly—*whump!*—a body fell face-down into the mud right next to his kneeling frame.

Race immediately opened his eyes and peered behind him—

—and saw Craterface standing there, with his G-11 aimed at the spot where the other Nazi's head had been only moments ago.

The dead Nazi now lay face-down in the mud with an ugly soup of blood and brains oozing out from a hole in the back of his head.

'Uli,' Renée said, standing up and running over to Craterface. She hugged him warmly.

Race's mind spun.

Uli . . . ?

Then Renée slapped the big pock-faced Nazi hard on the chest. 'Honestly, could you have waited any longer? I was almost jumping out of my skin there.'

'I'm sorry, Renée,' Craterface—Uli—said. 'I had to wait until we were far enough from the boat-house.

Otherwise the others would have known.'

Race turned suddenly to face the man named Uli.

'You're BKA,' he said.

'Yes,' the big man said, smiling. 'And *your* good intentions saved your life, Professor William Race of New York University. In your bid to save Renée on the catamaran, you tackled the right man. If I'd been a real Nazi, I would have put a bullet in your brain right away. My name is Special Agent Uli Pieck, but around here I am known as Unterscharführer Uli Kahr.'

And then suddenly in Race's mind, it all made sense.

'The manuscript,' Race said. 'You're the one who got the BKA their copy of the manuscript.'

'That's right,' Uli said, impressed.

Race recalled Karl Schroeder telling Frank Nash about the BKA's plan to beat the Nazis to the idol. He remembered Schroeder's words clearly: *'To do that, we obtained a copy of the Santiago Manuscript and used it to find our way here.'*

It was only now, though, that Race realised he should have known from that moment that the BKA had a man inside the Stormtrooper organisation.

The BKA's copy of the manuscript was a Xerox of the *actual* Santiago Manuscript. But the actual Santiago Manuscript had been *stolen* from the San Sebastian Abbey in the French Pyrenees several days earlier by the Stormtroopers. Hence, the Xerox of the manuscript that the BKA had in their possession must have been sent to them by someone *within* the Nazi organisation.

A spy.

Uli.

'Come on,' Uli said, hurrying over to the body of the fallen Nazi. He quickly stripped the dead man of his weapons, tossing his G-11 and a couple of conventional hand grenades to Renée, and then throwing the Nazi's black kevlar breastplate and Glock-20 pistol to Race. 'Hurry, quickly, we have to stop Ehrhardt before he arms the Supernova!'

Heinrich Anistaze and Odilo Ehrhardt were standing in one of the glass-enclosed offices inside the boat-house, surrounded by a bank of radio and communications equipment.

In front of them stood Dr Fritz Weber—the former member of Adolf Hitler's atomic bomb project, the Nazi scientist who during World War II had conducted experiments on human subjects and been sentenced to death for it. Although his body was eighty-seven years old, hunchbacked and gnarled, his mind was as alive as ever.

Weber held the Incan idol out in front of him.

'It's *beautiful*,' he said.

At eighty-seven, Fritz Weber was a decade older than Ehrhardt and two feet shorter. He was a small bespectacled man with hard appraising eyes and a wild Einsteinian mane of hair that flowed all the way down to his shoulders.

'What word from the European and American governments?' Ehrhardt asked him.

'The Germans and the Americans both asked for more time to raise the money. Nothing from the others,' Weber said. 'It's a ruse, a standard negotiator's stalling tactic. They're trying to buy more time until they know for sure that their own teams haven't found the idol first.'

'Then let's show them who has the idol,' Ehrhardt growled. He turned to face Anistaze. 'Make a digital image of the idol now. Time it and date it and then feed it into the computer and send it to Bonn and Washington direct. Tell the presidents that the device has been armed and set to detonate in exactly thirty minutes. It will only be *disarmed* when we have confirmation of the transfer of one hundred billion dollars into our account in Zurich within that time.'

'Yes, sir,' Anistaze said, crossing the room to switch on a digital camera.

'Doctor Weber,' Ehrhardt said.

'Yes, Oberstgruppenführer?'

'When the Obergruppenführer is finished taking the digital image, I want you to take the idol to the control booth and arm the Supernova immediately. Set a thirty-minute countdown and start the clock.'

'Yes, Oberstgruppenführer.'

Race, Renée and Uli hurried back up the dirt path toward the boat-house.

Uli and Renée carried G-11s, Race the small Glock that Uli had taken from the dead Nazi at the refuse pit.

He also now wore the dead Nazi's black kevlar breast-plate over his T-shirt. He hadn't really noticed the Nazis' body armour before. But now—now that he was wearing it—he looked at it more closely.

First of all, it was incredibly light and easy to wear—it didn't inhibit his movement at all. Secondly, however, he noticed a strange A-shaped unit attached to the *back* of the breastplate, covering his shoulderblades. The A-shaped unit was also light, and like a spoiler on a sports car, it had been smoothly incorporated into the design of the kevlar breast-plate so as not to ruin its slick aerodynamic appearance.

As always, and perhaps incongruously with his

high-tech body armour, Race was still wearing his damn Yankees cap.

'Digital image is complete,' Anistaze said from over by the bank of radio and electronic equipment. 'Sending it now.'

Ehrhardt turned to Weber. 'Arm the Supernova.'

Weber immediately snatched up the idol and, with Ehrhardt in tow behind him, quickly headed out of the office.

'Over there!' Renée yelled, pointing at one of the two incredibly long suspension bridges that connected the riverside buildings to the control booth in the centre of the crater.

Race looked out over the mine and saw two tiny figures—one large and fat, the other small and dressed in a white lab coat—bouncing across the modern steel-cabled bridge.

The smaller man was carrying something wedged underneath his arm. An object wrapped inside a purple cloth. The idol.

Uli and Renée left the dirt path, plunged into a section of low foliage, heading in the direction of the crater. Race followed them.

Seconds later, the three of them arrived at the rim of the gigantic mine and looked out over it.

'It's Ehrhardt and Weber,' Uli said. 'They're taking the idol to the Supernova!'

'What do we do?' Race asked.

Uli said, 'The Supernova is inside the control booth hanging over the mine. There are only two bridges that lead out to it—that one from the north, and the other

430

one from the south. Somehow we have to get to that cabin and disarm the Supernova.'

'But how do we do that?'

'To disarm the device,' Uli said, 'you have to enter a code into the arming computer.'

'What's the code?'

'I don't know,' Uli said sadly. 'No-one knows. No-one except Fritz Weber. He designed the device, so he's the only one who knows the disarming code.'

'Great,' Race said.

Uli turned. 'Okay now, listen, this is how I see it. I am the only one of us who can get to the control booth. If they see either of you running down one of the cable bridges, they'll drop them immediately and isolate the booth. Then, if they don't get their money, they'll blow the Supernova.

'But they're expecting me back soon, believing that I have killed the two of you. When I get back, I will try to get to the control booth. Then I will try to . . . *persuade* . . . Weber to disarm the device.'

'What do we do in the meantime?' Race asked.

'For this to work,' Uli said, 'I must be able to deal with Weber alone. I need you two to take out Anistaze and the remaining men in the boat-house.'

Exactly seven hundred feet above the floor of the mine, Dr Fritz Weber was punching buttons on a computer console. Beside him, a laser cutting device was carefully going to work on the thyrium idol inside a vacuum-sealed chamber.

Behind Weber stood Ehrhardt. And behind Ehrhardt, standing in the exact centre of the control booth, stood a very imposing, six-foot-tall silver-and-glass device.

Two thermonuclear warheads—each approximately three feet in height and roughly conical in shape—were positioned inside a clear glass cylinder. They were arranged in what was known as an 'hourglass formation'—the upper warhead pointing downwards, the lower one pointing upwards—so that the whole device looked like an enormous eggtimer. In between the two warheads, at the throat of the hourglass, sat a skeletal frame made of titanium into which a subcritical mass of thyrium would be placed.

It was the Supernova.

A pair of cylindrical lead-lined containers each the size of an ordinary garbage bin sat beside the device. They were warhead capsules—monumentally strong, radiation-proof containers that were used to transport nuclear warheads in safety.

Now, as Weber knew, a conventional nuclear weapon required about 4.5 pounds of plutonium. The Supernova, on the other hand, according to his calculations, would require much less than that, only a quarter of a pound of thyrium.

Which was why now, with the aid of two Cray YMP supercomputers and a high-powered laser beam that could cut to within a thousandth of a millimetre, he was extracting a small cylindrical section of thyrium out of the idol.

Nuclear science had come a long way since J. Robert Oppenheimer's masterwork at Los Alamos in the 1940s.

With the aid of multi-tasking supercomputers like the two Crays, complex mathematical equations regarding the size, mass and force ratios of the radioactive core could be done in minutes. Inert gas purification, proton enrichment and alpha-wave augmentation could all be done simultaneously.

And the mathematics of it all—the crucial part, the part that had taken Oppenheimer and his band of masterminds six whole *years* to master with the aid of the most primitive computers—could be done by the YMPs in seconds.

In truth, the hardest part for Weber had been the actual construction of the device itself. Even with the aid of the supercomputers, it had still taken him more than two years to build.

While the laser cut through the stone in accordance with a preset weight-for-volume ratio based on the atomic weight of thyrium, Weber entered some complex mathematical formulae on one of the nearby supercomputers.

Moments later, the laser cutter beeped loudly and reverted to stand-by mode.

It was done.

Weber came over, flicked off the laser cutter. Then, using a robotic arm—human arms being too inexact for such a task—he extracted the small cylindrical section of thyrium from the base of the idol.

The section of thyrium was then placed inside a vacuum-sealed chamber and bombarded with uranium atoms and alpha waves, turning the tiny section of thyrium into a subcritical mass of the most potent substance ever to have existed on earth.

Moments later, the robotic arm carried the entire chamber over to the Supernova where with the utmost precision it slid the chamber—with the subcritical mass of thyrium inside it—into the titanium frame that was suspended in between the two thermonuclear warheads.

The Supernova was complete.

The subcritical mass of thyrium now sat horizontally in its vacuum-sealed throne between the two warheads, looking for all the world as if it contained the power of God.

The thing was, it did.

Screens all around the control booth scrolled out massive amounts of data feed. On one screen, under the heading 'DUAL AXIS RADIOGRAPHIC HYDRODYNAMIC FACILITY' a neverending series of ones and zeroes scrolled downwards.

Weber ignored them, began typing on the computer keyboard that was attached to the front of the Supernova. A prompt appeared on the screen: INSERT ARMING CODE.

Weber did so.

SUPERNOVA ARMED.

Weber typed: INITIALIZE TIMER DETONATION SEQUENCE.

TIMER DETONATION SEQUENCE INITIALIZED. INSERT TIMER DURATION.

Weber typed: 00:30:00.

The screen changed instantly.

```
┌─────────────────────────────────────────────┐
│                                               │
│                 YOU NOW HAVE                  │
│                   00:30:00                    │
│        MINUTES TO ENTER DISARM CODE.          │
│            ENTER DISARM CODE HERE             │
│                                               │
│                  ────────                     │
│                                               │
└─────────────────────────────────────────────┘
```

Weber paused as he gazed at the screen, took a slow, deep breath.

Then he slammed his finger down on the 'ENTER' key.

00:29:59

00:29:58

00:29:57

'Where is Unterscharführer Kahr?' Heinrich Anistaze asked nobody in particular as he peered out from the boat-house office at the immense earthen crater outside. 'He should have been back by now.'

Anistaze turned. '*You*,' he said, tossing a radio to one of the two lab coat-wearing technicians standing at a computer terminal nearby. 'Go to the pit and see what is taking the Unterscharführer so long.'

'Yes, sir.'

Renée and Race slammed into the boat-house wall together.

Only moments earlier, Uli had left them. He had headed off down the side of the massive boat-house in the direction of the crater and the northern cable bridge.

Renée peered round the wide garage door next to her.

The interior of the enormous boat-house was clear—in particular, the wide section of floor between the glass offices to her right and the mooring slots on her left.

Nothing stirred. There wasn't a soul in sight.

She nodded to Race.

Ready?

Race acknowledged her signal by gripping his Glock a little more tightly.

Ready.

Then without a word Renée quickly ducked around the doorway, her G-11 held high, pressed against her shoulder.

Race made to follow her, but as he did so, *another* door behind him suddenly burst open and he dropped to the ground in an instant, taking cover behind an old oil barrel.

A young Nazi technician—dressed in a white lab coat and holding a radio awkwardly in his hand— rushed out through the newly opened door and hurried off down the path toward the refuse pit.

Race's eyes went wide.

He was going to the refuse pit—where he would find one dead Nazi and nothing else.

'Shit,' Race said. 'Uli . . .'

Decision time. He could go after the technician— and then do what? Kill him in cold blood? Despite all that he had done so far, Race wasn't sure if he could actually do that, kill a man. On the other hand, he could warn Uli. Yes, that was better—much better.

And so at that moment, instead of following Renée into the boat-house, Race headed off down the side of the big warehouse-like building, in the direction of the crater and Uli.

Uli came to the northern cable bridge.

It stretched away from him into the distance, swooping fearlessly over the vertiginous seven-hundred-foot drop, its steel-threaded handrails converging like a pair of railroad tracks disappearing into the distance, ending as tiny specks at the doorway to the control booth four hundred yards away.

'Unterscharführer,' a voice said suddenly from behind him.

Uli spun.

And found himself standing before Heinrich Anistaze himself.

'What are you doing?' Anistaze demanded.

'I was going to see if the Oberstgruppenführer and Doctor Weber required any assistance over in the control booth,' Uli answered, perhaps a little too quickly.

'Have you eliminated the two prisoners?'

'Yes, sir, I have.'

'Where is Dieter?' Anistaze asked.

'He, uh, had to go to the WC,' Uli lied.

At that exact same moment, the lab technician Anistaze had sent to the refuse pit arrived there.

He saw Dieter's body immediately, lying face-down in the mud, blood and brains seeping out from the hole in the back of its head.

No Americans. No Uli, either.

The lab technician lifted his radio to his lips.

'*Herr Obergruppenführer,*' the technician's voice came in over Anistaze's earpiece.

'Yes.'

Anistaze was still standing with Uli at the edge of the northern cable bridge. The four fingers of the Nazi commander's left hand tapped silently on his pants leg as he listened to the voice on his earpiece.

'*Dieter is dead, sir. I repeat, Dieter is dead. I can't see the prisoners or Unterscharführer Kahr anywhere.*'

'Thank you,' Anistaze said, staring at Uli. 'Thank you very much.'

Anistaze's cold black eyes bored into Uli's. 'Where are the prisoners, Unterscharführer?'

'I beg your pardon, Herr Obergruppenführer?'

'I said, *where are the prisoners*?'

It was then that Uli saw the Glock appear in Anistaze's right hand.

Renée moved silently through the boat-house, gun up.

Race hadn't come in behind her, and she wondered what had happened to him. But she couldn't wait, she still had a job to do.

The boat-house was silent, still. The conveyor belt that rose up out of the tunnel to her right sat motionless. She saw no-one standing in the office beyond it—

An engine turned over.

Renée spun.

And saw the rotor blades of the parked Bell Jet Ranger helicopter slowly sputter to life.

Then she saw the pilot—lying on his side on the floor of the cockpit, oblivious to her presence—carrying out some kind of repairs on the chopper.

Then suddenly with a shrill *bzzzzz!* the rotor blades of the helicopter snapped into overdrive and the deafening roar of their motion filled the enormous space of the boat-house. Renée almost jumped out of her skin.

If it hadn't been for the roar of the rotors, however, she probably would have heard him sneak up on her.

But she didn't.

For at that moment, as Renée moved toward the pilot and the chopper with her G-11 raised, something very heavy hit her on the back of her head, pitching her forward, sending her falling heavily to the ground.

'Herr Obergruppenführer,' Uli said as he stood at the edge of the massive crater, raising his hands. 'What are you—'

Blam!

Anistaze's Glock went off—a single shot that went thundering into Uli's stomach. Uli doubled over at once, fell to the ground.

Anistaze stood over him, gun in hand. 'So, Unterscharführer. Am I to assume that you are BKA scum, too?'

Uli rolled around on the ground at the Nazi commander's feet, clenching his teeth in agony.

'No answer,' Anistaze said. 'Well, how about this, then. How about I blow off every finger on your right hand, one by one, until you tell me who you work for. And when I am done with that hand, I shall start on the other one.'

'Argh!' Uli grunted.

'Wrong answer,' Anistaze said, aiming his gun at Uli's hand, squeezing the trigger.

The gun went off.

Just as William Race—bursting out from behind the nearby corner—crashed into Anistaze from the side, hitting him at speed, knocking the Glock from his hand.

But the two of them fell awkwardly, bouncing off one of the buttresses that held up the cable bridge. Anistaze's right foot slipped over the edge of the crater and he threw out a hand that gripped Race's arm like a vice and before Race even knew what was happening, both he and Anistaze were falling out over the edge of the mine.

440

Race and Anistaze fell.

Down the wall of the crater.

Fortunately, the earthen walls of the mine weren't perfectly vertical but rather were slanted at a very steep angle, maybe 75 degrees or so. As such, they still fell fast, but not straight down. Both men kicked up puffs of dirt as they slid wildly down the wall of the crater. They slid a full ninety feet before they both landed in a crashing heap on flat, solid ground.

In the boat-house, Renée hit the ground, too, and for a moment she saw stars.

She rolled onto her back—

—just in time to see a length of piping held by the second Nazi lab technician come rushing down at her face! She rolled again and the pipe clanged against the floorboards inches away from her head.

She quickly somersaulted to her feet, looking for her weapon. Her G-11 lay on the ground four feet away, out of reach, dislodged by her fall after being smacked on the back of the head with the pipe.

The technician swung at her again.

Renée ducked and the pipe went swiping over her

head, then she bobbed back up and punched the technician square in the face, sending him flying backwards into a wall.

The technician's back slammed into a control panel on the wall. He must have struck a button as he hit it, Renée guessed, because at that moment she heard an ominous clanking of machinery within the walls of the massive boat-house and suddenly—without warning—the big conveyor belt that ran down the length of the warehouse started moving.

Race and Anistaze jolted forward.

Both men were still in something of a daze after their ninety-foot drop into the open-cut mine, and they were only just getting to their feet when suddenly the ground beneath them lurched forward.

Race tottered slightly, looked down at the ground beneath his feet.

It wasn't *solid* ground at all. It was the low end of the conveyor belt—the same conveyor belt that reached the surface inside the boat-house!

Only now it was moving.

Upward.

Race spun—just in time to see Anistaze's four-fingered left fist come flying at his face. The German commando's blow hit its mark and Race dropped like a sack of potatoes onto the wide conveyor belt.

Anistaze stood over him and then, abruptly, the world went black.

At first Race didn't know what had happened. Then he realised. He and Anistaze—positioned on the moving conveyor belt—had just been drawn into the long dark tunnel that led back up to the boat-house.

442

Up in the boat-house, Renée fought with the technician as the deafening roar of the Bell Jet Ranger's rapidly-spinning rotor blades echoed throughout the cavernous interior space.

The tech swung at Renée with the pipe again just as she leapt backwards and the blow missed, but as she moved, Renée saw that the pilot over in the helicopter had seen what was going on over by the conveyor belt and was now looking directly at her!

The pilot began to shimmy out of his awkward position on the floor of the chopper—just as, at that exact same moment, the young technician who had gone to the refuse pit to search for Uli appeared in the doorway of the boat-house!

Renée saw them both. And then in one fluid motion, as she ducked underneath another blow from the first technician, she pulled two grenades from her belt—the grenades Uli had retrieved from the dead Nazi at the refuse pit—yanked out their pins, spun and *hurled them across the boat-house together*!

The two grenades skidded across the floor, fanned out at different angles—one heading for the helipad pontoon and the chopper, the other heading directly for the young technician standing at the doorway.

One, one thousand . . .

Two, one thousand . . .

Three, one thousand . . .

The tech in the doorway realised what the object bouncing toward him was a second too late. He tried to move at the last moment, but he wasn't fast enough. The grenade exploded. So did he.

The second grenade bounced onto the helipad pontoon and came to rest directly underneath the sleek white Bell Jet Ranger. It detonated—abruptly, powerfully—shattering the chopper's bubble in a nanosecond, killing the pilot on its floor instantly. The blast also blew the helicopter's landing skids to hell, obliterating them, causing the whole chopper to drop *four feet straight down* and crash down onto the pontoon. It came to rest on its belly, its rotor blades still whipping around above it in a blur of speeding motion.

As they rose through the darkness, Race and Anistaze struggled.

Race fought hard—as hard as he physically could— throwing punches wildly, some hitting, most missing. But Anistaze was by far the better fighter, and soon he had Race flat on his back, pinned to the ground, vainly fending off his blows.

And then Anistaze drew a Bowie knife from a sheath down by his ankle. Even in the darkness of the steeply-sloping tunnel, Race saw the long glistening blade as it came rushing down toward his face.

He caught Anistaze's wrist with his hands, held the blade at bay, but the Nazi had all the leverage and the blade came closer and closer to his left eye—

—abruptly, harsh white light assaulted both of them and just as suddenly, the steep slope of the conveyor belt dropped level beneath them, causing both men to lose their balance and giving Race the chance to swipe Anistaze's knife clear.

He looked quickly about himself.

He was inside the boat-house again!

Only now he was travelling *horizontally* on the conveyor belt, still pinned underneath Anistaze.

Unfortunately for both of them, however, the conveyor belt was now drawing them toward the rapidly-spinning blades of the Bell Jet Ranger helicopter, which now—owing to the fact that it had lost its skids in the grenade blast—whipped round like a horizontal buzzsaw *barely three feet* above the moving conveyor belt!

The rotor blades were ten feet away. Spinning fast.

Nine feet.

Anistaze saw them too.

Eight feet.

Race saw Renée struggling with the technician over by the wall. The roar of the chopper's blurring rotor blades thundered throughout the cavernous warehouse.

Seven feet.

And Anistaze decided on a horrifying new tactic. With tremendous strength, he yanked Race up by the lapels and held him out at arm's length so that Race's neck was level with the speeding blades of the helicopter.

Six feet.

Renée was still fighting with the first technician. In between blows she saw Race and Anistaze fighting on the conveyor belt, saw Anistaze lift the professor onto his knees and hold him out from his body.

Her eyes went wide with horror.

Anistaze was going to decapitate Race with the blades of the chopper!

Five feet.

And she saw the control panel on the wall. The panel that started and stopped the conveyor belt . . .

Four feet.

Race saw the rapidly-spinning rotor blades behind him, saw what Anistaze was trying to do.

Three feet.

He tried to move, tried to fight. But it was no use.

Anistaze was just too strong. Race looked into his assailant's eyes and saw nothing but hate.

Two feet.

Certain death was approaching. Race yelled in desperation. '*Arrggghhhh!!*'

One foot.

At that precise moment, Renée ducked another blow from the technician and swung in swiftly behind him, then she grabbed him roughly by the hair and *banged* his head hard against the control panel on the wall.

The conveyor belt stopped on a dime.

Race stopped, too—the nape of his neck jolting to a halt *an inch* from the speeding blur of the helicopter's rotating blades.

Anistaze's face went blank in surprise.

What the fuck—?

Race took the opportunity and kneed the Nazi hard in the crotch.

Anistaze roared.

Just as Race grabbed *him* by the lapels!

'Smile, motherfucker,' Race said.

And then he dropped down onto the conveyor belt and rolled quickly backwards, *underneath* the chopper's blurring blades, using his newfound leverage to yank Anistaze forward, neck-first, *right into the buzz-saw-like blades of the helicopter!*

The rotor blades of the chopper sliced through Anistaze's neck like a chainsaw through butter, removing his head from his body in a smooth, frictionless cut.

An explosion of blood splattered all over Race's face as he lay on the conveyor belt, still holding onto Anistaze's lapels.

Race quickly discarded the body—*yecch!*—and rolled himself off the conveyor belt.

He shook his head. He couldn't quite believe what he had just done. He had just *decapitated* a man.

Whoa . . .

He looked up and saw Renée standing over by the control panel, standing astride the unconscious body of the Nazi technician. The tech had been knocked out cold by the blow she'd given him against the control panel.

Renée smiled at Race, gave him the thumbs up.

For his part, Race just fell limp against the floor, exhausted.

No sooner had his head hit the ground, however, than Renée was at his side.

'Not yet, Professor,' she said, pulling him to his feet. 'No resting yet. Come on, we have to stop Ehrhardt from detonating the Supernova.'

In the control booth high above the mine, the timer on the Supernova's laptop screen continued to tick downwards.

00:15:01

00:15:00

00:14:59

Ehrhardt keyed his radio. 'Obergruppenführer?'

No response.

'Anistaze, where are you?'

Still nothing.

Ehrhardt turned to Fritz Weber. 'Something's wrong. Anistaze's not answering. Initiate protective countermeasures around the device. Seal the control booth.'

'Yes, sir.'

Renée and Race dragged Uli into the glass-walled office overlooking the mine and laid him down on the floor.

A large digital timer on the wall ticked downwards:

00:14:55

00:14:54

00:14:53

'Damn it,' Race said, 'they started the countdown!'

Renée immediately went to work on the gunshot wound to Uli's stomach. As she did so, however, a fax machine on the far side of the office began to clatter loudly.

Race, now carrying a G-11 assault rifle, went over to it as a fax began to scroll out. It read:

FROM THE OFFICE OF
THE PRESIDENT OF THE UNITED STATES
— — — — — — — — — — — — — — — — —

SECURE FACSIMILE TRANSMISSION
— — — — — — — — — — — — — — — — —

ORIGINATING FAX NO: 1-202-555-6122
DESTINATION FAX NO: 51-3-454-9775
DATE: 5 JAN, 1999
TIME: 18:55:45 (LOCAL)

SENDER CODE: 004 (NATIONAL SECURITY ADVISOR)

MESSAGE IS AS FOLLOWS:
Having consulted with his advisors, and in keeping
with his well-known views on terrorism, the President
has instructed me to inform you that he WILL NOT
UNDER ANY CIRCUMSTANCES pay to you any sum of
money to restrain you from detonating any device you
may have in your possession.

W. PHILIP LIPANSKI
National Security Advisor
to the President of the United States

'Jesus,' Race breathed. 'They're not going to pay . . .'

Renée came over, looked at the fax. 'God, look how forceful the wording is. They're trying to call his bluff. They don't think he'll blow the Supernova.'

'Will he blow the Supernova?'

'Absolutely,' Uli said from the floor, causing Race and Renée to spin around.

Uli spoke through clenched teeth. 'He talks constantly of it. He's insane. He only wants one thing—his new world. And if he *can't* have that, then he will simply destroy the existing one.'

'But why?' Race said.

'Because that is the currency he trades in. It is the currency he has always traded in—life and death. Ehrhardt is an old man, old and evil. He has no further use for the world. If he doesn't get his money—and hence his new world order—he will just destroy the old one without even thinking twice.'

'Wonderful,' Race said. 'And we're the only ones who can stop him?'

'Yes.'

'Then how do we do it?' Renée said, turning to Uli. 'How do we stop the countdown?'

'You have to enter the disarm code into the device's arming computer,' Uli said. 'But as I said before, only Weber knows the code.'

'Then somehow,' Race said, 'we're going to have to get that code out of him.'

Moments later, Race was running around the rim of the immense crater, heading for the southern cable bridge.

The plan was simple.

Renée would wait at the start of the northern bridge while Race ran around the crater to the southern bridge. Then, when he arrived there, they would both make a run for the control booth at the same time, from opposite ends.

The logic of their plan was based on the fact that the two cable bridges that stretched out to the control booth were quite advanced and very sturdy—each bridge was constructed of high-tensile steel threads and to drop either of them would require someone to uncouple four separate pressure couplings. If Race and Renée bolted down the two bridges at the same time, one of them might make it to the booth before Ehrhardt and/or Weber managed to uncouple *both* bridges.

After six-and-a-half minutes of running, Race arrived at the southern cable bridge.

It stretched away from him, out over the mine. It was so monstrously *long*—a feature which was accentuated by its narrowness. While it was only wide enough for one person to travel down at a time, it was easily as long as four football fields stretched end on end.

Oh God, Race thought.

'Professor, are you ready?' Renée's voice said suddenly in his earpiece. It had been so long since he'd used his radio gear, Race had almost forgotten he was wearing it.

'As I'll ever be,' he said.

'Then let's go.'

Race stepped out onto the rope bridge.

He saw the white box-shaped cabin at the far end of it, suspended high above the floor of the mine— saw the door sunk into its wall at the point where the bridge met it. At the moment, that door was closed.

There was no movement inside the control booth's long rectangular windows, either.

No. The booth just sat there—silent—hovering perfectly in the air, seven hundred feet above the world.

Race moved down the bridge.

At that very same moment, Renée was moving quickly down the northern cable bridge.

She moved with her eyes locked on the closed door at the end of her bridge—watched it with tense anticipation, waiting for it to burst open at any moment.

But the door remained resolutely closed.

Odilo Ehrhardt peered out from behind one of the windows of the control booth, saw Renée coming down the northern bridge.

Out the opposite window, he saw Race mirroring her movement, coming down the southern cable bridge.

Now Ehrhardt had to make a choice.

He chose Race.

The tiny figures of Race and Renée made their way down the two swooping suspension bridges, converging on the control booth.

Renée was moving a little faster than Race, running quickly, her gun up. When she was about halfway down her walkway, however, the door at the end of it burst open and Odilo Ehrhardt stepped out onto the bridge.

Renée stopped dead in her tracks, froze.

Ehrhardt was holding the tiny figure of Dr Fritz Weber in front of him, shielding himself with the little scientist's struggling body. Ehrhardt had one pudgy arm wrapped around Weber's throat. In his other hand, he held a Glock-20 semi-automatic pistol levelled at the scientist's head.

Don't do it, Renée's mind pleaded, willing Ehrhardt not to kill the only man who knew the code to disarm the Supernova.

She obviously wasn't wishing hard enough. For at that moment—that singular, chilling moment—Odilo Ehrhardt gave Renée a final sinister smile and pulled the trigger.

The gun in Ehrhardt's hand went off—loud and hard, echoing throughout the crater.

It sent a geyser of blood exploding out the side of Weber's head, sent his brains spraying out over the handrail and down into the crater.

Weber's body went completely limp as Ehrhardt tipped it over the railing and Renée could do nothing but stare in stunned horror as the corpse dropped—dropped and dropped and dropped—seven hundred horrible feet before it hit the bottom of the mine with a muted distant thud.

Race heard the gunshot too, and a second later, he caught sight of Weber's body as it went sailing down into the crater.

'Good God . . .'

He started moving more quickly toward the control booth, started running . . .

Back on the northern side of the control booth, Odilo Ehrhardt wasn't finished.

Having tossed Weber's body off the bridge, he now

hurriedly began uncoupling the pressure hoses that connected the cable bridge to the control booth.

'*No!*' Renée yelled, gripping the handrail on either side of her.

With a sharp *snap-hiss!* one of the pressure couplings came free, and the handrail to Renée's left just dropped away.

Renée did the calculations in her head. There was no way she could get to the control booth before Ehrhardt released the other three couplings.

She turned around and ran, ran for all she was worth, back up the cable bridge.

Snap-hiss!

Another coupling broke free, and the *other* handrail dropped away.

Two couplings to go.

Renée was running hard—now on a rail-less bridge—seven hundred feet above the ground.

A few seconds later, the third coupling went and the boards beneath her started to sag to the left.

Then, with a final grin of satisfaction, Ehrhardt snapped open the last coupling and the massive suspension bridge—connected to the northern rim of the crater, but now no longer connected to the cabin in its centre—fell into the abyss, with Renée Becker on it.

Renée was only about fifty feet from the rim when the bridge dropped away beneath her. As soon as she felt it give way, she dived forward, clutching onto the steel floorboards with her fingers, holding onto them for dear life.

The cable bridge fell flat against the slanted wall of the crater. Renée slammed into the mine's earthen wall, bounced off it, but—somehow—managed to hold on.

Race reached the door at the end of his cable bridge just as Renée's voice came blasting in over his headset.

'Professor, this is Renée. My bridge is down. I'm out of the equation. It's up to you now.'

Great, Race thought wryly. *Just what I needed to hear.*

He took a deep breath and gripped his gun tightly. Then he grabbed the doorknob and turned it, and pushed open the door with the barrel of his G-11 . . .

. . . tripping the wire.

Beep!

Race saw Ehrhardt before he saw the source of the high-pitched beep.

The big Nazi general was standing on the other side of the control room, over by the northern door, with his Glock hanging lazily by his side. He was smiling at Race.

To Ehrhardt's left, Race saw the Supernova—its silver-and-glass surfaces gleaming, the cylindrical section of thyrium situated in its core, suspended inside its vacuum-sealed chamber in between the two thermonuclear warheads.

Two Cray YMP supercomputers sat against the wall to the side of the Supernova. The two warhead capsules that had been used to transport the nukes sat on the floor beside the big device, and the idol—now with a hollowed-out section in its base—sat on a nearby bench, discarded.

On the laptop computer attached to the front of the Supernova—the source of the beep—Race saw the countdown timer ticking down toward zero:

00:05:00
00:04:59
00:04:58

Underneath the countdown, he saw the words: 'ALTERNATE DETONATION SEQUENCE INITIALIZED.'

Alternate detonation sequence?

'Thank you, Little Man Trying Desperately To Be Brave,' Ehrhardt sneered. 'By entering this cabin, you have just condemned yourself to death.'

Race frowned.

Ehrhardt's eyes flicked left.

Race followed them, and saw—situated along the eastern wall of the control booth—eight yellow 200-gallon drums. The words 'CAUTION!' and 'DANGER: HYPERGOLIC FLUIDS' screamed out from their sides.

Other words were stencilled across the front sections of the huge yellow drums:

'HYDRAZINE.'

'NITROGEN TETROXIDE.'

There were four drums of hydrazine. Four of nitrogen tetroxide. A complex web of cables and hoses connected each plastic barrel to the next.

Hypergolic fluids, Race recalled from his chemistry days, *were fluids that exploded on contact with one another.*

A second countdown timer sat on top of one of the hydrazine drums. This timer, however, sat motionless, frozen at five seconds.

00:00:05

And then—just then—Race saw that the eight yellow drums were connected to the *Supernova's* arming computer by a thick black cord that snaked its way across the floor of the cabin.

00:04:00

00:03:59

00:03:58

'How?' Race demanded, his G-11 pressed against his shoulder, trained on Ehrhardt's chest. 'How have I condemned myself to death?'

'By opening that door, you just triggered a mechanism that will, in one way or another, end your life.'

'*How goddamnit!*'

Ehrhardt smiled. 'There are two incendiary devices in this room, Professor: the Supernova and the hypergolic fuels. One will blow up the entire planet, the other will only blow up this cabin. I know you wish to disarm the Supernova, but if you succeed in doing that you will do so at a price.'

'What price?'

'Your life in exchange for the world's. By opening that door, Professor, you set off a mechanism that linked the Supernova's arming computer to the hypergolic fluids. Now, if for any reason the Supernova's countdown is terminated, the timer on the hypergolic fuels will be started. In five seconds, the fuels will mix and when they do they will detonate, destroying this cabin, destroying *you*.

'So now you have a choice, Professor, a singular choice, unique in the history of mankind. You can die with the rest of the planet in exactly three-and-a-half minutes—or you can save the world. But in doing so, you must sacrifice your own life.'

Race couldn't believe what he was hearing.

A singular choice . . .

You can save the world . . .

But to do so, you must sacrifice your own life . . .

The two men stood on either side of the control booth, Race standing in the southern doorway with his G-11 pressed against his shoulder, Ehrhardt over by the northern door, with his Glock by his side.

00:03:21

00:03:20

00:03:19

'The President has agreed to pay your ransom—' Race said quickly, trying a last-ditch ploy.

'No he hasn't,' Ehrhardt snapped, snatching a sheet of paper from the bench beside him and flinging it at Race.

The sheet fluttered to the floor. It was a copy of the same fax Race had seen in the mine's office earlier. Ehrhardt must have had a fax machine in here too.

'And even if he had said that he would pay,' the Nazi spat, 'I *still* wouldn't be able to disarm the device. Only Weber knew the disarming code and he, my friend, is dead. No. Now, it is *you* or it is *nothing*. Now, whatever happens, at least I will have the satisfaction of knowing that you will not be leaving this cabin alive.'

'But what about you?' Race said defiantly. 'You'll die too.'

'I am old, Professor Race. Old and decayed. Death means nothing to me. The fact that I can take the rest of the world with me, however, means *everything* . . .'

And at that moment, quick as a rattlesnake, Ehrhardt whipped his Glock up, aimed it at Race and pulled the—

Blam!

Race's G-11 bucked against his shoulder as he fired a single round.

The caseless bullet smacked into Ehrhardt's enormous chest, causing a gout of blood to explode out from it, the impact hurling the big man into the wall behind him.

Ehrhardt slammed into the wall and—*ba-blam!*—his Glock went off, firing into the ceiling, smashing a smoke alarm to pieces, and suddenly a series of fire sprinklers in the ceiling of the cabin burst forth with showers of water.

Ehrhardt sank to the floor in the teeming indoor rain—a dribbling, ugly mess—his mouth open, his eyes wide with shock.

Race just stood there in his doorway, frozen in the firing position, water hammering against his face, stunned.

He had never shot a man before. Not even during the river chase earlier. He felt ill. He swallowed back the bile welling in his throat.

And then he saw the Supernova's timer:

00:03:00

00:02:59

00:02:58

He snapped out of his trance, hurried over to examine the fallen Nazi leader.

Ehrhardt was still alive, but barely. Blood dribbled out from his mouth, bubbled out from his chest.

But his eyes still glimmered, glaring up at Race with a kind of mad delight, as if Ehrhardt were thrilled to have left him in this position—alone in a control booth in a foreign country, with nothing but a dying Nazi, a ticking Supernova, and eight drums of explosive hypergolic fuel that would kill him for certain even if he did manage to disarm the main bomb.

All right, Will, stay calm.
  00:02:30
  00:02:29
  00:02:28
Two-and-a half minutes to the end of the world.
Stay calm, my ass!
Race scrambled across the floor to the Supernova,
peered at the screen on its arming computer.

```
                    YOU NOW HAVE
                      00:02:27
        MINUTES TO ENTER DISARM CODE.
           ENTER DISARM CODE HERE

           _____
```

Race stared in dismay at the timer. Sprinkler rain
pounded against his head.
What are you gonna do, Will?
It wasn't like he had a choice now, was it?
He could die along with the rest of the world or he
could try to figure out how to stop the Supernova—
and die that way, too.
Damn it! he thought.

He wasn't a hero.

People like Renco and Van Lewen were heroes. He was just a nobody. *A guy.* A university professor who was always late for work, who always missed his train. Jesus, he still had outstanding parking fines to pay, for God's sake!

He wasn't a hero.

And he didn't want to die like one either.

Besides, he wouldn't know the first thing about cracking the code on the Supernova's arming computer. He wasn't a hacker. No, the simple fact of the matter was that Fritz Weber was dead, and *he* was the only one who knew the code that would disarm the Supernova.

00:02:01

00:02:00

00:01:59

Race shut his eyes, sighed.

Might as well die like a hero.

And so he sat up straight in front of the Supernova, and stared at its display screen with a fresh mind.

All right, Will, deep breaths. Deep breaths.

He looked at the screen, at the line that read:

ENTER DISARM CODE HERE

_ _ _ _ _ _ _ _

Okay.

Eight spaces to fill. To fill with a code.

Okay, so who knows the code?

Weber knows the code.

He was the *only* one who knew the code.

Just then a voice exploded in Race's ear and he almost jumped out of his skin.

'Professor. What's happening?'

It was Renée.

'Jesus, Renée. You scared the shit out of me. What's happening? Well, Ehrhardt shot Weber and then I shot Ehrhardt and now I'm sitting in front of the Supernova trying to figure out how to disarm it. Where are you?'

'I'm back in the office overlooking the crater. Ehrhardt cut my bridge.'

'Got any ideas on how to disarm this thing?'

'No. Weber was the only one—'

'I know that already. Listen, I've got eight spaces to fill and I need to fill 'em fast.'

'Okay. Let me think . . .'

00:01:09

00:01:08

00:01:07

'One minute, Renée.'

'All right. All right. They said in that telephone transcript that their Supernova is based on the US model, right? That means the code must be numerical.'

'How do you know that?'

'Because I know that the American Supernova has a numerical code.' She must have heard his silence. *'We have people inside your agencies.'*

'Oh, okay. Numerical code it is then. Eight-digit code. That leaves us with about a trillion possible combinations.'

00:01:00

00:00:59

00:00:58

'Weber was the only person who knew the code, right?' Renée said. *'So it has to be something to do with him.'*

'Or it could be a number that's completely random,' Race said dryly.

'Unlikely,' Renée said. *'People who use numerical codes rarely use random numbers. They use numbers that have significance to them, numbers that they can recall by*

thinking of a memorable event or date or something like that.
So what do we know about Weber?'

But Race wasn't listening anymore.

Something had twigged in the back of his mind as he'd been listening to Renée—something about what she had just said.

'All right,' Renée was saying, thinking aloud. *'He was a Nazi during the Second World War. He performed experiments on human subjects.'*

But Race was thinking about something else entirely.

They use numbers that have significance to them, numbers that they can recall by thinking of a memorable event or date . . .

And then it hit him.

It was the *New York Times* article that he had read on his way to work yesterday morning—before he had arrived at the university to find a team of Special Forces troops waiting for him in his office.

The article had said that thieves were finding it easier to break into people's bank accounts because 85 per cent of people used their birthdays or some other significant date as their ATM number.

'When was his birthday?' Race said suddenly.

'Oh, I know that,' Renée said. *'I saw it in his file. It was in 1914 sometime. Oh, what was it? That's it. August 6. August 6, 1914.'*

00:00:30

00:00:29

00:00:28

'What do you think?' Race yelled over the roar of the indoor rain.

'It's a possibility,' Renée said.

Race thought about that for a second. He scanned the room around him as he did so—saw Ehrhardt sitting with his back up against the wall, cackling through his blood-filled mouth.

'No,' Race said decisively. 'That's not it.'

'What?'

00:00:21

00:00:20

00:00:19

For some reason, Race was thinking with crystal clarity now.

'It's too simple. If he used a date at all, it would be a significant one, but one which would be in some way clever or smug. Something which shoved it to the rest of the world. He wouldn't use something as inane as his *birthday*. He would use something with meaning.'

'Professor, we don't have much time. What else is there?'

Race tried to remember everything he had heard about Fritz Weber earlier.

He had performed experiments on human subjects.

00:00:15

He had been tried at Nuremberg.

00:00:14

And sentenced to death.

00:00:13

And executed.

00:00:12

Executed.

Executed . . .

That's it, Race thought.

00:00:11

But when was the date?

00:00:10

'Renée. Quickly. What was the date of Weber's supposed execution?'

00:00:09

'Oh . . . November 22, 1945.'

465

00:00:08
November 22, 1945.
00:00:07
Do it.
00:00:06
Race leaned forward, punched in the numbers on the Supernova's keyboard.

ENTER DISARM CODE HERE

1 1 2 2 1 9 4 5

Once he had entered the code—with the sprinkler rain pounding down around him and the timer in front of him rapidly counting down to zero—Race slammed his finger down on the 'ENTER' key.

Beep!

Ehrhardt's cackling stopped as soon as he heard the beep.

Race's face broke out into a wide grin.

Oh my God, I did it . . .

And then suddenly the Supernova's screen changed:

```
DISARM CODE ENTERED.

DETONATION COUNTDOWN TERMINATED AT

00:00:04

MINUTES.

ALTERNATE DETONATION SEQUENCE ACTIVATED.
```

Alternate detonation sequence?

'Oh, *damn* . . .' Race breathed.

His eyes flashed over to the *other* timer—the one that sat on top of the hydrazine drums on the other side of the room—the timer that was set permanently at 00:00:05.

The second timer activated, ticked over to 00:00:04.

467

Ehrhardt's eyes went wide with surprise.

Race's went even wider.

'Oh, man,' he said.

Exactly four seconds later, at the expiration of the abbreviated countdown, the hypergolic fuels in the drums mixed and the walls of the control booth blew out with shocking force.

Its windows shattered as one, blasting out into the sky in a million fragments, closely followed by a roaring, billowing, blasting ball of flames.

Debris shot out in every direction—doors, pieces of the Supernova, torn segments of wooden benches, sections of floor—all dispatched with such monumental force that some of them even managed to clear the rim of the crater, landing in the thick foliage that surrounded the giant earthen mine. The cracked pieces of the two thermonuclear warheads that had comprised the Supernova landed harmlessly on the floor of the crater—the hypergolic blast far too crude to split the atoms inside them.

In a moment, all that was left of the control booth was a blackened skeletal frame—charred beyond recognition, hanging loosely above the mine—its walls gone, its windows gone, its floor and ceiling also gone.

William Race was gone too.

SIXTH MACHINATION

Tuesday, January 5, 1910 hours

The two rivercraft motored slowly across the river's surface toward the abandoned mine.

One of the vessels was a long sleek speedboat, the other, a battered-looking little seaplane, with only one pontoon hanging down from its right wing.

The world was silent, the river calm.

Leonardo Van Lewen and Doogie Kennedy peered out from their respective cockpits, stared at the deserted mine in front of them. Slowly, they both brought their vessels in toward the riverbank, ran them gently aground.

They had heard the hypergolic explosion and now they saw the mine—the immense brown earthen crater—and the plume of black smoke rising from the charred box-shaped shell hanging in its centre.

There was no-one in sight.

Nothing stirred.

Whatever had happened here was well and truly over.

The two Green Berets jumped out of their vessels and walked cautiously over to the collection of old warehouse-like buildings at the edge of the canyon, guns in hand.

Then, abruptly, Renée appeared from a door in one

of the buildings. She saw them instantly, came over, and the three of them stood together at the edge of the canyon, staring out at the blackened remains of the control booth.

'What happened here?' Van Lewen asked.

'Ehrhardt used the idol to arm the Supernova. Then he set it to detonate,' Renée said, her voice sad and soft. 'Professor Race managed to stop the detonation sequence, but no sooner had he neutralised the Supernova than the whole cabin just exploded.'

Van Lewen turned to look out at the destroyed control booth, at the last place William Race had been seen alive.

'The device was in there?' he asked.

'Uh-huh,' Renée said. 'You wouldn't have believed it. He stopped the countdown. He was amazing.'

'What about the idol?'

'Destroyed in the blast, I presume, along with the Supernova and Professor Race.'

There came a rustling sound from their right.

Van Lewen and Doogie spun, guns up.

But when they turned, they saw nothing but trees and foliage.

And then suddenly a drum-like cylindrical object—a capsule of some sort, about the size of a regular garbage bin—dropped out of the upper branches of a tree and bounced softly onto the thick foliage about twenty yards away from them.

Van Lewen, Renée and Doogie all frowned, went over to it.

The capsule must have been inside the control booth when it blew, and been blasted all the way here by the concussion wave.

The warhead capsule rolled to a halt in the foliage, and then, oddly, it began to wobble back and forth, as if there were someone inside it wriggling around, trying to get out—

Suddenly the lid of the capsule popped open and Race tumbled out of it and went sprawling butt-first onto the wet, muddy ground.

Renée's face broke out into a thousand-watt grin and she and the two Green Berets rushed over to where Race was lying in the foliage.

The professor lay on his back in the mud—soaking wet and exhausted beyond belief. He was still wearing his cap and his black kevlar breastplate.

He looked up at his three comrades as they came over, offered them a tired half-smile.

Then he pulled his right hand out from behind his back and placed an object on the ground in front of him. Droplets of water glistened all over it, but there was no mistaking the shiny black-and-purple stone and the fierce features of the rapa's head that had been carved into it.

It was the idol.

The Goose flew through the air, soaring gracefully over the Amazon rainforest.

It was heading west in the early dark of night. Back toward the mountains, back toward Vilcafor.

Doogie sat up front in the cockpit, flying the plane, while Van Lewen, Race, Renée and the wounded Uli sat in the back.

Race pondered his escape from the control booth.

In the five seconds he'd had between disarming the Supernova and the mixing of the hypergolic fuels, he had desperately searched the cabin for a way out.

As it happened, his eyes fell upon one of the warhead capsules—a container capable of withstanding 10,000 pounds-per-square-inch of pressure since its purpose was the protection of explosive nuclear warheads.

With nothing else to call on, he'd dived for it— snatching the idol sitting on the workbench on the way and snapping shut the capsule's lid just as the five-second countdown expired.

The fuels mixed and the control booth blew and he was launched high into the sky, inside the capsule. Thankfully, it had landed relatively softly in the trees surrounding the mine.

But he was alive and that was all that mattered.

Now, as he sat in his seat in the back of the sea-plane, Race also held in his hands a tattered leather-bound book that he had found in the boat-house after his spectacular escape. It had been sitting on a shelf inside the office overlooking the mine.

It was a book that he'd insisted on searching for before they headed back to Vilcafor.

It was the Santiago Manuscript.

The *original* Santiago Manuscript—written by Alberto Santiago in the sixteenth century, stolen from the San Sebastian Abbey by Heinrich Anistaze in the twentieth, and copied by Special Agent Uli Pieck of the *Bundes Kriminal Amt* not long after that.

As he sat in the back of the little seaplane, Race gazed at the manuscript in a kind of subdued awe.

He saw Alberto Santiago's handwriting. The strokes and flourishes were familiar, but now he saw them on beautifully textured paper and written in rich blue ink, not some harsh, scratchy photocopy.

He wanted to read it immediately, but no, that would have to wait. There were some other things he had to settle first.

'Van Lewen,' he said.

'Yes.'

'Tell me about Frank Nash.'

'What?'

'I said, tell me about Frank Nash.'

'What do you want to know?'

'Have you worked with him before?'

'No. This is my first time. My unit was pulled out of Bragg to come on this mission.'

'Are you aware that Nash is a colonel in the Army's Special Projects Unit?'

'Yeah, sure.'

'So you knew it was a lie when Nash came to my

office yesterday morning with a DARPA ID and a story saying that he was a *retired* Army colonel now working with the Defense Advanced Research Projects Agency?'

'I didn't know he said that.'

'You *didn't* know?'

Van Lewen looked at Race honestly. 'Professor Race, I'm just a grunt, okay. I was told that this was to be a protective assignment. I was told to protect *you*. So that's what I'm doing. If Colonel Nash lied to you, I'm sorry, but I didn't know.'

Race clenched his teeth. He was pissed as hell. He was furious at having been tricked into coming along on the mission.

In addition to being angry, however, he was also determined to know everything, for if Nash wasn't really with DARPA then it raised a whole lot of *other* questions. For instance, what about Lauren and Copeland? Were they with Army Special Projects, too?

Even closer to home were the questions regarding how Race himself had come to be a part of the mission. After all, Nash had claimed to have been put onto him by his brother Marty. But Race hadn't even seen his brother in almost ten years.

Strangely, Race found himself thinking about Marty.

They'd been close as kids. Although Marty had been a good three years older than him, they had always played together—football, baseball, just plain running around. But Will had always been better at sports, despite the age difference.

Marty, on the other hand, was easily the cleverer of the two boys. He'd excelled at school and been ostracised for it. He wasn't handsome, and even as a nine-year-old he was the image of his father, all hunched shoulders and thick dark eyebrows, with a permanently severe expression that was reminiscent of Richard Nixon.

Conversely, Race had his mother's easy good looks—sandy brown hair and sky blue eyes.

As teenagers, while Will would go out on the town with his friends, Marty would just stay at home with his computers and his prized collection of Elvis Presley records. By age nineteen, Marty hadn't even had a girlfriend. Indeed, the only girl he'd ever liked—a pretty young cheerleader named Jennifer Michaels—had turned out to have a crush on Will. It had devastated Marty.

College came and while his schoolyard tormentors went off to become bank tellers and real estate agents, Marty had headed straight for the computer labs at MIT—fully paid for by his father, a computer engineer.

Race on the other hand—intelligent for sure but always the lesser academically—would go to USC on a half sports scholarship. There he would meet, court and lose Lauren O'Connor and, in between all that, study languages.

Then came their parents' divorce.

It happened so suddenly. One day, Race's father came home from the office and told his mother that he was leaving her. It turned out he'd been having an affair with his secretary for almost eleven months.

The family split in two.

Marty, then twenty-five, still saw their father regularly—after all, he had always been his old man's son both in looks and manner.

But Race never forgave his father. When he died of a heart attack in 1992, Race didn't even go to the funeral.

It was the classic American nuclear family—nuked from within.

Race snapped out of it, returned to the present, to a seaplane flying over the jungles of Peru.

'What about Lauren and Copeland?' he asked Van Lewen. 'Are they with Army Special Projects too?'

'Yes,' Van Lewen said solemnly.

Son of a bitch.

'All right then,' Race said, changing tack. 'What do you know about the Supernova project?'

'I swear I don't know anything about it,' Van Lewen said.

Race frowned, bit his lip.

He turned to Renée. 'What do *you* know about the American Supernova project?'

'A little.'

Race raised his eyebrows expectantly.

Renée sighed. 'Project approved by the Congressional Armaments Committee in closed session: January 1992. Budget of $1.8 billion approved by Senate Appropriations Committee, again in closed session: March 1992. Project was intended to be a co-operative joint venture between the Defense Advanced Research Projects Agency and the United States Navy. Project leader's name is—'

'Wait a second,' Race said, cutting her off. 'The Supernova is a Navy project?'

'That's right.'

So Frank Nash had told more than one lie to get him to come along on the mission. The Supernova wasn't even an Army project at all.

It was a *Navy* project.

And then, suddenly, Race found himself recalling something he had heard the previous night, when he had been imprisoned inside the Humvee, *before* the cats had attacked the BKA team.

He recalled hearing a woman's voice—Renée's

maybe—saying something in German over the radio, a sentence that he had found quite incongruous at the time, a sentence which he *hadn't* translated for Nash and the others.

Was ist mit dem anderen amerikanischen Team? Wo sind die jetzt?

'What about the other American team? Where are they now?'

The other American team . . .

'I'm sorry, Renée,' he said, 'who did you say was the Supernova's project leader?'

'His name is Romano. Doctor Julius Michael Romano.'

And there it was.

The mysterious Romano, revealed at last.

Romano's team was the other American team. A Navy team.

Christ . . .

'So let me just get this straight,' Race said. 'The Supernova is a Navy project led by a guy named Julius Romano, right?'

'That's right,' Renée said.

'And Romano and his team are in Peru right now, searching for the thyrium idol?'

'That's right.'

'But Frank Nash has an Army team down here as well, *also* going after the idol.'

'That's correct,' Renée said.

'So why? Why is a team led by a colonel from the U.S. Army's Special Projects Division trying to beat a team of U.S. *Navy* people to an idol that is the key to a weapon that the Navy owns?'

Renée said, 'The answer to that question is a little more complex than it would at first appear, Professor Race.'

'Try me.'

'All right,' Renée said, taking a deep breath. 'For

the last six years, German intelligence has been looking on silently as the three branches of the United States armed forces—the Army, the Navy and the Air Force—have engaged in a very bitter but very secret power struggle.

'What they fight for is survival. They fight to be the pre-eminent armed service in the United States, so that when the U.S. Congress finally removes one of them—as it intends to do in the year 2010—it will not be their branch that takes the bullet. They fight to make themselves indispensable.'

'Congress intends to remove one of the armed services by 2010?' Race said.

'By a secret Department of Defense minute dated 6 September 1993 and signed by both the Secretary of Defense and the President himself, the Department of Defense recommended to the President that by the year 2010, one branch of the United States military be made redundant.'

'Okay . . .' Race said, doubtfully. 'And how is it that you know all this?'

Renée offered him a crooked smile. 'Come on, Professor. The U.S. Navy isn't the only navy in the world which secretly taps into other countries' undersea communications cables.'

'Oh,' Race said.

'The basis of the Department's decision was that war has changed. The old land-sea-air division of a country's armed forces no longer applies to the modern world. It's an anachronism from two world wars and a thousand years of hand-to-hand combat. The decision then becomes *which service goes*?'

'Ever since that time,' Renée went on, 'each branch of the armed services has attempted to prove its worth, at the expense of the other two.'

'For example?' Race said sceptically.

'For example, the Air Force claims it has the Stealth Bomber and a unique expertise in air superiority fighting. But the Navy counters by saying that it has Carrier Battle Groups. On top of that, it claims that not only are its regular fighters and bombers as stealthy as the B-3 anyway, but also that they have the added advantage of a transportable landing strip. With a dozen Carrier Battle Groups, the Navy says, who needs an Air Force?

'The Army, on the other hand, claims it has specialised ground troops and mechanised infantry forces. But both the Navy and the Air Force counter this by saying that modern warfare takes place in the skies and on the world's oceans, not on land. They say to look at the Gulf War and the Kosovo conflict—battles that were fought from the sky, not the ground.

'Add to that the Navy's close affiliation with the United States Marine Corps. Since the Marines Corps' existence is guaranteed by the American Constitution, they *cannot* be eliminated. And they have both ground *and* mechanised infantry capabilities, thus putting even more pressure on the Army to justify its existence.

'Hell, look at ICBMs. *All three* armed services maintain missile launch facilities: the Navy has submarine-launched systems; the Air Force air- and land-launched systems; and the Army land and mobile systems. Does a nation seriously need *three* separate nuclear missile systems when really only two—or even one—would do?'

'So who looks like being the loser?' Race asked, cutting to the chase.

'The Army,' Renée said simply. 'Without a doubt. Especially when the Constitutional guarantee for the Marine Corps is taken into account. In every analysis

I've seen so far, the Army has always come in third place.'

'So they need to prove their worth,' Race said.

'They *desperately* need to prove their worth. Or diminish one of the other service's worth.'

'What do you mean, "diminish one of the other service's worth"?'

'Professor,' Renée said, 'did you know that late last year there was a break-in at Vandenberg Air Force base?'

'No.'

'Some top-secret plans for the new W-88 nuclear warhead were stolen. The W-88 is a miniaturised warhead, state of the art. Six security staff were killed during the theft. The official investigative report into the break-in—and the subsequent media coverage of it—claimed that it was the work of Chinese agents. The *unofficial* report into the break-in, however, says that upon examination of the kill and entry techniques used, only one unit could have executed the crime. An Army Special Forces unit. Green Berets.'

Race shot a look at Van Lewen. The Green Beret sergeant just shrugged helplessly back at him. This was news to him.

'The *Army* broke into an *Air Force* base?' Race said in disbelief.

Renée said, 'You see, Professor, the Army are working on a new miniaturised warhead of their own. The successful completion of the W-88 would have seriously undermined their own project—and provided one less reason to keep them around in 2010.'

Race frowned. 'So how do we apply this to the Supernova project?'

'Simple,' Renée said. 'The Supernova is the ultimate weapon. Whichever armed service controls its use will ensure its survival in 2010. Quite obviously, although the Supernova is officially a Navy project, the Army has taken it upon itself to build its own device—in all likelihood using information that they have managed to obtain from a source inside the Navy project.'

'But no-one has any thyrium yet,' Race said.

'Which is why everybody's down here looking for that idol.'

'Okay, so let me get this straight,' Race said. 'Even though the Supernova is officially a Navy project, the Army has been secretly constructing its own device. Then, when it discovers that there might be a source of thyrium out there, it gives Frank Nash and the Special Projects Unit the task of finding that thyrium before the Navy does.'

'That's correct.'

'Goddamn,' Race breathed. 'How far up does a thing like this go?' He was thinking about yesterday's motorcade out of New York. For someone to make *that* happen required some serious rank.

'*All* the way up,' Renée said in a low voice. 'All the way to the highest-ranking officers in the U.S. Army hierarchy. And that's what really scares me. I've never seen the Army so desperate. I mean, God, look at this mission. This is *it*. This is the home run. If the Army gets that stone'—she nodded at the idol on the empty seat next to Race—'they *guarantee* their future existence. And that means that Frank Nash will do anything to get it. Anything at all.'

Race picked up the idol. It glistened in his hands, the rapa's head snarling with menace.

He just stared at it sadly, looked at the newly hollowed-out section in its base.

'Then I guess there's really only one problem, then, isn't there?' he said.

'What's that?' Renée said.

'This idol.'

'What about it?'

'You see, that's the thing,' Race said. 'This idol isn't made of thyrium. This idol is a fake.'

'It's a what?' Renée gasped.

'It's a fake?' Van Lewen echoed.

'It's a fake,' Race confirmed. 'Here, take a look.' He tossed the gleaming black idol to Van Lewen. 'What do you see?'

The big sergeant shrugged. 'I see the Incan idol that we came here to get.'

'Do you?' Race leaned forward, grabbing a water canteen that hung off Van Lewen's belt. 'Can I borrow this?'

He quickly unscrewed the lid and tipped the contents of the canteen onto the idol.

Water splashed all over the rapa's head, ran down its face, dribbled down onto the floor of the plane.

'Okay, so . . . ?' Van Lewen said.

'According to the manuscript,' Race said, 'when the idol gets wet, it's supposed to emit a low humming noise. This one isn't making a sound.'

'*So?*'

'So it's not made of thyrium. If it were made of thyrium, the oxygen in the water would make it resonate. This isn't the real idol. It's a fake.'

'But when did you know?' Renée asked.

Race said, 'When I took this idol off the workbench

a couple of seconds before the cabin blew, the sprinkler system inside the control booth was dousing the whole room with water. It splashed all over the idol, but ever since that time it hasn't hummed at all.'

'So the Nazis' Supernova *wouldn't* have destroyed the world?' Van Lewen said.

'Nope,' Race said. 'Just us, and maybe a few hundred hectares of rainforest with the thermonuclear blast. But not the world.'

'If it isn't made of thyrium,' Van Lewen said, 'what is it made of?'

'I don't know,' Race said. 'Some kind of volcanic rock, I guess.'

'If it's a fake,' Renée said, taking the idol from Van Lewen, 'then who made it? Who *could* have made it? It was found inside a temple that no-one's been inside for over four hundred years.'

'I think I know who made it,' Race said.

'You do?'

He nodded.

'*Who?*' Renée and Van Lewen asked at the same time.

Race held up the leather-bound manuscript in his hand—the original Santiago Manuscript—the same manuscript that Alberto Santiago himself had once laboured over a long, long time ago.

'The answer to that question,' he said, 'lies in the pages of this book.'

Race retired to the rear section of the little seaplane.

They would arrive back at Vilcafor soon. But before they did, he wanted to read the manuscript—to read it right to the end.

There were so many questions he wanted

answered. Like *when* Renco had substituted a fake idol for the real one, or how he had got the rapas back into the temple.

But most of all—more importantly than anything else—he wanted to know one thing.

Where the real idol lay.

Race settled into his seat at the back of the plane. Just as he was about to open the manuscript, however, he saw the emerald pendant hanging from his neck—Renco's pendant—and took it in his hand. He ran his fingers over the stone's glistening green edges. As he did so, he thought about the skeleton from which he had taken the leather neckpiece earlier that day—the filthy battered skeleton that he had found just inside the temple.

Renco . . .

Race blinked out of it, tried not to think about it. He released the emerald and collected his thoughts. Then he found the spot in the manuscript where he had last left the story:

Alberto Santiago had just saved Renco's sister, Lena, from the rapas, after which Lena had told Renco that the Spaniards would be arriving at Vilcafor by daybreak . . .

FOURTH READING

Renco stared at Lena for the longest of moments.

'Daybreak,' said he, repeating her words.

It was still dark outside, but it would be morning in a matter of hours.

'That is right,' said Lena.

In the dim firelight of the citadel, I could see the thoughts as they crossed Renco's face—his mission to save the idol conflicting with his desire to help the people of Vilcafor in their time of dire need.

Renco looked across the interior of the citadel. 'Bassario,' said he and sharply.

I turned to see Bassario sitting cross-legged on the floor in a darkened corner of the citadel, his back to the room as usual.

'Yes, oh, wise prince,' the criminal said, not looking up from what he was doing.

'What progress have you made?'

'I am almost finished.'

Renco strode over to where the devious criminal was sitting. I followed.

Bassario turned as Renco arrived at his side, and I saw on the floor beside him the idol that it was our sworn mission to protect. Bassario then offered Renco something to appraise.

When I saw what it was, I stopped dead in my tracks.

Then I blinked my eyes twice and looked again for I was sure that they were playing a trick on me.

But they were not.

They most certainly were not.

For there in Bassario's hands, right before my eyes, was an exact replica of Renco's idol.

Of course, Renco had planned it all, conceived it from the very beginning.

I remembered our brief stop in the quarry town of Colco very early in our journey, remembered seeing Renco obtain a sack full of sharp-edged objects. And I distinctly remembered wondering at the time why we were wasting our precious time collecting rocks!

But now I understood.

Renco had obtained a collection of rocks from the quarry which had most imitated the strange black-and-purple stone from which the idol had been carved.

Then he had given those stones to the criminal Bassario and commissioned him to carve an identical copy of the idol with which, presumably, he would bamboozle Hernando.

It was brilliant.

I also realised then what Bassario had been doing throughout our journey, at those times when he would skulk off to a corner of our camp and huddle over a small fire with his back to us.

He had been carving his copy of the idol.

And truly, it must be said, what a remarkable copy it was. The snarling jaws of the cat, the knife-like teeth. All of it carved out of a most lustrous kind of black-and-purple stone.

And for a moment, all I could do was stare at the false idol and wonder what kind of master criminal Bassario had been.

'How long until you are finished?' Renco inquired of Bassario. As Renco spoke, I noticed that the replica still required some finishing touches around the cat's jawline.

'Not long,' the criminal answered. 'It will be done by dawn.'

'You have half that time,' said Renco, turning away from Bassario and looking at the assembled group of survivors gathered behind him in the citadel.

It did not give him much hope.

Before him stood Vilcafor—old and vain and frail—and seven Inca warriors, those who had been lucky enough to be inside the citadel when the rapas had first attacked. In addition to the seven warriors, however, Renco saw only an assortment of frightened-looking older men, women and children.

'Renco,' I whispered. 'What are we going to do?'

My brave companion pursed his lips in thought. Then he spoke thusly: 'We are going to put an end to all this suffering. Once and for all.'

And with that, while Bassario worked feverishly to finish his replica of the idol, Renco began to organise the surviving members of Vilcafor.

'Now listen,' said he as they gathered around him in a tight circle, 'the gold-eaters will be here by sunrise. By my reckoning, that gives us less than two hours to prepare for their arrival.

'Women, children and older kin—you will enter the

493

quenko under the direction of my sister and get as far away from the village as possible.

'Warriors,' he said, turning to face the seven surviving warriors of the village. 'You will come with me, to this temple that Vilcafor speaks of. If these rapas come from within that building, then we will just have to put them back inside it. We shall lure them into the temple with the song of the wet idol and then we shall shut them back inside it. Now go, gather together whatever weapons you can muster.'

The warriors hurried off.

'Lena,' said Renco.

'Yes, brother?' His beautiful sister appeared at his side. She smiled at me as she arrived, her eyes gleaming.

'I'll need the largest bladder you can find,' said Renco. 'Filled with rainwater.'

'It will be done,' said Lena, hastening away.

'What about Hernando?' I inquired of Renco. 'What if he arrives while we are engaged in returning the rapas to their lair?'

Said Renco, 'If, as my sister reports, he is following us with Chanca trackers, then as soon as he arrives here, he will know in which direction we have gone. Trust me, good Alberto, I am counting on such action. For when he finds me, he shall find an idol with me . . . and by my word, I shall give him that idol.'

'Hernando is a cold, callous man, Renco,' said I, 'vicious and remorseless. You cannot expect honour from him. Once you give him the idol, he will kill you for sure.'

'I know.'

'But then why—'

'My friend, what is the greater good?' said Renco softly. His face was kind, his voice calm. 'That I live and Hernando gets my people's idol? Or that I die and he gets a worthless replica of it?'

He smiled at me. 'Personally, I would rather live, but I am afraid that there is more at stake here than just my life.'

The citadel became a hive of activity as the people of Vilcafor went about preparing themselves for what was to come.

Renco himself went off to brief the town's warriors more fully. As he did so, I took the opportunity to join Bassario for a short while and watch him fashion his replica of the idol. Truth be told—and God forgive me for this—I had an ulterior motive for speaking to him.

'Bassario,' I whispered hesitantly, 'does . . . does Lena have a husband?'

Bassario shot me an impish grin. 'Why, monk, you old rascal . . .' said he in a full voice.

I begged him in hushed tones not to speak so loudly. Bassario, as one would expect of such a rogue, was highly amused.

'She once had a husband,' said he eventually. 'But their marriage ended many moons ago, before the arrival of gold-eaters. Lena's husband's name was Huarca and he was a promising young warrior, and their marriage—insofar as an arranged marriage can be—was viewed as one of great promise. Little did anyone know, however, that Huarca was prone to fits of rage. After the birth of their son, Huarca began to beat Lena savagely. It was said that Lena would endure these beatings in order to protect Mani from his father's fury. Apparently she succeeded in this aim. Huarca never beat the boy once.'

'Why did she not leave him?' I inquired. 'After all, she is a princess of your people—'

'Huarca threatened to kill the boy if Lena told anyone about the beatings.'

Good Lord, I thought.

'So what happened then?' I inquired.

'It was all uncovered by accident, really,' said Bassario. 'One day Renco called on Lena unexpectedly—only to find her cowering in a corner of her home, cradling her son in her arms. She had tears in her eyes and her face was bloody and bruised.

'Huarca was captured immediately and sentenced to death. I believe he was ultimately dropped into a pit with a pair of hungry jungle cats. They tore him limb from limb.' Bassario shook his head. 'Monk, the man who beats his wife is the lowest form of coward—the lowest form. I should think Huarca met a fitting end.'

I left Bassario to his work and repaired to a corner of the citadel to ready myself for the coming mission.

After a short time, Renco joined me to do the same. He was still wearing the Spanish attire that he had stolen from the prison hulk many weeks ago—the brown leather vest, the white pantaloons, the knee-high leather boots. The extra clothing, he once told me, had been of immense value to him during our arduous trek through the rainforest.

He slipped a quiver over his shoulder, began putting his sword belt on around his waist.

'Renco?' said I.

'Yes?'

'Why was Bassario in prison?'

'Ah, Bassario . . .' he sighed sadly.

I waited for him to elaborate.

'Believe it or not, but Bassario was once a prince,' Renco said. 'A most esteemed young prince. Indeed, his father was no less than the Royal Stonemason, a brilliant builder and fashioner of stone, the most venerated engineer in the empire. Bassario was his son and protégé, and soon he too became a brilliant stonemason. Why, by the age of sixteen, he had surpassed his father in knowledge and skill, despite the fact that his father was the Royal Stonemason, the man who built citadels for the Sapa Inca!

'But Bassario was reckless. He was a brilliant sportsman—indeed as an archer he had no peer—but like many of his ilk, he was prone to drinking and gambling and disporting with the pretty young maidens of Cuzco's more raucous quarters. Unfortunately for him, however, his success with women was not mirrored at the gambling houses. He accumulated a monstrous debt with some less than reputable fellows. Then, when the debt became too great for him to repay, those rogues decided that Bassario would repay it another way—with his considerable talents.'

'How?'

'Bassario repaid them by using his brilliant stonemasonry skills to carve forgeries of famous statues and priceless treasures. Emerald or gold, silver or jade, whatever the substance, Bassario could replicate even the most complex object.

'Once he had copied a famous statue, his nefarious colleagues would break into the home of the real idol's owner and substitute Bassario's fake for the real one.

'Their scheme worked for almost a year and the

criminals profited immensely from it until one day, Bassario's "friends" were discovered in the home of the Sapa Inca's cousin, caught in the act of switching a fake idol for the real one.

'Bassario's role in the scheme was soon uncovered. He was sent to prison and his entire family disgraced. His father was removed as Royal Stonemason and stripped of his titles. My brother, the Sapa Inca, decreed that Bassario's family were to be relocated from their home in the royal quarter to one of Cuzco's roughest slums.'

I took this all in silently.

Renco went on, 'I thought that the penalty was too harsh and told my brother so, but he wanted to make an example of Bassario and he ignored my pleas.'

Renco gazed over at Bassario, working away in the corner of the citadel.

'Bassario was once a very noble young man. Flawed certainly, but essentially noble. That was why when it became my duty to rescue the idol from the Coricancha, I decided that I would use his talents to aid my quest. I reasoned that if the criminal elements of Cuzco could employ his skills to suit their own ends, then I most certainly could too, in my mission to rescue my people's Spirit.'

At length Bassario finished his replica of the idol.

When he was done, he brought the fake idol— together with the real one—over to Renco.

Renco held both idols out in front of him. I looked at them over his shoulder and truly such was Bassario's skill that I could not tell which was the real one and which was the fraud.

Bassario retired to his corner of the citadel and

began gathering his things together—his sword, his quiver, his longbow.

'Where do you think you are going?' inquired Renco, seeing him stand.

'I'm leaving,' said Bassario simply.

'But I need your help,' said Renco. 'Vilcafor says that his men had to remove a great boulder from the temple's entrance and that it took ten men to do so. I am going to need as many again if I am to roll it back into place. I need your help.'

'I feel that I have done more than my share in your quest, noble prince,' said Bassario. 'Escaping Cuzco, traversing the mountains, charging blindly through the perilous forests. And all the while making a fake idol for you. No, I have done my share, and now I am leaving.'

'Have you no loyalty to your people?'

'My people put me in jail, Renco,' Bassario retorted harshly. 'Then they punished my family for *my* crime—banished them to live in the filthiest, roughest quarter of Cuzco. My sister was molested in that slum, my father and mother beaten and robbed. The robbers even broke my father's fingers, so that he could no longer fashion stone. He was left to beg—to beg for scraps to feed his family. I have no grudge against my own punishment, no grudge at all, but then I also have no loyalty whatsoever to the society that punished my family for a crime that was mine and mine alone.'

'I am sorry,' said Renco softly. 'I did not know of these incidents. But please, Bassario, the idol, the Spirit of the People—'

'It is your quest, Renco. Not mine. I have done enough for you, more than enough. I think I have earned my freedom. Follow your own destiny and allow me to follow mine.'

And with those sharp words, Bassario shouldered his longbow and climbed down into the quenko and disappeared into the darkness.

Renco did not attempt to stop him. He just looked after him, his face awash with sadness.

Now it was that the rest of us were all prepared for our confrontation with the rapas. All that remained was one final touch.

I picked up the small bladder of monkey urine that the toothless old man had given to me earlier that night and opened its cap.

At once, an utterly vile odour assaulted my olfactory passages. I winced at the odour and despaired at the prospect of pouring the foul-smelling liquid over my body.

But I did so nonetheless. And oh, how putrid it was! It was no wonder the rapas detested it.

Renco chuckled at my discomfiture. Then he took the small bladder from me and began dousing himself in the stinking yellow liquid. The bladder was passed to the other warriors who would be venturing up into the mountains and they, too, began bathing themselves in the foul, reeking liquid.

As all was approaching readiness, Lena returned with a much larger animal bladder—a llama's bladder, I guessed—also filled with liquid.

'The rainwater you requested,' said she to Renco.

'Good,' Renco said, taking the llama's bladder from her. 'Then we are ready to go.'

Renco poured a trickle of rainwater from the llama's bladder over the real idol.

It hummed to life instantly, singing its melodious song.

The interior of the citadel was empty. Lena had already sent the women, children and old folk of the village down into the quenko to commence their journey into its labyrinthine tunnels, a journey that would ultimately take them to the waterfall at the edge of the tableland. Lena herself had stayed behind in the citadel, ready to shut the doorstone after us.

'All right,' said Renco, nodding to the pair of Incan warriors manning the doorstone. 'Now.'

At that moment, the two Incan warriors rolled the big stone aside, revealing the dark night outside.

The rapas were right there!

Waiting for us.

Gathered in a wide circle immediately outside the citadel's stone doorframe.

I counted twelve of them—twelve enormous black cats, each possessed of demonic yellow eyes, high pointed ears and powerful muscular shoulders.

Renco held the singing idol out in front of him and the rapas stared at it, transfixed.

Then, abruptly, the idol stopped its singing and

equally suddenly, the rapas broke out of their trances and started a low growling.

Renco quickly doused the idol with more water from the llama's bladder and the idol's song resumed and the rapas lapsed into their hypnosis once again.

My heart also started beating again.

Then, with the idol in his hands and the seven Incan warriors and myself in tow behind him, Renco stepped through the citadel's doorway and out into the cold night air.

The rain had stopped—at long last—and the clouds had parted somewhat, revealing the starry night sky and a brilliant full moon.

With flaming torches held high above our heads, we made our way through the village and onto a narrow path that ran alongside the river.

The rapas were all around us, moving with slow, deliberate steps, keeping their bodies low to the ground while at the same time keeping their eyes fixed on the singing idol in Renco's hands.

My fear was extreme. Nay, it must be said that I have never been more terrified in my life.

To be surrounded by a pack of such enormous, dangerous creatures—creatures totally devoid of pity or mercy, creatures that killed without the slightest hesitation.

They were so big! In the flickering firelight of our torches the muscles on their shoulders and flanks rippled orange. Their breathing was loud too—a kind of deep-chested braying sound not unlike that of a horse.

As we walked along the riverside path, I looked behind me and saw Lena standing at the edge of the village holding a torch, watching after us.

After a few moments, however, she vanished from my view—having decided, I imagined, to go back to the citadel and carry out her duties there. We continued on our journey up to the mysterious temple.

Along the path we went. Nine men—Renco, myself and the seven Incan warriors—surrounded by the pack of rapas.

We came to the mountainside, to a narrow passageway set into the rockface. One of the Incan warriors told Renco that the temple was to be found at the other end of this passageway.

Renco doused the idol once again. It sang loudly, its high-pitched tone cutting through the early-morning air. Then he entered the passageway, the cats trailing close behind him like children following a schoolteacher.

As we walked down the narrow passageway by the light of our flaming torches, one of the Incan warriors foolishly attempted to stab one of the entranced rapas with the point of his spear—but just as he was about to drive his weapon into the beast's flank, the rapa turned on him and snarled ferociously, stopping him in midlunge. The big cat then just turned forward and resumed its enraptured pursuit of the singing idol.

The warrior exchanged a glance with one of his companions. The rapas might have been entranced, but they were not totally defenceless.

Now it was that we emerged from the narrow passageway into a wide circular canyon of some kind. As the chieftain Vilcafor had said, a most incredible finger of stone shot up out of the middle of it, soaring high into the night sky.

A path was cut into the canyon wall to our left—the

escape path Vilcafor had ordered his people to build. It curled around the circumference of the cylindrical canyon, spiralling up and around the finger of stone in its centre.

Renco mounted the path, stepping slowly upward, holding the wet idol in his hands. The cats followed him. The Incan warriors and myself walked slowly up the path behind them.

Up and up we went. Round and round, following the steady curve of the path.

At length we came to a rope bridge that stretched out over the canyon, connecting the outer path to the finger of stone in the middle of the great canyon.

I looked out across the ravine at the stone tower opposite me.

On top of the tower, surrounded by some low-cut foliage, I saw a magnificent stepped pyramid not unlike those found in the lands of the Aztecas. A box-shaped tabernacle was mounted atop the imposing triangular pyramid.

Renco crossed the bridge first. The cats followed him, one by one, bouncing with supreme surefooted-ness across the long swooping bridge. The warriors went next. I crossed last of all.

Once I had navigated my way across the bridge, I mounted a series of wide stone steps which opened onto a clearing of some sort. At the head of this clearing lay the portal to the temple, the entrance.

Wide and dark, square and menacing, it yawned open as if daring all the world to enter.

With the wet idol in his hands, Renco approached the portal. 'Warriors,' said he and firmly, 'man the boulder.'

The seven warriors and my humble self hurried over to the boulder that stood to the side of the temple's yawning entryway.

Renco stood in the mouth of the portal, dousing the idol with rainwater, causing it to continue its melodious song.

The cats stood before him, staring at the singing idol, hypnotised.

Renco took a step inside the temple.

The cats followed him.

Renco took another step down and the first cat went inside after him.

Another step.

A second cat, then a third, then a fourth.

At which stage Renco tipped as much water as was left inside the llama's bladder over the idol, and then—after taking a final solemn glance at his people's most prized possession—he hurled it down into the dark depths of the temple.

The cats leapt inside the temple after it. All twelve of them.

'Quickly, the boulder!' Renco cried, hurrying out of the temple's entrance. 'Push it back into the portal!'

We pushed as one.

The boulder rumbled against the threshold.

I leaned on it with all my might, straining against the weight of the great stone. Renco appeared beside me, also heaving against it.

The boulder moved slowly back into the portal. A few more paces to go.

Almost there . . .

Just a couple . . . more . . .

'Renco,' a voice said suddenly from somewhere nearby.

It was a woman's voice.

Renco and I turned together.

And we saw Lena standing at the edge of the clearing.

'Lena?' Renco said. 'What are you doing up here? I thought I asked you to—'

At that moment, Lena was shoved roughly aside, thrown to the ground, and suddenly I saw a man standing on the stone steps behind her, and in that single, solitary instant, every ounce of blood in my veins turned to ice.

I was looking at Hernando Pizarro.

A stream of about twenty conquistadors poured out from the foliage behind Lena and spread out around the clearing, their muskets raised and pointed at our faces. The firelight of their torches illuminated the entire clearing.

They were accompanied by three olive-skinned natives who each had long, sharp spikes of bone protruding from their cheeks. Chancas. The Chanca trackers Hernando had employed to follow our trail to Vilcafor.

Last of all—nay, most ominously of all—came another olive-skinned man. He was taller than the others, bigger, with a long shock of matted black hair that came down to his shoulders. He also had a spike of bone thrust through his left cheek.

It was Castino. The brutish Chanca who had been in the same prison hulk as Renco at the beginning of our adventure, the one who had overheard Renco say that the idol was in the Coricancha in Cuzco.

The conquistadors and the Chancas formed a wide circle around Renco, myself and the seven Incan warriors.

It was then that I noticed how filthy they all looked. To a man, the conquistadors were covered in mud and grime. And they looked worn and exhausted, weary beyond measure.

Whence I realised—this was all that remained of Hernando's hundred-strong legion. On their march through the mountains and the forests, Hernando's men had died all around him. From disease, from starvation, or just from sheer exhaustion.

This was all that remained of his legion. Twenty men.

Hernando stepped forward, yanking Lena to her feet as he did so. Dragging her behind him, he approached the temple and stood before Renco, staring imperiously down at him. Hernando was a full head taller than Renco and twice as broad. He shoved Lena roughly into Renco's arms.

For my part, I cast a fearful glance at the temple's portal.

It was still partially open, the gap between the boulder and the great stone doorway easily wide enough for a rapa to fit through.

This was not good.

If the water drained off the idol and it stopped its song, the rapas would break out of their spells and—

'At last we meet,' said Hernando to Renco in Spanish. 'You have evaded me for far too long, young prince. You will die slowly.'

Renco said nothing.

'And you, monk,' said Hernando, rounding on me. 'You are a traitor to your country and to your God. You will die even more slowly.'

I swallowed back my fear.

Hernando turned back to Renco. 'The idol. Give it to me.'

Renco didn't flinch. He just slowly reached into the pouch on his belt and extracted the false idol.

Hernando's eyes lit up as he saw it. If I didn't know better, I would have sworn he began to salivate.

'Give it to me,' said he.

Renco stepped forward.

'On your knees.'

Slowly, despite the sheer humiliation that attended it, Renco knelt down and offered the idol to the standing Hernando.

Hernando took it from him, his eyes gleaming with greed as he stared at his long-sought-after prize.

After a few moments, he glanced up from the idol and turned to one of his men.

'Sergeant,' he said.

'Yes, sir?' the sergeant standing nearest to him replied.

'Execute them.'

My hands were bound together with a long length of rope. Renco's were too.

Lena was snatched away from Renco by two of the Spanish soldiers, and the two brutes goaded her with foul utterings of what they would do to her once Renco and I were dead, utterings which I dare not repeat here.

Renco and I were made to kneel before a large rectangular stone in the middle of the clearing, a stone that looked like a low altar.

The Spanish sergeant stood over me, his sabre drawn.

'You, Chanca,' said Hernando, tossing a sword to Castino. Ever since he had arrived in the clearing, the vile Chanca had been eyeing Renco with pure unadulterated hatred. 'You may dispose of the prince.'

'Gladly,' said Castino in Spanish, catching the sword and marching quickly over to the altar stone.

'Cut their hands off first,' said Hernando judiciously. 'I would like to hear them scream before they die.'

Our two executioners nodded as two more conquistadors pulled Renco and myself into position—yanking on our bonds so that our arms were stretched out across the wide altar. Our wrists were now totally exposed, our hands ready to be excised from our bodies.

'Alberto,' said Renco softly.

'Yes.'

'My friend, before we die, I would like you to know that it has been an honour and a joy to have known you. What you have done for my people will be remembered for generations. For that I thank you.'

'My brave friend,' I replied, 'if the circumstances were to repeat themselves, I would do it all again. May God look after you in heaven.'

'And you too,' said Renco. 'And you too.'

'Gentlemen,' said Hernando to our executioners. 'Remove their hands.'

The sergeant and the Chanca raised their glistening swords at the same time, raised them high above their heads.

'Wait!' someone called suddenly.

At that moment, one of the other conquistadors hurried over to the altar. He appeared older than his fellow soldiers—more grizzled—a wily old fox of a man. He ran directly over to Renco.

He had spied the emerald pendant looped around my companion's neck.

The old conquistador quickly lifted the leather necklace over Renco's head, smiling greedily at him as he did so.

'Thank you, savage,' he sneered as he placed the emerald pendant around his own neck and scurried back to his position over by the temple's portal.

Our two executioners looked over to Hernando for the signal.

But strangely, Hernando wasn't watching them anymore.

In fact, he wasn't even looking at Renco or myself either.

He was just staring off to our right—at the temple—his mouth agape.

I spun to see what it was he was looking at.

'Oh, my Lord . . .' I breathed.

One of the rapas was standing in the half-opened mouth of the portal, peering curiously at the assembled mass of humanity before it.

It loomed large in the doorway—its powerful forelimbs splayed wide, its shoulders bunched with muscle—but its appearance at that moment was oddly comical, chiefly because it was holding something in its mouth.

It was the idol.

The *real* idol.

The great black cat—previously so terrifying and vicious—now looked like a humble retriever bringing a stick back to its owner. Indeed, the rapa just held the idol dumbly in its mouth, as if it were looking for someone who might wet it again and thus make it sing.

Hernando just gazed at the cat—or rather, at the idol that it held between its mighty jaws. And then, all of a sudden, his eyes swept from the rapa and the idol in its mouth to the idol that he held in his own hands, and from it to Renco and myself, a wash of understanding spreading across his face.

He knew.

He knew that he had been deceived.

The big Spaniard's face went red with fury as he glared at Renco and me.

'Kill them!' he roared to our executioners. 'Kill them now!'

It was at that exact moment that a myriad of things happened at once.

Our executioners raised their swords again—re-aimed at our necks now—and had just begun to bring their blades down in two great swinging arcs when abruptly a sharp whistling sound cut through the air above my head.

Not a moment later, with a powerful thud, *an arrow* lodged itself in the nose of my executioner, sending a garish fountain of blood exploding from his face and hurling him clear off his feet.

For its part, the rapa in the portal—after seeing the crowd of people standing in the clearing before it and sensing another tasty human meal—immediately dropped the idol from its mouth and leapt ferociously at the nearest Spaniard, not a moment before the eleven *other* rapas rushed out from within the temple—one after the other after the other—and commenced their own attack on the crowd of conquistadors.

Castino had seen the other executioner drop to the ground beside him, struck by the arrow, and had momentarily halted his lunge at Renco's neck, a look of stunned incomprehension on his face.

I knew what he was thinking.

Who had fired the arrow? And from where?

Castino obviously decided he would answer these questions later, after he had killed Renco.

He quickly raised his blade again and brought it down with tremendous force—

—whence another arrow slammed into his sword's hilt and sent it flying from his grasp.

Not a moment later, a third arrow whistled down from somewhere above us and struck the rope binding Renco's hands together, cutting it cleanly in two, releasing him.

Renco immediately leapt to his feet, just as Castino—now swordless—swung at him with one of his gigantic fists. Renco quickly yanked the conquistador who had been holding him to the altar *in between* himself and the oncoming blow, and Castino's mighty knuckles hit the conquistador square in the face, shattering his nose in an instant, pummelling it into the back of his skull, killing him with a single blow!

Just then another conquistador levelled his musket at Renco and fired at exactly the same time as Renco pivoted on the spot—bringing the dead conquistador around in front of him, using him as a shield—and the musket's shot opened up a ragged red hole in the centre of the dead soldier's chest.

As Renco went off to join the fight, the conquistador holding my wrists across the altar drew his sword and glared at me with evil intent.

But then—faster than a man can blink—an arrowhead exploded out from the centre of his face and the conquistador flopped down onto the altar stone in front of me, face-down, an arrow sticking out from the back of his head.

I looked up into the darkness beyond him, searching for the source of the arrows.

And I saw him.

Saw the figure of a man positioned up on the rim of the canyon.

He was silhouetted against the moon, crouched on one knee with a longbow extended in the firing position and an arrow drawn back to his ear.

It was Bassario!

I gave a cheer, and then I immediately set about unravelling my bonds.

It cannot be understated the carnage that was going on around me at this time. It was mayhem. Pure and utter mayhem. The clearing in front of the temple had become a battlefield—a ferocious, bloody battlefield.

Fighting went on everywhere, in about a dozen separate battles.

Over by the temple, the rapas had already killed five of the conquistadors, and now they were attacking four more Spaniards and their three Chanca trackers.

Elsewhere in the clearing, the seven Incan warriors—avoided by the rapas due to the monkey urine that covered their bodies—fought with the remaining Spaniards. Some of them fell as the conquistadors fired their muskets into them, others hacked into their Spanish foes with rocks or stones or whatever weapons they could lay their hands on. Despite all the murder and bloodshed that I had seen on my travels throughout New Spain, this was indeed the most brutal and primal example of combat that I had ever witnessed.

Beside me, Renco and Castino had both picked up swords and were now engaged in the most ferocious of swordfights.

Castino, taller than my brave companion by at least

two heads, held his sword two-handed and unleashed upon Renco a rain of powerful blows.

But Renco parried well—one-handed, just as I had taught him—dancing backwards in the mud like a classical Spanish fencer, maintaining his balance as he retreated toward the foliage.

As I finally released the rope from my left wrist and stood, I realised just what a keen student Renco had been. It was clear to me now that the pupil by far outclassed the teacher.

His swordsmanship was dazzling.

For every mighty blow that Castino threw at him, Renco would quickly bring up his sword—just in time to stop it.

The two men's swords clashed with ferocious intensity.

Castino swung, Renco parried. Castino lunged, Renco danced.

And then Castino unleashed a devilish blow, a blow so hard and swift that it would have taken the head off any ordinary man.

But not Renco.

His reflexes were too quick. He ducked under the blow and in the fleeting instant that followed, he leapt forward, up onto a low rock and launched himself into the air, negating the height difference between himself and Castino, his blade cutting through the air so swiftly it whistled, and before I even knew what was happening, I saw his sword embedded horizontally in the tree trunk behind Castino's neck.

Castino just stood there, his mouth hanging open, his eyes wide. A moment later, his sword dropped out of his hand.

And then abruptly his *entire body* just dropped away from beneath his ugly head.

Renco had cut his head clean off his shoulders!

I almost cheered.

Which is to say I would have cheered, had I not had other things with which to deal.

I spun to survey the battlefield around me.

Small battles were still being waged all over the clearing—but the only obvious victors seemed to be the rapas.

It was then that I saw the idol.

The real idol.

It lay on the threshold of the portal, tilted over onto its side, at the exact spot where it had fallen from the rapa's mouth earlier.

With the length of rope still tied to my right wrist— it was about two paces long—I grabbed a sword and a torch from the ground beside me and ran for the temple, through the clashing of blades and the screams of the ravaged conquistadors.

I reached the portal and fell to the ground next to the idol, grabbed it—

—just as one of the Spanish soldiers rammed into me from behind, bowling both of us in through the portal and into the temple!

The two of us tumbled down a set of wide stone steps, down into the darkness of the temple, a tangled mix of arms, legs, idol and torch.

We hit the bottom of the stairs and fell apart. We were inside a dark stone-walled tunnel of some sort.

My foe clambered to his feet first so that he now stood against the wall, in front of a small alcove set into it. I was still sprawled out on the floor, flat on my behind, with the idol sitting in my lap.

As the Spanish soldier stood over me, I saw the

emerald necklace looped around his neck and I recognised him instantly. He was the wily older soldier who had relieved Renco of his priceless pendant earlier.

The old fox drew his sword, raised it high. I was defenceless, completely exposed.

At that moment, with an obscenely loud roar, something very large leapt over my head from behind and rammed into the conquistador at frightening speed.

A rapa.

The cat hit the Spaniard with such colossal force that he was thrown back into the alcove behind him. His head struck the wall with the most sickening of sounds and just exploded, cracking like an egg, a foul spray of blood and brains shooting out from the hole that was instantaneously created in the back of his skull.

The wily old soldier collapsed into the alcove, but he was well and truly dead by the time he reached the floor.

The cat began to ravage him on the spot, its tail licking back and forth behind its body as it did so.

I seized the moment, grabbed hold of the idol and charged back up the stairs, out of the temple.

I burst out into the night, thankful to have escaped death once again.

But my revelry was shortlived. No sooner was I out of the portal than I heard a sharp *click-click* from somewhere behind me, followed quickly by a coarse shout of 'Monk!'

I spun.

And saw Hernando Pizarro standing before me with a pistol in his hand, levelled right at my chest.

Then, before I could so much as move, I saw a flash

of fire flare out from the end of the pistol, heard its loud report echo out all around me, and almost immediately I felt a tremendous weight slam into my chest and I was thrown backwards.

I collapsed to the ground instantly, after which I saw nothing but clouds—dark storm clouds rolling across the starry night sky above me—and it was at that moment that I realised to my extreme horror that I had just been shot.

I lay on my back, my teeth clenched in agony, looking up at the cloud-strewn sky, a searing, burning pain shooting through my chest.

Hernando bent over me and took the idol from my loose grasp. As he did so, he slapped me lustily across the face and said, 'Die slowly, monk.' Then he was gone.

I lay on the stone steps in front of the temple, waiting for the life to drain out of me, waiting for the pain to become unbearable.

But then for some reason that was beyond my ken, my strength, rather than fading, began to return.

The searing pain in my chest subsided and I sat up instantly and patted my chest at the point where the bullet had created a hole in my cloak.

I felt something there.

Something soft and thick and square. I extracted it from my cloak.

It was my Bible.

My three-hundred-page, handwritten, leather-bound Bible.

In the centre of it was a tattered round hole that looked like the burrow of a worm. At the farthest extremity of the burrow I saw a warped sphere of dull grey lead.

Hernando's bullet.

My Bible had stopped his bullet!

Praised be the Word of the Lord.

I leapt to my feet, exhilarated in the moment. I looked for my sword, couldn't find it anywhere, gazed out over the clearing.

I saw Renco on the far side of the clearing, fighting with two swords against two sabre-wielding conquistadors.

Two Incan warriors grappled with a pair of Spaniards not far from where I stood—they seemed to be the only other men left alive on the rock tower.

And then I saw Hernando—with the idol in his hands—hurrying away into the foliage to my right, dashing down the stone stairway there.

My eyes went wide.

He was going for the rope bridge.

If he got there, he would almost certainly cut the bridge and leave us stranded on the tower, stranded with the rapas.

I hurried after him, bounding across the clearing, hurdling a rapa as it lay on the ground tearing into the body of a dead conquistador.

I flew down the stone steps two at a time, my heart racing, my legs pounding, chasing after Hernando. As I rounded a bend in the stairs, I saw him about ten paces in front of me, stepping out onto the rope bridge.

Hernando was large and muscular, and he moved as such. I was smaller, more nimble, faster. I gained on him quickly and dashed out onto the bridge after him, at which moment, with absolutely nothing else to call on, I hurled myself—swordless—at his back.

I collided with him most heavily and we fell together onto the thin floorboards of the rope bridge, high above the canyon floor.

But such was the weight of our landing that the floorboards beneath us shattered like twigs and to my utter horror we fell straight through them, down into the abyss . . .

But our fall was brief.

With a sudden, jarring jolt the two of us came to an abrupt halt. In the terror of our fall, Hernando had reached out for a handhold, had grasped for anything that would stop his fall.

What he had found was the free end of the rope that was still tied to my right wrist. Now the rope lay stretched over a lone floorboard on the rope bridge, with Hernando and myself dangling from both of its extremities!

And so we hung there like counterweights hanging from a pulley, at different ends of the same rope, with dangling cords of the partially-broken rope bridge hanging down all around us.

Through force of luck—bad luck in my case—I hung below Hernando, my head down near his dangling knees. Hernando hung up higher, just below the remaining floorboards of the bridge.

I saw that he had the idol in his left hand, while he held onto my rope with his right. He reached up with his left hand, trying desperately to loop the idol over the rope bridge's surviving floorboards and garner a handhold.

Once he succeeded in doing that, I realised, he would be safe to let me fall. At present, my weight—small though it was compared to his—was the only thing holding him up.

I had to do something. And quickly.

'Why are you doing this, monk!' Hernando roared

as he reached for his salvation, so close now. 'What do *you* care about this idol! I would kill for it!'

As he raged, I saw one of the thin cords dangling down from the rope bridge above us—one of the cords that had previously held up the bridge's handrail.

If I could just . . .

'You would kill for it, would you, Hernando?' said I, trying to distract him as I endeavoured to untie the length of rope that was tied around my right wrist— the rope that connected me to Hernando. 'That means nothing to me!'

'No?' he shouted. It was a race now, a race to see who would get to his objective first—Hernando to the floorboard above us, me to untie the rope that joined us together.

'No!' I called back—just as I succeeded in releasing myself from the length of rope.

'Why, monk?'

'Because, Hernando, *I would die for it.*'

And with that, having now freed myself from the rope tied to my wrist, I reached out for the thin cord dangling down from the bridge above me and grabbed hold of it—while at exactly the same moment I released my grip on the length of rope connecting me to Hernando.

The response was instantaneous.

With the counterweight at the other end of his rope now gone, Hernando fell. Straight down.

He fell past me, his body a streaking blur of screaming humanity, and as a fitting final insult, as he whistled by in front of me, I reached out and plucked the idol from his grasp.

'*Noooooo!*' Hernando screamed as he fell.

And as I hung there above the abyss—dangling one-handed from the rope bridge's cord, holding the sacred idol in my free hand—I watched the look of absolute terror on his face get smaller and smaller until, finally, it disappeared into the dark abyss beneath me and soon all I could hear was his screaming.

It would stop a moment later at the same time as I heard a distant, sickening splat.

I arrived back in the clearing some time later, the idol in my hand.

The sight which greeted me was like a glimpse of the underworld itself.

In the flickering light of the torches that littered the clearing, I saw the rapas kneeling over the ranks of dead conquistadors, gorging themselves on fresh human flesh. Pointed silver helmets lay strewn everywhere, glinting in the firelight.

It was then that I saw Renco and Lena and three of the Incan warriors standing over by the portal, holding swords and muskets in their hands—the only survivors of the carnage, thanks largely to their fighting skills and the layer of monkey urine that covered them. They appeared to be searching for something. The idol no doubt.

'Renco!' I called. 'Lena!'

I regretted it as soon as I did it.

One of the rapas lying on the ground in front of me immediately looked up from his feasting, disturbed by my shout.

The massive beast rose to its feet, glared at me.

Another cat beyond it did the same.

Then another, and another.

The pack of giant cats formed a wide circle around me. They held their heads low, their ears pinned back.

I saw Renco turn and see my predicament. But he was too far away to be of any help.

I wondered why my own layer of monkey urine was no longer keeping the cats at bay. Perhaps it had been scraped away during my scuffle with the wily old conquistador inside the temple or maybe it had rubbed off when I had fallen to the ground after being shot by Hernando.

Whatever the case, I thought, this was it, this was the end.

The lead rapa tensed its whole body, prepared itself to pounce. And then—

—the first drop of water hit the top of my head with a loud smack. It was closely followed by a second drop and then a third, then a fourth.

And then, like a gift from God himself, the skies parted and the rain came tumbling down.

Oh, how it rained! It came down in sheets—thick drenching sheets—big fat drops of water hammering down on the rock tower with tremendous force, smacking down against my head, smacking down against the idol.

And at that moment, thank the Lord, the idol began to sing.

Its song becalmed the cats instantly.

They all just peered at the dripping idol in my hands, their heads cocked to one side in response to its melodious high-pitched hum.

Renco, Lena and the three warriors came over to where I stood, shielding their torches against the rain, skirting around the pack of entranced rapas.

I noticed that Renco held Bassario's fake idol in his hand.

'Thank you, Alberto,' said he, taking the singing

idol from me. 'I think I shall take that now.'

Beside him, Lena smiled at me, her beautiful olive skin sparkling in the rainstorm. 'So, you defeated the big gold-eater to save our idol,' she said. 'Is there anything you cannot do, my brave little hero?'

As she said these words, she suddenly leaned forward and kissed me softly on the lips. My heart almost skipped a beat as her lips pressed themselves firmly against mine. My knees felt weak. I almost fell over, so delightful was the touch of her lips.

As Lena was kissing me so beautifully, however, a voice from somewhere behind me said: 'Come now, monk. I thought that wasn't allowed for men of your ilk.'

I turned to see Bassario standing on the stone steps behind me, his longbow slung over his shoulder, his face creased into a broad smile.

'We reserve the right to make exceptions,' said I.

Bassario laughed.

Renco turned to face him. 'Thank you for returning to help us, Bassario. Your arrows saved our lives. What made you return?'

Bassario shrugged. 'As I reached the waterfall at the end of the quenko, I saw the gold-eaters approaching from the other side of the river. Then I supposed that if by some miracle you survived all of this, people would sing songs about you. I decided that I wanted to be a part of those songs. To be remembered for something other than disgracing my family name, and at the same time, to restore that name to honour.'

'You succeeded on both counts,' said Renco. 'You truly did. Now, however, may I beg your indulgence one more time and ask of you one final favour.'

As he spoke, Renco—holding a torch in one arm and both idols in the other—began to back away from the rest of us and headed through the rain toward the portal. On his way, he picked up the llama's bladder from where it had been dropped during the battle and allowed it to fill with the pouring rain.

The cats immediately began to follow him—or rather, follow the singing idol in his hands.

'Once I am inside the temple,' said Renco as he walked, 'I want you all to shut the boulder behind me.'

I looked from Renco to the three remaining Incan warriors beside me.

'What are you going to do?' said I.

'I am going to ensure that no-one ever gets this idol,' said Renco. 'I will use it to lure the cats into the temple. Then, when they are all inside, I want you to push the boulder back into the portal.'

'But—'

'Trust me, Alberto,' he said, his voice calm as he moved slowly toward the portal with the pack of rapas slinking along behind him. 'We shall see each other again, I promise.'

And with that, Renco stepped up into the open mouth of the temple. The cats crowded in all around him, oblivious to the pouring rain.

Lena, Bassario, the three warriors and myself hastened over to the boulder.

Renco stood in the entrance to the temple and gave me one final look.

He smiled sadly. 'Take care, my friend,' said he.

And then he was gone, disappearing into the darkness between the boulder and the great stone portal.

The cats followed him into the temple one by one.

When the last cat disappeared inside the portal, Bassario called, 'All right, heave!'

The six of us leaned on the massive boulder, pushed against it with all our might.

The big boulder rumbled loudly against the stone floor. It was fortunate that we did not have to push it very far—only a couple of paces—otherwise we might not have been able to do it with only six people.

But Bassario and the Incan warriors were strong. And Lena and I pushed with all the strength we had, and slowly, very slowly, the boulder began to fill the square-shaped portal.

As we proceeded to seal the temple with the great stone, I heard the song of the idol inside it growing softer and softer.

Then abruptly the boulder sealed the portal fully, and as it did so, it stifled the song of the idol completely, and with the ceasing of that song, a great sadness came over me, for I knew then, in that moment, that I would never see my good friend Renco again.

Before I left that dreadful rock tower, I would perform one final act.

I grabbed a dagger from one of the fallen conquistadors and I scratched a message into the surface of the great boulder now lodged in the portal. I inscribed a warning for all of those who might contemplate opening the temple again.

I wrote:

> *No entrare absoluto.*
> *Muerte asomarse dentro.*

AS

Do not enter at any cost. Death looms within.

It has now been many years since those events transpired.

Now I am an old man, withered and frail, seated at a desk in a monastery, writing by the light of a candle. Snow-covered mountains stretch away from me in every direction. The mountains of the Pyrenees.

After Renco entered the temple with the two idols and the rapas, Bassario, Lena and I returned to Vilcafor.

It was not long before word spread throughout the empire of our deeds—word of Hernando's death, and of the idol being laid to rest inside a mysterious temple in the presence of a pack of deadly rapas.

Typically, the Spanish colonial government created some sham tale about the death of the Governor's brother, Hernando. They said that he died honourably at the hands of an unknown tribe of natives while he had been bravely navigating some uncharted jungle river. If only my countrymen knew the truth.

I also understand that the Incas did indeed sing songs about our adventure—and, yes, those songs mentioned Bassario's name—and the singing of those ballads continued even after the Spanish conquest of their lands.

The gold-eaters, they said, could seize their land, burn their houses, torture and murder their people.

But they could not take their spirit.

To this day, I do not know what Renco did inside that temple with the two idols.

I can only assume that in his wisdom, he anticipated the rumours that would spread after our victory over Hernando. Like Solon, he knew that people, hearing of the idol inside the temple, would seek it out.

I imagine that he placed the fake idol at some location nearer to the entrance of the temple, so that if someone did open it up in search of the idol they would come upon the wrong idol first.

But I speculate. I do not know for sure.

I never saw him again.

For my own part, I could no longer endure living in the horror that was New Spain. I decided to return to Europe.

And so after bidding farewell to the beautiful Lena and the noble Bassario, with the help of several Incan guides I embarked upon a trek through the mountains of New Spain, heading north.

I walked and walked, through jungles, mountains and deserts until finally I came to the land of the Aztecas, the land that Cortez had conquered in the name of Spain but a few years previously.

There I managed to bribe my way aboard a merchant ship, laden with stolen gold, bound for Europe.

I arrived in Barcelona some months later and from there I travelled to this monastery high in the Pyrenees, a place far away from the world of the King and his bloodthirsty conquistadors, and it was here that I grew old, dreaming every night of my adventures in New Spain and wishing every moment that I could have spent just one more day with my good friend Renco.

Race turned the page.

That was it. That was the end of the manuscript.

He looked forward through the cabin of the Goose. Beyond the windshield of the little seaplane he saw the sharp peaks of the Andes towering in front of him.

They would arrive back at Vilcafor soon.

Race sighed sadly as he thought about the tale he had just read. He thought of Alberto Santiago's bravery, and of Renco's sacrifice, and of the friendship that had developed between the two of them. He also thought about *two* idols resting inside the temple.

Race pondered that for a moment.

Something about it wasn't right.

Something about the way the manuscript had ended—so suddenly, so abruptly—and *also*, now that he thought about it, something he had seen yesterday, back when Lauren had done the original nucleotide resonance test to determine the location of the real thyrium idol. Something about the *result* of that test that wasn't quite right.

The thought of Lauren and Frank Nash's expedition gave rise to a whole other set of thoughts in Race's mind.

How Nash wasn't with DARPA. How he was actually in charge of an Army unit trying to beat the *real*

Supernova team—a Navy team—to the thyrium idol. And how he had deceived Race into coming along on the mission.

Race shook the thoughts away.

He was going to have to figure out how he would deal with Nash when he arrived back at Vilcafor—should he confront him, or would he be better served remaining silent and not letting Nash know just how much he knew?

Whatever the case, he would have to decide soon, for no sooner had he finished reading the manuscript than the seaplane tilted gently beneath him, dropping its nose.

They were beginning their descent.

They were returning to Vilcafor.

Special Agent John-Paul Demonaco walked carefully through the vault room examining the scene of the crime.

After the Navy captain, Aaronson, had gone off to give the green light to an assault on the suspected Freedom Fighter locations, the other Naval investigator—Commander Tom Mitchell—had asked Demonaco if he would take a look at the crime scene. Maybe he would notice something they hadn't.

'Aaronson's wrong, isn't he?' Mitchell said as they wandered through the vault room.

'What do you mean?' Demonaco said as he scanned the heavily-sealed lab facility. It was a very impressive laboratory. In fact, it was one of the most high-tech labs he had ever seen.

'The Freedom Fighters didn't do this,' Mitchell said.

'No . . . no, they didn't.'

'Then who did?'

Demonaco was silent for a moment.

When at last he spoke, however, he didn't answer the question. 'Tell me more about the device that the Navy was building here. This Supernova.'

Mitchell took a deep breath. 'I'll tell you what I

know. The Supernova is a fourth-generation thermo-nuclear weapon. Instead of splitting the atoms of terrestrial radioactive elements like uranium and plu-tonium, it creates a mega-explosion by splitting a subcritical mass of the *non*-terrestrial element thyrium.

'The blast caused by the splitting of a thyrium atom is so powerful that it would rip out nearly a third of the Earth's mass. Put simply, the Supernova is the first man-made device capable of destroying the planet we live on.'

'This element, thyrium, you say it's *non*-terrestrial,' Demonaco said. 'If it doesn't come from Earth, then where does it come from?'

'Asteroid impacts, meteorite landings. Segments of rocks that survive the journey through the Earth's atmosphere. But so far as we know, no-one's ever found a live specimen of thyrium.'

'I think you'll find,' Demonaco said, 'that someone has now. And I might just know who.'

Demonaco explained.

'Commander, for the last six months, my unit at the Bureau has been hearing rumours of an inter-militia war between the Oklahoma Freedom Fighters and another terrorist group calling themselves the Republican Army of Texas.'

'The Republican Army of Texas—aren't they the ones who skinned those park rangers up in Montana?'

'They're the prime suspects,' Demonaco said. 'We told the media that those two rangers stumbled on some hillbillies shooting illegal game, but we actually think it was worse than that. We think they stumbled on a secret Texan training camp.'

'A training camp?'

'Uh-huh. The Texans are a much larger group than the Freedom Fighters, and much better fighters—in fact, you can't even join the Texans unless you've been a member of one of the armed forces.

'They're also exceptionally organised for a terrorist group, more like an elite military unit than a weekend hunting club.

'They have a rigidly defined chain of command, with severe penalties for any member who breaks that hierarchy, a system that has been attributed to the influence of their leader, Earl Bittiker, a former Navy SEAL who was dishonourably discharged in 1986 for sexually assaulting a female lieutenant who gave him an order he didn't like. He raped her both vaginally and orally.'

Mitchell winced.

'Apparently, Bittiker was one of the SEALs' best men—a totally remorseless killing machine. But like a lot of those types, he lacked certain *civilising* virtues. Apparently in 1983, three years before the rape incident, he was diagnosed as being clinically psychotic, but the Navy allowed him to remain on active duty anyway. So long as his aggression was directed at our enemies, they figured it didn't matter. Great logic.

'After the rape, Bittiker was discharged from the Navy and sentenced to eight years in Leavenworth. When he got out in 1994, he founded the Republican Army of Texas with a couple of other disgraced ex-servicemen he'd met in jail.

'The Texans train constantly,' Demonaco said. 'In the desert, in the badlands of Texas and Montana, and sometimes, up in the mountains in Oregon. They figure that when the time comes to launch a full-scale war against the United States government—or the U.S. government in conjunction with the United Nations—they want to be ready to fight in all kinds of terrain.

'What makes it worse is that they have money too. After the government screwed him on an oil deal, the Texan oil tycoon Stanford Cole left Bittiker and the Texans something in the vicinity of forty-two million dollars and a note that said, "Give 'em hell". It's no surprise then that Bittiker and his cronies are often seen at black market arms bazaars in the Middle East and Africa. Hell, last year, they bought eight surplus Black Hawk helicopters from the Australian government.'

'Christ,' Mitchell said.

'Still,' Demonaco went on, 'that doesn't stop them *stealing* some heavy-duty hardware every now and then. For example, although we can't prove it, we believe that the Texans are responsible for the theft of an Abrams M-1A1 main battle tank while it was—'

'They stole a tank?' Mitchell said, incredulous.

'Off the back of a semi-trailer while it was being transported from the Chrysler plant in Detroit to Tank and Automotive Command in Warren, Michigan.'

'Why do you suspect them?' Mitchell asked.

'Because two years ago, the Texans bought an old Antonov An-22 heavy-lift cargo plane from an arms market in Iran. The An-22 is a damn big plane, the Russian equivalent of our biggest lifters, the C-5 Galaxy and the C-17 Globemaster. Now if you wanted a regular cargo plane, you'd go and buy yourself a smaller An-12 or a C-130 Hercules, not an An-22. You'd only need a '-22 if you were intending to move something big. Something really, *really* big. Something like a 67-ton tank.'

Demonaco paused, shook his head. 'But that's the least of our worries now.'

'Why?'

'Because lately we've been hearing some disturbing rumours about the Texans. It seems that they've found something of a soulmate in the Aum Shinrikyo cult in Japan, the group who released sarin gas in the Tokyo subway in 1995. After the Tokyo attack, some members of the cult came to America and infiltrated a few of our militia groups. We have reason to believe that several members of Aum Shinrikyo joined the Texans.'

'What does that mean for us?' Mitchell asked.

'It means that we now have a very big problem.'

'Why?'

'Because the Aum Shinrikyo cult is a doomsday cult. Its only goal—indeed, its only reason for being—is to bring about the end of the world. We only know about the Tokyo subway incident because the networks got film footage of it. Did you know that in early 1994 Aum Shinrikyo managed to seize control of a remote Chinese missile silo? They almost launched thirty tactical nuclear missiles at the United States in an attempt to initiate a full-scale thermonuclear war.'

'No, I didn't know that,' Mitchell said.

'Commander, we've never really had a genuine doomsday cult in America. We have violent anti-government groups, anti-UN groups, anti-abortion, anti-Semitic and anti-Negro groups. But we have *never* had a group whose sole ambition is to bring about the mass destruction of life on this planet.

'Now, *if* Earl Bittiker and the Texans have decided to adopt a doomsday philosophy, then that leaves us with a big problem. Because then we'll have one of the most dangerous paramilitary groups in America running around with a death wish.'

'Okay, then,' Mitchell said, 'so how does all this relate to this robbery?'

'Easy,' Demonaco said. 'The group which carried out this robbery was a highly trained, highly skilled assault squad. The tactics that they employed were pure Special Forces—large-scale SEAL stuff—which would point to an organisation more like the Texan Republican Army and not the Freedom Fighters.'

'Right.'

'But whoever did this left us a single tungsten-cored bullet—to point us toward the Freedom Fighters. If the Texans really did do this, don't you think it would make sense for them to throw us off the scent by framing their enemies—the Oklahoma Freedom Fighters?'

'Yeah . . .'

'What really scares me, though,' Demonaco said, 'is *what they were after*. Because if the Texans really have acquired doomsday tendencies, then this Supernova of yours is exactly the kind of thing they'd go for.'

'The other thing we have to think about,' Demonaco went on, 'is how they got in. They had someone on the inside, someone who knew the codes to, and who could get cardkeys for, all the security locks. Do you have a record of the names of everyone working on the project?'

Mitchell pulled a sheet of computer paper from his breast pocket and handed it to Demonaco.

'That's a list of all the people working on the Supernova project, Navy and DARPA.'

Demonaco looked at the list.

PROJECT NAME:	N23-657-K2 (SUPERNOVA)		
CLASSIFICATION:	RED (ABSOLUTE SECRET)		
RELEVANT AGENCIES:	NAVY / DARPA		

PERSONNEL INVOLVED:

NAME	POSITION HELD	AGENCY	SECURITY NO.
ROMANO, Julius M.	Nuclear physicist, PROJECT LEADER	NAVY	N/1005-A2

FISK, Howard K.	Theoretical physicist, DARPA PROJECT LEADER	DARPA	D/1546-77A
BOYLE, Jessica D.	Nuclear physicist	DARPA	D/1788-82B
LABOWSKI, John A.	Delivery system engineer	NAVY	N/7659-C7
MAHER, Karen B.	Secondary systems	DARPA	D/6201-22C
NORTON, Henry J.	Technical support	NAVY	N/7632-C1
RACE, Martin E.	Ignition system design engineer	DARPA	D/3279-97A
SMITH, Martin W.	Weapons electronics	DARPA	D/5900-35B

ADDITIONAL PERSONNEL:

KAYSON, Simon F.	Project security	NAVY	N/1009-A2
DEVEREUX, Edward G.	Language specialist	HARVARD	N/A

Mitchell said, 'We've checked them all out. They're all clean, even Henry Norton, the guy whose security card and PIN codes were used to get in.'

'Where was he on the night of the break-in?' Demonaco asked.

'In the Arlington morgue,' Mitchell said simply. 'Paramedic records confirm that at 5:36 am on the night of the break-in—exactly fifteen minutes before the thieves stormed this building—Henry Norton and his wife, Sarah, were found shot to death at their home in Arlington.'

'5:36,' Demonaco said. 'They got here quickly after they killed him. They knew his name would be flagged at the hospital.'

As both Demonaco and Mitchell knew, it was common for high-level government employees to have electronic flags attached to their names in the event that they unexpectedly arrived at a hospital. As soon as the important person's name was entered into the hospital's records, a flag screen would come up telling the doctor involved to call the relevant government agency.

'Did Norton have any links to militia groups?' Demonaco asked.

'Not a one. Been in the Navy all his life. Technical support systems expert—computers, communications systems, navigation computers. He has an exemplary record. Hell, the man's a goddamn boy scout. The man least likely to betray his country.'

'What about the others?'

'Nothing. None of them has any links to any para-military organisations. Every member of the team had to go through a comprehensive security check before they were cleared to work on the project. They're clean. Not a single one of them is believed to even *know* a member of a militia group.'

'Well, someone does,' Demonaco said. 'Find out who worked with Norton the most, anyone who could have watched him enter his PIN codes every day. I'll make some calls to my people and see what Earl Bittiker and the Texans have been up to lately.'

The Goose kicked up a shower of spray as it touched down on the surface of the Alto Purus River, not far from the base of the waterfall that cascaded out over the tableland.

Night had fallen and, mindful of the presence of the rapas in the village, Race and the others had decided that they would moor the seaplane down by the waterfall and re-enter Vilcafor via the quenko.

After Doogie had parked the Goose on the riverbank underneath a dense canopy of trees, the four of them disembarked. They left Uli in the plane, unconscious and dosed up on some methadone they'd found in a first-aid kit in the back of the plane.

Before they made for the path behind the waterfall, however, Race made them do something quite unusual.

Using a couple of wooden boxes they had found inside the Goose and a few energy bars that Van Lewen and Doogie had had on their persons, they set some primitive traps—traps that were designed to catch the monkeys rustling about in the trees above them.

Ten minutes later, they had a pair of furious primates trapped inside the two wooden boxes. The two monkeys screamed and shrieked as Van Lewen and Doogie carried them along the path behind the rushing waterfall and into the yawning stone doorway of the quenko.

Ten minutes later, Race climbed up into the citadel of Vilcafor.

Nash, Lauren, Copeland, Gaby Lopez and Johann Krauss were all gathered in a corner of the citadel watching Lauren as she tried to make radio contact with either Van Lewen or Doogie.

They all turned as one when they saw Race emerge from the quenko with the fake idol in his hands.

Renée, Van Lewen and Doogie came up into the citadel after him. They were all completely covered in mud and grime. Race still had dried droplets of Heinrich Anistaze's blood on his face.

Nash saw the idol in his hands immediately.

'You got it!' he exclaimed, rushing over to Race, snatching the idol from him.

He gazed at it adoringly.

Race just watched Nash coldly, and in that instant he decided that he wouldn't tell Nash what he knew about him. Rather he would just wait and see what Nash did from here. They might still get the idol—indeed, maybe even with Race's help—but Race was determined to ensure that Nash wouldn't end up with it.

'It's beautiful,' Nash said wondrously.

'It's a fake,' Race said flatly.

'What?'

'It's a fake. It's not made of thyrium. If you turn on your nucleotide resonance imager again, you'll find that there is still a source of thyrium is this area. But this idol isn't it.'

'But . . . how?'

'During his escape from Cuzco, Renco Capac got the criminal Bassario to craft an exact replica of the Spirit of the People. Renco planned to surrender to Hernando and hand over the fake idol to him. He knew Hernando would kill him, but he also knew that so long as Hernando got *an* idol, he would never suspect that it might be the *wrong* idol.

'As it happened, however, Renco and Alberto Santiago killed Hernando and his men, and Renco—so the manuscript says—proceeded to hide *both* idols inside the temple.'

Nash turned the idol over in his hands and saw for the first time the hollowed-out cylindrical section in its base. He looked up at Race.

'So the real idol is still somewhere inside the temple?'

'That's what Santiago says in the manuscript,' Race said.

'But . . . ?'

'But I don't believe him.'

'You don't believe him? Why not?'

'Does your NRI machine still work?' Race asked Lauren.

'Yes.'

'Set it up and I'll show you what I mean.'

They all moved to the open-topped roof of the citadel, where Lauren began setting up the nucleotide resonance imager.

While she went about setting up the machine, Race looked out over the village. It was dark, still raining lightly. He caught a glimpse of a large feline shadow peering up at him from behind one of the smaller buildings of the town.

After a few moments, Lauren had the NRI machine ready. She flicked a switch and the silver rod mounted on top of the console began to rotate slowly.

Thirty seconds later, there came a shrill *beep!* and the rod stopped abruptly. It was not, however, pointing at the idol in Nash's hands. Rather, it was pointing away from Nash, up at the mountains.

'I'm getting a reading,' Lauren said. 'Strong signal, very high frequency resonance.'

'What're the co-ordinates?' Race said.

'Bearing 270 degrees. Vertical angle 29 degrees, 58 minutes. Range 793 metres. Same as it was last time, if I remember it right,' she said, giving Race a look.

'You are remembering it right,' he said. 'You'll also remember that we thought it was inside the temple.'

'Yes . . .' Lauren said.

Race looked at her hard—harder than usual. He wondered if she had been party to Nash's deception, decided that she probably was. 'Do you remember *why* we thought it was in the temple?'

Lauren frowned. 'Well, I remember we climbed up the crater and saw the temple. Then we figured that the temple's location matched the trajectory of the NRI. Ergo, the idol was in the temple.'

'That's right,' Race said. 'That's exactly what we did. And that's exactly where we went wrong.'

They all came back inside the citadel.

Race grabbed a pen and a piece of paper from inside the ATV that was still parked flush against the doorway to the citadel.

'Copeland,' he said to the tall humourless scientist. 'Do you think that with all this technological gadgetry you've got here, you could find me a regular calculator?'

Copeland found one inside one of the American containers, handed it to him.

'All right,' Race said, allowing the others to crowd around him and watch.

He drew a picture on the sheet of paper.

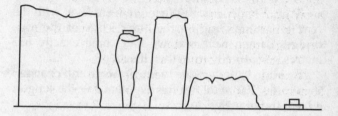

'Okay,' he said. 'This is a picture of Vilcafor and the plateau to the west of it as seen from the side. Okay?'

'Okay,' Lauren said.

Race drew some lines across the drawing:

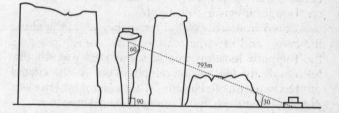

'And this is what we deduced yesterday from the reading that we got from the nucleotide resonance imager: 793 metres to the idol. Angle of inclination 29 degrees, 58 minutes—but I'll just use 30 degrees to keep it simple. The point is, when we climbed up the crater and saw the temple, we immediately thought that the temple must have matched the reading. Right?'

'Right . . .' Nash said.

'Well we were wrong to do that,' Race said. 'Do you remember when we were climbing up that spiralling path around the rock tower and Lauren took a reading from her digital compass?'

'Vaguely,' Nash said.

'Well, I remember it. When we were level with the rock tower, standing on the outer ledge of the rope bridge, Lauren said that we had come exactly 632 metres horizontally from the village.'

He added another line to the drawing and changed the words '793 m' along the hypotenuse—the longest side of the triangle—to '*x* m'.

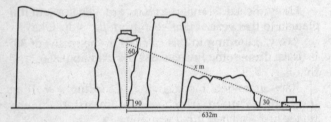

'Anybody remember doing trigonometry at school?' he asked. All the theoretical physicists in the citadel around him shrugged bashfully. 'Granted, it isn't nuclear physics,' Race said, 'but it does still have some uses.'

'Oh, I see it . . ..' Doogie said suddenly from the back of the small crowd gathered around Race. Clearly the others didn't.

Race said, 'Using simple trigonometry, if you know one angle of a right-angled triangle and the length of one of its sides, you will be able to determine the lengths of the other two sides by using the concepts of *sines*, *cosines* and *tangents*.

'Don't you guys remember 'SOHCAHTOA'? The sine

of an angle equals the length of the side *opposite* the angle divided by the length of the hypotenuse. The cosine equals the length of the side *adjacent* to the angle divided by the hypotenuse.

'In our example here, to find x—the distance between us and the temple—we would use the cosine of 30°.' Race then wrote:

$$\cos 30° = \frac{632}{x}$$

'Therefore,' he said,

$$x = \frac{632}{\cos 30°}$$

He punched some numbers into the calculator Copeland had given him.

'Now, according to this calculator, the cosine of 30° is 0.866. Therefore, x equals 632 divided by 0.866. And that is . . . 729.'

Race amended his drawing accordingly, writing feverishly. Lauren watched him in astonishment. Renée just watched him, beaming.

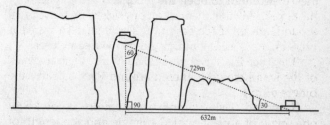

'Anybody see a problem here?' Race said.

Everyone was silent.

Race amended his drawing one last time, finishing with a flourishing 'X'.

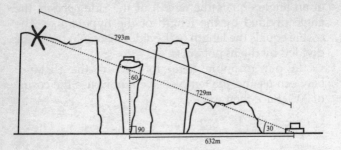

'We made a mistake,' he said. 'We assumed that because of its height the *temple* was 793 metres from the village and hence, that the idol was inside it. It was a good guess but it was a wrong guess. The real idol isn't inside the temple at all. It's *beyond* it, up on the plateau somewhere.'

'But where?' Nash said.

'I would imagine,' Race replied, 'that the idol is to be found in the village of the tribe of natives who built the rope bridge up on the rock tower, the same tribe of natives that attacked our German friends here when they were about to open the temple.'

'But what about the manuscript?' Nash said. 'I thought that it said *both* idols were inside the temple.'

'The manuscript doesn't tell the full story,' Race said. 'I can only guess that Alberto Santiago doctored the ending so that no-one reading it later would know the true resting place of the idol.'

Race held up the sheet of paper with his drawing on it. 'That's where the idol is. Your NRI says so, so does the math.'

Nash pursed his lips, thinking. Then at last he said, 'All right. Let's go get it.'

The two monkeys that Race and the others had caught down by the river had gladly—or perhaps angrily—obliged them with an ample supply of urine, urine which the two screaming primates had sprayed throughout the plastic bags that Race had lined their boxes with.

Put simply, the monkey urine reeked. Its sharp foul odour—the smell of ammonia—pervaded the interior of the citadel. It was no wonder the rapas despised it, Race thought as he and the others applied the warm stinking urine to their bodies.

When they were all done, Van Lewen handed out weapons. Since he and Doogie were the only Green Berets left—so far as anyone knew, Buzz Cochrane was still up on the tower top—they took the two G-11s. Nash, Race and Renée were given M-16s, complete with grappling hooks.

Race, still dressed in his black Nazi breastplate and his blue baseball cap, hung his grappling hook from his belt.

Copeland and Lauren were each given SIG-Sauer P228 semiautomatic pistols. Krauss and Lopez, the ordinary scientists, went gunless.

Once everyone was ready, Van Lewen stepped through the doorway of the citadel and into the ATV. Then he made his way to the rear of the all-terrain vehicle and opened the pop-up hatch.

His G-11 emerged first.

Then slowly, Van Lewen peered out from the open hatch and scanned the area. Immediately, his eyes went wide.

The big eight-wheeled vehicle was *surrounded* by rapas.

Their tails coiled and uncoiled behind their massive bodies. Their yellow eyes bored into him, hard and cold.

Van Lewen counted twelve of them, just standing there in the street, watching him.

Then all of a sudden, the nearest cat snorted— smelled the urine—and immediately reeled away from the ATV.

One after the other, the other cats did the same, turning away from the armoured vehicle and forming a wide circle around it.

Van Lewen stepped out onto the street, his gun up. One by one, the others came out behind him, Race among them.

Like everyone else, he moved slowly, cautiously, staring at the cats while he kept his finger poised on the trigger of his M-16.

It was a truly bizarre sensation, a kind of stand-off. Men armed with guns, the cats armed with sheer natural aggression. Despite their rifles and their pistols, Race was certain that the rapas could take them all down easily if they dared to fire a shot.

But the cats did not attack.

It was as if the humans were protected from them by some kind of invisible wall—a wall which the rapas simply refused to cross. Rather, they just followed Race and the others at a safe distance, paralleling them as they made their way toward the riverside path.

Christ, they're huge! Race thought, as he made his way through the ranks of massive black cats.

The last time he had seen them up close he had been on the other side of the Humvee's glass windows, but now—now that they were all around him, with no windows or doors separating them from him—they looked twice as big. He could hear their breathing. It was just as Alberto Santiago had described it—a deep-chested braying sound like that of a horse. The sound of a powerful beast.

'Why don't we just shoot them?' Copeland whispered.

'I wouldn't go doing that too quickly,' Van Lewen replied. 'At the moment, I think their dislike of monkey urine overrides their desire to kill us. If we open fire on them, I think it's likely that their desire to *survive* will override their dislike of monkey urine.'

The eight of them made their way up the riverside

path and into the narrow fissure in the plateau, the rapas following them at a distance.

They emerged from the passageway at the bottom of the crater and saw the shallow lake stretching away from them, with the rock tower soaring into the sky from its centre and the thin but incredibly tall waterfall pouring down from the south-west corner of the canyon.

For once it wasn't raining, and the full moon shone down on the crater with all its strength, bathing it in a kind of mystical blue light.

Led by Van Lewen, they climbed the spiralling path, up into the night.

The rapas slunk their way up the spiralling path behind them. With their dark black heads and high pointed ears, they looked like demons climbing up out of Hell itself, ready to yank Race and his companions down into the depths of the earth should any of them make one false step. But ultimately they just kept their distance, put off by the smell of the monkey urine.

At last the group came to the two buttresses that had once held up the rope bridge.

The rope bridge itself now lay flat against the wall of the tower on the other side of the ravine, exactly where the Nazis had left it.

Race looked across at the tower top. There was no sign of Buzz Cochrane anywhere.

Then, however, instead of crossing over onto the rock tower—which, at present, they couldn't do any-way—Van Lewen led them further up the spiralling path, toward the rim of the crater.

The path slid around and behind the thin waterfall at the south-western corner before it rose dramatically, arriving at the rim of the crater.

Race stepped up onto the rim and looked westward—

and saw the majestic peaks of the Andes towering above him, dark triangular shadows superimposed on the night sky. Off to his left, he saw the small river that fed the thin waterfall and alongside it, a section of dense rainforest.

A narrow muddy path—created by constant use rather than any deliberate design—ran away from him into the thick green foliage.

But it was what sat on either side of the slender path that seized his immediate attention—a pair of wooden stakes, driven into the mud.

Impaled on each stake was a fearsome-looking skull.

Race felt a chill as he shone his barrel-mounted flashlight onto one of the skulls.

It looked utterly horrific—an effect magnified by the copious amounts of fresh blood and rotting flesh that dangled from its sides. It was oddly shaped too—definitely not human. Rather, both skulls were strangely elongated, with sharp canine teeth, inverted triangular nostrils and wide eye sockets.

Race swallowed hard.

They were *feline* skulls.

They were rapa skulls.

'A primitive "Keep Out" sign,' Krauss said, looking at the two filthy skulls impaled on the stakes.

'I don't think they're meant to keep *people* out,' Gaby Lopez said, sniffing one of the skulls. 'They've been drenched in monkey urine. They're designed to keep the cats away.'

Van Lewen stepped past the skulls and pressed on into the dense foliage. Race and the others followed him, guided by the beams of their flashlights.

About thirty yards beyond the two skulls, Van Lewen and Race came to a wide moat not unlike the one that surrounded Vilcafor.

The only differences between the two moats were, firstly, that this moat wasn't dried up—rather, it was filled with water, the surface of which lay about fifteen feet below the rim of the moat. And secondly, it was inhabited by a family of very large caimans.

'Great,' Race said as he watched the giant crocodilians prowling around the bottom of the moat. 'Caimans again.'

'Another defensive mechanism?' Renée asked.

'Caimans are the only animals in this area with even a remote chance of defeating a rapa in a fight,' Krauss said. 'Primitive tribes do not have rifles or trip wires, so they look for other methods of keeping their feline enemies at bay.'

Beyond the moat—completely surrounded by it— Race saw another section of low foliage, beyond which lay a small collection of thatch huts nestled underneath a stand of tall trees.

It was a village of some sort.

The short stretch of foliage lay between the village and the moat, gave the cluster of primitive huts a quaint, almost mystical look. Some torches burned on high sticks, bathing the little town in a haunting orange glow. Apart from the burning torches, however, the village appeared to be completely deserted.

A twig snapped.

Race spun, and immediately saw the pack of rapas standing on the muddy pathway about ten yards behind his group. Somehow, they had managed to get past the urine-soaked skulls and now they were standing a short distance behind Race and the others— watching, waiting.

A narrow log-bridge lay flat on the ground on the village side of the moat. A length of rope was attached to one end of it in a manner not unlike that which had applied to the rope bridge down at the rock tower. It stretched out *over* the moat to Race's side, where it was tied to a stake in the ground.

Van Lewen and Doogie pulled on the rope, manoeuvred the log-bridge into position so that it now spanned the moat.

The eight of them then crossed the bridge and entered the section of low foliage surrounding the village.

Once they were all over the bridge, Van Lewen and Doogie quickly pulled it back onto the village side of the moat, so that the rapas could not follow them over.

They all came out from the foliage together, emerging onto a wide, town square-like clearing. They cast the beams of their flashlights over the thatch huts and tall trees that surrounded the bare dirt clearing.

At the northern end of the square stood a bamboo cage, its four corners comprised of four thick tree trunks. Beyond the cage—carved out of the muddy wall of the moat—was a large pit about thirty feet square and fifteen feet deep. A criss-crossing bamboo gate separated the pit from the moat itself.

In the very centre of the town square, however, stood the most arresting sight of all.

It was a shrine of some sort, a large wooden altar-like structure that had been carved out of the trunk of the widest tree in the village.

It was filled with nooks and small alcoves. Inside the alcoves Race saw a collection of relics that was nothing short of spectacular—a golden crown embedded with sapphires, silver and gold statues of Incan warriors and maidens, various stone idols, and one gigantic ruby that was easily the size of a man's fist.

Even in the semi-darkness, the shrine shone, its treasures glistening in the moonlight. Dense clusters of leaves hung down from the trees around it, framing it on either side like curtains in a theatre.

In the very centre of the wooden shrine—right where its heart would have been—sat the most elaborate nook of all. It was covered by a small curtain and was quite obviously the centrepiece of the whole altar. But whatever occupied it lay hidden from view.

Nash strode directly over to it. Race knew what he was thinking. With a sharp yank, Nash pulled the curtain covering the nook aside.

And he saw it. Race saw it too, and gasped.

It was the idol.

The *real* idol.

The Spirit of the People.

The sight of it took Race's breath away. Strangely, the first thing that struck him about the idol was what an excellent job Bassario had done in replicating it— his fake idol had been a perfect reproduction. But no matter how hard he had tried, Bassario had been unable to reproduce the *aura* that surrounded the real idol.

It was majesty personified.

The ferocity of the rapa's head inspired terror. The glint of the purple-and-black thyrium stone inspired wonder. The whole shining idol just inspired awe.

Entranced, Nash reached out to pick it up—at exactly the same moment as a sharpened stone arrowhead appeared next to his head.

The arrow was held by a very angry-looking native who had stepped out from the curtain-like foliage to the right of the shrine. He held the arrow poised in his longbow, its drawstring stretched taut back to his ear.

Van Lewen made to raise his G-11, just as the forest all around him came alive and out of it stepped no fewer than *fifty* natives.

Nearly all of them brandished bows and arrows, all of them aimed squarely at Race and the others.

Van Lewen still had his gun up. Doogie didn't. He just stood rooted to the spot a few yards away, frozen.

An uneasy stand-off materialised. Van Lewen—armed with a gun that could kill twenty men in an instant—facing off against the fifty-plus natives armed with bows and arrows that were all ready to be fired.

There are too many of them, Race thought. Even if Van Lewen did manage to get a few shots off, it wouldn't be enough. The natives would still kill them all, so overwhelming were their numbers.

'Van Lewen,' Race said. 'Don't . . .'

'Sergeant Van Lewen,' Nash said from over by the altar, where he stood with an arrow poised next to his head. 'Lower your weapon.'

Van Lewen did so. As soon as he did, the natives immediately moved forward, seized the Americans' high-powered weapons.

An older-looking man with a long grey beard and wrinkled olive skin stepped forward. He didn't bother carrying a longbow. He appeared to be the chieftain of this tribe.

Another man walked at the chieftain's side and as soon as he saw him, Race blinked in disbelief.

This second man wasn't a native at all, but rather

was a stout-looking Latin-American man. He was deeply tanned and dressed in the manner of the Indians, but even the liberal doses of ceremonial paint that he wore on his face and chest couldn't hide his decidedly urban features.

As the chieftain glared at Nash—standing in front of the shrine like a thief caught with his hands in the till—he growled something in his native tongue.

The Latin-American man at his side listened attentively and then offered some advice in reply.

'Hmph,' the chieftain grunted.

Race stood next to Renée, the two of them surrounded by five arrow-bearing Indians.

Just then one of the Indians stepped forward—curious—and touched Race on the cheek, as if testing to see if his white skin was real.

Race pulled his face away, jerking it clear.

As he did so, however, the Indian shrieked in astonishment, causing everyone to turn. He hurried over to the chieftain, shouting, 'Rumaya! Rumaya!'

The chieftain immediately came over to where Race stood, with his white adviser behind him. The old chieftain stood before Race, appraising him coldly while at the same time the Indian who had touched Race's face pointed at his left eye and said, 'Rumaya. Rumaya.'

Abruptly, the chieftain grabbed Race's chin and turned it hard to the right.

Race didn't resist.

The chieftain evaluated his face in silence, inspecting the triangular brown birthmark situated underneath his left eye. Then the chieftain licked his finger and began rubbing the birthmark, as if testing to see if it would come off. It didn't.

'Rumaya . . .' he breathed.

He turned to his Latin-American adviser and said something in Quechuan. The adviser whispered something in return, keeping his voice low and respectful, to which the old chieftain shook his head and pointed emphatically at the square-shaped pit that had been carved into the wall of the moat.

Then the chieftain turned on his heel and barked an order to his people.

The Indians quickly herded everyone except Race into the bamboo cage between the trees.

For his part, Race was shoved toward the muddy pit adjacent to the moat.

The Latin-American adviser fell into step beside him.

'Hello,' the man said in heavily-accented English, taking Race completely by surprise.

'Hey there,' Race said. 'You, ah, want to tell me what's going on here?'

'These people are the direct descendants of a remote Incan tribe. They observed that you are possessed of the Mark of the Sun—that birthmark under your left eye. They think you might be the second coming of their saviour, a man they know as the Chosen One. But they want to test you first to be sure.'

'And how exactly are they going to test me?'

'They will put you in the pit and then they will open the gate that separates it from the moat, allowing one of the caimans to enter the pit with you. Then they will see who survives the subsequent confrontation, you or the caiman. You see, according to their prophecy—'

'I know,' Race said. 'I've read it. According to the prophecy the Chosen One will bear the Mark of the Sun, and be able to fight with great lizards and save their spirit.'

The man looked at Race askance. 'You're an anthropologist?'

'A linguist. I've read the Santiago Manuscript.'

The man frowned. 'You've come here looking for the Spirit of the People?'

'Not me. Them,' Race said, nodding over at Nash and the others as they were placed inside the bamboo cage.

'But why? It's worthless in monetary terms—'

'It was carved out of a meteorite,' Race said. 'And now it's been discovered that that meteorite was made of a very special kind of stone.'

'Oh,' the man said.

'So who are you?' Race asked.

'Oh, yes, I'm very sorry, I completely forgot to introduce myself,' the man said, straightening. 'My name is Doctor Miguel Moros Marquez. I am an anthropologist from the University of Peru and I've been living with this tribe for the last nine years.'

A minute later, Race was shoved down a thin sloping path that descended into the mud.

The path was bounded on either side by high earthen walls and it ended at a small wooden gate that opened onto the pit. As soon as Race arrived in front of the gate, it slid open—pulled upward by a pair of Indians standing on the ground above—and he stepped tentatively out into the pit that adjoined the caiman-infested moat.

The pit was roughly square in shape and it was *big*—about thirty feet by thirty feet.

It was lined on three sides by sheer muddy walls. The entire fourth wall, however, was comprised of an enormous gate constructed of a latticework of bamboo 'bars'. Through it, Race could see the dark waves of the moat outside.

To make matters worse, the floor of the pit was covered in a layer of black water—water that sloshed freely in through the criss-crossing bars of the bamboo gate from the moat outside. Its depth where Race was standing was about knee-deep. Its depth in other parts of the pit was indeterminate.

Well, this is new, Will. What the hell did you do to get yourself into this situation?

Just then, a rectangular section of the enormous bamboo gate—a gate within the gate—was raised by some Indians standing at the rim of the pit and immediately a wide opening was created in the middle of the larger gate *between* the pit and the caiman-infested moat.

Race watched in horror as the gate was lifted higher and higher, making the opening wider and wider. After a few moments it reached its zenith and stopped and there followed a long silence.

The inhabitants of the village now lined the rims of the pit and peered down into it, waiting for the arrival of one of the caimans.

Race patted his pockets for any weapons he could use. He was still wearing his jeans and T-shirt and the kevlar breastplate that Uli had given to him at the mine, and of course, his glasses and Yankees baseball cap.

No weapons—except for the grappling hook that hung from his belt.

Race grabbed it. It had a length of rope attached to it, and at the moment its four silver claws were retracted, lying flush against the hook's handle like an umbrella in the closed position.

He looked at it for a moment, thinking. Maybe he could use it to climb out of here—

It was then that something very large slid in through the open gate from the moat.

Race froze.

Even though fully three-quarters of its body must have been *under* the surface, it was still absolutely enormous.

Race saw the nostrils and the eyes and the rounded armoured back protruding above the surface—all moving at the same speed as the big animal cruised ominously through the water. He saw its long plated tail swishing lazily back and forth behind it, propelling it slowly forward.

It was a caiman and it was *huge*.

At least an eighteen-footer.

Once the massive reptile was fully inside the pit, the bamboo gate behind it was lowered back into its slot and locked into place.

Now it was just Race and the caiman.

Facing off.

Good God . . .

Race sidestepped away from the big beast, backing into a corner of the square-shaped pit, his feet sloshing through the knee-deep water.

The caiman didn't move a muscle.

In fact, the enormous crocodile-like creature didn't even seem to be aware of his presence at all.

Race could hear his heart pounding loudly inside his head.

Kathump-kathump-kathump.

The caiman still didn't move.

Race stood frozen in the corner of the pit.

And then suddenly, without warning, the caiman moved.

But it wasn't a quick movement of any kind. It didn't rush forward. Nor did it lunge or leap at Race. Rather, it just lowered itself, slowly and ominously, beneath the surface of the muddy water.

Race's eyes went instantly wide.

Holy shit.

The caiman had just submerged itself completely! He couldn't see it. In fact, in the soft blue moonlight and the flickering orange light of the Indians' torches, he couldn't see *anything* but the small waves on the surface of the water.

More silence.

Wavelets slapped against the earthen walls of the pit.

Race's entire body was tensed, waiting for the caiman to appear. He gripped the steel grappling hook in his hand like a club.

The water's surface was completely still.

Total silence.

Race could feel the fear building up inside him.

Fuck-fuck-fuck-fuck-fuck-fuck-fuck-fuck.

He wondered how long the reptile could stay under—

The attack came from the left, just as Race was looking to the right.

With a loud roar, the caiman exploded up out of the water next to him, its jaws bared wide, its enormous two-ton body rolling through the air.

Race saw the reptile instantly and on a reflex dived sideways, splashing into the water as the caiman shot past him and slammed down into the slime again.

Race clambered to his feet, spun around, then dived again as the caiman made another lightning-quick pass at him, snapping its jaws in front of his face with a loud fleshy *smack!*

Race was covered in mud now, but he didn't care. He rose out of the water again—right next to the earthen wall of the pit—and turned just in time to see the caiman come rushing at his face.

He ducked—let his body drop straight down, *under* the surface—and the caiman went thundering over the top of him, slamming nose-first into the muddy wall of the pit.

Race surfaced to the cheers of the Indians standing

up on the rim of the pit. He waded right and found himself standing in deeper water. He began to unloop the rope attached to the grappling hook.

He looked up at the rim of the pit.

Fifteen feet, not far.

He was standing waist-deep in the water now, unlooping the rope. As he did so, he quickly glanced about himself, to see where the caiman was.

And he didn't see it.

The caiman was nowhere to be seen.

The pit was completely bare.

It must have gone under again . . .

Race looked fearfully at the water all around himself.

Oh, shit . . . he thought.

And then abruptly he felt something slam into his leg at tremendous speed, felt a searing pain shoot through his ankle. Then he was yanked beneath the surface.

Race went under, opened his eyes, and through the inky water all around him, saw that the caiman had his left foot *inside* its mouth!

But it didn't have a good grip on him and it opened its mouth for a split second to get a better one.

That was all Race needed. No sooner had the big reptile released his foot than Race yanked it clear and the caiman's jaws came chomping down on nothing.

Race surfaced, with the grappling hook's rope trailing through the water behind him, desperately gasping for air.

The caiman came up too, surging out of the water after him, snapping wildly, catching the grappling hook's rope in its jaws, slicing through it in an instant.

As the rope was cut, Race lost his balance and fell clumsily away from the reptile into shallower water.

He turned quickly, at exactly the same moment as he saw the caiman come rushing in at him from the side, its jaws wide, its tooth-filled mouth filling his field of vision, and with nothing else left to call on, Race just jammed the grappling hook—together with his entire right arm—*into the caiman's wide-open mouth!*

The big reptile's jaws came crashing down on his arm—

—just as Race hit the release button on the grappling hook's handle.

At that moment, a nanosecond before the caiman's razor-sharp teeth clamped down on his right bicep, the grappling hook's pointed steel claws *sprang* outwards with monumental force.

The caiman's head just exploded.

Two of the pointed steel claws burst out from its eye sockets, and in that single disgusting instant, both of the caiman's eyes were blasted out of its head—*from the inside*—replaced by the razor-sharp tips of the two steel claws.

The grappling hook's other two claws exploded out from the underside of the caiman's head, ripping through the softer skin there, puncturing it with ease.

The two claws that had shot through the big reptile's eye sockets must have penetrated its brain on their journey through the caiman's skull. As such, they'd killed the massive animal in an instant—freezing its jaws in mid-chomp—and now Race sat on the floor of the pit, with an enormous eighteen-foot caiman attached to his right arm, its long triangular mouth poised over his exposed arm—its teeth millimetres away from his skin—its immense black body stretching out into the pit, motionless.

The crowd of natives standing on the rim of the pit just stood there aghast, stunned.

And then, slowly, they started clapping.

Race emerged from the pit to the adulation of the Indians. They slapped him on the back, smiled at him through crooked yellow teeth.

The cage holding Nash and the others was opened immediately and a few moments later they joined Race in the centre of the village.

Van Lewen shook his head as he came up to Race. 'What the hell did you just do? We couldn't see a thing from that cage.'

'I just killed a great lizard,' Race said simply.

The anthropologist, Marquez, came over and smiled at Race. 'Well done, sir! Well done! What did you say your name was?'

'William Race.'

'Rejoice, Mister Race. You just made yourself a god.'

John-Paul Demonaco's cellular rang.

Demonaco and the Navy investigator, Mitchell, were still at DARPA headquarters in Virginia. Mitchell was taking another call himself.

'You say it came from Bittiker . . .' Demonaco said into the phone. Suddenly his face went ashen white. 'Call the Baltimore PD and get them to send the bomb squad over there right now. I'll be there as soon as I can.'

Mitchell came over as Demonaco hung up.

'That was Aaronson,' the Navy man said. 'They just raided the Freedom Fighter locations. Nothing in any of them. Empty.'

'Never mind,' Demonaco said, heading for the door.

'What is it?' Mitchell said as he hurried after him.

'I just got a call from one of my guys in Baltimore. He's at the apartment of one of our Texan informants. Says he's got something big.'

Ninety minutes later, Demonaco and Mitchell arrived at a decrepit old warehouse in the industrial sector of Baltimore.

Three police cruisers, a couple of nondescript beige

Buicks—FBI cars—and a large navy blue van with 'BOMB SQUAD' painted on its side were already parked out in front of the building.

Demonaco and Mitchell entered the warehouse, ascended some stairs.

'This place belongs to a guy named Wilbur Francis James, better known as "Bluey".' Demonaco said. 'He used to be a radio operator in the Army, but he got discharged for stealing equipment from the office—frequency scanners, M-16s. Now he's a small-time crook who acts as a liaison between the Texans and certain criminal elements who supply them with guns and intelligence. A couple of months ago, we caught him with three stolen canisters of VX nerve gas, but we decided to withhold pressing charges if he helped us with our own intelligence gathering. He's been very reliable so far.'

They arrived at a cramped little apartment on the top floor of the warehouse, guarded by a pair of Baltimore beat cops. They went inside. It was a crappy, disgusting apartment, with damp floorboards and peeling wallpaper.

Demonaco was met by a young black agent named Hanson and the leader of the Baltimore Police Department's Bomb Squad, a small squat man named Barker.

Bluey James himself sat in the corner of the room with his arms crossed. He chugged on a cigarette defiantly. He was a small unshaven runt of a man, with dreadlocked brown hair and a filthy Hawaiian shirt. On his feet he wore sandals—with socks.

'What have you got?' Demonaco asked Hanson.

'When we arrived, we found nothing,' the young agent said, eyeing Bluey James scornfully. 'But upon further examination we found this.'

Hanson handed Demonaco a package about the

size of a small book. It was wrapped in brown paper and was unopened. With it was an ordinary-looking white envelope which *had* been opened.

'It was hidden behind a false panel in the wall,' Hanson said.

Demonaco turned to Bluey. 'Inventive,' he said. 'You're getting smarter in your old age, Bluey.'

'Blow me.'

'X-ray?' Demonaco said to the man named Barker.

'It's clean,' the bomb squad man said. 'Judging by the scan, it looks like a CD or something.'

Bluey James snorted. 'I didn't know it was a fucking crime in this country for a man to buy himself a CD. Although it probably *should* be for the shit you'd listen to, Demonaco.'

'What, you don't like "Achy Breaky Heart"?' Demonaco said. He looked at the white envelope, pulled a slip of paper from it. It read:

WHEN WE HAVE THE THYRIUM, I WILL CONTACT YOU DIRECTLY. AFTER YOU RECEIVE MY CALL, E-MAIL THE CONTENTS OF THIS DISC TO EACH OF THE FOLLOWING ORGANISATIONS.

BITTIKER

After that there was a list of about a dozen names and addresses, all of them relating to television networks or channels—CNN, ABC, NBC, CBS, FOX.

Demonaco turned the brown-paper package over in his hands. What could Earl Bittiker want to e-mail to every major television network in the country?

He ripped open the package.

And saw a gleaming silver compact disc.

The first thing he noticed about it, however, was that it wasn't an ordinary CD.

It was a V-CD—a video compact disc.

He turned. 'Bluey, what the hell is this?'

'*The Best of Billy Ray Cyrus*. Just for you, asshole.'

'Hey, Demonaco,' Mitchell said, nodding at a V-CD player over by Bluey's trinitron television. Next to the TV stood a black IBM computer. All three objects looked completely out of place in the otherwise dilapidated apartment.

Demonaco slid the compact disc into the V-CD player and hit 'PLAY'.

The face of Earl Bittiker appeared on the television screen instantly.

It was an ugly face—an evil face—pitted with scars and hate. Bittiker had sanguine, hollow features, with stringy blond hair and cold grey eyes that showed nothing but the world of rage that existed behind them. In the background behind the terrorist, Demonaco and Mitchell saw the Supernova.

Bittiker spoke directly into the lens.

'People of the world. My name is Earl Bittiker and I am the Anti-Christ.

'If you are watching this message, then you are about to die. At exactly 12 noon today, Eastern Standard Time, you will all be killed at the hands of a weapon that was created by your own taxes. A weapon that in a few hours' time is going to send this whole vile world to the place where it belongs.

'To the people of the world—I have no quarrel with you. It is the world you inhabit that I hate, a world that no longer deserves to exist. It is a diseased dog and it must be put down.

'To the governments of the world—you are to blame for this state of affairs. Communists, capitalists and fascists alike, you all grew fat while the people you governed starved. You all grew rich while they grew poor, you lived in mansions while they lived in ghettos.

'Human nature is the desire of one man to rule over another. It comes in many guises, many forms—from office politics to ethnic cleansing—and it is performed by all of us, from the lowest foreman to the Chief Executive of the United States. But its character remains the same. It is about *power* and *ruling*. But it is a cancer on this world and that cancer must now be terminated.

'To the television networks who receive this message, contact the Navy or the Defense Advanced Research Projects Agency and ask them what has happened to their Supernova. Ask them about its existence and its purpose. Ask them about the seventeen security staff who died two days ago when my men raided DARPA headquarters in Virginia. I'm sure that no-one has informed you of this incident, because that's the way governments work today. After you've done all that, ask your government if *this*'—he pointed at the device behind him—'is what they're looking for.'

Bittiker stared hard into the lens.

'People of the world, I make no demands of you. I do not ask for a ransom. I do not want political prisoners released from their cells. There is *no way* you can stop me detonating this device. Not now. Not ever. There is nothing you can do to stop this from happening. At twelve noon today, we'll all be going to Hell together.'

The screen cut to hash.

A long silence followed as everyone digested what Bittiker had just said. Even Bluey James was aghast.

'*Fuck* me . . .' he breathed.

'Very clever,' Demonaco said. 'He only stated the time it'll go off. Twelve noon. Now all he has to do is find the thyrium and get in touch with Bluey and his plan is all set.'

He turned to face Mitchell. 'I think we just found your Supernova, Commander.' Then to Bluey: 'Am I to assume that you haven't got that call yet?'

'What do you think, fucknut?'

'What do you know about all this, Bluey?' Demonaco said, changing his tone.

'What I always know, man. Jack shit.'

'If you don't tell me something right now, I'm going to have you charged with aiding and abetting in the murder of seventeen security staff at a federal—'

'Hey, man, weren't you fucking listening? The world is about to end. What does aiding and abetting matter now?'

'I guess that all depends on who you think is gonna win this little contest, us or Bittiker.'

'Bittiker,' Bluey said flatly.

'Then it looks like you'll be spending your last few hours on this Earth in jail,' Demonaco said, nodding to the two cops at the door. 'Take this little weasel away.'

The two cops grabbed Bluey by the arms.

'Oh, now wait just a fucking minute . . .' Bluey said.

'Sorry, Bluey.'

'All right listen, man, listen! I had nothing to do with no murders, okay. I'm just the go-between, all right. I deal on Bittiker's *behalf*. Like a lawyer. Which I might say hasn't been so easy lately since he's been going off the fucking deep end.'

'He's been going off the deep end?' Demonaco waved the two policemen away.

'Like *yeah*. Where you been, man? First he lets a whole group of fucking chinks join the Texans. Japs, man. Fuckin' Japs. You should see these little fuckers. Fucking kamikazes, man. They're from some messed-up cult in Japan. Wanna destroy the world and all that shit. But Earl, he decides he likes what they got to say and he lets 'em in the movement. But then—*fuck*—then he goes and does the strangest thing of all. He goes and merges with the fucking Freedom Fighters.'

'*What?*'

'To get their technical know-how, like. You ask me, man, those Freedom Fighters are a bunch of cocksuckers, but they do know their technology. I mean, shit, messages to the world on V-CD. You think *I* went out and bought this player?'

'The Texans *merged* with the Freedom Fighters . . .' Demonaco said. 'Holy shit.'

Bluey was still yapping. 'It's all the Japs, you see. Ever since they got here, those slopeheads've been telling Earl that if he wants to fuck up the world, he's gonna need some serious hardware. Not guns and shit, but *bombs* and shit. Nukes. And then when they found out about that Supernova thing, well . . .'

But Demonaco wasn't listening anymore.

He turned to Mitchell. 'The Texans *absorbed* the Freedom Fighters. That's why your boss Aaronson didn't find anybody at the Freedom Fighter locations. They don't exist anymore. God, no wonder they used tungsten bullets. They bought themselves time by framing a terrorist group that no longer exists. The Texans and the Freedom Fighters weren't fighting a turf war. They were *merging* . . .'

'What are you saying?' Mitchell asked.

'I'm saying that we have just witnessed the union of three of the most dangerous terrorist organisations in the world. One is a brilliantly organised fighting unit, the second is perhaps the most technologically advanced paramilitary group in America, and the third is a doomsday cult from Japan.

'You add all that up,' Demonaco said, 'and you got yourself one hell of a problem, because those are the guys who stole your Supernova, and judging from that video we just saw, they're out there now trying to get themselves some thyrium.'

In the soft predawn light of the foothills, a banquet was being prepared.

After he had defeated the caiman, Race had politely begged off the adulation of the Indians and asked to rest. A sound sleep had followed—God, he needed it, it had been nearly thirty-six hours since he'd last slept—and he awoke just before the dawn.

The platter that was laid down before him was fit for a king. It was an assortment of raw jungle food set out on wide green leaves. Grubs, berries, corn. Even some raw caiman meat. It was raining lightly but no-one seemed to care.

Race and the Army people sat in a wide circle on the section of open ground that lay in front of the upper village's shrine, eating underneath the watchful gaze of the real idol as it sat proudly in its ornate wooden alcove.

Although the natives had returned their weapons to them, there was still a slight aura of suspicion in the air. A dozen or so Indian warriors stood ominously outside the circle of people, armed with bows and arrows, watching Nash and his people carefully—as they had been doing all night.

Race sat with the tribe's chieftain and the anthropologist, Miguel Moros Marquez.

'Chieftain Roa would like to express his utmost gratitude to you for coming to us,' Marquez said, translating the words of the old chieftain.

Race smiled. 'We've gone from thieves in the night to honoured guests.'

'More than you know,' Marquez said. 'More than you know. If you hadn't survived your encounter with the caiman, your friends would have been sacrificed to the rapas. Now your friends bask in your glory.'

'They're not really my friends,' Race said.

Gaby Lopez sat on the other side of the little anthropologist, her excitement at being in the presence of a legend obvious. After all, as she had said to Race on their first day in Peru, nine years ago Marquez had entered the jungles to study primitive Amazonian tribes—and had never returned. 'Doctor Marquez,' she said, 'please, tell us about this tribe. Your experiences here must have been fascinating.'

Marquez smiled. 'They have been. These Indians are a truly remarkable people, one of the last remaining untouched tribes in the whole of South America. Although they tell me that they have lived in this village for centuries, like most of the other tribes in this region they are nomadic. Often the whole village will just up and move to another location—in search of food or a warmer clime—for six months or even a year at a time. But they always return to this village. They say that they have a connection with this area—a connection with the temple in the crater and the cat gods that dwell inside it.'

'How did they come to possess the Spirit of the People?' Race asked, interjecting.

'I'm sorry, I do not understand?'

'According to the Santiago Manuscript,' Race said, 'Renco Capac used the idol to seal the rapas inside the temple. Then he shut himself inside the building with them. Did these Indians at some stage enter the temple and get the idol out?'

Marquez translated what Race had said for the Indian chieftain, Roa. The chieftain shook his head and said something quickly in Quechuan.

'Chieftain Roa says that Prince Renco was a very clever and brave man, as one would expect of the Chosen One. The chieftain also says that the members of this tribe take a special pride in being his direct descendants.'

'His direct descendants,' Race said. 'But that would mean Renco got out of the temple . . .'

'Yes, it would,' Marquez replied cryptically, translating the chieftain's words.

'But how?' Race said. 'How did he manage to get out?'

At that, the chieftain barked an order to one of his Indian warriors and the warrior scurried off into a nearby hut. He returned moments later carrying something small in his hands.

When the warrior arrived back at his chieftain's side, Race saw that the object in his hands was a thin leatherbound notebook. Its binding looked positively ancient, but its pages appeared uncreased, untouched.

The chieftain spoke. Marquez translated.

'Mister Race, Roa says that the answer to your question lies in the construction of the temple itself. After Renco and Alberto's famous battle with Hernando Pizarro, yes, Renco did enter the temple—*with* the idol. But he also managed to get out of it—*with* the idol. The full story of what happened *after* Renco entered the temple is contained in this notebook.'

Race looked at the notebook in the chieftain's hands. He craved to know what was inside it.

The chieftain handed the little notebook to Race.

'Roa offers it to you as a gift,' Marquez said. 'After all, you are the first person in four hundred years to pass through this village who would actually be able to read it.'

Race opened the notebook immediately, saw about a half-dozen cream-coloured pages filled with Alberto Santiago's handwriting.

He stared at it in awe.

It was the *real* ending to Santiago's story.

'I have a question,' Johann Krauss said suddenly, pompously, leaning forward from his place in the circle. 'How have the rapas managed to survive for so long inside the temple?'

After consulting with the chieftain, Marquez replied, 'Roa says you will find the answer to that question in the notebook.'

'But—' Krauss began.

Roa cut him off with a sharp bark.

'Roa says that you will find the answer to your question in the notebook,' Marquez said firmly. Clearly, while Roa's hospitality to Race was limitless, his grace toward his companions extended only so far.

The rain began to fall more heavily. After a few minutes, Race heard the rumble of distant thunder over the horizon. Doogie and Van Lewen also turned at the sound.

'Storm's coming,' Race said.

Doogie shook his head as he looked up into the sky. The rumbling of thunder grew louder.

'No it isn't,' he said, grabbing his G-11 out of the dirt.

'What are you talking about?'

'That ain't thunder, Professor.'

'Then what is it?'

At that moment, before Doogie could answer him, a massive Super Stallion helicopter *roared* by overhead.

It was closely followed by another, identical helicopter, swooping in low over the village, its rotors thumping loudly, shaking the trees with its powerful downdraft.

Race, Doogie and Van Lewen leapt to their feet, while at the same time all of the Indians reached for their bows.

The roar of the two Super Stallions hovering above the little village was deafening, all-consuming. And then suddenly eight zip-lines were hurled out from within each helicopter. In a second, sixteen men dressed in full combat attire began to slide quickly down the ropes, guns in their hands, ominous shadows against the predawn sky.

Bullets spewed out from the guns of the men abseiling down from the helicopters.

People ran every which way. The Indians dashed for cover in the foliage surrounding the village, snatching up their bows and arrows as they did so. Van Lewen and Doogie fired their G-11s as gunfire from above raked the mud all around them.

Race snapped about where he stood—saw Doogie take two brutal hits to his left leg—then he spun again just in time to see the German zoologist, Krauss, convulse violently as the whole front of his body—his face, his arms, his chest—became an indistinguishable mass of ragged bloody flesh, torn open by about a million rounds of devastating supermachine-gun fire.

The two Super Stallions hovered about twenty feet above the village, razing it with their cannons. As he leapt to his feet, Race saw a single word emblazoned across their sides: NAVY.

It was Romano's team.

They had arrived at last.

And then—just then—as he ran for cover from the two enormous choppers hovering menacingly over the village, Race had an unusual thought.

Wasn't Romano supposed to be flying three *Super Stallions . . .*

Abruptly, a spattering of gunfire strafed the ground all around him and Race scampered for the treeline, turning as he ran just in time to see Frank Nash hurry away from the shrine and dash off into the foliage beyond it with Lauren and Copeland right behind him.

Race's eyes zeroed in on the shrine. The idol was still there, sitting proudly in its alcove.

Or was it?

As the ground all around him exploded with bullet holes, Race hustled over to the shrine and grabbed the idol from its alcove, flipped it over in his hand.

A cylindrical section had been cut out of the base of this idol.

It was the fake.

'No . . .' Race breathed.

Gunfire rang out from the choppers above him. The gale-force wind created by their downdrafts whipped around him like a tornado.

Race ran through the powerful wind, charging into the foliage after Nash and the other two.

'Where are you going?' Renée called to him from her position behind a nearby tree.

'Nash has got the idol!' Race yelled back. 'The real one—'

At that moment—completely without warning— one of the big Super Stallion helicopters above them just exploded in mid-air. It was a staggering explosion, monstrous in its force. All the more so because it had been so unexpected.

Race looked up instantly and saw the mighty helicopter fall to the earth in a kind of horrific slow motion, *right on top of the men hanging underneath it.*

The men—they were Navy SEALs—hit the ground

first, followed a split second later by the massive helicopter as it came crashing down on top of them, crushing them in an instant, its awesome bulk slamming down against the ground with a resounding *whump!*

Race looked above the fallen, flaming wreck of the Super Stallion and saw a horizontal smoke-trail dissipating in the air above it.

It was the smoke-trail of an air-to-air missile. Race traced it back to its source.

And saw *another* helicopter!

Only this one wasn't a troop transport like the two Super Stallions. It was a two-man chopper—an attack bird—thin but not skinny, with a prism-shaped cockpit and an enclosed tail rotor. It looked like a mechanical preying mantis.

Although Race didn't know it, he was looking at an AH-66 'Comanche'—the U.S. Army's next-generation attack helicopter.

Nash's air support.

It, too, had finally arrived.

Race saw a second Comanche attack chopper materialise in the morning sky behind the first one, saw it open fire on the surviving Super Stallion with its twin-barrelled Gatling gun.

The second Super Stallion responded with its own burst of machine-gun fire, covering the eight SEALs still dangling from its zip-lines.

The first SEAL touched the ground—just as an arrow smacked squarely in his forehead, dropping him instantly.

The seven remaining SEALs continued down their zip-lines. Two more were taken out by arrows on their way down. The others hit the ground running.

In the air above them, their Super Stallion was in all

sorts of trouble. It swivelled laterally in the air, turning to face the two Army Comanches firing on it.

Then suddenly—*shoom!*—a single Sidewinder missile shot out from the Super Stallion's side-mounted missile pod. The missile traced a perfectly horizontal smoke-trail through the air behind it before it *slammed* at tremendous speed into the canopy of one of the Comanches, blasting the attack chopper out of the sky with a momentous explosion.

But it was a consolation goal. In fact, if it did anything at all, it only succeeded in sealing the Super Stallion's fate. Because there was still one Comanche left.

No sooner had the first Army chopper been hit, than the second one quickly pivoted in mid-air and released a Hellfire missile of its own.

The Hellfire rocketed through the air at phenomenal speed, zeroing in on the Super Stallion. It found its mark in seconds, ploughing at full speed into the side of the big Navy helicopter.

The Super Stallion's walls shattered in an instant, blasting out in every direction, showering the ground beneath it with firetrails of flaming debris. Then the massive Navy helicopter crashed down into the trees above the village, a billowing, flaming wreck.

Wet fern branches slapped hard against Race's face as he and Renée ran eastward through the dense section of low foliage to the south of the village square, chasing after Frank Nash.

They passed Van Lewen on their way. He was standing behind one of the huts, firing with his G-11 at three of the five Navy SEALs who had survived their dispersal from the second Super Stallion.

He fired low—trying to wound, not to kill. After all, they *were* his own countrymen, and after what he had heard from Renée on the plane earlier about Frank Nash and the Army's mission to undercut the Navy, he had started to question his allegiances. He didn't want to kill men just like himself—line animals who were just following orders—unless he really, *really* had to.

The three SEALs had hunkered down behind some trees near the shrine and their MP-5s, when used in co-ordination, were proving a good match against his lone G-11. Then abruptly the SEALs' fire stopped as they were overwhelmed from behind by a horde of Indians bearing axes, arrows, sticks and clubs.

Van Lewen winced.

'Where are *you* going?' he yelled when he saw Race and Renée run past him.

'We're going after Nash! He stole the real idol!'

'He what—?'

But Race and Renée were already hurrying off into the trees. Van Lewen took off after them.

Gaby Lopez was running too. Only she was running for her life.

As soon as the Navy Super Stallions had appeared, she had hurried off behind the nearest set of trees. But she had gone the wrong way. Everyone else had gone south while she had gone north and now she was racing through the chest-high foliage to the north-east of the upper village—alone—ducking as she ran, trying desperately to avoid the bullets that smacked against the branches around her head.

The two remaining Navy SEALs were somewhere behind her, firing hard with their MP-5s as they crashed through the undergrowth.

Gaby looked behind herself as she ran, searching fearfully for her pursuers. Then, as she turned to look behind her one more time, she abruptly felt the ground beneath her feet just fall away.

She dropped like a stone.

A second later, she hit water.

Muddy liquid flew everywhere. When it settled, Gaby opened her eyes and found that she was sitting on her butt in the moat that encircled the upper village! She leapt quickly to her feet and found that she was standing in a section of ankle-deep water.

The thought suddenly occurred to her: *caimans*.

She looked about herself desperately. She saw that the moat was roughly circular in shape, saw that it bent away from her in both directions like a road disappearing around a curve. Its sheer muddy walls towered above her, their rims a good ten feet above her head.

Suddenly submachine-gun fire raked the water all around her and on an instinct Gaby dived forward and the bullets shot over her head, smacking into the earthen walls of the moat.

Then abruptly she heard more gunfire—different gunfire this time, G-11 gunfire—and in an instant the first set of bullets stopped firing and there was silence. Gaby was still lying on her chest in the shallow water of the moat. A long silence followed. After a few seconds, she cautiously raised her head.

And found herself staring into the smiling face of a caiman.

Gaby froze.

It was just sitting there in the mud in front of her, watching her, its tail slinking slowly back and forth behind it. It had her. Had her dead to rights.

Then with a loud grunting roar, the giant reptile charged, baring its jaws savagely, lunging at her—

591

Splat!—something landed right on top of the caiman from above. Gaby didn't know what it was. It had looked like an animal of some sort and now it and the caiman were rolling around together in front of her in a splashing heap of mud and water.

Her jaw dropped when she realised what the animal was.

It was a man. A man in combat uniform. He had jumped down from the rim of the moat, tackling the caiman at the exact moment that it had lunged at her.

The caiman and the man rolled as they wrestled, the reptile bucking and snapping, the man gasping for air whenever he could.

And then Gaby saw who it was.

It was Doogie.

Doogie and the caiman fought, rolling and wrestling, grunting and thrashing. The caiman snapped wildly at Doogie while the injured Green Beret grappled desperately with its snout, trying to keep it closed as he had seen alligator wrestlers do when he was a child.

He still had his G-11, but it was useless now, empty. He'd reluctantly used his last few rounds to drop the two Navy SEALs who had been firing on Gaby. Then when he had seen the caiman appear in front of her and lunge, he had done the only thing he could think to do—he had leapt down on top of it.

Just then the caiman jerked its snout free from Doogie's grasp, bared its jaws and launched itself at his head. Out of sheer desperation, Doogie swung his G-11 around and without even thinking, *wedged it inside the big crocodilian's mouth*, propping it open, right in front of his own face!

The caiman grunted in surprise.

Its jaws were now propped wide open, like the bonnet of a car. The big creature couldn't close its mouth!

Doogie seized the opportunity and quickly unsheathed his Bowie knife.

The caiman stood stupidly in front of him, its long snout held open by the vertical G-11.

Doogie tried to get around the big reptile—behind it—so that he could drive his knife into its skull and kill it, but the caiman saw him move and it swung quickly sideways, bowling into him, knocking him off his feet, sending him splashing into the muddy water.

The caiman then stomped quickly forward, stepping *on top of* Doogie's legs with its stubby forelimbs, causing them to sink down into the mud.

'*Arggghhh!*' Doogie yelled as the weight of the caiman came down on his shins. The big reptile took another slow step forward, stepping onto his wounded left thigh. Doogie roared with pain as his legs sank further into the mud.

The caiman's propped-open mouth yawned before his face, two feet in front of his nose, held open by his G-11.

Fuck it, Doogie thought as, with a quick lunge, he reached deep inside the caiman's enormous jaws and wedged his Bowie knife *in behind* the G-11, positioning it vertically so that the knife's butt sat on the caiman's tongue while its blade rested up against the roof of the big beast's mouth.

'Eat this,' Doogie said as he swung his arm sideways, swiping the G-11 out of the giant reptile's mouth.

The response was instantaneous.

With the G-11 gone, the caiman's mighty jaws came rushing back together, the upper jaw chomping downwards, right on top of the Bowie knife in the back of its mouth, forcing it up into its brain.

The blood-stained blade of the knife burst up out of the reptile's massive head and the caiman's body went instantly limp, the life rushing out of it.

Doogie stared at it for a moment, stunned at what he had just done. The massive animal was still standing half on top of him, groaning involuntarily, expelling large amounts of air that it no longer needed.

'Whoa . . .' Doogie breathed.

Then he shook his head and pulled himself out from under the enormous creature and clambered over to where Gaby was still lying in the mud, completely dumbstruck at his act of chivalry.

'Come on,' he said, taking her hand. 'Let's get out of here.'

Frank Nash raced through the dense foliage between the upper village and the crater, holding the idol under his arm like a football.

Lauren and Copeland ran behind him, SIG-Sauer pistols in their hands.

Amid all the confusion of the aerial attack on the upper village, he and Lauren and Copeland had quickly laid one of the log-bridges over the moat and bolted across it into the dense underbrush.

'This is Nash! This is Nash!' he yelled into his throat microphone as he ran. 'Aerial team, come in!'

He looked up at the sky behind him, saw the surviving Army Comanche helicopter hovering over the smoking remains of the village. Behind it, he saw another chopper—a third helicopter that was fatter and stockier than the Comanche. It was a Black Hawk II, the third Army chopper.

'*Colonel Nash—is Captain Hank Thompson—read you,*' a static-ridden voice said over his earpiece. '*Sorry—took so long—lost your signal in—overnight electrical storm—*'

'Thompson, we have the prize. I repeat, we have the prize. I am currently about fifty metres due east of the village, heading eastward toward the crater. I need immediate extraction.'

'Negative on that, Colonel—nowhere to land up here—too many—trees.'

'Then meet us down in the other village,' Nash yelled. 'the one with the citadel. Just head due east, straight over the crater, and look down. You can't miss it. It's got plenty of room to land.'

'Ten-four, Colonel—see you there.'

The two surviving Army choppers immediately banked in the air above the upper village and thundered over Nash's head, heading toward Vilcafor.

Not a minute later, Nash, Lauren and Copeland came to the crater and took off down its spiralling pathway.

Race, Renée and Van Lewen dashed through the dense section of foliage between the upper village and the crater, chasing after Nash and the idol.

The rapas were nowhere to be seen.

They must have retired to the depths of the crater with the onset of dawn, Race thought. He hoped to hell that the monkey urine on his body still worked.

The three of them hit the crater's path running.

As Race, Renée and Van Lewen were starting down the path, Nash, Lauren and Copeland were arriving at its base.

They came to the fissure, ran down its length, their feet kicking up water with every step. They never noticed the dark feline heads pop up lazily from the shallow lake as they ran by.

The three of them burst out onto the riverside path to be met by a thin morning mist, but they didn't stop to admire it. They just kept moving forward, heading toward Vilcafor and the thumping sound of the choppers.

Another couple of minutes and they reached the moat on the western side of the village.

And they stopped.

Stopped dead in their tracks.

Before them—standing in the middle of Vilcafor, with their hands clasped behind their heads and the soft mist curling around their feet—stood a group of about a dozen men and women. They all stood motionless, oblivious to the *whump-whump-whump* of helicopter rotors that filled the morning air.

A couple of them were Navy SEALs. They were dressed in full combat attire. But they weren't holding any guns. Others wore blue Navy uniforms. Others still wore ordinary civilian clothing—the DARPA scientists.

And then Nash saw their helicopter. It was standing behind the small crowd of people.

A lone Super Stallion.

The third Navy chopper.

It sat in the centre of the village, silent, motionless, its seven rotor blades still. Nash saw the word 'NAVY' plastered across its side in bold white lettering.

And then he looked upwards, searching for the source of the loud whumping sound that filled the air above the village.

And he saw them.

Saw the two Army helicopters—the Comanche and the Black Hawk II—that he had sent down from the upper village. They were hovering over Vilcafor, with their twin-barrelled Gatling guns and their fearsome-looking missile pods aimed squarely at the hapless Navy–DARPA team on the ground.

Race and the others emerged from the riverside path a couple of minutes later.

By the time they arrived at the main street of Vilcafor, the two Army choppers had landed and Nash was strutting around like a peacock in front of the Navy men, holding the gleaming idol in one hand and a silver SIG-Sauer pistol in the other.

The crews of the Army choppers—six men in all, two from the Comanche, four from the Black Hawk—held M-16s levelled at the Navy–DARPA crowd.

'Ah, Professor Race, nice of you to join us,' Nash said as Race and the others stepped out onto the main street of the village, staring at the odd mix of Navy men and civilians standing with their hands clasped behind their heads.

Race didn't answer Nash. His eyes just swept over the dozen or so Navy people, searching for someone.

He figured if they were Romano's team, the *real* Supernova team, then maybe . . .

He froze.

He saw him.

Saw a man, a civilian, standing among the group of Navy men, dressed in ordinary hiking clothes and boots. Despite the fact that he hadn't seen him in almost ten years, Race recognised the dark eyebrows and the stooped shoulders instantly.

He was looking at his brother.

'*Marty . . .*' Race breathed.

'Professor Race—' Nash said.

Race ignored him as he strode over to his brother. They stood before each other—no embrace—two brothers but two vastly different men.

For one thing Race was a mess. While he was covered in mud and stank of monkey urine, Marty was perfectly groomed, his clothes pristine clean. He stared wide-eyed at Race—at his filthy clothes, at his battered, mud-stained cap—as if he was the creature from the Black Lagoon.

Marty was shorter than Race, stockier. And while Race always wore a very open, easy expression, Marty's face was perpetually set in a deathly serious frown.

'Will . . .' Marty said.

'Marty, I'm sorry. I didn't know. They tricked me into coming along. They said that they were with DARPA and that they knew you and that—'

And then, abruptly, Race cut himself off as he saw another member of the Navy team whom he recognised.

He frowned.

It was Ed Devereux.

Devereux was a short, bespectacled black man, and at forty-one was one of the most highly-regarded ancient languages professors at Harvard. Some said he was the best Latin scholar in the world. At the moment, he stood silently in the line of Navy and DARPA people, holding a large leather-bound book under his arm. Race guessed it was the Navy's copy of the manuscript.

It was then that Race remembered meeting Frank Nash in his own office two days ago, at the very beginning of all this—remembered recommending to Nash that he take Devereux on the mission instead of himself since the Harvard professor was much better at medieval Latin than he was.

But now . . . now Race knew why Nash had insisted on taking *him* and not Devereux.

It was because Devereux had already been taken. By the real DARPA team.

'You'll never get out of this alive, Nash,' one of the older Navy–DARPA men said. He had a completely bald head and the bearing of a man in charge—Doctor Julius Romano.

'Why do you say that?' Nash said.

'The Armed Services Committee will hear about this,' Romano said. 'The Supernova is a Navy project. You have no business being here.'

'The Supernova ceased to be a Navy project the moment it was stolen from DARPA headquarters two days ago,' Nash said. 'Which means that now the *Army* is the only armed force in the United States with a Supernova in its possession.'

Romano said, 'You son of a—'

It was at that moment that Romano's head exploded—bursting like a tomato—sending a fountain of blood spraying out in every direction. A split second later, his body dropped to the ground—limp, lifeless, dead.

Race whirled around at the sound of the gunshot, just in time to see Nash standing there with his SIG-Sauer pistol extended in the firing position. Nash took a step along the line of Navy and DARPA people and levelled his pistol at the next man's head.

Blam!

The gun went off and the man fell.

'What are you *doing!*' Race yelled.

'Colonel!' Van Lewen shouted, incredulous, making to raise his G-11.

But no sooner had he moved than another silver SIG-Sauer appeared next to *his* head. At the other end of the pistol stood Troy Copeland.

'Drop the gun, Sergeant,' Copeland said.

Van Lewen clenched his teeth, dropped the G-11 and glared at Copeland.

Lauren had Renée similarly covered.

Completely confused, Race spun to look at Marty, but his brother just stood at the end of the line of Navy and DARPA people, staring stoically forward, his only movement a blink with every gunshot.

'Colonel, this is outright murder,' Van Lewen said.

Nash stepped up in front of another Navy man, levelled his pistol.

Blam!

'No,' he said. 'It is merely a process of natural selection. Survival of the fittest.'

Nash came to Ed Devereux.

The small Harvard professor stood before him, trembling. His eyes were wide behind his wire-framed glasses, his whole body shaking with fear. Nash levelled his SIG at the little man's head.

Devereux screamed, '*No—!*'

Blam!

The scream cut off abruptly and Devereux crumpled to the ground.

Race couldn't believe this was happening. American killing American. It was a nightmare. He winced as he saw Devereux fall to the ground, dead.

It was then that he saw the leather-bound book that Devereux had been holding when he had been shot. It lay in the mud, face-up, open, revealing a set of crusty old pages filled with ornate medieval artwork and calligraphy.

It was the Santiago Manuscript.

Or rather, Race corrected himself, the partially-completed *copy* of the manuscript that had been made by another monk in 1599, thirty years after Alberto Santiago's death.

'Colonel, what the hell are you doing?' Race said.

'I am merely eliminating the competition, Professor Race.'

Nash slowly made his way down the line of men and women, calmly shooting each of them at point-blank range, one after the other. His eyes were hard, cold, devoid of any emotion as he clinically executed his enemies—his fellow Americans—one by one.

Some of the Navy–DARPA people started to pray as Nash levelled his pistol at their faces. Some of the civilians started to sob. Race, helpless to stop the slaughter, saw tears well in Renée's eyes as she watched the shocking series of executions.

Soon there was only one man left, the last man in the line.

Marty.

Race just watched as Nash stood in front of his brother. He felt completely helpless, powerless to assist Marty.

And then, strangely, Nash lowered his pistol. He turned to face Race, didn't take his eyes off him as he spoke: 'Lauren, would you get me my laptop from the ATV, please?'

Race frowned, confused.

What the hell—?

Lauren hurried off to the ATV, still parked in front of the citadel. She returned a minute later with Nash's laptop computer, the one he had been using during the early stages of the mission. She handed it to Nash who—strangely—passed it on to Race.

'Turn it on,' Nash said.

Race did so.

'Click on "U.S. ARMY INTERNAL NET",' Nash said.

Race did so.

A title screen appeared.

U.S. ARMY INTERNAL MESSAGE NETWORK

The screen then changed to reveal a list of secure-line e-mail messages.

'Now there should be a message there with your name on it. Do a search for the name "Race",' Nash instructed.

Race punched in his own name and hit the 'SEARCH' button. He wondered where Nash was going with this.

Suddenly, the computer beeped: '2 MESSAGES FOUND'.

The long list of e-mails shortened to two.

DATE	TIME	SUBJECT
3.1.99	1801	SUPERNOVA MISSION
4.1.99	1635	WILLIAM RACE ISSUE

'See the one with your name on it?' Nash said.

Race eyed the second message, double-clicked on it. A message screen appeared:

4 JAN 1999 16:35 US ARMY INTERNAL NET 617 5544 89516-07 NO.187

From: Special Projects Division Leader

To: Nash, Frank

Subject: WILLIAM RACE ISSUE

Do not leave Race in Cuzco. Repeat. Do not leave Race in Cuzco. Take him with you to the jungle. Once the idol has been obtained, liquidate him and dispose of the body accordingly.

GENERAL ARTHUR H. LANCASTER

U.S. Army Special Projects Division Leader

'I just wanted you to know that you should have been dead a long time ago, Professor Race,' Nash said.

Race felt his blood run cold as he stared at the e-mail.

This was a death warrant—*his* death warrant. A missive from the general in charge of the Army Special Projects Division ordering that he be killed.

Jesus Christ.

He tried to remain calm.

He looked at the time of the message.

16:35, January 4.

Late in the afternoon on the day he'd left New York.

Hence this message must have arrived while he had been flying to Peru on board the cargo plane.

The flight to Peru.

Jesus, it seemed like years ago now.

And then suddenly Race recalled when, at one point during the flight, the little sing-song bell on Nash's laptop computer had tinkled. He remembered it clearly—it had been just after he'd finished translating Nash's partial copy of the manuscript.

And then it dawned on him.

This was why Nash had brought him to Vilcafor—despite the fact that at the very start of the mission Nash had said that if he finished translating the manuscript before they landed Race wouldn't even have to get off the plane. But Nash had brought him along anyway. And why?

Because Nash couldn't have *any* witnesses.

Since his was a secret mission—an Army mission trying to undercut a Navy mission—Nash couldn't risk leaving any witnesses alive.

'I was going to kill you two days ago,' Nash said, 'after we opened the temple. But then that German BKA team arrived and interrupted my plans. They opened the temple and, well, who could have guessed what they'd find inside it. But then, *then* we got those extra sections of the manuscript, and I was glad I hadn't killed you.'

'I'm so pleased you were happy,' Race said flatly.

Just then, out of curiosity more than anything else, while he had the computer in front of him, Race double-clicked on the other message that mentioned his name, the one titled 'SUPERNOVA MISSION'.

The full message appeared on the screen.

Oddly, however, it was a message that Race had seen before, right at the start of the mission, back when he had been travelling through New York in the motorcade.

3 JAN 1999 22:01 US ARMY INTERNAL NET 617 5544 88211-05 NO.139

From:	Nash, Frank
To:	All Cuzco Team Members
Subject:	SUPERNOVA MISSION

Contact to be made with Race ASAP.

Participation crucial to success of mission.

Expect package to arrive tomorrow 4 January at Newark at 0945. All members to have equipment stowed on the transport by 0900.

Race frowned at the words.

Contact Race ASAP.

Participation crucial to success of mission.

When he had first seen the message, Race hadn't really paid much attention to it. He had just assumed it was a reference to himself—William Race—and that it was *he* who should be contacted immediately.

But what if it actually meant *someone else* the Army had to get in touch with. Some other Race.

In which case it meant that contact should be made with . . .

Marty.

Race looked up from the computer in horror, just as his brother stepped out of the line of dead Navy and DARPA people and shook hands with Frank Nash.

'How are you, Marty?' Nash said familiarly.

'I'm well, Frank. It's good to finally catch up with you.'

Race's mind was in a spin.

His eyes flashed from Nash and Marty to the dead bodies on the muddy street, and from them to—

—the copy of the manuscript lying in the mud next to Ed Devereux's body.

And then suddenly it all made sense.

Race saw the ornate calligraphy on the text, the stunning medieval artwork. It was identical to the Xeroxed copy of the Santiago Manuscript that he had translated for Nash on the way to Peru.

Oh, no . . .

'Marty, you didn't . . .'

'I'm sorry you had to get caught up in all this, Will,' Marty said.

'We had to get a copy of the manuscript somehow,' Nash said. 'God, when those Nazis raided that monastery in France and stole the real manuscript, they set off a chase like you wouldn't believe. Suddenly, everybody in the world who had a Supernova had the chance to get a live sample of thyrium. It was the opportunity of a lifetime. Then, when we intercepted a DARPA transmission saying that there was a *second* copy of the manuscript in existence, we simply arranged for someone at DARPA to get a Xerox of it for us—Marty.'

But how? Race thought. *Marty was with DARPA, he wasn't with the Army. Where was the link? How was Marty associated with Nash and Army Special Projects?*

At that moment, he saw Lauren go over to Marty and kiss him lightly on the cheek.

What the . . . ?

It was then that Race saw the ring on Marty's left hand.

A wedding ring.

He looked at Lauren and Marty again.

No . . .

Then he heard Lauren's voice in his head: '*My first marriage didn't exactly work out. But I've recently remarried.*'

'I see you've met my wife, Will,' Marty said, stepping forward holding Lauren by the hand. 'I never told you I got married, did I?'

'Marty—'

'Do you remember when we were teenagers, Will? You were always the popular one and I was always the loner. The geek with the thick eyebrows and the hunched shoulders who stayed at home on Saturday nights while you went out with all the girls. But there was one girl you *didn't* get, wasn't there, Will?'

Race was silent.

'And it looks like I got her,' Marty said.

Race was stunned. Was it possible that Marty had been so bitter about his childhood that he had pursued Lauren just to get even with Race?

No. Not possible.

Such a theory failed to give *Lauren* any credit. She wouldn't have married anybody she didn't want to marry—which really meant she wouldn't have married anyone who didn't advance her own career.

It was then that another image leapt into Race's mind.

The image of Lauren and Troy Copeland standing in the Huey two nights ago, kissing like a pair of teenagers before Race had stumbled onto them.

Lauren had been having an affair with Copeland.

'Marty,' he said quickly. 'Listen, she's going to betray you—'

'Shut up, Will.'

'But Marty—'

'I said, *shut up!*'

Race fell silent. After a moment, he said in a low voice, 'What did the Army give you to sell out DARPA, Marty?'

'They didn't have to give me much,' Marty said. 'My wife simply asked me to do her a favour. And her boss, Colonel Nash here, offered me an executive posting in the Army's Supernova project. Will, I'm a design engineer. I design the computer systems that control these devices. But at DARPA that makes me nothing. All my life, Will—*all my life*—all I've ever wanted was recognition. At home, at school, at work. Recognition of my ability. Now, finally, I'm going to get some.'

'Marty, please, listen to me. Two nights ago, I saw Lauren with—'

'Drop it, Will. Show's over. I'm really sorry it had to happen like this, but it has and I can't help that. Goodbye.'

And with that Frank Nash stepped in front of Race—cutting off his view of Marty—replacing it with a view down the barrel of Nash's SIG-Sauer.

'It's been a pleasure, Professor, really it has,' Nash said, squeezing the trigger.

'*No,*' Van Lewen said suddenly, stepping forward— in between Race and Nash's pistol. 'Colonel, I cannot allow you to do this.'

'Get out of the way, Sergeant.'

'No, sir, I will not.'

'Get out of the fucking way!'

Van Lewen straightened as he stood before the barrel of Nash's pistol. 'Sir, my orders are clear. They came from you, yourself. I am to protect Professor Race at any cost.'

'Your orders just changed, Sergeant.'

'No, sir. They did not. If you want to kill Professor Race, then you're going to have to kill me first.'

Nash pursed his lips for a moment.

Then—with shocking suddenness—the SIG in his hand discharged and Van Lewen's head exploded, showering Race all over with blood.

The Green Beret's body fell to the ground in a heap, like a marionette that had just had its strings cut. Race stared down at Van Lewen's fallen frame.

The tall, kind sergeant had sacrificed his own life for his—had stared down the barrel of a gun for him. And now, now he was dead. Race felt like he was going to be sick.

'You son of a bitch,' he said to Nash.

Nash re-aimed his gun at Race's face. 'This mission is bigger than any one man, Professor. Bigger than him, bigger than me, and definitely bigger than you.'

And with that, Nash pulled the trigger.

Race saw the flash of brown shoot across in front of his face before he even heard the whistling sound.

Then, just as Nash pulled the trigger on his pistol, a miniature explosion of blood flared out from the Army colonel's forearm as it was penetrated by a primitive wooden arrow.

Nash's gun-hand was knocked sideways and the SIG discharged wildly to Race's left. Nash roared with pain and dropped the pistol just as a volley of about twenty more arrows rained down all around them, killing two of the Army crewmen instantly.

The wave of arrows was quickly followed by a blood-curdling battle-cry that ripped through the early-morning air like a knife.

Race spun at the sound and his jaw dropped at the sight that met him.

He saw all of the natives from the upper village—all the adults, *fifty* of them at least—*charging* out from the trees to the west of Vilcafor. They were shrieking wildly as they rushed forward, brandishing whatever weapons they could muster—bows, arrows, axes, clubs—and they wore on their faces some of the angriest expressions Race had ever seen in his life.

The charge of the natives was nothing short of terrifying.

Their fury was intense, their anger almost tangible. Frank Nash had stolen their idol and now they wanted it back.

Abruptly the crack of M-16 gunfire rang out from somewhere close behind Race.

A couple of the helicopter crewmen had opened fire on the Indians. Almost instantly, four of the natives at the front of the rushing horde were hit. They stumbled and fell, crashing face-first in the mud.

But the others just kept on coming.

Nash—now with an arrow lodged in his right forearm, complete with a ragged piece of his own flesh dangling from its point—turned instantly and, with his people behind him, abandoned the village and made for the two Army choppers.

Race hadn't even moved. He just stood there in the centre of the street, rooted to the spot, staring dumbstruck at the horde of charging natives.

Then suddenly someone grabbed him roughly by the shoulder.

It was Renée.

'Professor, come on!' she yelled as she dragged him toward the empty Super Stallion on the other side of the village.

The Army people reached their choppers.

Nash, Lauren, Marty and Copeland leapt up into the rear compartment of the Black Hawk II at the same time as the chopper's two crewmen threw themselves into the pilot's and gunner's seats.

The Black Hawk II's rotors began to turn instantly.

Nash looked out from the rear compartment, saw Race and Renée running for the Super Stallion.

He yelled to the crewman manning the chopper's rear-mounted Vulcan minigun. 'Take out that chopper!'

As the Black Hawk II's rotors whipped into overdrive and the big helicopter slowly began to lift off, the co-pilot jammed down on his trigger and a blazing barrage of gunfire blasted out from the Vulcan.

The hail of gunfire that assailed the Super Stallion was shocking in its intensity. It pummelled the reinforced walls of the helicopter with thousands of bullet holes, each the size of a man's fist.

And then—just as Race and Renée were coming toward it—the Super Stallion exploded into a billowing ball of flames.

The two of them dived to the ground a split second before a storm of burning-hot metal whizzed over their heads, shooting out in every direction. Two stray shards of red-hot metal, however, slammed into Renée's shoulder, sizzling on contact. She roared with pain.

'Now take *them* out!' Nash yelled, pointing down at Race and the injured Renée.

The Black Hawk II was about fifteen feet off the ground now, rising quickly into the sky. The gunner immediately whirled the massive Vulcan around and drew a bead on Race's skull.

Blam!

The crewman's head snapped violently backwards, shot right between the eyes.

Nash spun around in surprise, searching the ground below for the source of the shot that had killed his gunner.

And he saw him.

It was Doogie.

Crouched on one knee over by the moat with a stolen

Navy MP-5 pressed against his shoulder, aimed directly up at the Black Hawk II! Behind him stood Gaby Lopez.

Just then Doogie loosed another shot and it pinged off the steel roof above Nash's head.

Nash yelled at his pilot, 'Get us the fuck out of here!'

With his arm looped underneath Renée's good shoulder, Race scrambled for the ATV.

The crowd of natives was now standing underneath the two Army helicopters, shouting angrily at them, waving their sticks, firing their arrows in vain at the armoured underbellies of the flying steel beasts.

Race leapt up onto the back of the ATV, yanked open the small circular hatch set inside it and helped Renée in through it.

Just as he was about to follow her, however, he saw Doogie and Gaby hurrying across the main street toward him, waving their arms wildly. Gaby was helping Doogie as he limped along as fast as he could.

They arrived at the ATV, clambered up onto it.

'What the fuck is going on here?' Doogie said in between breaths. Race saw his bloodied left leg. It had a makeshift tourniquet tied around it. 'We got here just in time to see *the colonel* shoot Leo in the fucking head!' Doogie's face was contorted with a mixture of rage and helpless confusion.

'The colonel had other priorities,' Race said bitterly. 'Priorities that didn't include us.'

'What are we going to do?' Doogie said.

Race bit his lip in thought.

'Come on,' he said. 'Get inside. We're not out of this yet.'

The two Army helicopters—the Comanche and the Black Hawk II—rose into the sky above the main street of Vilcafor.

Nash looked out the side door of his chopper at the crowd of angry natives beneath him, yelling and screaming and waving their fists at the helicopters. He snorted a laugh as he turned away from them and looked out through the forward windshield of the chopper.

The two Army helicopters cleared the treetops.

And Nash's smile went flat.

There were eight of them—Black Hawk I helicopters—similar to his own but older; superseded models that the Army had discarded years ago. They were all painted black, with no markings on them whatsoever, and they hovered menacingly in a wide, 500-yard circle around Vilcafor like a pack of hungry jackals waiting on the periphery of the battle, waiting to pick up the scraps.

There came a sudden puff of smoke from one of the unmarked Black Hawks as, without warning, a missile shot out from one of its stub-like wings.

A long finger-like trail of smoke extended through the air in front of the helicopter as the speeding missile cut a bee-line for the Army Comanche. The Comanche exploded in an instant and dropped clumsily out of the sky. It smashed down onto one of the stone huts on the main street of Vilcafor, flames spilling out from its charred, twisted shell.

Race and the others were inside the citadel and about to climb down into the quenko when they heard the sudden explosion outside.

They hurried back into the ATV and peered out through its narrow slit-like windows to see what had happened.

They saw the blazing wreck of the Comanche lying awkwardly on its side on top of one of the small huts of Vilcafor.

They also saw Nash's Black Hawk II hovering above the village, not daring to move.

The rotors of the Army Black Hawk thumped rhythmically as the big helicopter hovered over Vilcafor, in the centre of the circle of ominous black helicopters.

Suddenly, two of the unmarked choppers banked out of their formation and flew in toward the village.

Black-clad soldiers sitting in their doorways opened fire on the natives on the ground and the Indians scattered immediately, hurrying over the log-bridges, darting into the dense foliage around the town.

A voice came over a loudspeaker from one of the choppers. A man's voice, speaking in English.

'Army Black Hawk. Be advised, missile lock has been established on your aircraft. You are to land immediately. I repeat, you are to land immediately and prepare to hand over the idol. If you do not land immediately, we will blast you out of the sky and pick it out of the wreckage later.'

Nash and Marty exchanged a look.

Lauren and Copeland did the same.

'They're not lying about the missile lock, sir,' the pilot said, turning to Nash.

'Take us down,' Nash said.

Flanked by the two unmarked Black Hawks, Nash's Black Hawk II slowly descended back to earth.

The three choppers hit the ground together. The moment the Army chopper's wheels touched the mud the voice on the loudspeaker came again.

'Now exit the helicopter with your hands up.'

Nash, Lauren, Copeland and Marty did so, accompanied by the chopper's pilot.

From the safety of the ATV, Race and the others stared out at the scene before them in awe.

Race couldn't believe what was happening. It was like one of those fables where a big fish eats a smaller fish, only to be eaten itself by an even bigger fish moments later.

Frank Nash, it seemed, had just come across a bigger fish.

'Who the hell are these guys?' Doogie asked.

'I would guess,' Renée said, a strip of gauze pressed firmly against her bloody shoulder, 'that they are the people who were responsible for the break-in at DARPA headquarters two days ago. The break-in that involved the theft of the Navy's Supernova.'

Half a world away, Special Agent John-Paul Demonaco and Commander Tom Mitchell were sitting inside Bluey James' filthy Baltimore apartment, waiting for the phone to ring. They were waiting for the call that would instruct Bluey to send out the V-CD of Bittiker's message to all the TV networks. Naturally, Bluey's phone had been hooked up to a bank of FBI tracing equipment.

There was a knock at the door.

Mitchell opened it to reveal two agents from Demonaco's Domestic Terrorist Unit—a man and a woman, both young, clean-cut thirtysomethings.

'What have you got?' Demonaco said.

'We checked out Henry Norton,' the female agent said. 'The guy whose cardkeys and codes were used in the break-in. Our own investigations have confirmed that he had no known paramilitary contacts.'

'So who did he work with, then? Who could have seen him enter his codes and then pass them on to somebody?'

'Apparently he worked closely with a guy named Martin Race—Martin Eric Race. He was one of the DARPA people working on the project, the ignition system design engineer.'

'But we checked him out too,' the male agent said. 'And he's clean. No militia links, not even a history of contact with any extremist groups. He's even married to a high-ranking Army scientist named Lauren O'Connor. She's technically a major, but she's had no combat experience. The rank is purely honorary. Race and O'Connor were married late in 1997. No kids. No apparent discord. *But . . .*'

'But what?'

'But exactly three weeks ago, *her* FBI file was flagged when she was spotted leaving a motel in Gainesville with this man'—the agent handed Demonaco an 8 x 10 black-and-white photo of a man leaving a motel room—'Troy Copeland. Also a major with the Army's Special Projects Unit. Seems Ms O'Connor has been having an affair with Mr Copeland for the last month.'

'So . . . ?' Demonaco said expectantly.

'So. *Copeland* has been under periodic surveillance for the past *year*, under suspicion of passing Army security codes to certain militia groups, one of which is—wait for it—the Republican Army of Texas.'

'But since the affair is only a month old,' the female agent said, 'DARPA probably hasn't picked up on it with any follow-up checks.'

Demonaco sighed. 'And the Army and the Navy aren't exactly the best of bedfellows. They've been pulling the rug out from under each other for years.' He turned. 'Commander Mitchell?'

'Yes.'

'Does the *Army* have a Supernova?'

'They're not supposed to.'

'Answer the question.'

'We think are working on one, yes.'

'Is it possible, then,' Demonaco said, 'that this

O'Connor woman was getting her husband to pass secret DARPA codes to her and the Army, and then *she* was passing them on to her lover Copeland, not knowing that he was giving them to the Texans?'

'That's what we figure,' the male agent said.

'Damn it!'

With the Spirit of the People in his hands, Frank Nash stepped out of his grounded Black Hawk II. Lauren, Marty, Copeland and the pilot did the same.

The two unmarked Black Hawks that had landed on either side of the Army chopper kept their rotor blades turning swiftly.

'*Step away from the helicopter!*' the voice on the loudspeaker demanded.

Nash and the others did so.

An instant later another finger-like trail of smoke raced down from the sky at incredible speed—from one of the other Black Hawks hovering above the village. The missile slammed into the Army Black Hawk II, blasting it to smithereens.

Nash winced.

A long silence followed, the only sound the rhythmic *whump-whump-whump* of the rotors that still turned atop the two unmarked helicopters.

After nearly a full minute had passed, a lone man got out of the nearer of the two unmarked choppers.

He was dressed in full combat attire—boots, fatigues, combat webbing—and he carried in his left hand an odd-looking semi-automatic pistol.

It was a big gun, black in colour, and easily bigger

than the famous IMI 'Desert Eagle', the largest production-made semi-automatic pistol in the world. This gun, on the other hand, had a sturdy grip and an unusually long slide which ran for the entire length of its barrel.

Nash recognised it instantly.

It wasn't a *semi*-automatic pistol at all. It was a rare—and very expensive—Calico pistol, the only truly *automatic* pistol in the world. You depressed the trigger and a stream of bullets blazed out from the barrel. Like an M-16, the Calico could be set to fire either short three-round bursts or full auto. But whatever mode you chose, the result was still the same. If you shot someone with a Calico, you opened them up big-time.

The man with the Calico stepped up to Nash while the men in the unmarked chopper behind him kept their M-16s trained on the others.

The man held out his hand.

'The idol, please,' he said.

Nash appraised him for a moment. He was middle-aged but thin, gaunt, with muscly, wiry arms. He had a hollow, sanguine face that was pitted all over with scars, and a messy shock of thinning blond hair that came down to his eyes—blue eyes that brimmed over with hate.

Nash didn't hand over the idol.

It was then that the man with the Calico calmly raised his pistol and blew the Army pilot's skull open with a short three-round burst.

'The idol, please,' the man repeated.

Reluctantly, Nash gave it to him.

'Thank you, Colonel,' the man said.

'Who are you?' Nash demanded.

The man cocked his head slightly to one side. Then, slowly, the edge of his mouth curled into a sly smile.

'The name's Earl Bittiker,' he said.

'And who the fuck is Earl Bittiker?' Nash snorted.

The man smiled again, that same supercilious smile.

'I'm the man who's gonna destroy the world.'

Race, Renée, Gaby and Doogie were all peering out through the windows of the ATV, watching the drama outside unfold.

'How did they know how to get here?' Renée said. 'Surely there can't be *another* copy of the manuscript out there.'

'No, there isn't,' Race said. 'But I think I know how they got here.'

He began to look around the ATV, searching for something. A few seconds later, he found it. The BKA team's laptop. He turned it on. After a few seconds, he brought up a familiar screen, written in German.

COMMUNICATIONS SATELLITE TRANSMISSION LOG 44-76/BKA32

NO.	DATE	TIME	SOURCE	SUMMARY.
1	4.1.99	1930	BKAHQ	PERU TEAM REPORT STATUS
2	4.1.99	1950	EXT SOURCE	SIGNATURE UHF SIGNAL
3	4.1.99	2230	BKAHQ	PERU TEAM REPORT STATUS
4	5.1.99	0130	BKAHQ	PERU TEAM REPORT STATUS
5	5.1.99	0430	BKAHQ	PERU TEAM REPORT STATUS
6	5.1.99	0716	FIELD (CHILE)	ARRIVED SANTIAGO, HEADING FOR COLONIA ALEMANIA
7	5.1.99	0730	BKAHQ	PERU TEAM REPORT STATUS

8	5.1.99	0958	FIELD (CHILE)	HAVE ARRIVED COLONIA ALEMANIA; BEGINNING SURVEILLANCE
9	5.1.99	1030	BKAHQ	PERU TEAM REPORT STATUS
10	5.1.99	1037	FIELD (CHILE)	CHILE TEAM URGENT SIGNAL; CHILE TEAM URGENT SIGNAL
11	5.1.99	1051	BKAHQ	PERU TEAM REPORT IMMEDIATELY

It was the screen they had seen yesterday, before the Nazis had arrived, the one showing every communication signal that had been received by the BKA's Peruvian team.

Race saw the line he was looking for immediately. The second line:

| 2 | 4.1.99 | 1950 | EXT SOURCE | SIGNATURE UHF SIGNAL |

'Doogie,' he said, 'you said something about a UHF signal yesterday. What exactly is it?'

'It's a standard homing signal. I sent one to our air support team yesterday, so they'd know where to pick us up.'

Renée pointed at the screen. 'But this UHF signal was sent out *two days* ago—at 7:50 pm on January 4. That was well before my team arrived here.'

'That's right,' Race said. 'And that time has significance.'

'How?' Doogie asked.

'Because at exactly 7:45 pm on the first night, Lauren did her nucleotide resonance scan of the area and determined that there was thyrium in the immediate vicinity of this village. This UHF signal was sent out exactly five minutes *after* that successful scan. And what were we doing at that time?'

'We were unloading the choppers,' Doogie said, shrugging. 'Getting our gear ready.'

'Precisely,' Race said. 'The perfect opportunity for someone to send up a UHF signal while nobody was looking, a signal that would tell his friends that the presence of thyrium had been confirmed.'

'But who did it?' Gaby asked.

Race nodded out the window. 'I think we're about to find out.'

Earl Bittiker pulled another Calico pistol from his spare holster and tossed it to Troy Copeland.

'Heya, Troy,' he said.

'Nice of you to join us,' Copeland replied, cocking the massive pistol.

Lauren's face went ashen white. 'Troy?' she said in disbelief.

Copeland smiled at her. It was a cruel, nasty smile. 'You should be careful about who you fuck, Lauren, 'cause they might just be fucking *you* over. Although I imagine it's not often that *you're* the one who gets fucked over.'

Lauren's face darkened.

Beside her, Marty blanched. 'Lauren?'

Copeland started to chuckle. 'Marty, Marty, Marty. Little fucking Marty who sold out DARPA so he could get himself some goddamn respect—you oughta be more careful about who you give your information to, my friend. But then, you didn't even know that your own wife was screwing another man.'

Race watched the scene outside, his entire body tense, still.

He could hear what Copeland was saying to Marty, humiliating him.

'She liked it, too,' Copeland said. 'In fact, I can't think of many things I liked better on this earth than hearing your wife scream as she orgasmed.'

Marty's face reddened, both in anger and humiliation.

'I'll kill you,' he growled.

'Not likely,' Copeland said, pulling the trigger on his Calico, sending a rapid-fire burst of bullets into Marty's abdomen.

Race almost jumped out of his skin when he heard the gun go off.

Marty's shirt was ripped open by the sudden three-round burst, his stomach raked into a ragged mass of red. Race saw him fall to the ground hard.

'Marty . . .' he breathed.

Out on the main street, Copeland turned his gun on Lauren, while Bittiker turned his on Frank Nash.

'What did you call it, Frank?' Copeland said to Nash. 'The law of unintended consequences—terrorist groups getting their hands on a Supernova. Face it, you only saw this weapon as a bluffing tool—a weapon that you possess, but which you will never have the courage to use. Maybe you should have thought about it another way: *don't build it if you don't intend to use it.*'

Copeland and Bittiker fired at the same time.

Nash and Lauren fell together, splashing into the mud. Lauren was killed instantly, shot clean through the heart. Nash, on the other hand, was hit in the stomach and he fell to the ground screaming with pain.

Then, with the idol in their possession, Bittiker and Copeland hurried back to one of the unmarked Black Hawks and leapt aboard.

No sooner were they on board than the two big

black choppers rose quickly into the sky. Once they had cleared the treetops, they both tilted sharply forward and powered off, heading south, away from Vilcafor.

As soon as the Texan choppers were gone, Race threw open the rear hatch of the ATV and charged out onto the main street. He slid to his knees beside the fallen figure of Marty.

When he arrived at his brother's side, Marty was feebly trying to put his intestines back in his stomach. Blood gurgled from his mouth, and as Race looked down into his brother's eyes, he saw only fear and shock.

'Oh, Will . . . Will,' Marty said, his lip quivering. He grabbed Race's arm with one blood-smeared hand.

'Marty, why? Why did you do this?'

'Will . . .' he said. 'Ignition . . .'

Race held him in his arms. 'What? What are you trying to say?'

'I'm . . . so sorry . . . ignition . . . system . . . please, stop . . . them.'

And then slowly Marty's eyes glazed over, settling into a frozen vacant stare. His bloodied body went limp in Race's arms.

It was then that Race heard the soft gurgling sound from somewhere behind him.

He turned and saw Frank Nash lying on his back a few yards away. Nash's mid-section was also torn to pieces. He was coughing up blood, gagging on it.

And then suddenly, beyond Nash, Race saw movement.

Saw the first curious native emerge slowly from the trees.

'Professor,' Doogie called softly from the ATV, 'I, ah, think it might be a good idea to step away from there.'

The other natives emerged from the forest. They still carried their primitive weapons—their clubs and sticks and axes—and they looked angry as hell.

Slowly, Race lowered Marty's body gently to the ground. Then he stood and slowly—very slowly— walked back to the ATV.

The natives hardly even noticed him.

They only had eyes for one person—Nash—lying in the middle of the street, gurgling blood.

And then with a savage, high-pitched shriek, the Indians rushed forward as one and converged on Nash like a swarming school of piranha. In a moment Race lost sight of the murderous Army colonel and soon all he could see was a roiling mass of olive-skinned natives crowding around Nash, hacking violently with their clubs and their sticks and their axes, and then suddenly, horrifically, above it all he heard a single ear-piercing scream—a scream of such pure terror that it could only have come from one man.

Frank Nash.

Race slammed the rear hatch of the ATV behind him and looked at the three faces before him.

'All right,' he said. 'Looks like we're gonna have to do this all over again. We have to stop these assholes before they get that idol to a Supernova.'

'But how?' Doogie asked.

'The first thing we have to do,' Race said, 'is find out where they're taking it.'

Race and the others flew through the narrow tunnels of the quenko, running as fast as their injured bodies would carry them.

They had practically no firepower—just a couple of SIG-Sauers and the single MP-5 that Doogie had found in the upper village. As far as armour was concerned, Doogie still wore his combat fatigues and Race still wore his unusual kevlar breastplate. That was it.

But they knew where they were going and that was all that mattered.

They were heading for the waterfall.

And the Goose that lay hidden on the riverbank there.

After about ten minutes of running, they came to the waterfall at the end of the quenko. Another four and they arrived at the Goose—parked exactly where Race, Doogie and Van Lewen had left it—underneath the overhanging branches of the riverside trees. Uli, Race was pleased to see, was still sleeping safely inside it.

Four more minutes and the little seaplane was back in the water, skipping across the waves, shooting across the wide brown surface of the river. It accelerated to take-off speed quickly before suddenly, gloriously, it lifted off the surface and soared into the sky.

Once it was airborne, Doogie banked the plane sharply around so that it was pointing directly south, in the direction that the Texan Black Hawks had gone.

After about ten minutes of flying, Doogie caught sight of them—eight black specks on the horizon. They were veering right, heading south-west over the mountains.

'They're going for Cuzco,' Doogie said.

'Stay on them,' Race said.

An hour later, the eight Black Hawk helicopters landed at a private airfield just outside Cuzco.

Sitting majestically on the dusty dirt runway waiting for them was a massive Antonov An-22 heavy-lift cargo plane.

With its powerful quadruple propeller system and a wide rear loading ramp, the An-22 had long been one of the Soviet Union's most dependable tank-lifters. It was also a valuable export commodity, having been sold regularly to countries who couldn't afford—or who weren't allowed to buy—American cargo-lifters.

With the end of the Cold War and the crumbling of the Russian economy, however, many An-22s had found their way onto the black market. While movie stars and professional golfers bought Lear Jets for $30 million, paramilitary organisations could buy a second-hand An-22 for little more than $12 million.

Earl Bittiker and Troy Copeland leapt out of their chopper and strode over to the rear loading ramp of the massive cargo plane.

When he arrived at the back of the plane, Bittiker looked up into its cavernous cargo bay and beheld his pride and joy.

An M-1A1 Abrams main battle tank.

It looked awesome. The picture of brutal, untameable strength. Its black-painted composite armour didn't shine, its monstrously wide tracks stood planted on the cargo deck, splayed wide.

Bittiker gazed at its imposing trapezoidal gun turret. It faced resolutely forward, toward the front of the plane, its long-bodied 105mm cannon pointing upward at a 30-degree angle.

Bittiker stared at the Abrams with cool satisfaction. It was the perfect place to keep the stolen Supernova. It was impregnable.

He handed the idol to one of the Freedom Fighter techs and the little man went scurrying back up into the plane, heading for the tank.

'Gentlemen,' Bittiker said into his radio, addressing the men in the other helicopters. 'Thank you very much for your loyal service. We'll take it from here. See you in the next life.'

Then he discarded his radio and pulled out his cell phone, and dialled Bluey James' number.

The phone rang in Bluey's apartment. The FBI's digital tracing equipment lit up like a Christmas tree.

Demonaco slipped on a pair of headphones, then nodded to Bluey.

Bluey picked up the telephone. 'Yo.'

'Bluey, it's Bittiker. We have the thyrium. Send the message out now.'

'You got it, Earl.'

Bittiker hung up his phone and, with Copeland in tow behind him, headed up the loading ramp and into the back of the Antonov.

It was 11:13 am.

'Jesus! They took off already!' Doogie exclaimed, pointing down at the old Antonov as it thundered along the dirt runway and lifted off into the sky.

'Look at the *size* of that thing,' Renée said.

'I think we just found out where they're keeping their Supernova,' Race said.

The Antonov soared into the sky, its outstretched wings glinting in the morning sun.

In the womb-like silence of the Abrams main battle tank that sat inside its cavernous cargo bay, two Freedom Fighter technicians were working carefully at a vacuum-sealed work chamber, slowly excising a small cylindrical section from the base of the thyrium idol with a laser cutter.

Behind the two technicians, taking up nearly all the room inside the big tank, sat the Supernova—the Supernova that until two days previously had resided in the vault room at DARPA headquarters.

After they had extracted the cylindrical section of thyrium, with the aid of two IBM supercomputers that lined the walls of the cargo bay outside, they subjected it to alpha-wave augmentation, inert gas purification and proton enrichment, transforming the section of thyrium into a subcritical mass.

'How long till it's ready?' a voice said suddenly from above them.

The two men looked up and saw Earl Bittiker staring down at them through the tank's circular upper hatch.

'Fifteen more minutes,' one of them replied.

Bittiker looked at his watch.

It was 11:28 am.

'Call me as soon as you're done,' he said.

'Doogie,' Race said as he stared up at the enormous cargo plane above them. 'How do you open up the loading ramps on those big cargo planes?'

Doogie frowned. 'Well, there are two ways. Either you press a button on a console inside the cargo bay, or you use the exterior console.'

'What's the exterior console?'

'It's just a pair of buttons, hidden inside a compartment on the outside of the plane. Usually, they're located on the left-hand side of the loading ramp and covered by a panel to protect them against the wind.'

'Do you need a code or anything to open the panel?'

'No, not at all,' Doogie said. 'I mean, it's not like anyone's going to open the loading ramp from the outside in mid-air, now is it?'

He turned to Race. And then suddenly his eyes opened wide. 'You can't be serious.'

'We have to get that idol before they put it in their Supernova,' Race said. 'It's as simple as that.'

'But how?'

'Just bring us up behind that plane. Stay right underneath it so they don't see you. Then bring us in nice and close.'

'What are you going to do?'

Race turned, looked back at the sorry group of people in the plane around him: Doogie—gunshot wounds to the leg and shoulder; Renée—wounded shoulder; Gaby—still slightly in shock from all their recent skirmishes; Uli—out for the count.

Race snuffed a laugh. 'What am I going to do? I'm going to save the world.'

And with that, he stood up and grabbed the only submachine-gun they had, the Navy MP-5.

'All right, now. Take us up.'

The two planes soared through the bright morning sky.

The Antonov was cruising at about 11,000 feet— three kilometres above the Earth—coasting along at an easy cruising speed of 200 knots as it rose steadily into the sky.

Although the Antonov didn't know it, rising through the air behind it, closing in quickly on its tail section, was a much smaller plane—the Goose.

The little seaplane's panels shuddered violently as it hit its maximum speed of 220 knots. Doogie gripped his steering vane as hard as he could, trying to keep her steady.

This was bad. The Goose's operational ceiling was 21,300 feet. If the Antonov kept rising, it would soon be physically out of the Goose's reach.

The little seaplane gradually closed in on the massive cargo-lifter, the two aircraft acting out a bizarre kind of aerial ballet—the sparrow chasing the albatross. Slowly—very slowly—the Goose moved up behind the Antonov and edged its nose right in behind the bigger plane's hindquarters.

Then suddenly, without any warning, the hatch on

the nose of the Goose popped open and the tiny figure of a man appeared out of it from the waist up.

The blast of wind that assaulted Race's face as he stuck his head out through the Goose's forward hatch was absolutely *colossal*.

It slammed into his body, pounded against him. If he hadn't been wearing his kevlar breastplate it almost certainly would have knocked the wind out of him.

He saw the Antonov's sloping hindquarters looming large in front of him, about fifteen feet away.

Christ, it was enormous . . .

It was like looking at the rear-end of the biggest bird in the world.

And then Race caught sight of the earth below him.

Ooooh . . . fuck!

The world was a long way down—a *long* way down. Immediately beneath him, he saw a rolling patchwork quilt of hills and fields and, away to the east—ahead of the two planes—the neverending sea of rainforest.

Don't think about the fall! a voice inside him screamed. *Keep your mind on the job!*

Right.

Okay. He had to do this quickly, before he ran out of air, and before the two planes rose to a height where the combination of thin air and wind-chill would freeze him to death.

He waved at Doogie through the Goose's windshield, instructing him to bring the little seaplane closer to the Antonov.

The Goose edged further forward.

Eight feet away.

Earl Bittiker and Troy Copeland sat in the cockpit of the Antonov, oblivious to what was going on in the air behind their plane.

Abruptly, the wall-mounted phone next to Bittiker buzzed.

'Yes,' Bittiker said.

'Sir,' it was the tech in charge of arming the Supernova. 'We've placed the thyrium in the device. It's ready.'

'All right, I'm coming down,' Bittiker said.

The Goose was three feet away from the Antonov—and 15,000 feet above the world and still rising.

Race was standing with his entire upper body protruding from the Goose's nose hatch. He saw the Antonov's loading ramp in front of him. The ramp was still firmly shut, its existence betrayed only by a set of thin grooved lines that ran in a square around the rear of the massive plane.

Then Race saw a small panel to the left of the ramp lying flush against the exterior wall of the plane.

He waved for Doogie to bring the Goose closer still.

Bittiker emerged from the upper deck of the Antonov and looked down upon the cargo bay from a thin metal catwalk. He saw the gargantuan tank beneath him, saw the barrel of its mighty cannon pointing directly up at him.

He looked at his watch.

It was 11:48. The V-CD would have gone out a good half-hour ago. The world would be in a panic. Judgement Day had arrived.

Bittiker slid down a rung-ladder and then stepped

up onto the turret of the tank, climbed down into it.

He arrived in the belly of the Abrams and saw the Supernova—saw the two thermonuclear warheads suspended in their hourglass formation, saw the cylindrical section of thyrium lying horizontally in the vacuum-sealed chamber in between them.

He nodded, satisfied.

'Start the detonation sequence,' he said.

'Yes, sir,' one of the techs said, leaping for the laptop computer on the front of the device.

'Set it for twelve minutes,' Bittiker said. 'Twelve noon.'

The tech typed quickly and within seconds a countdown screen appeared:

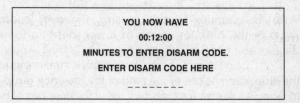

```
        YOU NOW HAVE
          00:12:00
MINUTES TO ENTER DISARM CODE.
  ENTER DISARM CODE HERE

      _ _ _ _ _ _ _ _
```

The tech hit 'ENTER' and the timer began to race downwards. As it did so, Bittiker pulled out his cellular phone and dialled Bluey James' number again.

The digital tracing equipment in Bluey's apartment lit up like a Christmas tree again.

Bluey picked up the phone. 'Yo.'

'Has the message gone out?'

'It's out there, Earl,' Bluey lied as he stared into the eyes of John-Paul Demonaco.

'Is there panic in the streets?'

'Like you wouldn't believe,' Bluey said.

The Goose edged closer to the Antonov's hindquarters, two feet separating the two speeding, rising planes.

In the face of the battering, pounding wind, Race held onto the Goose's hatch with one hand while he reached out with the other for the panel on the cargo plane, stretching out as far as he could.

It was still too far away. Doogie brought the Goose in closer still, as close as he dared . . .

. . . and Race grabbed the panel, flipped it open.

He saw two buttons inside it—one red, one green—and without so much as a second thought, he slammed his fist down on the green button.

With an ominous rumbling whir, the rear loading ramp of the Antonov began to lower, right on top of the Goose's nose!

With the reflexes of a cat, Doogie quickly manoeuvred the little seaplane out of the path of the lowering ramp—in doing so, almost flinging Race *out* of the nose hatch! But Race's grip and balance held firm and he remained standing half-in-half-out of the Goose's hatch while Doogie deftly swung the little seaplane in behind the Antonov as the giant cargo plane's ramp yawned open before them.

The two planes continued to fly in tandem through the Peruvian sky—the massive Antonov and the tiny Goose flying barely two feet apart, hitting 18,000 feet—only now the Antonov's rear loading ramp was *open*, right in front of the little seaplane's nose!

Then, at the precise moment that the ramp came fully open and despite the fact that he was 18,000 feet above the earth, the tiny figure of William Race climbed up out of the hatch—into the roaring wind—and *leapt across* from the nose of the Goose onto the open loading ramp of the Antonov!

Race landed flat on his face on the loading ramp of the giant cargo plane.

He clawed for a handhold to stop himself getting sucked out the back of the plane, grappled his way along the length of the ramp—flat on his belly, hand over hand, the wind roaring all around him—crawling on his stomach with nothing but the Goose and 18,000 feet of clear open sky behind him.

It's funny where life takes you . . .

The enormous cargo bay opened up before him.

He saw the massive Abrams tank sitting proudly in the middle of it—saw the whipping wind scooping up anything that wasn't nailed down—saw the flashing red warning lights and heard the hysterical wail of the alarm klaxons that were no doubt alerting whoever was on board the plane that its loading ramp was now illegally open.

Earl Bittiker already knew.

No sooner had the loading ramp opened a foot than he had heard the whoosh of the wind rushing into the cargo bay. It was followed a split second later by the high-pitched wailing of the klaxons.

Bittiker spun where he stood in the belly of the Abrams tank, his cellular phone still pressed against his ear.

'What the *fuck* is this?' he said as he stormed up the ladder of the tank, heading outside.

On his feet now, Race unshouldered his MP-5 and sidestepped his way down the narrow passageway between the enormous tank and the wall of the cargo hold.

Abruptly, a man's head popped out from the hatch on top of the tank to his left.

Race whirled around, levelled his gun at the man.

'*Freeze!*' he yelled.

The man froze.

Race's eyes went wide as he realised who it was.

It was the man who had taken the idol from Frank Nash back at Vilcafor, it was the *leader* of the terrorists.

Holy shit.

Strangely, the man was holding a telephone in his hand, a cellular phone.

'Get down from there!' Race yelled.

At first, Bittiker didn't move, he just stared at Race in a kind of slack-jawed wonder—stared at this bespectacled man dressed in blue jeans and a filthy T-shirt, a battered New York Yankees cap and a black kevlar breastplate, ordering him around with an MP-5.

Bittiker glanced at the open loading ramp behind Race, saw the little Goose seaplane hovering in the air about twenty yards behind the Antonov, trying vainly—but unsuccessfully—to keep up with the giant cargo plane as it rose higher into the sky.

Slowly, Bittiker stepped down from the turret of the tank, until he stood in front of Race.

'Give me that damn phone,' Race said, snatching the cellular phone from the terrorist. 'Who the hell are you talking to anyway?'

Race held the phone to his ear as he kept his eyes and gun trained on Bittiker. 'Who is this?' he said into the phone.

'*Who am I?*' a nasty little voice snapped back at him. '*Who the fuck are you is the more appropriate question.*'

'My name is William Race. I'm an American citizen who was brought to Peru to help an Army team get a sample of thyrium to put inside a Supernova.'

There came a loud shuffling from the other end of the line.

'*Mister Race,*' a new voice said suddenly. '*My name is Special Agent Demonaco of the FBI. I am investigating the theft of a Supernova from the offices of the Defense—*'

'You can't stop it,' Bittiker said to Race, his voice laced with a slow Texan drawl—'you *cain't* stop it.'

'Why not?' Race said.

'Because not even I know how to disarm it,' Bittiker said. 'I made sure that my people only knew how to arm it. That way, once it was set to go off, no-one could stop it.'

'No-one knows the disarm code?'

'No-one,' Bittiker said. 'Except, I imagine, some Princeton-fuck scientist up at DARPA, but that ain't gonna help us now, is it?'

Race bit his lip in frustration.

The alarm klaxons were still ringing. Any second now, more Texans would come out to see what was going on—

Gunfire.

Loud and sudden.

It slammed into the deck all around him, kicking up sparks. Race dived out of the way, rolled across the deck, jammed the cellular phone into his back pocket and looked up—and saw Troy Copeland standing on the catwalk overlooking the cargo bay with two other Texans beside him, all three of them firing their Calico pistols down at Race.

Bittiker saw the chance and ducked behind the forward corner of the tank, out of Race's sight.

Race pressed his back against the massive tracked wheels of the tank, out of the line of fire, at least for the moment.

He was breathing hard, his heart pounding loudly inside his head.

What the hell are you going to do now, Will?

And then suddenly, he heard someone shouting his name.

'Is that you, Professor Race?' It was Copeland. 'God, you're a persistent little son of a bitch.'

'It's better than being a complete *asshole*,' Race muttered under his breath as he popped up from behind the tank and fired a short burst at Copeland and the other two terrorists, missing them by miles.

Damn it, he thought. *What did he do now? He hadn't really thought that far ahead.*

The Supernova, a voice said inside his head.

Disarm it! That's what you have to do.

After all, he thought, he'd already managed to disarm one Supernova on this trip.

And with that, Race leapt to his feet, and jammed down on the trigger of his MP-5, firing wildly up at the catwalk as he clambered onto the skirt of the Abrams tank. Then he climbed up onto the tank's turret and jumped down through the hatch and into the belly of the massive steel beast.

He was met by the stunned faces of the two Freedom Fighter technicians in charge of the Supernova.

'Out! Now!' he yelled, pointing his MP-5 at their noses.

The two techs hurried up the ladder and out through the hatch in the turret, banging it shut behind them. Race bolted it behind them, locking it, and suddenly he found himself alone in the command centre of the tank.

Alone with the Supernova.

He was beginning to get a terrible sense of *déjà vu*.

He felt the bulge of the cellular phone in his back pocket, grabbed it.

'FBI-man, are you still out there?' he said.

John-Paul Demonaco leapt for his microphone.

'I'm here, Mister Race,' he said quickly.

'*What did you say your name was?*' Race's voice said.

One of the other agents said, 'Trace is coming through. What the hell—? It says they're somewhere in *Peru* . . . and that they're *20,000 feet* off the ground.'

'My name is Demonaco,' Demonaco said. 'Special Agent John-Paul Demonaco. Now, listen to me very carefully, Mister Race. Wherever you are, you *have* to get out of there. The people with you are very dangerous individuals.'

No shit, Sherlock.

'*Uh*—' Race's voice said.

'—I'm afraid that getting out of here isn't an option,' Race said into the phone.

As he spoke, however, he saw the Supernova's timer counting down.

00:02:01

00:02:00

00:01:59

'Oh, you gotta be kidding me,' he said. 'This just isn't fair.'

'*PROFESSOR RACE, GET OUT OF THE TANK!*' a hideously loud voice boomed from a loudspeaker outside the Abrams. It was Copeland's voice.

Race looked out through the gunner's sights of the massive vehicle and saw Copeland standing up on the catwalk at the forward end of the cargo bay holding onto a microphone.

Wind whipped wildly around the hold. The loading ramp behind the tank was still open.

Race looked about the interior of the enormous tank.

The Supernova took up the entire central section of the command centre. Above him, he saw the entry hatch in the turret. Forward were the firing controls for the tank's 105mm cannon and beyond those—*beneath* them, half-buried in the floor in the very centre of the forward section of the tank—he saw a padded seat and a steering vane, the tank's drive controls.

There was something very odd about the drive

controls, though. The top of the driver's seat practically *touched* the low section of roof above it.

And then it hit Race.

In a tank like this, the driver drove with his head sticking out from a small hatch above his seat.

Race felt a sliver of ice shoot up his spine.

There was another hatch up front!

He dived forward—sliding into the driver's seat—and looked up instantly to see that it was true. There *was* another hatch up here. And at the moment it was open.

And standing astride it at that very instant, pointing his Calico pistol directly down at Race's head, was Earl Bittiker.

'Who the hell are you?' Bittiker asked slowly.

'My name is William Race,' Race said, looking up through the hatch at Bittiker. His mind was racing now, searching for an escape route.

Wait a second, there was one possibility . . .

'I'm a professor of languages at New York University,' he added quickly, trying to keep Bittiker talking.

'*A professor?*' Bittiker spat. 'Jesus fucking Christ.'

Race figured that from where he was standing, Bittiker couldn't see his hands—concealed as they were beneath the hatch—couldn't see that right now Race was feeling around underneath the steering controls of the tank.

'Tell me, poindexter, what did you think you could achieve by coming here?'

'I thought I could disarm the Supernova. You know, save the world.'

Still feeling.

Damn it, it had to be down here somewhere . . .

'You seriously thought you could disarm that bomb?'

Found it.

Race looked up at Bittiker with hard eyes. 'While I've still got one second left, I'm going to try to disarm that bomb.'

'Is that right?'

'Yeah, that's right,' Race said. '*Because I've done it before.*'

At that moment, unseen by Bittiker, Race jammed his thumb down hard on the rubber-sealed button that he'd found on the underside of the steering controls of the Abrams. The same rubber-sealed button that was fitted on every American-made field vehicle.

VROOOOM!

Immediately, the tank's monstrous Avco-Lycoming engine roared to life, the throb of its powerful engine reverberating throughout the enormous cargo bay.

Bittiker was jolted off balance by the sudden roar of the tank's engine. Up on the catwalk in front of the tank, Troy Copeland also looked up in surprise.

Inside the driver's hatch, Race looked around for anything he could—

Oh yeah. That's nice.

He found a control stick, complete with trigger, on which was written the words: MAIN GUN.

Race grabbed the stick and squeezed the trigger and hoped to God that there was a round inside the Abrams' main cannon.

There was.

The *boom* of the tank's 105mm cannon going off inside the cargo bay of the Antonov was perhaps the loudest thing Race had ever heard in his life.

The entire cargo plane shuddered violently as the Abrams' mighty cannon went off in all its glory.

The 105mm shell blasted through the plane like a runaway asteroid. First, it sheared Troy Copeland's head off—cleanly, quickly—removing it in an instant, like a bullet taking off the head of a Barbie doll, decapitating Copeland in a nanosecond, leaving his body standing for a full second *after* his head had been removed.

But the shell just kept on going.

It shot like a missile through the steel wall behind Copeland's body, rocketing up into the passenger deck of the Antonov, ploughing at colossal speed into the cockpit walls, exploding right *through* the pilot's chest before it blasted out through the plane's windshield in a spectacular shower of glass.

With its pilot now well-and-truly dead, the Antonov banked wildly, entering the first stages of a nosedive.

In the cargo bay, the world tilted crazily. Race saw the damage that he'd done, saw where this plane was going.

While I've still got one second left, I'm going to try to disarm that bomb.

Bittiker was still standing on the skirt of the tank, still holding his Calico pistol, but he'd been thrown wildly off balance by the discharge of the cannon.

Race crunched the tank's gears, found the one he wanted.

Then he jammed his foot down on the accelerator, slamming it against the floor.

The tank responded immediately—its tracked wheels leaping into motion—and the massive steel beast shot off the mark like a racing car. The only thing was, it shot *backwards*—out along the loading ramp, shooting off its edge, tipping over it and falling out into the clear open sky.

The Abrams tank fell.

Fast. *Really, really* fast.

Indeed, no sooner had it dropped off the loading ramp of the Antonov than the cargo plane—gutted by the blast of the tank's cannon—just banked away into a nose-dive and exploded in a gigantic, billowing ball of flames.

The Abrams fell through the sky—rear-end first—at *phenomenal* speed. It was so big, so heavy, it just cut through the air like an anvil, a screaming 67-ton anvil.

Inside the tank, Race was in a world of trouble.

Everything was tilted on its side and the whole tank shook violently as it was buffeted by the friction it created with the air outside.

For his part, Race lay awkwardly in the middle of the command centre, having been thrown there when he had reversed the tank off the loading ramp. Next to him was the Supernova. It now sat horizontally, wedged firmly in between the ceiling and floor.

Race saw the timer on its display screen counting down:

00:00:21
00:00:20
00:00:19

Nineteen seconds.

About the same time he had before the tank smashed into the ground from a height of about 20,000 feet.

Aw, fuck it.

Either the Supernova went off and he died along with the rest of the world—or he disarmed it and died alone when the tank slammed into the earth in about seventeen seconds' time.

In other words, he could sacrifice his own life to save the world's.

Again.

Goddamn it! Race thought. *How could the same thing happen to him twice in two days?*

He looked at the computer screen:

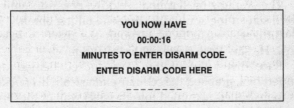

```
YOU NOW HAVE
00:00:16
MINUTES TO ENTER DISARM CODE.
ENTER DISARM CODE HERE
_____
```

Sixteen seconds . . .

The tank screamed through the sky.

Race looked forlornly at the timer as it counted inexorably downwards.

And then suddenly, out of the corner of his eye, he saw movement. He snapped to look up—and saw Earl Bittiker crawling in through the driver's hatch up at the top of the falling tank, his Calico pistol in his hand!

Oh fuck!

00:00:15

Forget about him!

Just think!

Think? Christ, how the hell is a guy supposed to think inside an Abrams tank that's plummeting to earth at about a hundred miles an hour, with a guy climbing in through the driver's hatch carrying a gun?

00:00:14

Race tried to clear his mind.

All right, last time he had known that *Weber* had set the disarm code. But this time, he didn't have the first clue who had set the code, principally because he didn't know who had designed the device's ignition system.

00:00:13

Ignition system . . .

Those were Marty's last words, the words he had spoken as he lay dying in Race's arms.

00:00:12

The Abrams hit terminal velocity, began to emit a shrill screaming sound like that of a falling bomb.

Bittiker was halfway through the driver's hatch now. He saw Race, fired his pistol at him.

Race dived out of the way, ducked behind the Supernova, grabbed the cellular phone from his pocket as more bullets slammed into the steel wall of the tank beside him.

'Demonaco!' he yelled over the din of the falling tank.

'*What is it, Professor?*'

'Tell me quickly! Who designed the ignition system on the Navy's Supernova?'

Three thousand miles away, John-Paul Demonaco snatched up a nearby sheet of paper. It was the list of the members of the Navy–DARPA Supernova team.

His eyes zeroed in on one line.

RACE, Martin E.	Ignition system design engineer	DARPA	D/3279-97A

'A guy named Race. Martin Race!' Demonaco shouted into the phone.

Marty, Race thought.

00:00:11

Marty had designed the ignition system. That's what he'd been trying to tell him before he died.

Therefore Marty had set the disarm code.

00:00:10

Eight-digit numerical code.

Bittiker was fully inside the tank now.

What code would Marty use?

00:00:09

The tank was still falling, screaming through the air at a thousand feet per second.

Bittiker saw him, raised his Calico again.

What code did Marty always use?

00:00:08

Birthday? Significant date?

No. Not for Marty.

If he had something that required a numerical code, an ATM card or a PIN number, he always used the same number.

Elvis Presley's Army serial number.

00:00:07

Bittiker levelled the Calico at Race.

Christ, what was it!

It was on the tip of his brain . . .

00:00:06

Race ducked behind the Supernova—Bittiker wouldn't dare shoot him through *it*—found himself standing in front of the device's arming computer.

God, what was the number?

533 . . .

Think, Will! Think!
00:00:05
5331 . . .
. . . 07 . . .
. . . 61 . . .
53310761!
That was it!

Race started punching the keys on the arming computer, typed: **53310761** and then he slammed his finger down on the 'ENTER' key.

The screen beeped.

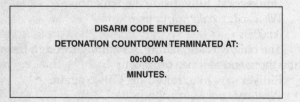

> **DISARM CODE ENTERED.**
> **DETONATION COUNTDOWN TERMINATED AT:**
> **00:00:04**
> **MINUTES.**

But Race didn't bother to stay and look at the screen.

Rather, he just clambered quickly away from Bittiker—shielded by the now-disarmed Supernova—and headed along the short ladder that led to the tank's turret hatch.

He didn't know why he headed that way. It was just a completely illogical notion that if he was on the *outside* of the tank when it hit the ground, he might have a better chance of surviving the impact.

They must be close to impact now.

On his way across the horizontal ladder, he came across the idol—now with a hole in its base—and scooped it up as he crawled.

He came to the hatch, pushed it open. Speeding wind assaulted his face instantly—wind that moved so fast it blinded him.

Clutching onto the now-vertical roof of the Abrams, he quickly kicked the hatch shut behind him, shutting Bittiker inside, just as the steel hatch itself was assailed by a barrage of automatic fire from inside.

Race looked down, into the face of the onrushing wind, as it pounded against his glasses—

—and saw the green rainforest rushing up at him at about a million miles per hour!

The tank screamed towards the earth.

Two seconds to impact.

This was it.

One second.

The earth rushed up toward him.

And in that last second before the Abrams tank slammed into the earth at incredible speed, William Race shut his eyes and offered up a single, final prayer.

And then it happened.

Impact.

The tank's impact with the earth was absolutely stunning in its force.

The world seemed to shudder as the 67-ton tank slammed into it at terminal velocity. The tank imploded on contact with the ground, flattening in a millisecond, sending whole sections of it shooting out in every direction.

Earl Bittiker had been inside the Abrams when it hit the ground. As the giant steel tank slammed into the earth, its walls came rushing in toward him at shocking speed, sending a thousand jagged corners of metal shooting into his body—penetrating him from every side in the nanosecond before he was crushed into nothing. One thing was for sure, Earl Bittiker had been screaming when he died.

William Race, on the other hand, hadn't been anywhere near the tank when it hit the ground.

In that second *before* the tank smashed into the earth—when it was about eighty feet above it—Race had experienced the strangest sensation.

He had heard a sound not unlike a sonic boom come from somewhere very close behind him and then suddenly, out of nowhere—*shoom!*—he had felt himself get *yanked* up into the sky by some powerful unseen force.

But the yank had not been rough or whip-like—rather it had been abrupt but smooth, as if he had been connected to the heavens by some invisible bungee cord.

So as the tank—and Bittiker—hit the ground in a smashing, blazing heap, Race had *hovered* thirty feet above the explosion, safe and sound.

And then he looked over his shoulder and saw what had happened.

He saw two plumes of white gas shooting out from the bottom of the A-shaped unit that was attached to the back of his unusual kevlar breastplate. In fact, the twin puffs of propellant shot out from two small exhaust ports situated at the base of the 'A'.

Although Race didn't know it, the black kevlar breast-plate that Uli had given him at the refuse pit was in fact a J-7 jet pack, the cutting-edge aerial insertion unit created by DARPA in conjunction with the United States Army and the 82nd Airborne Division.

Unlike the Army's current MC1-1B parachutes, which allowed their wearers to be suspended in full view of the enemy for at least several minutes before landing, jet packs allowed their wearers to free-fall to within eighty feet of the ground before swooping to a sudden stop just above the landing zone, in much the same fashion as a bird landing.

Like parachutes, however, all J-7 jet packs were equipped with altimeter switches—altitude-triggered safety mechanisms that engaged the pack's propulsion systems in the event that the wearer failed to engage them himself before he fell below eighty feet. As Race had just failed to do.

There was no way he could have known that on December 25, 1997, at the same time as forty-eight chlorine-based isotopic charges had been stolen from a DARPA truck travelling along the Baltimore beltway by agents of the Stormtroopers, also stolen were sixteen J-7 jet packs.

Slowly, gently, the jet pack lowered Race down to earth.

He sighed, breathless, and allowed his body to go limp as he descended into the canopy of lush rainforest trees.

Seconds later, his feet touched the ground and he just fell to his knees, exhausted.

He looked at the rainforest around him and in a distant corner of his mind wondered how the hell he was going to get out of here.

Then he decided that he didn't care anymore. He had just disarmed a Supernova while falling from a height of 19,000 feet inside a 67-ton main battle tank.

No, he didn't care in the slightest.

And then suddenly the solution to his problem revealed itself in the form of a small seaplane swooping in low over the trees above him. A man's hand waved happily from the pilot's window.

It was Doogie and the Goose.

Beautiful.

Thirty minutes later, thanks to a conveniently placed stretch of river nearby, Race was back on board the Goose with the others, soaring through the clear afternoon sky high above the rainforest.

He rested his head against the cockpit window,

stared vacantly through it as they flew. He was absolutely exhausted.

Beside him, Doogie said, 'You know what I think, Professor, I think it's high time we got the hell out of this damned country. What do you think?'

Race turned to face him. 'No, Doogie. Not yet. There's still one more thing we have to do before we go.'

SEVENTH MACHINATION

Wednesday, January 6, 1730 hours

The Goose touched down on the river next to Vilcafor shortly before sunset on January 6, 1999.

After dousing themselves in monkey urine again, Race and Renée headed back to the upper village. They left Doogie and Gaby in the Goose, to allow Gaby to tend to the young Green Beret's many wounds.

As the two of them trudged through Vilcafor, tired and exhausted, Race saw that there were no bodies lying on the street.

Despite the fact that about a dozen Navy and DARPA scientists—plus Marty, Lauren, Nash and Van Lewen—had been killed here only a few hours previously, no bodies remained.

Race looked at the empty street sadly. He had an idea where the bodies had gone.

He and Renée entered the upper village just as dusk was beginning to settle over the Andean foothills.

The natives' chieftain, Roa, and the anthropologist, Miguel Moros Marquez, met them at the moat at the edge of the village.

'I think this belongs to you,' Race said, holding the idol out in his hands.

Roa smiled at him. 'You truly are the Chosen One,' he said. 'My people will sing songs about you one day. Thank you, thank you for returning our Spirit.'

Race bowed his head. He didn't think he was any kind of Chosen One at all. He'd just done what he had thought was right.

'Just promise me this,' he said to Roa. 'Promise me that when I am gone, you will leave this village and disappear into the forests. Men will come searching for this idol again, of that I am certain. Take this idol far away from here, where they will never find it.'

Roa nodded. 'We will, Chosen One. We will.'

Race still hadn't actually handed the idol to Roa yet.

'If you will permit me, sir,' he said, 'there is one more thing I have to do here, and to do it, I will require the use of the idol.'

The tribe of natives assembled on the spiralling path that encircled the rock tower.

Night had fallen and they were all thoroughly doused in monkey urine.

The rapas, Marquez said, unable to return to their lair inside the temple, had spent the day hiding in the heavy shadows at the base of the crater.

Race stood on the spiralling path, looking out across the ravine that had earlier been spanned by the rope bridge.

The rope bridge still hung flat against the side of the tower, in the same place the Nazis had left it when they had unlooped it from its buttresses twenty-four hours ago.

One of Roa's nimblest climbers—doubly soaked in monkey urine—was sent down to the base of the canyon where he embarked upon a skilful climb up the rock tower's near-vertical wall.

After a while, he came to the long retrieval rope that dangled from the bottom of the rope bridge. He tied it to another rope that was held by natives standing on the spiralling path and they then pulled the retrieval rope over to their side of the ravine.

The rope bridge was quickly secured back into place.

'Are you sure you want to do this?' Renée said to Race as he gazed across at the tower top.

'There's a way out of that temple,' he said. 'Renco found it. I will, too.'

Then, with the idol in one hand and a torch in the other and a leather satchel slung over his shoulder, Race led the way across the swooping bridge.

A team of ten of Roa's strongest warriors followed him, bearing flaming torches of their own.

Once they were all on the rock tower, Race led them up to the clearing in front of the temple. There he pulled a water bladder out of his leather satchel and used it to douse the thyrium idol.

The idol hummed instantly. A pure, mesmerising sound that cut through the night air like a knife.

Within minutes, the first rapa arrived at the clearing.

Then a second, and a third.

The massive black cats gathered around the clearing, forming a wide circle around him.

Race counted twelve of them in total.

He doused the idol again and it emitted its even harmonic tone with renewed vigour.

Then he took a step backwards, entering the temple.

Ten steps down and he was surrounded by blackness.

The rapas—big, black and menacing—followed him inside, blocking the shafts of blue moonlight that entered the tunnel from without.

Once all the cats were fully inside the temple, the ten Indian warriors outside began to heave on the boulder—as Race had instructed them to do.

The massive stone groaned loudly as it was pushed slowly back into place.

Race watched its movement from within the temple. Gradually, all the moonlight from outside was replaced by the shadow of the massive rock and then, with a final ominous thud, the boulder would move no more.

It now filled the portal, sealing it shut, at the same time sealing William Race inside the temple with the pack of ferocious rapas.

Darkness.

Total darkness, save for the flickering orange glow of his torch.

The walls of the tunnel around Race glistened with moisture. From somewhere deep within the temple, he heard a steady, echoing *drip-drip-drip*.

It was absolutely terrifying, but strangely Race felt no fear. After all he'd been through, he was beyond being afraid.

The twelve rapas—visions of evil in the strobe-like light of the torch—just stared at the humming idol in Race's hand, entranced.

With his torch held high above his head, he made his way down the spiralling tunnel at the base of the stairs. It bent down and to the right in a slow, descending curve. Small alcoves lined its walls.

Race passed the alcove that he'd seen the last time he had been inside the temple, saw the mangled skeleton with the cracked skull lying in it. The skeleton that he had assumed was Renco but which he now knew to be the wily old conquistador who had stolen Renco's emerald pendant.

He came to the bottom of the spiralling passageway and saw a long straight tunnel stretching ahead of him.

It was the tunnel in which von Dirksen and his men had met their grisly end.

The rapas emerged from the ramp behind him—silent, looming, ominous—barely even making a sound as they slunk along on their soft padded paws.

At the end of the long straight tunnel, Race came across an enormous hole in the floor. It was roughly square in shape and at least fifteen feet wide, taking up the entire tunnel before him.

Out of it came one of the most repulsive odours he had smelled in a long, long time.

He winced at the smell as he evaluated the wide hole in the floor in front of him.

On the far side of it he saw nothing but wall—solid, stone wall—and inside the hole itself he saw nothing but inky blackness.

Just then, however, he saw a series of hand and footholds that had been cut into the hole's right-hand wall. They'd been carved in such a fashion—one on top of the other—that they created a ladder-like mechanism which a person could use to climb down into the hole.

After dousing the idol once again with his bladder full of water, Race put his flaming torch in his mouth and then, using the hand and footholds cut into the wall, slowly began to climb down into the dark stinking hole.

The rapas followed him, but they didn't bother using the footholds. They just used their scythe-like claws to climb down the walls of the hole after him.

About fifty feet later, Race's feet touched solid ground again.

The foul stench was stronger here, to the point of being overwhelming. It smelled like rotting meat.

Race grabbed the flaming torch from his mouth and turned away from the wall he had just scaled.

What he saw took his breath away.

He was standing inside an enormous hall of some kind, a gigantic stone-walled cavern that had been carved out of the belly of the rock tower.

It was absolutely spectacular.

An enormous, rock-walled cathedral.

Its high vaulted ceiling soared into the air at least fifty feet above the floor, disappearing into darkness. It was supported by a set of stone columns that had been fashioned out of the rock. A flat stone floor stretched away from Race. It also disappeared into shadow.

The walls of the cathedral, however, were its most stunning feature.

They were covered with primitive carvings—pictographs similar to those that adorned the portal up on the surface.

There were pictures of rapas, pictures of people, pictures of rapas killing people. Tearing their limbs off, ripping their heads off. In some of the carvings, the screaming humans being mauled by the cats clutched piles of loot in their hands, even as they were being killed.

Wanton greed, even at the moment of death.

Interspersed among the carvings on the walls were a series of stone alcoves that had all been carved in the shape of rapas' heads.

Thick cobwebs covered each alcove, so that it looked as if see-through grey curtains had been lowered over the carved rapas' jaws.

Race went over to one of the alcoves, sliced through the cobweb across the rapa's mouth.

His eyes widened.

A small shelf-like podium had been carved into the wall inside the rapa's bared jaws. On it sat a lustrous golden statue that had been fashioned in the shape of a fat man with an enormous erection.

'Good God...' he breathed as he stared at the statue.

He scanned the hall around him. There must have been forty such alcoves scattered around its walls. And if there was an artefact in each one, then it would be a treasure that was worth...

It was Solon's treasure.

Race looked at the ornate alcove in front of him, looked at the carved rapa's head, snarling viciously at him.

It was as if the builder of this temple were *daring* the greedy adventurer to reach inside the cat's mouth to grab its treasure.

But Race didn't want any treasure.

He wanted to go home.

He stepped away from the fearsome-looking alcove, out into the centre of the enormous stone cathedral, holding his torch aloft.

And then he saw the source of the foul odour that had assaulted his nose.

'*Oh, Christ,*' he breathed.

It lay on the far side of the cathedral, and it was huge.

It was a pile of corpses—a high, ugly mountain of bodies.

Human bodies.

There must have been at least a hundred of them, and they were all in various states of dismemberment. Blood slicked the walls all around them in such copious quantities that it seemed as if someone had *painted* them with it.

Some of the bodies were naked, others were partially clothed—some had had their heads ripped off, others their arms, others still had had their entire torsos gnawed in two. Bloodied bones littered the area, some of which still had chunks of uneaten flesh clinging to them.

To his horror, Race recognised a few of the bodies.

Captain Scott—Chucky Wilson—Tex Reichart—the German general, Kolb. He even saw Buzz Cochrane's body lying upside-down on the pile. The entire lower half of his torso had been chewed off.

More curiously, however, Race saw a large number of *olive*-skinned corpses on the pile.

Natives.

And then suddenly he saw a small hole in the wall beyond the grisly pile of bodies.

It was roughly circular in shape, about two-and-a-half-feet in diameter, the width of a broadshouldered man.

Race immediately recalled seeing a similarly shaped *stone* up on the surface earlier—on the balcony-like path behind the temple—a peculiar round stone amid all the square-shaped ones, a stone that appeared to have been slotted into a cylindrical hole of some sort.

Oh, no, Race thought, realising.

It wasn't a hole . . .

It was a *chute*.

A chute that started up on the surface and ended here, in the enormous stone cathedral.

And in an instant, the question as to how the rapas had survived for four hundred years inside the temple had an answer.

In his mind's eye, Race recalled Miguel Marquez's words: *'If you hadn't survived your encounter with the caiman, your friends would have been sacrificed to the rapas.'*

Sacrificed to the rapas.

Race stared at the circular hole in the wall, his eyes widening in horror.

It was a sacrificial well.

A well into which the natives from the upper village threw offerings to the rapas.

Human offerings.

Human *sacrifices*.

They would throw their own people down here.

But it probably didn't stop at that, Race thought as he gazed at the inordinate number of olive-skinned bodies that lay on the pile of corpses.

The natives probably threw their dead—and the dead of their enemies—down here as well, as another way of appeasing the rapas.

And in times of real shortage, Race imagined, the rapas probably ate each other.

Just then, he saw five more rapas lying on the stone floor beyond the pile of corpses, next to a small, square-shaped hole in the floor.

The five rapas were staring right at him, entranced by the steady hum of the wet idol.

Standing in front of them were about ten much smaller cats—cubs, rapa cubs—each about the size and shape of a tiger cub. They also stared at Race. It seemed as if they had all stopped in mid-play as soon as they had heard the idol's mesmerising drone.

Jesus, Race thought, *there was a whole community down here. A community of rapas.*

Come on, Will, get on with it.

Right.

It was then that Race extracted something else from the leather satchel that he had slung over his shoulder.

The fake idol.

Race left the fake idol on the floor at the base of the large square-shaped hole that had opened onto the cathedral, so that anyone entering the temple would find it immediately.

He didn't know for sure, but he imagined that that was exactly what Renco had done four hundred years previously.

All right, he thought, *time to get out of here.*

Race saw the smaller hole in the floor over by the five female rapas and their cubs and figured that his best option—apart from climbing up the sacrificial chute and hoping someone opened it for him—was to just keep going downwards.

And so with the real idol still humming in his hands, he cautiously made his way past the five female rapas and their cubs and over to the small, square-shaped hole in the floor next to them.

He looked down into the hole.

It was about six feet square and it just disappeared straight down into the rocky floor. Like the larger hole before it, it also had foot and handholds carved into its vertical walls.

What the hell, Race thought.

With his torch held firmly in his mouth again and the humming idol shoved inside his satchel, Race climbed down into the narrow shaft.

After a minute or so, he lost sight of the hole's opening above him. From then on, except for the small circle of flickering orange light that illuminated the shaft around him, he was surrounded by impenetrable darkness.

A couple of the rapas followed him down, slinking down the walls of the shaft at the edge of the torch's circle of light, hanging upside-down above him, keeping pace with him, glaring at him with their cold yellow eyes.

But they never attacked.

Race kept climbing. Down and down. It felt like he climbed for miles, but in reality it was probably only a couple of hundred feet or so.

Then, finally, his feet touched ground again.

Race grabbed his torch and held it aloft and found that he was standing in a small cavern of some sort, bounded on every side by solid stone walls.

Filling the cavern, however, was a body of water.

It was a pool of some sort—a small pool, bounded on three sides by walls of stone. On the fourth side of the pool was the flat section of ground on which Race now stood.

He walked over to the water's edge, bent down to touch it, as if to see if it was real. The two rapas stepped slowly out from the shaft behind him.

Race dipped his hand in the water.

And suddenly, he felt something.

Not an object or anything like that, but rather a gentle surge in the water itself.

Race frowned. The water was *flowing*.

He looked at the entire pool once again and saw that its tiny wavelets actually moved ever-so-slowly from right to left.

And in that instant, he realised where he was.

He was at the very bottom of the rock tower, at the point where it met the shallow lake at the bottom of the crater. Only—*somehow*—water was flowing in and out of this cavern.

The idol was still humming in his satchel.

The two rapas watched Race intently.

Then, with a confidence that he had no reason to

possess, Race discarded his flaming torch and stepped into the pool of inky black water—satchel, clothes and all—and ducked beneath the surface.

Thirty seconds later, after breaststroking his way through a long underwater tunnel, he surfaced in the shallow lake at the bottom of the crater.

He gulped in air and breathed a thankful sigh of relief.

He was outside again.

After he emerged from the base of the rock tower, Race returned to the upper village. But before he did so, he stopped at the tower top, at the entrance to the temple. The warriors who had pushed the boulder back into the portal were gone now, having already departed for the village, and Race stood before the ominous stone structure alone.

After a few moments, he grabbed a nearby stone and approached the boulder wedged inside the portal. Then, beneath Alberto Santiago's inscription, he scratched a message of his own:

> *Do not open at any cost.*
> *Death lies within.*

> *William Race, 1999*

When he arrived back at the upper village, he found Renée waiting for him at the edge of the moat, standing with Miguel Marquez and the chieftain, Roa.

Race handed the idol to Roa. 'The rapas are back inside the temple,' he said. 'It's time for us to go home.'

'My people thank you for all that you have done for

them, Chosen One,' Roa said. 'If only there were more in the world like you.'

Race bowed his head modestly, just as Renée looped her good arm in his.

'How are you feeling, hero?' she said.

'I think I must have suffered another hit to the head,' he said. 'How else am I going to explain all those feats of derring-do? Must have been the adrenalin talking.'

Renée shook her head, looked him squarely in the eye. 'No,' she said. 'I don't think it was adrenalin.'

Then she kissed him—nicely—pressing her lips firmly against his. When at last she pulled away, smiling, she said, 'Come on, hero. It's time to go home.'

Race and Renée left the upper village to the cheers of the natives.

As they disappeared down into the crater and headed back to Vilcafor, a muffled scream could be heard from somewhere within the village far behind them.

It came from the bamboo cage that was tied to the four post-like trees.

In the cage, lying on the ground, rolling around in agony from the wounds to his stomach and with both of his hands hacked off, lay the wretched—and gagged—figure of Frank Nash.

The natives hadn't killed him on the main street of Vilcafor earlier. Rather, they had cut off his thieving hands and brought him up here for more appropriate treatment.

An hour later, the last Indian procession to go to Solon's temple began. Bodies were carried aloft on ceremonial litters as the procession made its way across the rope bridge and over to the temple.

Nash lay writhing in agony on one of the litters, while a series of other corpses—Van Lewen, Marty, Lauren, Romano, and the corpses of the entire Navy–DARPA team—occupied other litters. Dead or alive, any kind of human flesh would appease the cat gods that dwelled inside the temple.

The whole village gathered around the rear of the temple—chanting in unison—as two strong warriors lifted the cylindrical stone from its slot in the path, revealing the sacrificial chute.

The dead bodies were cast into the hole first—Van Lewen, then Marty, then Lauren and the Navy people.

Frank Nash was brought over to the sacrificial well last of all. He had seen what had been done with the other bodies and his eyes widened as he realised what was going to happen to him.

He screamed through his gag as the sacrificial priests bound his feet together. He writhed about maniacally as two Indian warriors brought him over to the chute.

They put him in feet-first and as he saw the sky for the last time, Frank Nash went bug-eyed with horror.

The two warriors dropped him into the chute.

Nash screamed all the way down.

The cylindrical stone was placed back into its slot and the natives left the tower top for the last time, never to return. Once they arrived back at their village, they began preparations for a long journey, a journey that would take them to a place deep within the rain-forest, a place where they would never be found.

The Goose soared over the Andes, heading for Lima, heading for home.

Doogie sat up front in the cockpit, bandaged but alive. Race, Renée, Gaby and Uli sat in the back.

After about an hour or so of flying, Gaby Lopez joined Doogie in the cockpit.

'Hey,' she said.

'*Hey*,' Doogie replied when he saw who it was. He swallowed, nervous. He still thought Gaby was seriously pretty and seriously out of his league. She'd done a great job bandaging his wounds, treating them with gentle hands. He'd stared at her the whole time.

'Thanks for helping me with that caiman back in the moat,' she said.

'Oh,' he blushed. 'It was nothing.'

'Well, thanks anyway.'

'No problem.'

There was an awkward silence.

'Say, I was wondering,' Gaby said nervously. 'If you weren't—you know—seeing anybody back home, maybe you'd like to come over to my place and I could cook you dinner.'

Doogie's heart almost skipped a beat. He smiled a broad, beaming smile.

'That'd be great,' he said.

Ten feet behind them, in the passenger section of the plane, Renée lay nestled up against Race's shoulder, fast asleep.

For his part, Race was speaking to John-Paul Demonaco on Earl Bittiker's cellular phone—care of the redial button. He brought Demonaco up to speed on everything that had happened at Vilcafor. From the BKA to the Nazis, to the Navy and the Army, and then finally, the Texans.

'*So, wait a minute,*' Demonaco said. '*Have you had any military experience?*'

'None at all,' Race said.

'*Jesus. What are you, some kind of anonymous hero?*'

'Something like that.'

After they spoke some more, Demonaco gave Race the telephone number and address of the American embassy in Lima and the name of the FBI liaison there. The FBI, he said, would take care of the trip back to the States.

After he hung up, Race just stared out the window at the mountains swooping by beneath him, his battered Yankees cap pressed up against the glass, his right hand fingering the emerald necklace that hung from his neck.

After a while, he blinked and extracted something from his pocket.

It was the thin leather-bound notebook that Marquez had given him that morning during the banquet.

Race flicked through it. It wasn't very thick. In fact, it was only made up of a few handwritten pages.

But the handwriting was familiar.

Race turned to the first page, started reading.

FIFTH READING

To the worthy adventurer who finds this notebook.

I write to you now by the light of a torch in the foothills of the glorious mountains that dominate New Spain.

By my amateur reckoning, it is now approximately the Year of Our Lord 1560, nearly twenty-five years after I first came to these foreign shores.

To many who might read this work, it will mean nothing to you, for I write it in anticipation of penning another, fuller account of the remarkable adventures that befell me in New Spain—an account that I may not even write at all.

But if I do write it, and if you, oh, brave adventurer—having come across this notebook through the ministrations of some most noble natives—have indeed read that account, then what follows will certainly have meaning for you.

It is close on twenty-five years since my incredible adventure with Renco, and all of my friends are dead.

Bassario, Lena, even Renco himself.

But fear not, dear reader, they did not die of any foul deeds or subterfuge. They died in their sleep, all of them, victims to that villain no man can escape—old age.

Now, I am the last one left alive.

Sadly, as such, I have nothing left to live for in these mountains and so I have decided to return to Europe. I intend to end my days in some distant monastery far away from the world, where God willing, I shall write my amazing tale in full.

I leave this notebook, however, in the good hands of my Incan friends—to pass on to their children and their children's children—and to give it only to the most worthy of adventurers, indeed, only those of a stature commensurate with my good friend Renco.

That said, owing to the pedigree of those who will read this account, I shall endeavour in this notebook to dispel some of the fictions that I intend to include in the larger recounting of my tale.

After the death of Hernando on the enormous stone tower, Renco did indeed enter the temple with the two idols, but he would emerge soon after, from an under-water passage at the base of the giant finger of stone, safe and sound.

The inhabitants of Vilcafor would abandon their village at the base of the plateau and relocate to higher ground, to a new site above the enormous crater that housed the temple.

I would live with them for the next twenty-five years, enjoying the company of my friend Renco. Why even that rogue Bassario, who proved his worth in our final confrontation with Hernando and his men, became a faithful companion of mine.

But, oh, how I enjoyed my time with Renco. Never have I had such a good and loyal friend. I feel fortunate to have been able to spend the greater part of my life in his company.

Oh, and another small tale for you, noble reader—
but one which I beg of you not to tell my holy brethren.

After a time, I would marry.

And to whom, you might ask? Why, none other
than the beautiful Lena.

Yes, I know!

While I had admired her from the first moment I
laid eyes on her, I was not to know that she entertained
similar feelings toward me. She thought I was a brave
and noble man and, well, who was I disabuse her of
that impression?

With her young son Mani—whom Renco doted
upon in the manner of uncles the world over—we
made for a wonderful family, and indeed, soon Lena
and I would expand our brood to include two delightful daughters who, I say with pride, were the spitting
image of their mother.

Lena and I would be married for twenty-four years,
the most wonderful twenty-four years of my life. It
ended but a few weeks ago, when she fell asleep by my
side, never to wake.

I miss her every day.

Now, as the guides prepare to take me north through
the forests to the land of the Aztecas, I think of my
adventures, and of Lena, and of Renco.

I think of the prophecy that brought us together
and I wonder if indeed, I am one of the people mentioned in it.

> There will come a time when he will come,
> A man, a hero, beholden of the Mark of the Sun.
> He will have the courage to do battle with great lizards,
> He will have the jinga,

He will enjoy the aid of bravehearted men,
Men who would give of their lives, in honour of his noble
cause,
And he will fall from the sky in order to save our spirit.
He is the Chosen One.

I ask myself, am I a 'bravehearted man'?
It is strange—most strange—but now, after all that I have been through, I actually think that I am.

Worthy adventurer, this tale is at an end.
May these writings find you in good health and I wish you every happiness in life and love.
Farewell.

A.S.

Race sat in the back of the Goose, staring at the last page of Alberto Santiago's notebook.

He was pleased that the kind-hearted monk had found happiness after his adventure. He deserved it.

Race thought about Santiago's transformation—his transformation from timid monk to stalwart defender of the idol.

Then Race looked at the prophecy again and thought about Renco. And then for some reason that he couldn't fathom, he began to think about the similarities between Renco and *himself*.

They both bore the Mark of the Sun.

And they had both fought with caimans, and they had each displayed cat-like balance and movement.

Both of them had most certainly enjoyed the aid of bravehearted men, and they had both risked their lives for their cause.

And lastly, of course, they had both fallen from the—

Wait a second, Race thought.

Renco had never fallen from the sky . . .

AN INTERVIEW WITH MATTHEW REILLY

When did you begin writing your first novel, Contest?

I wrote *Contest* in my first year out of high school. I was 19 when I started it and 20 when I finished it. My motivation at the time was to write a book that was all action—action from start to finish—a book that thrust the reader back into his or her chair because of the sheer pace of the storytelling. To be quite honest, I'd been finding that the books I was reading were too slow, or taking too long between action scenes. I also saw no reason why books couldn't have really *massive* action scenes, action scenes that were even bigger than those you see in blockbuster Hollywood movies. Movies are constrained by budgets. But with books, the limit of your budget is the limit of your imagination. I like to think I have a big imagination.

What is Contest *about?*

Contest is the story of a man who is placed inside the New York State Library and told that he has been chosen to represent the human race in a contest that is held once every thousand years. He is told that six aliens have been placed inside the building with him and that all the entrances and exits to the building have been sealed. No-one is allowed out until only one contestant is left alive. Seven enter, only one leaves. In other words, it's a good old-fashioned fight-to-the-death. Lots of really scary aliens and clever escapes. More so even than either *Ice Station* or *Temple*, I like to think of *Contest* as a roller-coaster ride on paper, a non-stop series of hold-your-breath, foot-to-the-floor thrills. The movie version will be great—kind of like *Die Hard* meets *Aliens*.

What led you to self-publish Contest?

Simple. I offered it to every major publisher in Sydney and they all rejected it! What drove me to go down the path of self-publishing was my desire to see it get picked up. I honestly thought it had the goods and, on top of that, I kind of thought that the publishers I'd offered it to hadn't given it a fair go (some, I am certain, didn't even read it).

So I figured that I had to get the attention of a major publisher some other way. I reasoned that publishers go to bookstores to see where their books are placed etc, so if I could get *Contest* onto the shelves of major bookstores, maybe someone in the publishing industry would see it. And so, with the help of my brother, Stephen, I published *Contest* myself—complete with blockbuster-style cover art—and offered it to bookstores in person. It cost me $8,000 to print 1,000 books at a place called Image Desktop Publishing (a free plug for them but, hey, they did do a great job. Oh, and folks, these are 1996 prices).

In any case, *Contest* was seen in a city bookstore by the Publisher of Mass-Market Fiction at Pan Macmillan, the kind folk publishing this tome. She called me up and asked if I was writing anything else. As it happened, only a few weeks before I had decided to commence work on a new book, a little action ditty set in Antarctica about a team of United States Marines sent to defend a spaceship found buried deep within the ice. I sent the first 50 pages to Pan Macmillan and they signed me up on the basis of those pages. That book was *Ice Station*.

I understand that you've sold the film rights to Contest. *Is that right?*

That's correct. I optioned off the movie rights to *Contest* in early 1999. I've recently seen some of the ideas the movie guys have for the film, too. The special effects will be absolutely out of this world. Cannot wait to see it.

Will Contest—*the novel, that is—be reissued by Pan Macmillan?*

Yes, yes, yes, yes, yes, yes! Pan are going to re-release *Contest* in late 2000. My humble apologies to anyone who tried to get it after they read *Ice Station*. I only printed 1,000 copies and by the time *Ice Station* came out, there were none left!

Where did the idea for Ice Station *spring from?*

For me, any novel starts with the question *What would happen if...* You ask yourself that question, and the answer is your novel. The idea for *Ice Station* came when I asked myself *What would happen if someone discovered a spaceship somewhere on earth?* My answer: the country in whose territory it was found would grab it and hide it—a kind of Area 51 answer, really, and as a novel, not very satisfying.

So I extended the question to ask, *What would happen if that spaceship was discovered in Antarctica, the only place on earth that isn't any country's territory?* The answer to that question was much more interesting: it would be a free-for-all. An all-or-nothing race to see who could get the ship first. By making some of America's traditional allies (such as the French)—countries which most Westerners don't usually see as threats—the villains in *Ice Station*, I felt I made the story a little more geopolitically complex. Funnily enough, I wrote *Ice Station* in 1997 and only this year—1999, two whole years later—an Australian spy was caught by the FBI selling American secrets to the French! How about that!

Has Ice Station *been sold overseas?*

Yes, it has. *Ice Station* has been sold to publishers in 10 countries, including the US, the UK, Germany, China, the Netherlands, and Japan. Very cool. Can't wait to see a Japanese edition of it.

Will Shane Schofield appear in another book?

Yes. In fact, I am writing a rampaging sequel to *Ice Station* right now. And if anyone wants a hint as to the story, I'll only say this: it is set in a desert.

William Race is a very different hero to Shane Schofield, isn't he?

William Race *is* very different to Shane Schofield. While Schofield is a hero for all seasons—a pure Indiana Jones type—William Race is more of an ordinary guy who must discover his heroic nature in the most *extraordinary* of circumstances. As many people would guess, I like to picture my heroes in terms of the actors who might play them in movie versions of my books. Schofield was always written with Tom Cruise in mind for the role (he's even described in the book as being five-foot-ten with spiky black hair!). William Race, on the other hand, was always Brad Pitt—Brad Pitt with glasses and an unloseable New York Yankees cap.

By making Race an ordinary man, however, I found I could have a lot of fun with his fear. He is not a hero. He is just a guy. He gets frightened, even when he is doing the most death-defying stuff imaginable (lowering himself under speeding riverboats, leaping from one moving aeroplane to another . . .). At one point in *Temple*, he sees a skeleton in the temple which he thinks belongs to Renco—who most certainly *is* a hero—and he thinks: *that's what happens to heroes.* But, like Alberto Santiago, the monk in the manuscript story, he discovers that being a hero is really about one simple thing—doing what is right, whatever the circumstance.

How did Temple *come about?*

The genesis of *Temple* was a little different to that of *Ice Station*.

With *Temple*, I asked myself: *What if I could write a book that switched between two stories set in different times?* But on top of that I asked: *What if those two stories had twists that affected each other?*

In other words, I wanted to write a book that was set in two different time periods, but in which twists in Story 1 would actually affect Story 2 (for example, the mangled skeleton in the present day story found by Race suggests to the reader that Renco has met a grisly end in the past; conversely, in the past story, Alberto learns about the quenko underneath Vilcafor, but it is Race who uses this information for his benefit in the present).

The added bonus was with two stories I could get double the action!!!

And besides, I have always had a fascination with the Incas. So I figured I could write a no-holds-barred swashbuckling adventure set in 1535 at the same time as I wrote an explosive high-tech modern-day thriller like *Ice Station*. Sure, at times I felt like my head was about to explode, what with all those characters running around in it, but it was worth it.

Will William Race make another appearance?

Barring any unforeseen creative detours (such as George Lucas calling me up and asking me to write *Episode III* for him—it could happen . . . George, are you reading this?), yes, William Race will definitely be returning in a new adventure.

In fact, I recently dreamed up a new story for Race to be in—a story that will involve him having to translate another manuscript, thereby giving us a new split story to get into. Although, given my desire to write a new Schofield book, I might have to alternate between Schofield and Race books in the future.

Where do you want to be in ten years, Matthew?

I have several goals in life, nearly all of which are pretty much based on the acts of the two creative people I admire the most, Michael Crichton and George Lucas.

I want to write novels, I want to write and direct feature films, and I want to create TV shows. So in ten years time, I'd like to:

- have had modest success with my novels world-wide;
- have had at least one Hollywood film made from my books (just because you sell the film rights doesn't actually mean your film will get made, or made well for that matter, just ask Stephen King); and
- have directed at least one feature film.

In any case, I always aim high, since I subscribe to the maxim, 'If you aim for the stars, you might reach the moon'. And besides, you only live once, so I figure I might as well do it all.

Any final words?

Yes. To everyone reading this, I just hope you enjoyed the book.

MR
June, 2000